✳ 9/01

"I'm not going to let anyone hurt you, Sara Brand.

"Do you understand that? I promise I'll keep you safe."

Her damp eyes seemed trusting. Imagine that, trusting...of him. She had no reason in the world to trust him.

Mocking laughter seemed to fill Jake's mind, and the stinging words came back to him in the voice of officer Marty Kendall. *Right. Convict turns hero. Dream on, Jake Nash. You're going down, pal. And who's gonna protect her then? Hmm?*

Hell. Jake held Sara a little closer, realized he would be in jail right now if it hadn't been for her. He wanted to ease her fears. He wanted to be her hero. And that was a joke, because he knew damn good and well that he was no hero.

Dear Reader,

This is a very special month here at Intimate Moments. We're celebrating the publication of our 1000th novel, and what a book it is! *Angel Meets the Badman* is the latest from award-winning and bestselling Maggie Shayne, and it's part of her ongoing miniseries, THE TEXAS BRAND. It's a page-turner par excellence, so take it home, sit back and prepare to be enthralled.

Ruth Langan's back, and Intimate Moments has got her. This month this historical romance star continues to win contemporary readers' hearts with *The Wildes of Wyoming—Hazard,* the latest in her wonderful contemporary miniseries about the three Wilde brothers. Paula Detmer Riggs returns to MATERNITY ROW, the site of so many births—and so many happy endings—with *Daddy by Choice.* And look for the connected MATERNITY ROW short story, "Family by Fate," in our new Mother's Day collection, *A Bouquet of Babies.* Merline Lovelace brings readers another of the MEN OF THE BAR H in *The Harder They Fall*—and you're definitely going to fall for hero Evan Henderson. *Cinderella and the Spy* is the latest from Sally Tyler Hayes, an author with a real knack for mixing romance and suspense in just the right proportions. And finally, there's *Safe in His Arms,* a wonderful amnesia story from Christine Scott.

Enjoy them all, and we'll see you again next month, when you can once again find some of the best and most exciting romance reading around, right here in Silhouette Intimate Moments.

Yours,

Leslie J. Wainger
Executive Senior Editor

Please address questions and book requests to:
Silhouette Reader Service
U.S.: 3010 Walden Ave., P.O. Box 1325, Buffalo, NY 14269
Canadian: P.O. Box 609, Fort Erie, Ont. L2A 5X3

ANGEL MEETS THE BADMAN

MAGGIE SHAYNE

Published by Silhouette Books

America's Publisher of Contemporary Romance

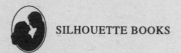 SILHOUETTE BOOKS

ISBN 0-373-27070-4

ANGEL MEETS THE BADMAN

Copyright © 2000 by Margaret Benson

All rights reserved. Except for use in any review, the reproduction or utilization of this work in whole or in part in any form by any electronic, mechanical or other means, now known or hereafter invented, including xerography, photocopying and recording, or in any information storage or retrieval system, is forbidden without the written permission of the editorial office, Silhouette Books, 300 East 42nd Street, New York, NY 10017 U.S.A.

All characters in this book have no existence outside the imagination of the author and have no relation whatsoever to anyone bearing the same name or names. They are not even distantly inspired by any individual known or unknown to the author, and all incidents are pure invention.

This edition published by arrangement with Harlequin Books S.A.

® and TM are trademarks of Harlequin Books S.A., used under license. Trademarks indicated with ® are registered in the United States Patent and Trademark Office, the Canadian Trade Marks Office and in other countries.

Visit Silhouette at www.eHarlequin.com

Printed in U.S.A.

MAGGIE SHAYNE,

a national bestselling author whom *Romantic Times Magazine* calls "brilliantly inventive," has written more than fifteen novels for Silhouette. Her Silhouette single title release *Born in Twilight* (3/97) was based on her popular vampire series for Shadows, WINGS IN THE NIGHT.

Maggie has won numerous awards, including a *Romantic Times Magazine* Career Achievement Award. A three-time finalist for the Romance Writers of America's prestigious RITA Award, Maggie also writes mainstream contemporary fantasy.

In her spare time Maggie enjoys collecting gemstones, reading tarot cards, hanging out on the Genie computer network and spending time outdoors. She lives in a rural town in central New York with her husband, Rick, five beautiful daughters and a bulldog named Wrinkles.

IT'S OUR 20th ANNIVERSARY!
We'll be celebrating all year,
Continuing with these fabulous titles,
On sale in April 2000.

Romance

#1438 Carried Away
Kasey Michaels/Joan Hohl

#1439 An Eligible Stranger
Tracy Sinclair

#1440 A Royal Marriage
Cara Colter

#1441 His Wild Young Bride
Donna Clayton

#1442 At the Billionaire's Bidding
Myrna Mackenzie

#1443 The Marriage Badge
Sharon De Vita

Desire

#1285 Last Dance
Cait London

#1286 Night Music
BJ James

#1287 Seduction, Cowboy Style
Anne Marie Winston

#1288 The Barons of Texas: Jill
Fayrene Preston

#1289 Her Baby's Father
Katherine Garbera

#1290 Callan's Proposition
Barbara McCauley

Intimate Moments

#997 The Wildes of Wyoming—Hazard
Ruth Langan

#998 Daddy by Choice
Paula Detmer Riggs

#999 The Harder They Fall
Merline Lovelace

#1000 Angel Meets the Badman
Maggie Shayne

#1001 Cinderella and the Spy
Sally Tyler Hayes

#1002 Safe in His Arms
Christine Scott

Special Edition

#1315 Beginning with Baby
Christie Ridgway

#1316 The Sheik's Kidnapped Bride
Susan Mallery

#1317 Make Way for Babies!
Laurie Paige

#1318 Surprise Partners
Gina Wilkins

#1319 Her Wildest Wedding Dreams
Celeste Hamilton

#1320 Soul Mates
Carol Finch

Chapter 1

Sara Brand saw the devil waiting for her on the wide, white veranda when she arrived at the plantation known as Sugar Keep in Gator's Bayou, Louisiana. Beyond the shimmering heat waves—which she figured probably heralded his presence everywhere he went—he sat in a wicker chair, sipping something cold, the glass dewy and small in his big, coppery hand. He rose when she got out of the car, came down the steps to the driveway. His jeans were tighter than sin. His shirt hung untucked and unbuttoned, and even then it stuck damply to his skin in places. And where it gaped open, the exposed skin was tanned, sweat dampened. Sara's gaze slid over his smooth, broad chest and dipped to his dark, shadowy navel, rippled over his washboard abs and explored the little dusting of dark hair that started just above the button-fly of those jeans and went lower…

"I can take them off if you want a better look."

She jerked her head up fast, realizing she'd been standing beside her car with the door still open, staring at him for a full minute. He was only a foot away now, looking darkly amused, but deadly serious. Black eyes—devilish black eyes—probed hers. He had the thickest lashes she'd ever seen on a man. "Um…no. I mean. Sorry. I was…thinking."

"I could see that. Care to elaborate?" His words flowed as slowly as molasses, drawn out by his slight Southern drawl, while his eyes raked her head to toe. The glance was suggestive. Appreciative. Devilish.

Mentally she reviewed her appearance. She was wearing the same things she always wore. A loose, flowery skirt of thin material, in deference to the smothering heat. A sleeveless, cotton, button-down blouse. Her hair was in a ponytail, and her sunglasses covered her eyes. It was an everyday look for her. So why did she suddenly feel so self-conscious? So nervous?

She automatically took a step backward, her back hitting the hot metal of the still-open car door.

His eyes narrowed for a moment. Then he shrugged almost imperceptibly. "So I take it you're Sara Brand?"

"Y-yes."

He nodded. "Jake Nash," he said. He offered a hand.

Sara reluctantly put hers in it. She knew she had no reason to be afraid of the man. *That* feeling was automatic and far more familiar to her than that other feeling that had swamped her when she'd set eyes on him. *That* had been…new. Different. Totally unlike her. To be afraid of him for no good reason…that was like her. All her instincts, honed from years of living in fear of strangers, were kicking into high gear. And it was almost a relief—despite the fact that her well-meaning sister-in-law, Chelsea, had told her she could let go of it now. That no one was out to get her anymore. That it was time to move on.

Jake Nash's big hand closed around hers. It was hot and moist and strong. It totally enveloped her hand, and he held it a moment too long.

Licking her lips nervously, she tugged free of his grip, knowing it was rude, knowing it would probably offend him.

Apparently it did. Lips thinning as he looked down at his now empty hand, he asked, "Bags in the trunk?"

"Um…yes."

He held out a hand, palm up. She only stared at it. At the lines in his palm, at the callused mounds at the base of each long, strong finger.

"Keys, Miz Brand?"

"Oh!" She fumbled in her oversize crocheted shoulder bag, found them and held them out. Even as he took the keys from her, she was looking past him at the empty-looking, stately house and the abandoned veranda, searching for other people. Safety. Witnesses. The brochure had said this old Louisiana plantation was owned by an older couple, the La Fleurs, and run by them with help from a daughter and son-in-law. Nowhere had it mentioned that guests would be greeted in the driveway by a devil in denim.

"They'll be along, don't you worry," he said. He

moved to the back of the car, opened the trunk, hauled out her small case and smaller satchel, then looked at her with brows raised. "That's it?"

"That's all. I'm…only staying for a week…and I don't plan to do much besides, um, you know. Relax."

"Uh-huh." He looked her up and down again. "That'll be a sight to see, won't it? Come on, your bungalow is this way."

He started off along a path that curved away from the big house and the gravel driveway, leaving Sara to catch up. "What's that supposed to mean?" she asked his back, maybe a bit defensively.

Broad shoulders shrugged. There was a dark spot right between them that kept drawing her eye. God, it was hot here. The air seemed…weighted down. Utterly still and heavy and hot.

"What's what supposed to mean?"

"What you said." She had to take two steps for every one of his. "About my relaxing being a sight. What did you mean by that?"

He shrugged, sent a backward glance over his shoulder at her. "You're wound tighter than a seven-day clock, lady. I doubt you know how to relax."

She swallowed hard. Chelsea had been right, then, hadn't she? Her fears were getting to be too much. If they were that obvious to a stranger…

"I've always found it odd, myself, that some people think they need to get away from home in order to relax," he drawled, as if he hadn't just insulted her. Maybe he didn't think he had.

"I was perfectly relaxed at home," she told him.

He stopped walking, turned to face her, a puzzled

frown creasing his deeply tanned forehead. "Then why'd you leave?"

She looked at him, acutely aware that they were alone here on this isolated path. To the left was a meadow, rife with grasses and wildflowers nearly as tall as he was. She could hear the buzz and hum of insects. To the right, cypress trees, hung with veils of ghostly moss, and God only knew what beyond them. The swamp, the bayou, as they called it here? The main house and her car were behind them now. And ahead, past more shimmering heat waves, she could see that the bungalow, a small white building with clapboard sides and red shutters, was an equal distance away.

When she brought herself to look at him again, it was to find him watching her intently. He looked...pissed off. But he said nothing.

"I can, um, take the bags from here," she said.

His lips thinned. He nodded. "Who you been talking to, Miz Brand? Hmm? Just what have you heard about me?"

"What?" She gave her head a shake. "I—no one...nothing. Why would you ask something like that?" Unless he has something to hide.

There she went again. Suspicious of everyone. Seeing evil secrets in the most innocent places. Chelsea was right.

Jake Nash blew out a sigh, shook his head. "Nothing. Never mind." Turning, he trudged onward toward the bungalow, not speaking another word to her all the way.

The small square building had a front porch like a miniature of the one on the main house. He dug a key out of his jeans pocket, unlocked the door, and dropped the bags inside. Then he stood back to let her pass.

"Dinner's at seven, up at the main house," he said. "I'd offer to come for you then, but I wouldn't want you to spend the next two hours dreading my appearance. Meanwhile you can have free run of the grounds." He nodded once and turned to head out the door.

"Wait."

He stopped in the doorway, his back to her.

"I offended you," she said. "I didn't mean to."

"Hell, lady, I'm used to it." Then he moved through, pulling the door closed behind him.

Sara went to the windowed door, parted the soft, white curtain and watched him go. He didn't turn around, never looked back, just strode away with broad, hurried steps. As if he couldn't get away from her fast enough.

Only when he'd rounded a bend in the path, taking him out of sight, did she let the curtain fall back into place. "I'm sorry," she whispered, closing her eyes. And she meant it.

With a sigh of self-disgust she straightened her spine. "Well, that's what this trip is about, isn't it?" Biting her lip, she called to mind the affirmations that Chelsea had given her and spoke them aloud as Chelsea had told her to do whenever irrational fears rose up. "No one is out to get me anymore. All those years of hiding and jumping at shadows are in the past. No one has any reason to want to hurt me in any way. I am perfectly safe. I am perfectly secure. I am not afraid of strangers."

There. That was better.

She opened her eyes.

Jake Nash was standing on the other side of the glass looking back at her. She shrieked. She didn't mean to; it just came out. At the same time, she lurched backward so suddenly that she fell over her bags and landed on her backside on the floor, with her skirt bunched up around her thighs.

The door flew open, and he stood over her, staring down at her, looking just about as disgusted with her as she felt with herself. "You okay?" he asked as if he really didn't care. His gaze roamed down her legs, lingered on her thighs.

Licking her lips, she nodded and held out her hand. "You startled me."

"Sorry." Looking doubtful about doing so, he closed his hand around hers and helped her to her feet.

"No," she said, straightening her skirt, heat flooding her cheeks. "I'm the one who should be apologizing here, Mr. Nash."

"For being afraid of me?" His eyes were so intense they almost burned her. "Why should you be any different from anyone else? It's pretty obvious you've heard about me. I don't make excuses for what I did, Miz Brand, but I don't apologize for it, either. I paid for it. If you don't see it that way, that's your problem." He looked down at their joined hands and, shaking his head, let hers go. "And your loss," he added darkly. "Just tell me one thing, will you?" He returned to performing exploratory surgery on her eyes with his own. "Why would a woman as damned jumpy as you are pick a place that comes complete with an ex-con in residence? Hmm?"

She flinched. She knew it, felt it, saw him react to it. "Ex...con?"

He was silent for a moment, studying her. "Then you *didn't* know." Lowering his head, he shook it slowly. "What, is *bad man* stamped across my forehead or something?"

She just shook her head. If she went a shade paler, she couldn't help it. He looked down at her hands. She did, too. Saw them shaking, fisted them to stop it.

"Don't worry, Miz Brand," he said softly. "The time I did in the pen wasn't for rape."

She lifted her head, met his eyes, tried to tell herself not to be afraid. But maybe the fear was no longer irrational. Maybe her instincts were right this time. She wanted to ask what it *was* for but couldn't quite muster the nerve. "Why did you come back?" she asked, trying hard not to sound as terrified as she felt. Her skin was tingling, and she wanted to run.

"I came back because I forgot to tell you to stay clear of the bayou. It's dangerous out there. Gators. Snakes. No doubt you'd prefer their company to mine. Maybe they don't scare you quite as much as I seem to. But trust me, Miz Brand, they bite." He let his eyes move down her, stared at her breasts. "A lot harder than I would."

A little swell of insight rose up, and brought a hint of irritation with it. "Are you trying to *frighten* me, Mr. Nash?" she said.

"Come on, Sara. That's not what you want to ask me. Not really. Go on," he said. "Ask me. You know you're dying to. Ask me what I did time for."

She tried to look away. Found she couldn't. His

eyes had a powerful hold on hers. "It's...really none of my business."

"No," he said. "It isn't. And I probably wouldn't tell you anyway. But I'm sure you'll find someone else who will."

Again he left her alone. But this time she locked the door behind him.

Jake Nash got halfway back along the path and stopped. He stood stock-still and he said, "You are a bastard, Nash. You're a mean, bitter, burned-out bastard, and you'd better get a handle on it before you alienate the whole damned world."

He stuffed his hands into his jeans pockets, lowered his head. He hadn't meant to lose his temper with little miss faint-heart out there. Hell, when he'd first seen her getting out of her little convertible, he'd thought she was just about the prettiest thing he'd seen. He'd been half-convinced he was looking at an earthbound angel.

And then...when her eyes had been eating him up the way they had, he'd thought maybe she wasn't feeling very angelic. And that maybe he would make nice with her, maybe give her a little vacation fling she wouldn't forget for a long time to come. God knew he was due for one.

Not that he hadn't been with a lot of women since he'd been out of prison. He had. He was not a monk. But it was always the same—quick, dirty, meaningless. Just like his life had been up to now.

He'd never once been with a woman like Sara Brand.

She was different. Delicate. Clean. Good. There was an aura of innocence about the woman that was so real she nearly glowed with it. Her halo, he thought with a wry smile.

And she'd been scared to death of the big, bad convict almost from her first glance of him, even before he'd spilled the beans. Hell, he supposed he had his own aura, his own nimbus, though few would call it a halo. More like a dark, dreary cloud. A woman like her wouldn't miss that in a man. She'd seen or smelled or sensed it in him right off. He was no good.

She was obviously a classy woman, the kind he'd always felt was out of his league. He didn't belong with her kind any more than he belonged here at Sugar Keep. Oh, his aunt and uncle had done a good job of pretending he was just like them, just like everyone else, over the past year. Too good a job, maybe. Maybe he'd forgotten for a minute there, who he *really* was.

He'd spent almost half his life in prison. He'd gone in at seventeen, and come out a year ago, thirty-three and naive enough to think he could start over. Get a new chance. A fair shake. It hadn't taken long to realize that there was no such thing as having paid his debt to society. Not in the eyes of the righteous, upstanding citizens on the outside. They would always see him as no good.

Just the way Sara Brand had seen him, even without knowing a thing. She was as repulsed by him as everyone else around here was. Hell, he couldn't even blame her.

But for some reason, with her, it stuck in his craw. It burned his pride, and so he fought back. Just like any animal would do. It was the base reaction, wasn't it? A cur dog would bite if you kicked it. A bastard-born convict would do the same. What the hell did she expect?

"Jacob, honey-love, you get on up here and tell me all about our new arrival," Flossie chirped as he neared the main house and the veranda.

Jake looked up to see his aunt in a tent-size floral muumuu and a big-brimmed hat, sitting in the chair he'd been in himself an hour ago. She vigorously waved a fan made of ostrich feathers in front of her face.

"She arrived while you were at mass," Jake said. He nodded hello to Uncle Bertram, who was just coming out the door with a mint julep in hand.

"Well thank the Lawd we have one heathen in the family, then," Flossie declared with a robust laugh. "I don't know how we ever got along without you, Jacob."

He forced a smile. Tante Flossie went overboard on the efforts to make him feel welcome. It wasn't that he didn't appreciate it. Just that he knew it wasn't genuine. He walked up the steps to the veranda but didn't sit. If he did, Flossie would keep him there all day.

"So tell me about her," she insisted. "She's a schoolteacher you know. Kindergarten. Isn't that just sweet?"

Jake shrugged and recalled her timidness, her skittishness. "Why am I not surprised?"

"What's that, hon?"

"Nothing." He gave his head a shake. "She's got dark hair and darker eyes. She's in her mid-twenties, and she's jumpy as hell," he said, dutifully complying with the status quo. Keeping his aunt informed was a matter of form around here. It was what was done. You didn't get away from her otherwise.

Flossie's brows went up, making her forehead pucker. "Jumpy, you say? Well, now, I wonder why that is." She sent Bertram a glance as if expecting him to answer, when she knew full well he wouldn't. He was a man of few words, Bertram was. He only shrugged and sent Jake a look of amused indulgence.

No doubt Tante Flossie would make it her business to find out why, Jake thought dryly.

"She comes from a large family in Texas, you know," she said.

Uncle Bertram sat down in the porch swing, his white suit immaculate. He pushed off with his feet, sipped his julep and muttered, "Quinn."

"Yes, Quinn's the town where most of her family lives," Flossie went on. "They have a ranch there."

"That's real interesting, Tante Flossie," Jake said. Naturally Flossie would have done all the research she could on Sara Brand before her arrival. It was Flossie's way. She did it with all the guests who came here...made no secret of it, either...but few ever seemed to mind it much. "But you know," Jake went on, not in the mood to gossip, "I ought to be fixing that plumbing in the vacant bungalow. Can't rent it out until I finish."

"Of course you should, hon. So you say she's jumpy? Did you get any idea why?"

He shrugged, turning to go back down the front steps. "Oh, I dunno. I got the feeling it was me that made her nervous."

"Oh, don't be silly. Why would she be nervous around you?"

He turned to look back at his aunt and sent her a half smile. "You're a gem, Flossie. Just a gem."

She smiled and fluttered her fan harder. "Well, Jacob, hon, so are you. But I wasn't trying to sweet-talk you. That girl's been around so many kinds of men, I can't imagine her being nervous, is all. Why, she has that brother, of course—although no one seems to know too much about what he does. But then there are all those cousins! One has a dude ranch, and one teaches all that judo kind of fol-de-rol. Another one raises horses and thinks he's some kind of medicine man or some such—you know, he's half Comanche? And one is a policeman, for heaven's sake!"

At the bottom step, Jacob went still.

"Sheriff," Uncle Bertram muttered. Then he sipped some more.

Swallowing hard, Jake shook it off. It didn't mean anything. And he told himself the guy could be a perfectly decent human being. That not all cops were like the ones he'd dealt with here. He thought it; he just wasn't sure he believed it.

He stepped off the bottom step onto the flagstone walk.

"So you don't know anything at all about her, then?" Tante Flossie called after him.

He shook his head. "You seem to have the girl's entire family history, *chère*. What more could there be to know?"

"Oh, go on!" She waved her fan at him, and Jake sent her a wink, then headed out to the shed for his toolbox.

But he couldn't help the little shiver of unease that worked up his spine. A cop in the lady's family.

He'd never liked cops. They still made him nervous, even though he hadn't so much as run a stop sign since he got out of prison. Cops. Hell, no wonder she'd seen him for what he was right off.

She'd probably seen enough men like him to know them on sight. She'd probably taken one look at him and thought she had him all figured out. And if she hadn't before, then she certainly would have once he'd told her he was an ex-con. Just like every cop he'd ever met, Sara Brand probably figured that was *all* he was. That there was no more to him than that label.

He didn't care, he told himself. He didn't care in the least what that flighty little, uptight female thought of him. Not in the least.

Chapter 2

Jake carried the toolbox back along the path. The cabin with the leaky pipes was farther away than the one where *she* was staying.

In spite of himself, he felt his gaze drawn to Sara Brand's bungalow as he passed. He didn't like that she was afraid of him. He didn't like that she was related to a cop or that she seemed to have judged him on sight and found him lacking.

He didn't like anything about her.

He *especially* didn't like what she was doing just now.

She had changed into a pair of cutoff denim shorts and a tank top, and was lying in the swamp grass in the shade of a cypress tree, just at the edge of the bayou, reading a book. She must be pretty engrossed in that book, too, he thought. So much so that she hadn't seen him walking past and didn't feel his eyes on her right now. And she *should* feel them.

Because when they roamed her body, Jake felt as if he were touching her.

Hell.

He wasn't going to go out there. God knew he'd already seen way too much of those legs to want to see any more. He knew they were shapely, slender but not skinny. Sexy but not long. Thanks to her little tumble when he'd startled her at the bungalow, he'd seen just about all there was to see of those legs, including the very sensible white cotton panties where they ended.

No, he didn't want to see any more.

Besides, she was perfectly safe out there. The gators wouldn't venture so near. And he didn't imagine she would be dumb enough to wander any farther.

Would she?

Shoot, she might.

Shoot, she already was.

Even as Jake looked on, that ridiculous female sat up, rolled her neck, stretched her arms—which made her breasts seem to strain for freedom against the tank top, and made Jake want to close his eyes and groan. He did groan. Didn't quite manage to close his eyes, though. Then she looked curiously into the darkness behind her.

Jake set the toolbox down on the path and watched her. Her back was toward him now. Her hands, small hands, he recalled, and soft, reached back to brush at her perfect, rounded backside, and he got a rush imagining what that would feel like under *his* hands.

She took a couple of steps past the first cypress

tree, looked around. She craned her neck and looked farther.

Hell. Jake sighed heavily and started forward.

Sara liked to walk. It helped her to think. And the fact that the unpleasant Jake Nash had warned her not to go into the bayou made her want to walk there. He was so sure he could scare her. He didn't have a clue about her. She'd been scared by the scariest, and he didn't even begin to measure up, with his ex-con talk and his dark looks.

He'd probably done time for some barroom brawl. Shoot, who hadn't? All her cousins had. Even Garrett, and he was a sheriff, for crying out loud! And Wes had even served a prison term. Didn't make him scary.

No, her fears were her own and had nothing to do with Jake Nash or his deep dark past. To hell with him.

She had so much to deal with just now.

She just wanted to walk.

The smooth ground just beyond the trees looked to Sara like a trail. Like a well-trodden path of some kind that went right into the bayou. Certainly alligators didn't make paths like this one. So she decided to examine it more closely. Oh, she wouldn't go far. Just in case those grim warnings delivered by Jake Lucifer Nash had been intended to do more than just frighten her. She was 99 percent sure that was his only reason for delivering them, though. He'd disliked her from the moment he'd set eyes on her, and while she knew her jumpiness had slightly offended him—okay, *deeply* offended him, especially given his past—she still didn't think his nastiness was warranted.

He was touchy. She probably should be a bit more understanding. Her cousin Wes was still extremely sensitive about having spent time in prison. Teasing him about it was the best way to get him to lose his temper. Not that anyone ever dared do that. But she knew it was a sore subject with Wes even now, and it had been a long, long time ago.

Then again, he should be defensive. Wes had been convicted of a crime he hadn't committed. If he was still bitter, then it was no wonder, was it?

But this man—this dark-eyed, intense, *rude* stranger—what about him? she wondered in spite of herself as she walked along the odd little path. What crime had he been convicted of? And had he been guilty of it?

He was, she admitted to herself, a handsome man. So dark and so sinewy that he seemed to exude some kind of sexual aura. A musk or an electrical charge that would make even the most reserved female feel tingly when he looked at her. Or maybe it was just those eyes…the way he used them. Like hands. Having him look at her the way he had was like being touched in some uncharted erogenous zone.

In college, some of her friends had told tales about certain men who could bring a woman to orgasm just by looking at her. She'd always laughed it off as one of those urban legends so many people would swear were true. Now she wondered. If it could be done…she rather thought Jake Nash might be the kind of man who could do it.

Her stomach was clenching and her blood heating. Even though it was marginally cooler here in the trees. Maybe he didn't even need to look at her, she thought wickedly. Maybe just thinking too long about him could do it. Then she smiled at her uncharacteristic thoughts and tried to shake them off. Maybe she was crazier than Chelsea thought she was, to be so turned on by the first strange man she met, while simultaneously wondering whether he were a reformed ax murderer.

A sound brought her head up sharply. A funny little sound. Like a...grunt.

Or...maybe a man, clearing his throat.

The old fear crept up her nape. She commanded it to go away. "No one is after me now," she reminded herself. Still, she stopped walking, since the noise had come from ahead of her. She probably ought to turn around and go back. But for some reason the thought of turning her back to whatever was up there was an unpalatable one. Instead she started walking backward so she could keep her eyes on the trail ahead and the source of that sound.

The grunt came again, this time accompanied by skittering footsteps.

Okay, she thought, backtracking faster. Alligators don't run. So maybe whatever was coming wasn't anything dangerous, and maybe—

It came into sight. Dark, bristly, with coal-chip eyes and sharp, yellow tusks poking out from its snout. It was running right toward her.

"What in the name of—"

"Wild boar," a deep voice said, even as a hot, powerful arm snagged her around the waist and lifted her off her feet. She squeaked in alarm but quickly realized he was pushing her up onto the low-hanging limb of a nearby tree. And in a second, Jake Nash, that dark ex-con who hated her guts, was scrambling up into the tree with her.

She clung to the tree trunk, staring at him in confusion as the bristly, mean-looking wild pig came running, grunting and snuffling in undisguised fury. Jake put his back to the tree trunk, wrapped his arms around her waist and pulled her against him. "Get your feet up here," he said gruffly into her ear.

"Oh, my God." She pulled her feet up, wondering how in the name of all creation a man's breath bathing her ear, the touch of a deep voice and the slight rasp of whiskers on her neck, could *possibly* feel so unbearably delicious.

The boar stood beneath the tree now, not fooled in the least by their evasive maneuvers.

Her back was pressed to the naked portion of Jake's incredible chest. His body heat was rapidly melting her insides. And it didn't help to realize that she was nestled snugly between his legs, while he had each foot braced on a limb on either side. She turned her head to look at him.

"Yeah, I know, you don't like this, but it was me or him, lady."

Her brows went up. "Did you hear me complaining?"

"I *told* you to stay out of the bayou."

"I *thought* you were just trying to scare me."

"Now why would I do that, when I managed to scare you just fine without trying in the least?"

She blinked and lowered her gaze. He had her on that one. The pig grunted and snorted and ploughed around the leaves with his nose. It really didn't seem so different from an ordinary hog-farm type pig. She imagined what her sister would say when she relayed this particular tale. Looking up at Jake again, Sara felt her lips twitch. She tried not to, but in a second she was smiling.

"What?" he snapped. "You find this amusing?"

"Jake, we've been chased into a tree by a pig. You have to admit it's funny."

"It wouldn't have been funny if that pig had gotten to you before I did," he said. But she did think she saw his eyes flash with just a hint of amusement, though he tried to sound very stern and serious.

She looked down again. The pig looked up, and Sara got a better look at the nasty little tusks protruding from the animal's snout as it paced underneath them. Then her smile died. "I guess I owe you one. You might have saved my life."

He met her eyes. She had to look away from their touch. "You're welcome."

"Thank you," she replied. Then she smiled again. "But it's still going to sound like a comedy when I tell my family how I was rescued from the mean old killer pig."

"Go on, pig. Get lost." Jake chipped pieces of bark off the tree and whipped them at the pig. When one piece finally hit the animal near its eyes, it turned and lumbered away, grunting all the way out of sight.

"Safe to get down now?" she asked. She was a little breathless. Pressed to his chest like this, his arms still latched around her waist, it was no wonder.

He looked at her. "Better wait a few minutes. Make sure he's not coming back." Then he settled into a more-comfortable position. And before she knew she was going to do it, Sara leaned farther back against his chest.

She stiffened, started to straighten up, but he pulled her back again. "It's okay," he said. "Relax. You said that's what you came here to do, right?"

"Well...yes, but not exactly like this."

"No. I don't imagine this is what you had in mind. So...what is it with you, anyway? Split personality?"

She felt her smile change to a frown as she tilted her head. "What do you mean?"

"I mean, as jumpy as you were earlier, I expected you to scream bloody murder over being chased up a tree by a dangerous animal. What gives?"

"Oh, that." She sighed, shaking her head slowly. "I'm not scared of animals. It's people I have trouble with."

"Oh yeah?"

She looked at him by tipping her head back. "Well, not all people. Just—"

"Don't finish. I gotcha. Just ex-cons, right?"

She tilted her head. "The only thing I have against ex-cons is that they're all so darn touchy about it."

His brows went up. "So you know a lot of us, do you?"

"Only my cousin Wes. But he's as oversensitive about it as you are. For the record, Jake Nash, my being a little...afraid of you earlier had nothing to do with your past or anything else about you. It's about me."

"Yeah?"

She nodded. "Yeah. And, I'm sorry you took it wrong."

"So you're not afraid of me, then?"

She shrugged. "Shoot, you just saved me from the big, bad pig, didn't you?"

"A little role reversal, isn't it? The Big Bad Wolf saving Little Red for a change?"

She swallowed hard. His eyes were all intense again. "I never said you were the Big Bad Wolf," she told him, softly. It was those eyes of his. They made her want things....

Suddenly he slid out from behind her, steadied her with one hand and jumped out of the tree, landing on his feet just below it. He looked around, listened, then reached up. "I think it's safe now."

"All right." She pushed herself off the limb.

Jake caught her. His hands closed around her waist, thumbs digging into her breasts as her body plastered itself against his. Her arms automatically linked around his neck, and her feet hovered a foot above the ground. He didn't lower her right away, either. He just stared at her. Her face was close to his, and his eyes probed hers like spies in search of secrets. Then they slid lower, to linger on her lips.

"Don't you, um, want to put me down?" she managed to say.

"No, frankly, I don't. But I will."

And he did. Slowly he clamped his arms tightly around her waist, slid her body down the front of his. It was blatantly sexual. It was a full-body caress. He was stroking her, slowly and masterfully—with his body. And when her feet touched the ground, he leaned down, and she thought he was going to kiss her.

But he didn't. He stopped with his mouth just a hair's breadth from hers. And he said, "Maybe you were better off being scared of me, Sara Brand. Maybe it would be better if you stayed that way."

"I...don't be silly. I'm not—I mean—"

"Yeah, you are," he whispered. "And just so you know, I *am* the Big Bad Wolf, Sara Brand. If you aren't careful with me, I'm liable to eat you alive."

Her stomach clenched into a knot so tight she thought it was turning to stone. He was so close. Why hadn't he kissed her yet? What was he waiting for?

"So?" he asked her softly, so close now she swore she felt the feathery touch of his lips as they moved to form the words. "Are you ready to ask me yet? Because I really think it's time you knew, little Sara. I think it would be best for both of us."

She knew what he meant. She didn't pretend not to. "All right," she whispered, her heart fluttering wildly in her chest, her eyes falling closed. "I'll ask you, even though I really don't care. What were you convicted of, Jake?"

His lips touched hers, all too briefly. Just a fleeting touch, then they skimmed over her cheek, to her neck, to her ear. And he whispered, "Murder."

Then he let her go all at once and turned to start walking back along the path.

Chapter 3

He walked briskly all the way to her bungalow and right on past it, pausing only long enough to snatch his toolbox up off the path and then continuing on his way.

Sara watched him go, head tilted to one side. Her conditioning seemed to be at war with her hormones here, she thought silently. She ought to be scared to death of him. And yes, she had been—for about the first ten minutes she'd known him. That, she realized, had been her conditioning kicking in. The years she'd spent—her whole life, really—being wary of strangers wasn't a phobia but a necessity. It had kept her alive.

Now that she no longer needed it, she'd found it irritatingly difficult to get rid of. But this...this thing going on inside her now was different.

She wasn't afraid of Jake in the same way she'd been afraid of other strangers. It was a tingling kind of fear. He was dangerous, but incredibly sexy, and she was drawn to him in spite of her fears. Maybe even…because of them.

In her experience, she thought idly, men out to do harm were sneaky. They lied. They didn't come right out and tell you their criminal past. Jake pulled that history of his out and used it like a weapon to fend her off.

In her experience men out to do harm didn't yank careless women up into trees to save them from rampaging wild boars, either.

She smiled to herself. There was a lot more going on with Jake Nash than met the eye. It would probably be stupid and self-destructive of her to try to find out what.

"But I'm perfectly safe here," she muttered, repeating Chelsea's mantra yet again. "No one here has any reason to want to hurt me. No one's after me anymore."

She went into her bungalow, opened her suitcase and took out her laptop. Then she looked for the phone jack.

An hour later she was skimming the newspaper reports on what had happened to Jacob Nash in the town of Gator's Bayou more than fifteen years ago. He'd been seventeen years old. He'd held up a liquor store, and the owner, a sixty-eight-year old man by the name of Bill Kendall, had suffered a fatal heart attack during the robbery. There was a very brief mention that Jake had called the paramedics and stayed with the old man, trying to perform CPR until help arrived. When he was arrested. There was a lot more mention of the fact that Mr. Kendall had been a local police officer for most of his adult life, until he'd retired and opened the little convenience store. The list of those surviving him sounded like a who's who of local politics.

So that was Jake's deep, dark secret. Oh yeah, Sara thought. He was the very epitome of evil.

Frowning, she wondered why he seemed to want her to think he really was that.

Biting her lower lip, she decided to go back to the main house a bit earlier than she needed to for dinner, maybe see if any of the owners had returned yet. Maybe she would have time to visit with them before dinner. She glanced down at herself. Her legs were a bit skinned up, thanks to that rough tree bark. She was hardly dressed for meeting new people. Okay, so she would change first.

As she saved the files to her hard drive and closed down the little laptop computer, she mentally reviewed every article of clothing she'd packed and told herself that being nervous about what to wear had nothing whatsoever to do with Jake Nash.

Nothing.

But she knew she was lying.

By the time he finished fixing the leaky pipes in bungalow two, Jake had skinned his knuckles, banged his thumb and managed to smear pipe dope in his hair. He was hot, and he was dirty, and he was frustrated as hell.

That woman. Damn her. There was a saying he'd heard once: When someone shows you who they are, believe them the first time. Well, she'd shown him who she was right off the bat. A delicate little flower of a female who was scared to death of men like him. A woman who took one look and decided she was way too good for the likes of him. And who was probably right.

That was fine with him. He'd received her message loud and clear. Hadn't liked it, but it wasn't anything he couldn't deal with. God knew he'd been dealing with attitudes like hers for well over a year now.

So why did she have to go and change tactics on him? Why did she have to get that wide, innocent-but-damned-interested kind of look in her big brown eyes? Hell. He'd seen that kind of thing before, too. She was a "good girl" looking for a walk on the wild side. She was bored with her safe little life and probably thinking a vacation fling with the local "bad boy" would be an adventure. And a safe one, because she could run right back to her cocoon in Texas and never have to set eyes on him again once she'd had her fill.

It, too, was a situation he'd faced before. It made him just as angry now as it had every time some bored housewife had shown up here and put the moves on him. He wasn't good enough to be seen with in public, but he would do fine for a night of hot, sweaty sex. A quick game of The Ex-convict and the Warden's Wife, with a real, live ex-convict for authenticity. It galled him. And every other time it had happened, he'd let the she-wolf in question know exactly what he thought of her plans.

At least when he had meaningless flings with local bad girls, they were on the same level. Both knew what they wanted, both knew it didn't mean a damn thing. There was an understanding, unspoken, but there. Neither was using the other.

These vacationing housewives were different.

Thought themselves his better in every way and just wanted excitement. They were slumming. Looking for a dirty rat to turn them on for a night and probably intending to wash themselves in iodine afterward. He never had any trouble telling those kinds of women where to get off.

This time he was having a little bit of trouble.

This time he was sorely tempted to oblige.

Where was his pride, anyway?

He closed his eyes when he passed bungalow one on his way back to the house. He kept his head down and moved straight ahead, refusing to look left or right. And he walked fast. He was pretty pleased with himself when he rounded the bend and the big house came into view, because he'd managed not to even look back.

That feeling of satisfaction vanished, though, when he saw that it had all been a wasted effort. Sara Brand sat in the porch swing, sipping iced tea and laughing with what remained of his family. If he knew Tante Flossie at all—and he *did*—she'd probably spilled the entire tale of Jake's sordid life by now.

He swallowed the dryness in his throat, looked down at the streak of dirt across his sweaty belly and the stains on his shirt and wished he'd stayed away just a bit longer. But they'd seen him now. Tante Flossie was waving her arm so hard it was rippling, and she was smiling ear to ear.

Hell.

Jake drew a breath and strode forward. When he walked up the steps to the veranda, he tried to keep his spine straight and his pride intact.

Sara looked at him. Her eyes managed to hold his

for about ten seconds before they skimmed lower, sliding over his belly just the way they had earlier. He expected to see a tiny wrinkle of distaste appear in her little nose. But he didn't. Instead he saw the tip of her tongue dart out to moisten her lips.

"We've been having the nicest talk," Flossie sang. "Sara told me how you rescued her from that boar, Jacob. I declare, those animals can be such a nuisance. You and Trent ought to take the shotgun out later on, see if you can't track him down. I'd hate to have someone get hurt!"

He only nodded, his eyes on Sara. She looked as fresh as early-morning sunlight. Yellow sundress, with straps that left her tanned arms bare. Sandals, one of which sort of dangled from her toes. Her hair was down. Shoulder length and shiny and almost as dark as his own. She was so damned clean she would squeak, he thought. She'd even polished up her halo.

"So are you pretty much recovered from that scare in the woods?" he managed to ask her.

"Completely," she said.

"I meant the part with the pig." He watched her face, saw her eyelids lower to half mast.

"That part didn't scare me to begin with."

"And the rest?"

"My gracious, what else *was* there?" Flossie asked.

Not missing a beat, Sara Brand said, "Being up in the tree with Jake. I've got this longtime fear of…heights. So…it shook me some."

"Well, mercy, no wonder!" Flossie pressed one hand to her chest while the other one picked up the pace in flapping the fan she was rarely without.

"But as it turned out, that gnarly old tree wasn't half as scary as it was trying to make me think it was."

Jake held her gaze and hoped it didn't show when he flinched inwardly. So she thought she could see right through him, did she? They would see about that.

Flossie was tilting her head, frowning from one of them to the other, and the last thing he needed was for her to get ideas, so he decided it would be a good time to change the subject.

"Have you met the others yet?"

"Just your uncle Bert," Sara replied. "He's inside making a fresh pitcher of pink lemonade."

With a nod, Jake glanced at Flossie. "Are we expecting Vivienne for dinner?"

"Oh, with that daughter of mine, who knows what to expect?" she replied, her fan slowing, eyes flicking just a little. The antics of her only child hurt the woman, no doubt about that. But not as much as they hurt Viv's husband. Trent had become Jake's only real friend over the past year, and Viv's behavior didn't sit well with Jake at all.

But Flossie was sending an apologetic glance toward Sara now and remembering her manners. "Vivienne is my daughter. She keeps awfully late hours these days. But my son-in-law will be here. Oh, you'll love Trent. He's just as sweet as…why, just as sweet as Jacob is."

Jake shot a look Sara's way and saw the amusement in her eyes. She looked right back at him, too, not bothering to hide it. "I can hardly imagine there being two like Jake in one family," she said, those pink lips curving just a little at the corners.

"Don't worry," Jake said. "There aren't." Then he glanced down at himself again. "I'd best go clean up. See you two ladies at dinner."

Flossie La Fleur loved to talk. She loved to have an avid listener, and she loved her nephew, Jake. All of that was obvious to Sara. Her husband, Bertram, on the other hand, seemed to be her opposite in every way. Reserved, all but silent, skinny as a rail, he treated Jake coolly. But then, he seemed cool toward everyone.

By the time dinner was served, though, Sara felt as if she had become Flossie's new best friend. The woman had told her about her daughter's five-year marriage to Trent and the couple's frustration at being unable to have children. She'd told her about her own gall bladder surgery two years ago and her plans to redecorate the dining room. She'd told her that the bungalows stood on the same site where slave quarters had once been, and that Sugar Keep had been in her family for five generations.

What she didn't tell Sara was anything about Jake Nash. And that was what Sara was dying to know. Sure, she'd gleaned the barest of facts about one life-altering incident from the newspaper reports she'd dug up on the Internet. But nothing personal. Why had he been trying to rob that store in the first place? How long had his sentence been, and when was he released? What had he been doing since then? How did he *feel* about all that had happened to him?

They were all sitting at the dining room table, and Jake was in the seat next to hers, and she couldn't seem to focus on anything else but him. Trent had shown up, as promised. He was, Sara saw at a glance, nothing like Jake. He wore a suit and tie, though he took the jacket off the second he arrived. He took her hand gently when they were introduced, and he pulled her chair out for her when she went to sit down.

He was polite and soft-spoken and clean-cut. And invisible compared to Jake. He was pastel. Jake was neon. But he was friendly, and she liked him at once. He wasn't the kind of man she would ever have been afraid of...even before she'd begun working to get rid of her fears.

"I'm sorry about Vivienne being late again," Trent said to Flossie as he settled into his chair. "I did call her, but she said she'd be tied up until late."

He didn't meet his mother-in-law's eyes when he said it. Just looked down at his plate. Sara got an icky feeling. She glanced quickly at Jake and saw his jaw tense just slightly as he eyed his cousin.

"Did she say why?" Jake asked.

Trent smiled weakly. "Oh, you know Viv. Probably hitting the clubs with her friends. She can't get enough of the New Orleans nightlife." He looked around the table as if in search of his favorite food. "She'll be along when she gets tired out."

"She always is," Jake muttered. And from the venom in his tone, Sara knew something was going on. Poor Trent. Vivienne must be a real problem.

She bit her lip, gave herself a mental kick. She shouldn't be thinking that way about a woman she hadn't even met.

Then she looked around the table. Just the mention of Vivienne's name seemed to have cast a pall here. Even the always-smiling Flossie seemed melancholy for a few moments.

Yup, Sara thought. Vivienne was a problem. No question.

"Speaking of the New Orleans nightlife," Trent began after a strained silence, "do you plan on sampling it, Sara? I'm sure any of us could suggest some places—"

Sara held up a hand. "I'm not exactly a nightlife kind of girl," she said, offering him a smile. "I'll do some sight-seeing while I'm here, but during the day."

"Jake will take you," Flossie said.

Jake's fork clattered to his plate, and when Sara glanced sideways at him it was to see that he'd gone still and was staring at his aunt in what looked like horror.

"Don't look like that, Nephew," Flossie said with a grin. "It'll do you a world of good. You've been working nonstop around here, and a day off is just what you need."

"Oh, but…I don't want to…impose," Sara said, suddenly nervous at the thought.

Jake sighed, closed his eyes slowly, opened them again. "I don't suppose it occurred to you that Miz Brand might not want or need my company?"

"It's not that," Sara argued. "I mean, it's just that I—"

"If she needs an escort around town, I'm sure she can dig up somebody she'd feel a little safer with than she would with me, don't you think, Flossie?"

Now *that* pissed Sara off. "I've known you a day, and already *that's* getting old, Nash," she muttered so softly that only he could hear her.

He frowned at her. "What?" he asked.

She shook herself. Forced a smile. Fluttered her lashes. "Actually, Jake, I'd be glad of your company," she said with exaggerated sweetness. Then she added, in a darker tone, "That is, if you think you can stand to be around me for that long." Maybe it was because he got to her and she wanted to get to him right back, or maybe she said it just to see if he would squirm. She didn't like him slamming himself for having a record, because each time he did, she felt as if he was slamming her favorite cousin, Wes. Besides, why did Jake hate the idea of spending time with her so much, anyway? He certainly hadn't seemed to hate her company out in the woods this morning.

He looked at her as if she'd grown horns. His expression more confused, perhaps, than angry. "Fine."

"Fine," she parroted.

"Lovely," Flossie said with a wide grin and a clap of her hands. "How about tomorrow?"

Sara licked her lips and met Jake's eyes. He was looking right back at her, almost daring her—to do what, she didn't know. "Tomorrow is fine by me," she said.

"Perfect." Jake said it like a swear word.

"I can see you're looking forward to this," Sara said.

"Yeah, like a toothache."

"Gee, I'll try not to let all this flattery go to my head."

Dead silence finally registered on her—on him, too, she thought. They both looked around the table, and she felt her face heat when she saw the way everyone was staring at them. With a sigh Sara pushed her chair away from the table. She was more than a little humiliated by her behavior, and even more so by having him react to her the way he had in front of everybody. "I'm...not very hungry, after all," she said. "I think I'll just head back to the bungalow."

"Oh, please stay," Flossie cried. "Jake's not himself at all today." There was a sound under the table, and when Jake flinched, Sara knew he'd been kicked. "Are you, Jake?" Flossie asked.

"No. Not myself at all," he muttered.

"Neither am I," Sara said. "Maybe it was just the drive out here, or the heat. God knows there's been a lot going on at home. Really, I'd just like to go to my bungalow and turn in early."

"All right, then. If you insist."

When she got up, Bertram and Trent rose automatically. Jake sat there until Flossie bored holes into him with her eyes, then he got up, too, moving as if every muscle in his body were protesting the effort. "Good night," he said.

"Night."

His eyes seemed to delve into hers for just a moment. Then he looked away, and Sara turned and left.

"Mr. Jacob Nash," Tante Flossie said, "if you don't go after that girl right now and make a proper apology, I'll...I'll..."

With a long-suffering sigh, Jake rolled his eyes. "Yeah, I kind of figured that would be the case. Why don't you fix her up a plate, and I'll take it on out there to her, after dinner."

Flossie sniffed. Trent just looked curiously at Jake, but Jake ignored the speculative look and went back to eating.

Sara took a long, cool shower, and that helped alleviate the sticky heat that had been clinging to her ever since her walk back to the bungalow. She got out of the tub, wrapped herself in a towel and took a more thorough look around her temporary home.

It was small. The furnishings were made of white wicker for the most part. Big chairs with floral cushions, matching footstools. A white wicker coffee table and end tables with glass tops. Even a white wicker lamp and magazine rack. The bungalow was lined all the way around by windows and screens. No air conditioning out here. But now that darkness had fallen and most of those windows were cranked wide open, a cooling breeze wafted in and swept some of the sultry heat away.

Sara's suitcases still lay on the floor just inside the front door, where Jake had dropped them. The big one was open. She'd rummaged through it for her laptop earlier, and then for the sundress she'd worn to dinner. But everything else remained packed. She felt a bit lazy, but then again, that was what vacations were about, right? Being laid-back and a bit lazy? Leaving responsibilities behind? Doing things you normally wouldn't do?

Like fantasizing about dark, dangerous men with shady pasts who ought to scare the hell out of you.

Sara shook that thought away and decided maybe Chelsea's cure was working far better than her sister-in-law would have wanted it to. She zipped up the big case, then picked it up and carried it through the bungalow, crossing on the cocomats that were scattered here and there over the hardwood floors.

The living room took up the whole front half of the small, square building. The back half was divided in two. On the left side was a small kitchenette. Minifridge mounted on a wall, a pair of tiny cupboards and a rectangle of countertop barely big enough to make a peanut butter sandwich on. There was a hot plate, a toaster and a small table with two chairs. The right half was the bedroom. Big windows, like those in the living room, lined it on two sides. It had a double bed and a nightstand with a glowing clock radio on it. The pair of small doors on the end led to a minuscule closet and a bathroom the same size as one. Shower, seat and sink. That was basically it. Clean towels were on the racks, though, and plenty of soaps and shampoos on the shelf inside the shower stall. Hey, it wasn't bad at all for what she was paying.

Off the back of the bungalow was another porch, but this one was fully screened in, where the one on the front was open.

She dropped the cases on the bed and started taking her clothes out and tucking them into the little closet. She hung some and left others folded, moving them onto the shelves. Somewhere in the process she shed her towel in favor of a lightweight nightgown of silky, cool, peach fabric, with spaghetti straps. The coolest thing she had brought along. Then she finished unpacking. It didn't take long. She hadn't brought all that much. She unloaded her brushes, combs, makeup and such onto the nightstand with the mirror attached. No room for anything other than her toothbrush in the bathroom.

Finished, she shoved both cases under the bed and then stood in the dim room looking around her. "Well, Sara, now what?"

She could use the time to think, she supposed. There was that problem at home to deal with. But she wasn't certain she was ready for that just yet. She wanted to be distracted.

A glance at the clock told her it was only a little after eight. Hardly bedtime. But there was no TV. She hadn't brought a book along—an oversight she could remedy when she went out tomorrow...

...with Jake.

Licking her lips, she wandered out onto that big back porch. The sounds of chirping, whirring insects, along with buzzing ones, and other noises, odd high-pitched sounds from the bayou—and low droning ones, too—were surprisingly loud. It was like walking into an orchestra pit during warm-ups.

For a moment she stood still, listening.

It was dark outside. She'd never liked the dark. Especially being alone in the dark. But that was before. When her fears hadn't been foolish, because someone really *had* wanted her dead. Now she felt again the familiar tingle along the back of her neck. The little shivery feeling creeping up her spine. The slight catch in her breathing. But she knew she didn't need it anymore.

"Go away and leave me alone," she whispered.

It didn't. She needed distraction. She needed to think about something else.

Jake.... He slipped into her mind like the serpent slipping into Eden. Tempting her. Sighing, she sat down on yet another wicker chair, closed her eyes, and, while the bayou's fragrant night-breath bathed her face, she let herself imagine him. Just for a little while. What could it hurt, anyway? It wasn't as if she was going to do anything about it. Besides, it would keep her from thinking about…other things.

So she thought. And the thoughts took on the quality of a daydream. In her mind, Jake, that handsome, dangerous devil, came out here to her cabin, after everyone else at the main house had gone to sleep. She saw him standing over her, looking down at her. He was wearing those tight jeans and that sweaty shirt hanging unbuttoned. And he was dirty, the way he'd been when he'd returned to the main house today. Hair damp and tangled, face streaked. He just stood there, staring at her where she lay in the little wicker chair. Her feet were up on a matching footstool. Her legs bare. Her nightie barely hiding a thing.

He came closer in her mind's eye, until he stood just beyond the footstool. Then, slowly, he took off his shirt. She watched, transfixed, as he peeled the fabric from his arms, revealing them to her. Strong, tanned, muscled. He flung the shirt aside, and, bending down, he closed one hand around her right ankle, the other around her left. She shivered as he parted them and stepped over the little footstool, then sat on it, between her ankles. Reaching for her, he closed those big, hot hands around her waist and pulled her to him, until she was sitting on his lap, her legs wrapped around him. He closed his arms around her, his hands sliding up to cup the back of her head, and then he kissed her.

"Sara?"

Lazily she opened her eyes, a soft smile tugging at her lips, and she said, "Jake..."

"Flossie asked me to bring this out to you," Jake said.

He was standing just beyond the little footstool, holding a plate of food in his hands.

Wait a minute. He was *really* standing there.

Sara's eyes widened as she realized she must have fallen asleep mid-fantasy. Her feet came off the little footstool and slammed onto the floor as she came to attention in her chair. "What do you want!"

He tilted his head to one side. "I told you already." He lifted the plate a little higher, nodding toward it. "Flossie asked me to bring this to you. You want it or not?"

Swallowing hard, she managed to nod. "Sure. Fine. Whatever."

"Right." He set the plate on the now-vacant footstool and turned to leave.

"Hey, don't get all touchy again," she said, scrambling to her feet. "I was sleeping, and you startled me, that's all."

"So you want me to do what? Wear bells on my shoes from now on so you'll know when I'm coming? I knocked, Sara. I called, and you didn't answer, so I came in."

"Yeah." She nodded, thinking about it. "The Big Bad Wolf came in to see if Little Red was all right. Huh, Jake? Isn't that a little out of character? Or is it that you're not quite as big and bad as you're trying so hard to make me think you are?"

He drew a breath, letting his eyes slide down her body slowly. "Maybe I just came in to see what you were wearing.'' Then he nodded. ''Nice choice, by the way.''

''You aren't scaring me, Jake.''

''I'm not trying to, Sara.''

''Yes, you are,'' she said. ''What I want to know is, why? Why are you trying so hard to make sure I dislike you?''

His eyes narrowed. Then he sighed, lowering his head. ''Okay,'' he said finally. ''Okay, fine. I give up. You win, all right? You just tell me how you want it, lady, and I'll oblige you.''

She frowned, tilted her head to one side. *''What?''*

''You heard me. You want a walk on the wild side, go for it. Shoot, I'm no Boy Scout, honey. Why the hell should I be? I'm not the one who initiated this. So come on. Come here and let's get on with it. And then you can rush on home to your sewing circle and tell the other aging virgins about your down-and-dirty, one-night stand.''

She stood perfectly still. She closed her eyes slowly, opened them again. Then, finally, she met his eyes again. ''You're that full of yourself, are you? Hmm? You really think that's what I've been sitting here plotting?''

''You gonna tell me it's not?''

She smiled very slowly. ''In your dreams, maybe. Then again, you don't need me coming on to you. You're your own best lover, aren't you?''

He swore at her. A really nasty little two-word slam that made her flinch. Instead of showing it, she just replied, ''You'd like to.'' Then, shaking her head, she snatched up the plate of food and headed for the door back into the bungalow. ''It's a real shame, you know that, Jake? I thought maybe you were a decent human being who was only acting like such an ass because he'd been judged too often on the basis of an unfortunate past. But, thanks for showing me the truth. You weren't acting at all. You really *are* an ass.''

She let the door bang behind her when she went inside.

But then she paused and bit her lip. She really had been fantasizing about him...exactly the way he thought, although not for exactly the reasons he'd concocted in his mind.

Damn. Why did he have to be such a jerk?

Chapter 4

So then, she *wasn't* coming onto him?

Jake stood on the screened-in porch staring at the door that had just banged shut and tried to review what had just happened here. But he really didn't get it. Why did women have to be so damned complicated, anyway? She either wanted to have a fling with him or she didn't. What was so hard about that? They were the only two options possible. She certainly wouldn't be interested in anything else with a guy like him. So why did she have to keep running hot and cold? One minute looking at him as if she wanted to leap on him right there, and the next, acting all huffy and slamming doors? What was up with the woman, anyway?

Hell, he couldn't make any sense of her at all. Maybe she would be more rational in the morning, when he showed up to take her sight-seeing.

With a frustrated sigh he went out the screen door,

down the little back steps and then walked around front to the path and the lonely walk to the main house.

Sara barely closed her eyes all night long. That man—that nasty, smart-mouthed, full-of-himself Jake Nash—made her so mad she couldn't even think straight. The nerve of him, assuming that just because she'd been nice to him—or tried to be nice to him—it meant that she wanted to...

In the morning she was no better. She slammed things, banged things and still hadn't vented half her anger. "Aging virgins, huh? I'll give him some aging virgins, right upside his head," she said as she showered, then stood in front of the mirror in the bathroom, looking herself over. "Twenty-five is *not* aging!" Then she yanked her clothes on and stomped barefoot into the kitchenette, where the coffee pot was just finishing up.

She filled her cup and stood still for a minute, staring at her face reflected back at her in the dark brew. She'd vented, she'd thrown things and slammed things and stomped around the place. She'd let off some steam. What was left was the truth. She'd been lying out there dreaming of making love to him, and when he'd woken her and said what he'd said, she'd gotten the feeling he knew. That he'd looked right inside her head somehow and seen the hot, sweaty images that had been playing in her mind. And it had mortified her.

Then he'd followed up with his insulting assumptions and flat-out insults. Pursing her lips, she glared at the coffee. "Aging virgin," she said again, and her hand clenched tighter on the coffee cup.

"We're all aging, sugar." That detestably cocky voice came from just beyond the front door, which was open to let the morning air in through the screen. She looked up to see him standing there, clean, shaved and wearing a shirt that was actually buttoned. "And the virgin part is obvious," he said.

"If you came for a hot-coffee facial, just step through that door, Jake, and I'll be happy to give it to you."

He eyed the cup in her hand, and his lips thinned. "I...might have been out of line last night."

"Might have been?" She lifted her brows.

"Hey, look, lady, cut me some slack here. I've been hit on by so many bored barracudas since I came to work here that it's become routine. Can you blame me if I read you wrong?"

She tilted her head to one side. "So that's how you solve the problem, then? You make sure they know it's a big inconvenience to you, and then you tell them you'll oblige them all the same?"

"No!" he said quickly. "I tell them to go to hell. For crying out loud, what do you think I am, some kind of stud service?"

"Yeah? Well you didn't tell *me* to go to hell!" she shot back.

They both went silent. His eyes clashed with hers, and his mouth opened to say something in his own defense, but then he closed it again, saying nothing.

She blinked twice and averted her eyes. Her voice a lot lower, she said, "Just for the record, Jake, I don't *do* one-night stands or vacation flings, and I'm not looking for any...stud service. Just because I'm...attracted to you doesn't mean that I want a quick night of meaningless sex. Okay?"

When she looked at him again, he looked kind of puzzled, a little crease between his brows. "What other kind is there?" he asked.

Her jaw fell open. She clamped it shut again. "You're a pig."

"And you're a princess. So once again, for the record as it pertains to you and me, what other kind of sex could there be besides meaningless?"

"None," she snapped. "None at all." She turned back to her coffee, looked for creamer in the little fridge and didn't see it, even though she knew damned well it was there.

"If that's the way you want it."

"It is."

"Good. Now that we've got that out of the way, why don't you put on some shoes and grab your moneybags so we can get going. I don't have all day."

Slowly she looked over her shoulder. "What are you talking about?"

"I'm talking about our date. What? You don't remember? I said no, but then you said yes, so I had no choice in the matter. If I don't follow through now, Flossie will never let me hear the end of it."

"Tell her I'm not feeling well."

"Okay. You can expect the local doctor at your door by noon."

"I don't need any doctor, and you damn well know it."

He shrugged. "Flossie won't see it that way."

Swallowing hard, she closed her eyes and sighed.

"It won't be so bad," he said. "I think now that we know where we both stand, we'll get along just fine."

"Now that we know where we both stand," she repeated, still wanting to smack him.

"Yeah. You're hot for me and knocking yourself out trying to fight it."

Pursing her lips, she nodded slowly. "And you'd be incapable of turning me down, should I decide to *stop* fighting it," she said.

"Now who's full of herself?"

She shrugged. "Well, you didn't tell me to go to hell, now did you, Jake?"

"Day's not over yet, lady."

"No. It's not." She looked around, spotted her sandals by the door and crossed the room to step into them. Then she snagged her straw bag off the little glass-topped table, yanked out her sunglasses and stuck them on her face. Turning to Jake, she said, "So, are we going or what?" She started for the front door.

"Wait a minute."

Sara turned, wondering what on earth he could possibly want now. He stood there, leaning on her wicker chair, looking maybe just a little bit thoughtful for once. And he said, "I, um, I'm sorry."

She blinked, waiting for the punchline or the slam or whatever would come next. But he didn't elaborate. "You are?" she asked stupidly.

"Look, um, you're obviously not here with the same motives as any other woman I've met, so—"

"I'm *nothing* like any other woman you've met, Jacob Nash," she snapped.

His lips quirked at the corners, as if he were battling a smile. "No, I guess maybe you're not."

"I'm glad you realize it."

* * *

He almost liked her, he decided.

They'd spent the morning pigging out at his favorite pancake house, then they'd done some sightseeing. He took her to lunch at a Cajun place where the music was as spicy as the food. She'd wanted to try everything and damn near burned her taste buds off. But even then, she had still kept her sense of adventure, though he figured she had drunk a gallon of water in between samplings.

It was late afternoon now. Jake drove Trent's Miata into the French Quarter, all the windows down, and watched Sara Brand not fussing with her hair. He thought maybe he *did* like her. At least, he liked her when she was too busy biting his head off to be afraid of him.

And he liked that she'd admitted to being "attracted to him," even though she denied being out for a quick tumble and a kiss goodbye. He thought she was probably a bit confused on that score...as far as what she wanted and didn't want from him sexually. But that, too, was understandable. She hadn't, after all, denied being a virgin, either.

He parked the car and got out, and she did the same. She didn't wait for him to come around and open her door for her, and he thought for a minute on that. Was it because she preferred doing it herself or because she doubted he had enough class to bother? Well, if it were the former, good for her. If it were the latter—hell, he hadn't exactly given her any reason to think otherwise, now had he?

"So what's the plan?" she asked him.

He actually had other reasons for being in this part of New Orleans. He was hoping to run into his cousin, Vivienne. He had it on good authority that this was where she liked to hang out with her lovers. And he was dying to give the woman an ultimatum and end her antics once and for all. But he wasn't going to tell Sara Brand any of that. "We walk, and if we pass someplace interesting, we go inside," he told her instead. "You'll get a lot more out of it that way than you would on any organized tour."

"Sounds good to me."

Jake started walking and she fell right into step beside him. He pointed out various landmarks. The famous restaurants. The historical homes. The jazz club he liked best.

That was where she wanted to go inside. His approval of her jumped another notch. Then he saw the person he'd been looking for and was doubly glad the lady had a weakness for jazz.

Vivienne. His beautiful cousin wore tight, yellow capri pants and a blouse that was little more than a handkerchief with straps. Stiletto heels. Platinum blond hair twisted and slick. Horn-rimmed sunglasses that were black. Just like her heart, Jake thought.

She went into the club without seeing him, on the arm of some empty-headed pretty boy Jake imagined was an aspiring actor or a professional model.

He took Sara's arm when they passed through the bright-red doors and entered the dark, smoky room, where already the sultry sounds of a tenor sax were waiting to greet them. Jake scanned the crowd in search of Vivienne and the bastard she was with.

"I wouldn't think the bands would start playing until night," Sara said. She had to lean close and speak loudly, near his ear. The shiver of pleasure that gave him was sizable, and it shook him right out of thoughts of Vivienne.

"It's always night in here, sweetheart," he said. He was still holding her arm. It was crowded, and he didn't want to lose her. Or that was what he told himself, anyway. He made a path through the bodies and sidled up to the bar. "Whisky," he said. Then he looked at Sara. "And what do you want?"

"The same."

He raised his brows.

"Well...I've never had whisky before."

He shrugged while the bartender poured. "You won't like it."

"Why not? You do."

Blinking at her, he allowed a small smile. "This isn't a contest sugar. Yeah, I like whisky. I even keep a bottle at the house, for my own private use. No one else can stand the stuff...except for Viv, on occasion." Actually, he'd noticed the level in his private bottle dropping drastically the past few days. Someone was drinking two or three shots every night, and it wasn't him.

Maybe what Viv was up to was making her nervous. Good. Served her right.

"Viv. That's your cousin, Trent's wife, right?"

"Yeah." Jake spun his stool around, putting his back to the bar, scanning the room. He finally spotted his cousin. She was cuddled up nice and cozy with her hunk at a corner table. Practically in his lap.

"What does she do?" Sara asked.

"She doesn't exactly do anything. Bertram and Flossie are pretty wealthy, though you wouldn't know it to look at them. They give her all the money she can spend and will probably leave her the entire plantation when they're gone. Not that she'll ever do anything but run it into the ground. Of course, Trent wouldn't. Trent would take care of the place…but not if it meant going against the little wife. He's devoted to Viv and her whims.''

Sara swallowed hard. ''I get the feeling she's not very nice.''

''She's not.''

Nodding slowly, Sara asked, ''In what way?''

He glanced at her. ''I don't like airing the family's dirt, *chère*. You'll think less of us than you already do.''

''I happen to like your family very much. Besides, every family has dirt.''

''Yeah. Right. You saying the pristine Brands have skeletons in their family closets?''

Sara's smile was a little bit shaky. ''You don't believe me?''

He shook his head.

Sara looked him square in the eye. ''My parents were killed when I was very small. I don't remember much. But I do recall my dad being away a lot. On business, they used to tell me. Well, just the other day, I found out where he really was on those business trips.''

''Really? Where?''

Sara's eyes got a little damp, and Jake almost regretted asking.

''Oklahoma,'' she said. ''Turns out my daddy was a bigamist. He had another wife, another family. I have five illegitimate half-sisters I knew nothing about. And now I have to decide if I even want to.''

''Hoo-ey,'' Jake said automatically. ''Shoot, Sara.

I'm sorry. I didn't know." He gave his head a shake. "No wonder you're so tense and testy."

"Hell, Jake, that's not even the half of it. But it's your turn. Come on, what could be so bad that I'd think less of your family if I knew about it?"

"You really want to know?"

She nodded. And while it wasn't like him to share family matters with outsiders, he found himself perfectly willing with her. Because...she was different. And she'd pretty much convinced him that she wasn't going to judge anyone. And she'd trusted him with a little bit of her own dirt.

"Look right over there," he said, and he pointed. "Corner booth. Vivienne."

He watched Sara instead of Vivienne. Watched her brown eyes scan the faces, fall on the couple and then widen. Saw her wet pink lips part on a gasp. "But...but that's not Trent."

"No," he said. "It's not."

"Oh... Oh, damn," she whispered. "Poor Trent." She bit her lower lip, lowered her eyes. "Maybe we shouldn't be here, Jake."

"No." Jake's gaze was on Vivienne now, and he was getting madder than hell. "She's the one who shouldn't be here." He started to slide off the stool, unable to sit still any longer. Trent was his best friend, his *only* friend.

Sara's hand closed around Jake's bicep, her grip surprisingly strong for such a small hand. "Jake, don't."

He paused, looked at her.

"It's just not smart. Besides—" she nodded at the bar, where the tender was just setting down two shot glasses ''—our drinks are here.'' She gave him a shaky little half smile.

He returned it. ''You're probably right.'' He settled back onto his stool, closed his hand around his glass, lifted it. She mimicked him. ''All in one gulp. Ready?''

She picked up her glass and nodded. Jake caught the bartender's eye, and the man gave him a nod. Then Jake clicked the rim of his shot-glass to the rim of Sara's and said, ''Bottom's up.''

He slugged his shot back. She did, too. Then she smacked the glass on the table, and her eyes widened to the size of silver dollars. She opened her mouth and went, ''haaaaaaaa,'' and thumped the glass on the bar three more times. The bartender handed her the glass of water he had waiting, and she gulped from it.

''Told you you'd hate it,'' Jake said.

She made such a funny face that he laughed. He couldn't help it. The bartender chuckled, too. ''Yech,'' she said. ''That must be what paint thinner tastes like.''

''It's…pretty close, actually.'' Jake was still grinning. And for just a moment his rage faded. Amazing.

Sara turned to the bartender. ''The water isn't cutting it. I need some…milk or something.''

''*Milk?*''

She nodded.

Jake shrugged and the bartender lifted his hands in surrender and went off to get the lady a glass of milk. She drank it all down, smacked the glass on the bar and said, ''Now that's a drink.''

She had a milk mustache.

It was at that very moment that Jake felt it. An odd sort of squishy feeling right in the middle of his chest. All warm and gooey. And a bubbling sort of frothy feeling in his belly. And a kind of a tightness in his throat. It came on all at once, without warning, and it scared him more than a sudden, crushing chest pain would have done. When he shook it off, he was left with a kind of aftershock.

He reached up without a thought and with his thumb, he wiped the milk from her upper lip. "You're too damn wholesome, you know that?"

She shrugged. "I'm a kindergarten teacher. I have a *degree* in wholesome."

"Yet you're slugging back shots with an ex-con."

Her smile was slow. "I'm on vacation." Then her expression grew a bit more serious. "Maybe you being such a big, scary ex-con is what's letting me enjoy myself so much."

He frowned at her. "You're gonna have to explain that one."

She turned around, wiggled her milk glass in the air. The bartender took it and brought her a refill. He handed her a chocolate chip cookie and said, "This is on the house, kid."

The smile she gave him would have been thanks enough for any man, Jake thought.

"I'm usually a nervous wreck in crowds, especially in strange places. You know, away from home. Around strangers. But I don't think I've looked over my shoulder once all day."

Was she saying she felt…safe…*with him?* Man, that was a laugh. "Why is that, Sara?" he asked her. "That you're usually so nervous, I mean?"

For the first time all day, he saw a shadow fall

over her eyes, and he regretted the question immediately. "I'm not gonna talk about that today," she
said. "I don't want to even *think* about that today.
Besides, it doesn't matter. It's in the past."

"The past always matters," he told her.

"Oh, no. You're way off base on that one. The
past is gone with the tick of a second hand. Blown
away like a stray breeze. Every day is a chance to
start over."

"That's quite the philosophy."

A loud, high-pitched giggle drew his gaze. He
looked at Vivienne with her lover and lowered his
head.

"If you go over there and make a big scene,
you'll ruin the whole day, Jake," Sara said very
logically. "She's not worth ruining such a great day
over, is she?"

"She's not worth ruining a bad day," he said.
"And you're right. This isn't the time or the place
for me to have this discussion with her. But believe
me, I am going to put a stop to this. One way or
another, this was Viv's last rendezvous with Mister
Wonderful there."

Sara looked at him, frowning hard. He shook his
head. "Let's get out of here," he said.

She nodded, grabbed her cookie and jumped off
the stool. Until then, he'd been sinking fast into a
murky haze of anger. But when he saw the way she
snatched a napkin up, carefully wrapped her cookie
inside it and then tucked it into her straw shoulder
bag as if she were tucking away the Hope diamond,
that angry haze dissipated. He felt lighter again. Felt
himself inclined toward grinning again.

They stepped outside, into the sunlight, which

was blinding after being in the darkness for so long. "So what do you want to see next?" he asked.

She shrugged, then inhaled. "I can't believe how good it smells here! It's like everyone in New Orleans is cooking their favorite dish all at once. And all the smells are being fanned out at innocent by-standers, and—" She stopped talking and looked back at the doorway they'd just exited.

Jake looked, too. Vivienne stood there, watching as her hunk walked away. When he got around a corner, she turned and looked right into Jake's eyes.

"We came so close, too," Sara muttered.

Viv came forward. "Well, I didn't expect to see you here Jake. Who's your...friend?"

"Her name is Sara. She's renting a bungalow for the week, and you'd have met her by now, if you ever bothered coming home to your family."

Sara elbowed him, but it was too late now to stop.

"Who was *your* friend?" he asked.

Vivienne lifted her painted-on brows in a perfect mimicry of innocence.

"Oh, come on, Viv, we both saw you in the club sucking face with that guy. And I've got news for you. It ends here. Today."

Vivienne's innocent expression vanished. Now she looked more like herself. Mean and selfish. "What I do and with whom I do it is none of your business, Jake Nash. Just who do you think you are, anyway?" She turned as if to go.

Jake grabbed her wrist and jerked her back around. He heard Sara gasp and tried to ignore it. "End it, Viv. Today. I mean it."

"Like I'm going to listen to some washed-up criminal? Let go of me, Jake."

"I'm not gonna let you ruin Trent like this. If you don't want him, then leave him. But don't do this."

"I said *let go!*" She hauled off and slapped Jake hard across the face.

He let go. All around them, people were looking, watching. It burned him to know what they saw. A low-life jerk manhandling a nice lady. "If you don't end it, I'm going to go to Flossie and Bertram, and I'm going to tell them what you've been up to."

The fury drained from her face, along with the color. "You...wouldn't."

"I'm so close you wouldn't even believe it. They'd disinherit you and you damn well know it."

"They...would never believe you over me!"

"I'm not so sure about that. But even if it were true, don't forget that Sara saw it all, too."

Vivienne's hate-filled eyes raked Sara briefly before returning to Jake. "If I leave Trent, they'll disinherit me, anyway," she said, all but hissing.

"So stay with him. Treat him half as well as he treats you. He'll think he's in freaking heaven."

"You're a son of a bitch, you know that?"

"I mean it, Vivienne. You give me a reason, I'll spill it all."

She spun on her heel and stomped away, not looking back. The crowd around them dissipated the second Jake swung his gaze over them. They couldn't get out of there fast enough.

Finally he remembered Sara and turned toward her. She was pale. The light was gone from her eyes; the smile from her lips. He didn't think they would be coming back anytime soon.

"I'm sorry."

"For what? Making a big, noisy horrible scene in

the middle of the street? Grabbing a woman hard enough to bruise her wrist? Yelling like a maniac? Using me to threaten your cousin? Or just generally ruining my day?''

He licked his lips, lowering his head. ''I guess dinner's out of the question, then, huh?''

''I want to go back. Now, Jake.''

''All right,'' he said. ''I'll take you back.''

He honestly couldn't remember when he'd regretted anything quite as much as he regretted screwing up Sara Brand's good day. She had been having fun with him. She had been relaxing with him, letting some of that tension she'd brought with her drain away. She had trusted him with her family secrets, and she'd listened to his as if she really did give a damn.

And then she'd turned nervous and sullen and jittery again. All because he was a hot-tempered jerk who didn't know when to leave well-enough alone.

Maybe it was for the best, though.

He hadn't liked that feeling that had come over him very much at all. It had been too big. Too hopeless. Too...everything.

Chapter 5

Was she afraid of him a little bit, after all?

No.

Was she wrong not to be?

Sara sighed deeply and thought on that for a moment. Jake had been furious at Vivienne, and when his pretty cousin had slapped him, Sara had seen something flare in his eyes…as if maybe he'd been thinking of hitting her back.

Maybe not. But…*maybe*.

And maybe Sara had been pretty damn stupid to be running all over New Orleans with a man who was an admitted criminal, who'd done time in prison and whom she barely knew. Maybe she'd been a complete idiot.

But she didn't really think so. As logical as it sounded when she told herself those things, she honestly didn't believe them.

So what was that? Instinct? Or wishful thinking? Could she trust her own gut feelings in this matter?

The logical solution would be to leave here. Get away from him and his slutty cousin and his family drama and not look back. But the more appealing course of action would be to find out for herself exactly what Jake Nash was made of, just what kind of man he really was. But how?

"You're awfully quiet." His deep voice broke into her thoughts. The long straight stretch of cypress-lined highway, broken only by dense shimmering heat waves, had been having a hypnotic effect. She'd almost forgotten she was in the car with him.

Sara gave herself a mental shake but didn't look at him. "Maybe I don't feel like talking."

"Maybe you're mad at me for ruining your day."

"No *maybe* about that one, Jake." She darted a glance at him. He looked troubled, intense.

"I couldn't just let it slide, Sara. She was making a fool out of my only friend, for crying out loud. *Publicly.* What did you expect me to do?"

Her head swung around when he said the words *only friend.* And a surge of ridiculous emotion welled up inside her, rising in her chest like a thick, warm tide. "I don't know what I expected," she said very softly, seeing beyond the hard glint in his eyes now to the pain behind it. In spite of herself and her mind's constant warnings, she kept imagining him as a boy. Just a boy. Seventeen or eighteen years old, being sent to prison for what must have seemed to him like the rest of his life. "Whatever I expected, Jake, it wasn't that you'd attack Vivienne the way you did."

"Hell, if I'd *attacked* her, they'd be scraping her off the sidewalk by now."

That warm tide turned cold and drained like a whirlpool. Sara trembled, and there was a brief flash of memory—buried deep, but alive still. Bodies on the floor. Blood pooling. All seen through the eyes of a four-year-old child, playing hide-and-seek in the kitchen cabinet with the door that didn't close quite all the way. A child who, even in her innocence knew her mamma wasn't going to come find her this time.

Then Jake swore, snapping her out of the nightmares of her past. "Damn it, woman, don't look like that. It was sarcasm, all right? Haven't you ever heard it before?"

"Of course I have. I just...I just—"

"You just never heard it from an ex-con."

Swallowing hard, she looked at him slowly. Her eyes burned, but she blinked them dry. "Why don't you quit feeling sorry for yourself, Jake? It's really wearing thin, you know."

"You should try living it for a couple of decades."

"*Living* it? You *wallow* in it."

He'd turned off the highway, onto the side road that led out to the plantation. She was glad of that, because there was less traffic here, and he was too busy gaping at her to look at the road. "I *wallow* in it?"

"Yeah. You do. You wallow in it. You bring it up at least once in every conversation we have. Why is that, Jake? Huh? I couldn't care less about it, so why do you think you have to keep waving it around like a big red flag? Are you warning me away, or just hiding behind it?"

He hit the brake. The car stopped, and Sara lurched forward, hands shooting to the dash automatically as the seat belt pulled tight. Then she sat straight again, only to find those dark eyes boring into her. "What exactly do you think I'm hiding from? Hmm? A prim-and-proper little kindergarten teacher?"

She looked at him for a long moment. His tanned face, stubble painting it with soft shadows now, in the late-afternoon light. His eyes, gleaming and dark and boiling over with feelings he kept locked tight inside. Pain. Old, rusty pain that he probably thought he couldn't even feel. But he *was* feeling it. It was eating him up inside. She'd seen it before, in her cousin, Wes. In her brother, Marcus. Old pain could just about kill a man if he let it. He wasn't the bad guy. He wasn't like the men who'd butchered her family. He was like her brother. His life torn apart before it had a chance to get started. She knew she was right. She *had* to be right.

She pressed the button to release her seat belt and slid closer to him, and she saw the flare of alarm in his eyes.

"No, Jake," she said. "I don't think you're afraid of a kindergarten teacher. I think you're afraid of this." And she leaned up just enough to brush her lips across his. She let her lashes fall to her cheeks, touched his mouth with hers, and wished he would respond instead of sitting there like a rock.

He didn't.

She drew back, lowering her eyes, unable to look at him. He obviously hadn't...wanted that kiss.

Jake was silent for a long moment. Then he sighed loudly. *"That?"* he said at last. "You think I'm afraid of *that?"* When she managed to lift her gaze to his, she saw something that hadn't been in his eyes before. Something dark, frightening and exciting all at once. "Come here," he said, his voice low and rough against the raw surface of her senses. He snapped his arms tight around her waist and drew her hard against him. "I'll show you something worth being afraid of."

And she *was* afraid, in the heartbeat before his mouth captured hers. After that the fear left her. Everything left her. Every coherent thought, every emotion. There was only the sensation of his mouth on hers, nudging it open; of his tongue thrusting inside, taking and tasting what it would; of his arms holding her crushingly to him.

When he finally let her go, she was breathless. Her heart pounded like the hooves of a runaway horse, and her vision seemed distorted and blurry. Hand to her chest, she leaned back in her seat.

Without a word Jake put the car into gear and drove the rest of the way back to Sugar Keep.

Dinner was tense. Sara tried to make conversation to lighten the mood, but it was having no effect. Vivienne sat beside her husband, acting for all the world as if nothing out of the ordinary had happened today, except for the daggers she occasionally shot at Jake. Jake looked as if he would like to strangle her. Trent seemed oblivious to it all, for which Sara was thankful.

There was just as much tension—maybe more— between Jake and Sara. Every time she looked at him, she could feel that kiss again. The passion building inside her in a way it had never done before. And when he looked back at her, she swore she saw the same thing in his eyes. She wanted so much to talk to him alone, to make him tell her what had happened to him when he was a teenager. What had happened to make him resort to robbing that store. She wanted him to be able to explain it away so that these feelings coming to life inside her would be all right. Would be sane and logical and good, as she was already convinced they were. Rather than self-destructive and foolish and blind, as she half feared they might be. And she wondered if it would matter which they were, because she would feel them, anyway.

"Did you enjoy your trip into the city, child?" Flossie asked, with a smile that appeared forced.

"Very much. I'm glad you suggested it."

"Jake needed a day off. He tends to take life far too seriously for his own good, don't you, Jake?" Flossie beamed when she looked at her nephew. "Admit it, now. You had a good time, too, didn't you?"

He glanced sideways, his gaze touching Sara's lips very briefly. Then meeting her eyes. A secret message. "Oh, I don't know. I think the little bit of New Orleans life we sampled today was just a teaser. There's a lot more to be savored."

She couldn't take her eyes away from his as he went on.

"I really expected our Sara would be a little bit afraid of the spicier selections. But she surprised me. Today I think she was willing to try just about anything."

Vivienne made a snorting sound but covered it by pretending to clear her throat.

Flossie shot her a glance but said nothing. Sara felt heat creeping into her cheeks and decided it was time to call it a night. "I should go. The gumbo was delicious, Flossie."

"Oh well, don't give me the credit. Berty made it. Didn't you, hon?"

Bertram smiled and nodded, quiet as always.

"Don't go yet," Flossie said. "Stay for an after-dinner drink. Berty's gonna make mint juleps for us, or you can have whisky, as Jake and Vivienne prefer."

"I think Sara's had plenty to drink already today," Jake said, still eyeing her. This time, though, there was a hint of a smile in his eyes. And she knew he was remembering her first taste of whisky and the milk chaser.

"It's dark outside," he said. "I'll walk you back to the bungalow."

Her stomach flip-flopped. What would happen if he did? She didn't know...yes, she did, and she didn't think she was ready. "I...I think I'd like to go alone, Jake," she said. "Maybe do a little exploring before I turn in."

He held her gaze for a long moment, and she half expected him to get all defensive again. But he didn't. He finally sighed and nodded. "Okay. I'll walk you out to the path, then."

"All right."

He pushed his chair away from the table, then glanced back at Vivienne. "The whisky's all yours tonight, Cuz. I'm gonna have milk." Turning back, he winked at Sara, then took her arm and led her outside.

They crossed the veranda, went down the steps and stopped on the sidewalk. Overhead the night sky was dense with stars, and the air was still heavy, if slightly cooler now. It smelled of magnolia and roses.

"The reason I want to walk back alone—"

"I'm sorry about today—"

They both spoke at once, then looked at each other and smiled. "Was that an apology, Jake? I can't believe it."

He lowered his head. "Why be surprised? It seems to me I spend almost as much time apologizing to you as I do insulting you."

She shook her head. "We just...keep poking each other's sore spots, I think."

"You think?" he asked.

"Yeah."

Jake drew a breath, blew it out. "Why don't you go first? The reason you don't want me walking back with you is...?"

"That I'm trying to take my time and use my head where you're concerned. And tonight I'm not sure I could do that."

He looked up again, smiled very slightly. "I'm not sure whether to be thrilled or heartbroken."

Her face heated, and she bit her lower lip, then spoke again. "Just so we're clear on this...that's the only reason. Your past mistakes have nothing to do with it."

He nodded. "You were right about that, Sara. I have been wallowing in it. It's just that I've butted heads with so many people who can't seem to get past it. I feel as if I'm branded for life. Like no one's ever going to see beyond the time I did, the mistakes I made."

"Well, you're wrong about that, Jake. I can see past them. Most people could, if you'd bother showing them what else there is to see."

"I think maybe you do. But that doesn't mean most people would. You're...not like anyone else, Sara. I don't know where the hell you came from, but you're not the poster girl for humans in general, that's for *damn* sure."

She lifted her brows. "Was there a compliment hiding in that twisted-up mess of nonsense?"

One corner of his mouth quirked upward. "I like you, Sara Brand."

"I like you, too," she said, but it came out kind of raspy. She cleared her throat.

"So, uh, about that apology," Jake said. "I'm sorry I spoiled our day together. Not sorry I gave Viv an ultimatum...never that. Someone has to put a stop to what she's doing, and I guess I'm the only one willing to take on the job. But...I shouldn't have involved you."

"Apology accepted," she said. "I disagree totally on the rest."

"I'm not done yet." Drawing a deep breath, Jake went on. "I'm sorry about that kiss, too."

Sara quickly pressed her forefinger to his lips. "No, Jake. Don't you dare apologize for that."

His eyes probed hers. "No?"

She shook her head slowly from side to side.

He took the cue, sliding his arms around her, pulling her close and kissing her again. But it was tender this time. It was soft, deep—hot, yes, but not as demanding, not as angry. Almost as if he were kissing her with every part of him this time, with all five senses savoring every nuance of the act. His lips nuzzled and nibbled and tasted, and he took his time about it. When he lifted his head, there was fire in his eyes. "You're…real sure about not wanting me to walk you back, I suppose?"

"Oh, I *want* you to. I just…"

"I know. You're not ready."

"I don't know what's between us yet, Jake. I told you already, I don't do physical attractions or one-night stands or vacation flings. If this is any of those things it'll pass soon enough, and I'll know that's all it was. But if it's more…then…then we have time. Because it's not going to be over when my week here runs out." She licked her lips nervously. "Do you understand what I'm telling you?"

He stood there staring down at her, looking surprised and more than a little bit shaken. "You're crazy. I'd be crazy to think this could lead to anything even remotely close to what you— You're *crazy*."

She shrugged. "Well…we'll see." Then she turned to go.

Jake caught her arm, turning her back around. "Wait. I want to show you something. Come here." He closed his hand around hers and drew her around the corner of the house, then pointed upward. "That second window from the back is mine. I have a clear view of the bungalow from there. If you…if you change your mind…put a light in the kitchen window. Turn off all the others and just put that one on. I'll see it."

Sara closed her eyes, already knowing she would

be battling the urge to do just that all night long. "You're not making this very easy, Jake."

"I wasn't trying to."

Looking up at the windows again, she said, "I can see this side of the house from the bungalow, too. Especially after dark, if the lights are on in the house. I saw Vivienne come home last night, late. She turned her light on and was moving around her bedroom. That one there." She pointed.

"Yeah. That's her room. Hers and Trent's. Though it's seldom they're in there at the same time lately. Tonight he's going out of town yet again."

"I heard him mention it at dinner. Why doesn't he take her with him?"

"Probably assumes she'd say no."

With a deep sigh Sara lowered her head.

"What?"

"Nothing. I just…well, I wonder if Vivienne's as much to blame in all of this as you think she is. Maybe if Trent were all over her the way that guy at the bar was, then…"

"Oh, come on, Sara. Nobody acts like that once they've been married six months."

"You haven't seen my brother and sister-in-law, or any of my cousins with their wives," she countered. "They all act like that."

"With *each other?*"

She scowled at him.

"No one's capable of that kind of closeness over the long haul," Jake said.

Sara shook her head. "Everyone is capable of it…helpless against it, even, when they find their soul mate."

Jake sighed, and his smile was a little bit sad. He

came closer and ran a hand over her hair. "I don't know what you think I am, Sara, but I wish to hell I could be it for you. I really do."

"But...?"

"But I can't. I'm not a nice guy. I'm a criminal with a record. I'm the black sheep of my family— what's left of it, anyway. And they only put up with me because my mother managed to lay a big guilt trip on Uncle Bert from her deathbed."

She stepped back, gaping. Then she snapped her jaw shut. "You really think that? My God, Jake, you're blind if you believe that. Flossie practically glows when she talks about you, and there's real caring in Bertram's eyes when he looks at you. I don't know how things were when you first came here, Jake, but those two love you now."

He rolled his eyes.

"They *do!*" she insisted.

He looked at her. "Maybe...they like me a little bit. I've been here a year now. I suppose they could be getting attached."

"You're like a son to them, Jake. Take my word on that."

He shook his head, looking away.

Licking her lips, she sighed. "I should go."

"Yeah, and I should let you." Then he lifted his head, met her eyes and said, "In a minute." He kissed her again, then. He held her tight to him and kissed her mouth, backing her up against the side of the house. Honeysuckle vines embraced her there, and she twisted her arms around Jake's neck, let him crush her body to his, met his tongue when it came sliding between her lips. Even opened her mouth wider to receive it. His hands slid down to cup her buttocks and pulled her hips forward, so that the hard bulge between his legs could press into her. And she rubbed against that hardness as he set her on fire inside.

Sliding his lips over her jaw, he moved lower, to her neck, sucking and nipping at the tender skin there as he rocked against her in a desperate mimicry of lovemaking. His hands squeezed her buttocks, his teeth scraped her skin. Heat rose to enfold them like a sodden blanket. And she wanted in a way she'd never wanted before.

Lifting his head, he kissed her mouth again and whispered, "I'm not a good guy, Sara Brand. I can give you what you need...just not what you think you want. No tender emotions or hearts and flowers. But I can give you screaming fits of pleasure that you'll never forget. I can give you that."

Opening her eyes, breathless with need and a burning hunger, Sara looked deeply into his. "I'm holding out for the man who can give me both," she whispered. Then she pushed at his chest, and when he released her, she hurried away.

Running helped burn off the biting edges of the raw desire Jake Nash had awakened in her tonight. Helped...but didn't totally erase it. Still, by the time she reached the bungalow she was a bit more in control of herself.

Or she thought she was.

Why, then, did she keep eyeing the oil lamp by the kitchen window? Why did she go so far as to reach for the matches sitting beside it, even picking them up...then putting them down again only by an incredible act of will? Why did she pace the floors and then the porches and then the lawn outside, rather than go to sleep that night?

Why had she let Jake Nash get under her skin?

Jake went back into the house feeling more torn and hot and frustrated than he'd ever felt in his life.

"So what's up with you two?" Trent asked him.

Jake gave his head a shake. "Nothing."

"Nothing, huh? Didn't look like nothing to me."

"Well, it's nothing. Trust me, pal."

Trent nodded and started for the door. Jake noticed then that he had a suitcase in his hand. "So you're heading out?"

"Yeah. It's a cotton-growers' seminar. I think this ground has lain fallow long enough. Sugar Keep ought to be paying for itself instead of syphoning off Bert and Flossie's fortune." He nodded, affirming his own words. "Just want to make sure we choose the right crop."

"I think you're right."

"Well, that means a lot to me, Jake." Trent clapped Jake on the shoulder and turned toward the door.

"Trent...why don't you go on upstairs and ask Viv to go with you?"

Turning slowly, Trent frowned at him. "What do you mean?"

"I just... Just do it. Just go up there and tell her you want her with you. You guys are letting it fall apart. Maybe...maybe some time alone together, on a trip like this, would—"

Trent looked at the floor, his expression so sad that Jake almost ached for him. "It's too late for that, my friend. It's just...it's too late."

"You telling me you don't love her anymore?"

"Come on, Jake, I don't want to talk about this with you."

"Do you love her or don't you? Because if you don't, you two would be better off calling it quits than going on like you've been doing. You're just torturing each other, for crying out loud."

"You can forget it, Jake. It's not gonna happen."

His tone made Jake look up slowly. "What do you mean?"

Trent blinked, seemed to shake himself, plastered a smile back on his face. "Never mind, my friend. I just...I overreact where Viv's concerned. I mean, I love her, of course I love her. I want to fix things. But...well, maybe when I get back."

Sighing, Jake lowered his head. "I guess you have to do it the way you think is best."

"Yeah. I guess I do. But...well, thanks for caring, bud."

Jake just nodded. "Yeah. Good trip, okay?"

"See you when I get back." Trent stepped outside, and Jake closed the door.

Jake went on up to his room, but despite a cool shower and an excellent action video, he was unable to put thoughts of Sara Brand out of his mind. He paced his floor that night and asked himself what the hell he thought he was doing, making out with her outside in the dark, like a teenager with his first crush. Had he lost his mind? Hadn't he learned anything? He was not good enough for a woman like Sara Brand. He wasn't even close. His world and hers did not mix. Oh, they could touch briefly, they could rub up against each other like a gator against a willow tree, but nothing more. A gator lived in the sludge and slime of the bayou. A willow needed fresh air and clean water and rich dark soil to thrive. Put her in the swamp and she would die. Take the gator out…ditto.

So why was he getting all soft where Sara was concerned? Why was it that when she talked about her cousins and their wives, about family and about men like him having a second chance—why did he find himself seeing it all in his mind? As if there were an ice cube's chance in New Orleans of it ever happening?

She was hypnotic. She was…she was special. Too special for a guy like him. And the sooner he got that through his head, the better.

He wanted her. Maybe he would even have her before she went back home to her pure and unsullied life. But on his terms. Not hers. No commitments. No promises. No future.

Basically those were the rules of his entire existence.

Chapter 6

If only she'd gone to bed, gone to sleep…stopped staring longingly up at the lighted bedroom windows on the south side of that big old house.…

But the shadows, the silhouettes moving beyond those mist-like curtains, were too enticing to allow her to look away. And Jake knew it, damn him. He had to know it. That was why he stood there for a long, long time, staring toward her bungalow. Searching for her signal. All she had to do was light the little oil lamp that sat on the windowsill. That was all. For hours she'd tried to put that thought from her mind, but it was still there, teasing and taunting. Still there. And the matches and lamp on the windowsill were putting out tractor beams to draw her hands.

No.

She stared back at him instead, from the safety of her darkened haven. The bedroom light was on, but only the faintest glow spilled into the kitchen where she stood.

Jake moved, and Sara's gaze remained riveted. He peeled his shirt off as she stood like a guilty voyeur. Like a sex-starved tramp. She licked her lips, felt her breath come stuttering in and out as if she were ill. Her blood heated, and she reached one trembling hand toward the lamp...

...removed the globe...

...picked up the matches...

Sweat popped out on her forehead, and the shaking that had begun in her hand moved down her arm and spread through her body. She ripped a match free, eyes still glued to that dark body in the distance. She felt possessed. As if Jake Nash really were the devil she'd believed him to be, and he'd taken over her soul.

Then his head lowered, and he turned away. His form vanished from her hungering eyes, and a second later the light in his window blinked out.

The breath rushed out of Sara's lungs as her body seemed to go limp. The spell was broken. She looked at the match in her hand, could barely believe how close she'd come to lighting it. Dropping the matches, she backstepped, as if they might burn her. They very nearly had.

If she were smart, she would put the matches far away from the lamp. Just in case she was tempted again. At least now he was gone. At least now her temptation wasn't right before her eyes. Of course, all she'd had to do was look away. But she hadn't been able to.

Even now her gaze was drawn back to that window. She forced herself to look away, marching to the bedroom and snatching a light robe, pulling it on over the flimsy nightgown she'd worn just in case.

What was wrong with her?

Barefoot, she stepped out of the bungalow, down the steps, burying her toes in the moist grass. Insects chirped, and all sorts of exotic and frightening sounds came from the bayou behind her. She had no idea what most of them were and decided she didn't really care. They were far less dangerous to her than the pleas of her own body right now.

She sucked in the fresh night air in greedy gulps, telling herself it would snap her out of the state into which she'd fallen. The breeze picked up for once, moving her hair, drying the sweat on her nape. But it was a bad wind that carried rank, decaying, swampy smells. She shivered all over, her entire body going cold. And when she saw the light go on in the distant window again from the corner of her eye, a sense of foreboding told her not to look.

Sara looked, anyway.

Two forms, not one. Shadow people, embracing in the window…not Jake's window. No. The one beside it. Vivienne's room. Sara almost smiled at the thought of Vivienne and Trent perhaps mending their tattered marriage, but her lips froze mid-motion, and her heart seemed to stop beating. Trent was out of town tonight. And…and that was not an embrace she was seeing.…

As the shadows turned, she saw in profile what she had not seen before—the man's hands clasped firmly at the woman's throat. The way her hands clawed at his, the way he shook her, so her head snapped back and forth…

"My God..." Sara's mind rebelled against what she was seeing, and the past seemed to draw closer, as if it would take over her mind.

The memory of what she'd seen as a little girl in the kitchen cabinet. And the killer's eyes when he'd finally spotted her there....

She shook the memory away. "Stop!" she shouted, even as she ran barefoot through the grass to the path. "Let her go!"

The form in the window froze, and the head turned. She couldn't see the man's eyes, but she could feel them on her. And she knew she stood in the moonlight and was probably more visible to him than he was to her—especially a second later when he dropped Vivienne's now-still body to the floor and reached out a hand to extinguish the light.

Sara felt the icy blade of fear skewering her, and the instinct to spin around and run in the opposite direction was almost too strong to resist.

He saw you, her mind screamed. *He's coming for you now...just like before.*

She fought her terror. Vivienne might still be alive. She had to do something. Run. Run toward the killer—not away. Try to help. Grating her teeth, she did.

Her feet pounded over the packed earth of the path, jarring her teeth, and her heart pumped harder with every step. Her breath came faster, and her lungs burned, and yet she didn't slow.

"Hurry!" she cried. "Someone help!"

She could no longer see that gruesome scene in the window, for the trees lining the path blocked her view. She was almost grateful for that. Dammit, why couldn't anyone hear her? She finally reached the yard, the sidewalk, the steps, shouting and shrieking all the way. It seemed to take forever to get there, and then on to the house, to climb the steps and cross the veranda. To haul open the screen. She reached for the door and yanked on the handle, only to find it locked. She pounded and yelled and yanked on the knob. She jammed her finger again and again on the bell. Tears streaming down her face, hoarse from her mad dash and her seemingly endless shouting. She kicked at the door in frustration, only to be sharply reminded that her feet were still bare. A sob was wrenched from her throat just as the door flew open.

Jake stood there, shirtless, wearing a pair of sweat pants and nothing else. He was damp, sweaty, as if he'd been exerting himself. And he was searching her face with a deep frown on his.

Then his hands closed on her shoulders, and drew her inside. "Sara, what the hell happened to you? Are you all right? What's—"

"Vivienne!" she rasped. "Go to Vivienne!"

"What?"

"The window! I saw through the window! He's *killing* her!"

She heard a pained gasp and looked up, spotted Flossie and Bertram standing at the bottom of the broad curving staircase in their nightclothes. Sara wished she could retract the words, but Flossie was already turning and hurrying back up. Bertram gripped her shoulders, held her firm. "No, love," he said.

Jake was already crowding past them, heading up the stairs. "Keep her down here—keep them both down here," he told Bert as he passed. Then he hit the top and lunged out of sight. His footsteps pounded, and a door creaked open. She didn't hear anything more for a long moment.

Sara was shaking all over. The memories wanted her…they wanted to claim her. Why must her eyes have to see so much violence? Why? She couldn't stand it. She couldn't—

"Call 9-1-1." Jake's voice was firm and eerily calm, coming from the top of the stairs.

Flossie bit her knuckle and sank toward the floor, and Sara rushed to help Bert get her to a chair and settle her into it. The woman didn't want to sit, though. Her pale face and wide, wet eyes were turned toward the staircase as Jake came slowly down. Sara reached for the phone and thumbed the buttons.

"I'm sorry, Tante Flossie, Uncle Bert," Jake said coming closer, as Sara spoke softly to the woman on the phone, asking for police and paramedics, giving the address, barely hearing the operator's questions, because she was so focused on Jake. He sank to one knee in front of Flossie's chair, gathered her hands in his. "Vivienne…" He lowered his head. "She's gone, Flossie. I'm sorry, there was nothing I could do."

The woman sat there in stunned silence, just looking at Jake with a plea in her eyes. Silently she begged him to tell her it wasn't true, that this was a mistake. "B-but…b-but…"

Bertram sank into a chair himself, lowering his head to his hands. His shoulders began to shake, and his tears were noisy ones. Inelegant, unreserved and messy.

"I want to go to her!" Flossie said suddenly, surging to her feet.

Jake put his hands on her shoulders. "No, you don't, hon." Then he looked at Sara as she put the phone down. "Can you stay with them? I need to have a look around. Don't leave this room, Sara. I mean it."

The killer could still be here, he told her with his eyes, not his words. She nodded, but thought about asking if there were a cupboard in the kitchen big enough for her to crawl into. They made great hiding places. At least...for a little while. Her throat went tight. Her oldest fears clawed at her senses. But she took Jake's place beside Flossie and convinced the woman to sit down again, while Jake stalked off in search of a murderer.

And after what seemed like forever, she finally heard sirens.

Jake knew in his gut what was coming. He knew damned well after searching Viv's room and finding nothing unusual, one slightly opened window, no evidence of any intruder, only the limp body of his pretty cousin lying on the floor. He knew what was going to happen next. While Sara sat with Flossie and Bert, he searched the house, went outside, had a look around underneath Vivienne's bedroom window. No footprints. No ground soft enough to leave any, but that wouldn't matter.

He ought to run. Every muscle in his body was twitching to run. He knew it would be the only sane thing to do. And there was no reason not to, for crying out loud.

But he couldn't. He couldn't do it, because he

couldn't stand the idea of leaving Tante Flossie and Uncle Bert believing the worst of him. Not that he didn't fully expect that, anyway. But running would make it look even worse. And what about Sara? What was she going to believe when the cops got here and said what he had no doubt they would say?

Why the hell did he care?

The sirens came wailing closer. Jake closed his eyes and licked his lips, and already he could feel the cold, cruel rub of metal on his wrists, could see the bars and smell the sweat-and-disinfectant scent of a prison cell. Dammit. Dammit straight to hell.

"And where is Jacob Nash right now?" one of the officers asked, with a look at the other one.

"He's right here." Jake's voice came from the doorway, and Sara felt a flood of relief to see him there. But he looked odd. He looked angry. Defiant. As if prepared to do battle. But still, she was glad he was back. Because her brave front was wearing very thin just now, and for some reason just seeing him in the same room seemed to bolster her somehow.

"And where have you been, Mr. Nash?" Officer Kendall asked.

"You think you already know the answer to that, so why bother asking me?" His tone was so bitter it made Sara suck in a breath.

She got to her feet, crossing the room to stand at Jake's side. "Jake, don't. Officer Kendall, we thought the killer might still be lurking, and Jake went to have a look around." Then she searched Jake's face. "Did you find anything?"

He only shook his head.

"And how do we know you weren't out there destroying evidence, Nash?" Kendall asked, looking at Jake as if he were looking at week-old garbage.

"You're gonna have to take my word on that."

The cop made a sound, a snort of air escaping him. "Right. The word of ex-cons is gospel. Everyone knows that."

"How about the word 'misconduct'?" Sara snapped.

The cop gaped at her, snapped his book closed, reached for his cuffs. "Turn around and put your hands behind your back, Nash."

"Go to hell," Jake growled.

"You can't arrest him!" Sara's voice broke in disbelief. "What are you? This is— I *told* you I saw the killer through the window!"

"You also told us you could only see him in silhouette. That you couldn't have identified him even if you knew him."

"I...I..."

"Up against the wall, Nash."

"No!" Sara said. "Look, I said I couldn't tell you who the killer *was.* But I can certainly tell you who he *wasn't,* and he wasn't Jake!"

The cop, cuffs dangling from one hand, eyed her sternly. "Would you swear to that in a courtroom?"

Her eyes shot to Jake's. The memory of his fight with Vivienne yesterday hit her hard—the memory of that brief moment when she'd glimpsed fury in his eyes and believed him capable of violence.

"He's killed before, you know," the second cop said.

What if he had done it? What if...what if...?

"I've seen a killer, Officer Kendall," Sara said

slowly. "I've stared right into his eyes, and I'm telling you, this man is no killer." She reached out to Jake then. "Give me your hands," she said.

"Don't bother, Sara. These two have already—"

"Give me your damned hands," she all but growled at him.

Looking surprised and confused, Jake complied.

Sara closed her hands around Jake's. Turning them over, she looked at the backs of them. Smooth, tanned, unmarred. "I saw—" Then she stopped herself, glanced up at Flossie and bit her lip. Still holding Jake's hands, Sara walked to the far side of the room, taking him with her. The two cops followed. "I saw Vivienne clawing at the hands on her throat," Sara whispered. "Check her nails, and you'll see I'm right. You're going to find blood and tissue under them. She had long nails. She'd have torn some skin. But there's not a mark on Jake's hands. I'm telling you, he didn't do it."

The cops looked at each other. One seemed relieved, but the other, Kendall, only looked angry. He glared at Jake. "You'd better hope I don't get so much as a kernel of evidence you did this, Nash, 'cause if I do, you're going right back behind bars where you belong. You hearing me?"

Jake said nothing, just glared back at the man.

Sara felt her demons fade into the background for just a moment as she tried to figure out why the man was being such a jerk—and then it hit her. "Wait a minute...Kendall? It just occurred to me...you're related to Bill Kendall, aren't you? The man who died in the convenience store holdup?"

The cop's eyes narrowed. "The man Jake Nash

killed, you mean? He was my grandfather. You have some kind of problem with that?''

"You bet your badge I do, mister.'' Sara squared her shoulders and leaned into the man in a way she'd never done to anyone in her life. "You're biased, and you shouldn't be within a hundred miles of this case,'' she said, pointing at him with a forefinger.

"Sara,'' Jake said. "Dammit, stay out of this.''

But she kept right on. "Don't you think for one minute that I won't be reporting this to your superiors, Kendall. I know the law. My cousin's a sheriff.''

"Yeah?'' Kendall said, leaning right back at her so his nose almost touched hers. "Well, my cousin's the D.A. So good luck.'' Then he backed up, turned on his heel and stomped away.

The other cop said, "Look, you all might as well get out of here for the night. The forensics team is gonna have to comb the place and…is there somewhere you can all go to get some rest? I mean…without leaving town?'' he added with a quick look at Jake.

Jake just nodded.

"I'll, uh, need to know where to reach you,'' the cop said.

"End of the path, bungalow two,'' Jake replied. He crossed the room, tugged a blanket off the back of the sofa and draped it around his aunt's shoulders. "It's gonna be okay, Flossie,'' he told her. "Come on, you just come with me, now. It'll be okay.'' Gently he drew her to her feet and then to the door, but she kept looking back, starting to speak, then stopping again. The poor thing was in shock.

"She ought to have a sedative,'' Sara said.

"Got any on you?" Jake asked, his tone sarcastic, as he helped Flossie down the porch steps and into the backseat of the SUV that sat in the driveway. Then he helped Bert get in beside her.

Sara stood next to the vehicle and got in the driver's door when Jake opened it. He didn't ask her why. Maybe it was obvious that she didn't want to be alone. Not even long enough to go to the other side of the car to get in. She slid across the seat and said, "Not on me. But I have some tranquilizers in my bungalow. If you stop there, we can run in and get them."

He stopped in the middle of backing the vehicle up, and she turned to find him staring at her. "Tranquilizers?" he asked.

She nodded. "I...haven't needed them in a long time," she said, and if it sounded a bit defensive, well, it probably was, because that was how she felt.

He looked at her for a long moment. "I guess there's a lot we don't know about each other yet, isn't there, Sara?"

"More than you could even imagine."

"How did you know...about Kendall?"

She grated her teeth, drew a breath. "After you told me you'd done time for murder, I got on the Internet and found the old newspaper articles about the case."

"Why?"

She turned her head to look at him. "Jake, please get us out of here. You have no idea how close I am to falling apart right now, and I'd really rather not do that in front of your aunt and uncle."

He looked at her for a long moment, finally nodded and said, "Okay." He put the SUV in gear and drove over the bumpy footpath out to the first bungalow. And there he stopped.

"Sara?"

She was sitting stiffly. All she kept seeing in her mind were the killer's eyes. Not the one who'd killed Vivienne. The one who'd killer her mother, her father…who'd looked right into her own terror-stricken eyes and started to come for her. The man she'd spent the rest of her life fearing, hiding from.

"Sara?" Jake shook her this time.

Sara blinked and turned her head.

"We're at your bungalow. Where are those tranquilizers?"

Swallowing hard, she said, "On the nightstand, beside the bed."

He was frowning as he studied her face. "You stay here, okay? I'll only be a minute."

She nodded, the motions stiff and jerky. Jake got out of the SUV, and Sara locked the doors behind him.

She was terrified right now and glad if it showed a little bit, because maybe that meant Jake wouldn't ask her to go anywhere or do anything alone for the next day or two. Or even the next hour or two. He didn't even suggest she might want to get out here, go to her own bed. She wouldn't have gone if he had.

She sat silent on the seat, fought the memories, but knew it was a battle she would never win. Glancing down at her clenched, trembling hands, she tried to remember how many tranquilizers remained in the little bottle she'd brought along in case of emergency. She hoped there would be enough for her and Flossie both. She wasn't sure she was going to make it through this night without something.

He'd seen her. The killer had looked right into her eyes. He'd seen her.

Just like before.

Sara shivered and clenched her fists more tightly.

Jake was a bit rattled. Not just by being the only suspect in his own cousin's murder, but by Sara Brand. First defending him like a pit bull to the meanest cop he'd ever met. Then doing a total turnaround. In the SUV she'd gone as rigid and fragile as pottery. He sensed a storm going on inside her, one she was fighting. And he sensed there was a whole lot more to the woman than he'd even begun to suspect.

"I've seen a killer," she'd told Kendall. "I've looked right into his eyes." What the hell did she mean by that? And was that why she'd been on tranquilizers?

She'd locked those doors so fast his feet had barely touched the ground when he heard the clicks.

Hell. Okay, so there was more to Sara Brand than met the eye. A lot more. And maybe he was as guilty of judging her by her surface appearance as he'd believed she'd been of judging him by the same.

He went into the bungalow and stopped just inside the door, because he'd heard, distinctly, the back door creak closed. Then what sounded like footsteps running softly through the grass out back. He flicked on a light and ran through the bungalow, looked out back. But saw nothing. Sighing, nervous, not liking this a bit, he went to the bedroom, snatched the pill bottle off the nightstand and turned to leave.

But as he moved back through the kitchen again, he noticed something else that gave him pause.

The oil lamp that sat in the window…its globe was off. And beside it was a book of matches, one match ripped out and lying atop the rest.

His throat went dry at what that implied. He tried to swallow, then hurried back out to the waiting vehicle.

Chapter 7

"They're finally asleep," Jake said. He dragged his gaze away from the bed in bungalow two, where Flossie and Bertram lay beneath the covers, resting thanks to some help from Sara's bottle of little white pills.

Sara said nothing. She was still sitting on the other side of the small bedroom, curled up in a wicker chair with her knees drawn to her chest and her arms wrapped around her knees. Her lips were pale, and her eyes were wide, and every once in a while a little tremor would ripple through her. Or she would start at some sound, like the wind blowing a twig over the front porch.

She was scared to death. Of what she'd seen tonight? Of the killer? Or of him?

And why the hell was he worrying about that, anyway? He certainly had better things to think about—more pressing things, at least. The main one being that by this time tomorrow he was going to be behind bars as the cops stamped "solved" on his cousin's murder case. Because it was only a matter of hours before the cops talked to someone about that huge asinine scene Jake had made out in front of the jazz club, when he'd grabbed Vivienne and Vivienne had slapped him. And that was gonna be damn near all the evidence they would need to lock him up for life.

Or worse.

He had to get the hell out of here. Now. Tonight.

Right, he thought, and leave everyone certain of his guilt?

But what choice did he have? There was no way he was going to get out of this mess. No way in hell. Kendall...dammit, Kendall would fry him. And as for any samples that might be found under Viv's nails—well, when a cop hated you the way Kendall hated him, evidence could easily disappear. And he couldn't even blame the bastard. The old man whose blood stained Jake's hands had been Marty Kendall's grandfather, after all.

Jake glanced at Sara again, shook off his own worries and crossed the room to her. "Why don't we find someplace for you to catch a few hours' rest, hmm?"

She looked up at him, shook her head. "I'll never sleep." But she got to her feet, anyway. Her knees didn't look too steady, though. Jake put an arm around her and helped her out of the room. This bungalow was a bit larger than the one she was in. It had two bedrooms and brought in a higher rental price. He was glad as hell it wasn't rented out this week. "Right in here," he said, pushing open the door to the second bedroom.

Sara's knees buckled a little, so he tightened his grip. When he got her to the bed, he yanked back the covers and eased her down onto the clean sheets. She immediately curled into a ball on her side, her back to him. She pulled the covers up to her ears. He could see her shoulders shaking underneath the blankets, and he knew it was too damn hot to want to cover up at all, much less cover up and still be shivering.

With a sigh he turned, took a single step away from the bed.

"No, don't."

Fear made her voice thin and tight, but soft for all that. He turned to face her again. "Don't what?"

"Don't go. Please, Jake, I...I need to ask you something."

With a sigh that felt suspiciously like relief, he returned to the bedside and lowered himself to sit on the edge of the mattress. She didn't want him to leave. That must mean she didn't think he'd killed Vivienne. Oh, sure, she'd said she believed he was innocent—to the cops. But what she really believed, way down deep in her gut, was what mattered. So maybe this meant she honestly, truly believed him. Or...or maybe that was what she was about to ask him—the big question: Did you do it?

He didn't think he could stand it if Sara Brand asked him that.

"Tonight, earlier," she said, "before all this happened, you stood in your bedroom window."

He searched her eyes. "Yeah. And you stood in the kitchen window."

She flinched. "You could see me, then?"

"I could see you a little. Not enough. I turned my light off so I could see you better." He tried a hint of a smile, thinking maybe he could distract her from whatever was eating her up inside. It didn't have any effect on her. In fact, she seemed to be getting paler. "When I went into your bungalow just now to get the pills, I saw the lamp in the window. The matches. One pulled out of the book. Did you really come that close to lighting the lamp, or is this just wishful thinking on my part?"

Teasing her didn't seem to help, either. She was shaking her head. Not even hearing him, he thought. "Sara?" he asked.

Her throat moved as she swallowed. "When you turned your light off…you could see me?"

"Yeah."

She closed her eyes slowly. "Then the killer saw me, too."

Jake sat there, stunned into silence.

"I saw him…choking her…and I screamed.…" Jake put his hand to her shoulder. "He— The window must have been slightly open, because he seemed to hear me. He looked out…right at me, and then he dropped her and he…he turned off the light."

So he could see her better, Jake thought. No wonder she was scared to death.

"I can't believe this is happening again," she whispered.

"Again?"

"Jake, hold me," she whispered. "Hold me, please. I'm so afraid."

Swallowing hard, and knowing that this invitation

into her bed had nothing whatsoever to do with sex, Jake nodded and crawled underneath the covers. He spooned against her, draped an arm around her, wondered how the hell he was supposed to slip away in the dead of night to save his own skin when she'd just given him reason to believe the killer might come after her next.

"I was four years old," she began. "I was playing hide-and-seek with my mamma. I used to do it all the time...crawl into the cupboard underneath the kitchen sink and pull the door almost closed. Then I'd crouch there and peek out at her while she pretended to look for me. That's where I was when it happened."

She rolled onto her opposite side and, facing him now, snuggled closer. Jake stroked her hair. He felt as if he were holding a child. A frightened, traumatized child, like the little girl she'd just described to him. In a way maybe he was.

"A man kicked the front door in. I...heard the crashing sound and peeked out the crack of the cupboard door. I could see into the living room. I could see his gun spitting fire, and the little explosions that came from my father's back as the bullets ripped through him. The noise was— It was so loud. And...and Mamma screamed...and then he shot her, too. And then it just got quiet. Just...so quiet."

Jake had gone stiff as the words poured from her. But now he pulled her even more tightly against him and held her close. God, no wonder this had her so upset. No wonder she was so afraid.

"I was so scared I couldn't move. But I couldn't look away, either. I wanted to pull the cupboard door shut the rest of the way, close off that tiny crack, huddle as far back as I could. But I couldn't move. I could only sit there, frozen…watching… because I couldn't look away.''

"My God, Sara…''

"The man, he dragged my mother's body across the floor and out of the house. I remember the blood, the way it smeared and made such a mess, and I sat there wondering who would clean that up. I knew Mamma couldn't. Then the man dragged my father away, too. And I thought it was over. I thought I was safe. But…he came back one last time…and he saw me. I met his eyes right through the crack in the cupboard door, and I knew he saw me. He even started to come for me. To kill me, too.''

"I'm sorry…God, I'm so sorry, Sara,'' Jake whispered, and his arms were holding her tighter than before, and he knew it, but didn't remember tightening them. Somehow his hand had begun stroking her hair, while his other hand rubbed her back.

"But then there were sirens…the police. The man had to run. And even when he was gone I couldn't move…or even speak. I…I was still in that cupboard when the police found me hours later.''

Jake swallowed hard. "What happened to you then?''

She sniffled. "I was taken away and put into the witness protection program. They gave me a new name, a new family. The newspapers were told that my entire family had been killed. In fact, I thought it was true. I thought my brother had died, as well. All the bodies had been taken away, so when they couldn't find him, they assumed…''

She lifted her head, and Jake saw that her eyes

were wet. "He wasn't dead, though. Marcus was in the basement when the shooting started, and he'd wandered away in shock before the police searched down there. He thought I'd been killed, and I thought he had. We only found each other again a year ago."

Jake didn't like the feeling that was suffusing his chest or the ideas that were spinning around in his head. Ideas about protecting the little girl who still lived inside Sara Brand. Who still hid in cupboards every once in a while. He'd seen that old fear. He'd thought it was him she was afraid of. But it wasn't. It had never been him.

"I spent my whole life being afraid, looking over my shoulder, waiting for that killer to finally track me down."

Jake blinked. "You mean he wasn't caught?"

Sara shook her head. "No. Not until last year, when he finally found out where I was. He came for me, just as I'd always known he would. And my brother killed him. My entire family's been trying to convince me that I'm finally safe—really, truly safe—ever since." Lifting her head, she stared into his eyes. "I was even starting to believe it."

"And now this... Dammit, Sara, I'm sorry. I'm so sorry." Her eyes were so wide he thought he could fall into them, so full of hurt that it was almost painful to look at them, and every single tear track on her silken cheeks was like a knife right through his heart. He cupped her face in his palms and said the words he'd been telling himself not to say—not to even think. They seemed to tumble from his lips without giving a damn what he told himself. "I'm not going to let anyone hurt you, Sara Brand. Do you understand that? I promise, I'll keep you safe.''

Her damp eyes seemed trusting. Imagine that, trusting…him. She had no reason in the world to trust him.

Mocking laughter seemed to fill his mind, and the stinging words came to him in the voice of officer Marty Kendall. *Right. Convict turns hero. Dream on, Nash. You're going down, pal. And who's gonna protect her then? Hmm?*

Hell. He held Sara a little closer, realized he would be in jail right now if it hadn't been for her. He wanted to ease her fears. He wanted to be her hero. And that was a joke, because he knew damn good and well that he was no hero.

"Maybe you should take one of those tranquilizers yourself, hmm? Get some rest?"

Sara shook her head fast. "I can't. If he comes for me, Jake…I need to be ready."

Tough talk from a scared little girl. "No one's going to come after you, Sara. Not tonight. Not while I'm here."

"Yes, he will. He came before, and he will again."

He ran a hand down her arm. "It's not the same guy, Sara."

"They're all the same guy, Jake." Her eyes looked into his, and he saw a hard-won wisdom in them. Too hard-won.

"Hot tea, then?" he said. "Decaf, or something herbal? So you can rest just a little bit?"

Looking up into his eyes, she nodded. Jake got up, opened the bedroom door, pointed into the small kitchen. "I'll be in sight the whole time, okay?"

Nodding shakily, she burrowed more deeply into the pillows, pulled the covers tight around her. Jake stepped into the kitchen, rummaged in the cupboards and found a few decaffeinated teabags. Not that the caffeine content, or lack thereof, was going to matter all that much. He knew what he had to do.

When the water was hot, he poured it, and while his back was to Sara, he pulled a couple of the tranquilizers out of the bottle and dropped them into the steaming water. Then he stirred in some sugar to mask the taste. She would never rest in the state she was in. And if he had any hope at all of staying out of jail himself, he had to act. Now. Tonight. Either figure this thing out on his own or get the hell out of Dodge before the posse came back with a rope. He figured he had until sunup. And maybe not even that long.

He went back to the bedroom and sat beside her, stroking her and soothing her until she'd drained every last bit of tea from the cup and passed out cold as a stone.

There was something he hadn't mentioned to Sara, and now that he'd seen the fear—heard it in her voice—he knew he couldn't tell her. Not without scaring her even more. He hadn't mentioned that when he'd been inside her bungalow, he'd heard the creak of the back door and the sound of footsteps in the grass... Since he'd seen no one, he'd chalked it up to raw nerves, the wind, a hundred other things.

Now, though, he realized it hadn't been any of those things. It had been the killer. And Jake couldn't for the life of him run away and leave her behind—not knowing that she was right. The killer had seen her. He probably thought she'd seen him, as well. And now he was planning to come after her next. Jake would be damned if he would run away to save himself and let the bastard get to her.

But he couldn't stay here, either. There was only one choice left, the way he saw it.

Sara woke with a groggy, head-stuffed-full-of-cotton sensation. Her head felt heavy, her limbs like lead. She drew a deep breath and found the air moist and pungent. The sound of lapping water made its way into her consciousness, followed by birds making rude screeching noises, and sudden bursts of movement—rustling, flapping sounds. The hard, misshapen bed beneath her seemed to be rocking gently.

She was outside.

Blinking her eyes open, she looked around, spying the wooden sides of whatever conveyance she'd been put into, then the booted feet and blue jeans of the man who'd put her into it, and beyond that, nothing but slate-gray fog.

She sat up fast, sucking in a gasp as memory returned, her heart leaping into her throat.

The man bent down. "It's okay, Sara. It's me. It's all right. You're safe."

"'Safe…'" She repeated the word as if it were foreign. Indeed, that was what it had been for most of her life. And from the looks of things, it would be for a while longer. "We're in a boat."

Jake nodded, straightening again. He was standing in one end of a small, box-nosed wooden boat, pushing it along with a long pole that vanished into the murky water. Sara squinted through the fog, even as she got herself up off the floor of the tiny vessel and onto the bench-like seat. It was a struggle because someone had mummy wrapped her in a soft blanket. Jake, she assumed. She freed her arms, settled the blanket more comfortably around her shoulders and got upright on the bench. But she could see little more than before. The darker shapes of trees dripping with moss, combined with the water, told her they were in the swamp. The bayou, as he called it. Gator's Bayou. The place he'd warned her repeatedly not to enter.

"Jake, what's going on?"

He drew a breath, let it out slowly. "I couldn't stay, Sara. Marty Kendall would have had me behind bars before breakfast time if I'd stayed."

She licked her lips, lowering her head. "Oh, no."

"I didn't have a choice."

"You're wrong, Jake."

"No, I'm not. I've spent almost half my life in prison, Sara, I don't plan on going back."

"Half your...my God, Jake, how long was your sentence for that robbery?"

Jake met her eyes. "Twenty years."

"But that's—"

"Excessive? I killed the town's favorite former cop, Sara. The guy was a hometown hero." Jake shrugged. "So I did seventeen, and they finally granted my parole."

"Who was your lawyer?" she asked. "Bozo the Clown? Because that's just—"

"Didn't have a lawyer. Couldn't afford one."

"But, Jake, if you can't afford a lawyer, they appoint one for you."

He shrugged. "I wouldn't have trusted any lawyer they'd picked out."

"So you defended yourself?"

He nodded.

"Well, there you go. That's why you wound up with such a ludicrous sentence."

He crooked an eyebrow at her. "You really think letting their guy defend me would have resulted in anything less?"

She tilted her head to one side. "Their guy? God, Jake, you really don't trust the system at all, do you?"

"Nope."

"But you have to. Jake...look what you're doing here. Running away isn't the answer."

"Bull."

"You have to go back. You have to fight this thing, clear your name, help find the real killer..."

He crouched down, his face inches from hers. "And what kind of fairy-tale world do you live in, where that's the way things work, Sara Brand? Hmm? I've got a record. I'm a convicted killer, who was seen having an altercation—some might even call it a *physical* altercation—with the victim only hours before she was murdered. I was the last one to see her alive. I was the only one in the house physically capable of strangling a grown woman to death. And I don't have anyone to vouch for my whereabouts at the time. Add to that the fact that the cop on the case has a hankering for my head on a platter, and you've got yourself a surefire conviction. If I go back there, Sara, I go to prison. Period."

"There will be blood under the nails, Jake. The DNA tests—"

"Don't kid yourself, Sara. Kendall won't let that evidence see the light of day."

She said nothing. Just stared into his eyes for a long moment. They were dark, and they were scared. Angry, furious, frustrated, yes...but scared, too. "I can understand why you believe that. But what's the alternative, Jake? Do you really want to spend the rest of your life running? Always looking over your shoulder? Always waiting for them to find you?"

"If that's what it takes."

"Then why did you bring me with you?"

He lowered his gaze quickly. Too quickly. Then he got back to his feet, resuming his pole pushing.

She frowned, searching his face as the mist around them paled to a lighter shade. The sun must be rising...somewhere. There was certainly no sign of it here. "This is like crossing the River Styx," she whispered.

"Yeah. I was thinking that."

She drew a breath, sighed. "You think he's going to come after me too, don't you?"

"Who?"

"You know who. The killer. You said you didn't think he'd seen me, but you know he did, and you know I was right about that. For all he knows, I can identify him. He's going to try to silence me before I can do that, and that's why you didn't leave me behind back there. Isn't it, Jake?"

There was a long pause. Then, slowly, he looked down at her, his face expressionless. "You trying to make me into some kind of hero, Sara? I'm not, you know. I'm an ex-con running from a murder rap. And it ought to be pretty obvious why I'd drag you along."

She only frowned at him.

"Think about it, Sara."

Blinking slowly, she lifted her brows. "Are you saying I'm some kind of a hostage?"

He looked at her, didn't affirm or deny it, just looked at her.

"Jake, if that's the idea, here, it's a bad one. My cousin's a sheriff. He'll have every cop in the country on your trail."

Jake closed his eyes slowly. "I'd…let that slip my mind." Then he smiled slowly, a bitter smile that held no hint of amusement. "I can pick 'em, that's for sure."

Thinning her lips, she shook her head. "Jake, please listen to me. You have to go back."

"No, Sara. I don't. And you can either talk about something else or keep quiet."

Sighing heavily, she let her shoulders slump. She didn't believe he'd taken her as a hostage, though that was obviously what he wanted her to think. He'd brought her along for some other reason.

"Fine," she said at last. "Kendall's in charge of the case and he has it in for you."

"How'd you guess?" he asked dryly.

"So we get him removed from the case," she said. "It shouldn't be hard to convince the authorities that he's biased." She tilted her head. "Was he on the force during the investigation of his grandfather's death?"

"Kendall was a rookie cop. His old man was a cop. His uncle worked in the D.A.'s office."

"My God…you were railroaded!"

"Murder is murder, Sara. The old man was just as dead, and I was just as responsible, whether he had relatives in high places or not."

"What did you do when that old man fell on the floor, Jake?"

Jake looked down at her, shook his head, looked away again.

"Did you hit him over the head with a crowbar to make sure he wouldn't get up again? Clean out the register and run like hell? What?"

He still didn't answer.

"Did you go through his pockets for loose change, Jake?"

His gaze leaped to hers. "I called an ambulance," he snapped.

"I know. I know you did, Jake. And then you stayed with him until it got there. You tried to do CPR on him, didn't you, Jake? When you could have run. You could have been long gone, free and clear. Dammit, Jake, why didn't you tell me this in the first place, instead of trying to make me think you were some kind of violent criminal? Why did you make me have to go snooping like some kind of busybody just to learn the truth about your past?"

"I didn't think you'd bother with the snooping. And I didn't think it would make any difference if you knew the truth. You're still an unspoiled school-teacher with a cop in the family, and I'm still a convicted killer." He shook his head. "If that wasn't enough, Sara, now I'm a fugitive, to boot."

"So...so you didn't tell me because you didn't want me to feel anything for you?"

"I didn't tell you because I wanted you to keep your damned distance. Trouble like you, I don't need. I knew that from the first time I set eyes on you, but you just couldn't take the hint, could you? You had to keep sending me sidelong glances with those doe eyes. You walk around with your secret written all over your face. I'm only human, Sara." He shook his head. "Problem is, a woman like you can't ever accept sex for its own sake. You always have to read more into it. Start attaching silly romantic notions to everything a man does."

She nodded slowly. "So you thought if I just went on believing you to be a cold-blooded killer, I'd be less prone to...silly romantic notions?"

"That's right."

Again she nodded. "I see." Then she shrugged. "Well, I don't know why, Jake, but your plan is just backfiring all over the place. Because I never fell for your big, scary ex-con act. And I knew from the start there was more to the story than you were saying. Even before I went digging on the Internet."

"How?" he challenged.

She lifted her chin. "Just like I told Kendall, Jake, I've seen the eyes of a killer. I've stared right into them. I know what they look like."

He grunted, but other than that, he didn't reply.

"And I'm not falling for this hostage story you're trying to make me believe, either. You brought me along for one of two reasons. Either you want me too badly to leave me behind, or you're protecting me from that maniac who murdered your cousin." She tilted her head to one side. "Or maybe both."

Jake stared at her, blinking in what looked like shock. The boat bumped up against something, rocking her a bit, and the mist grew steadily thinner, lighter.

"I was scared to death last night, Jake," she said. "I let it all come back to me for a little while there. Became the little girl I'd been before. But it was just temporary. I'm not that scared little girl anymore. Just like you, I've had a taste of freedom...freedom from fear. And I'm not going back. I'm not ever going to run or hide from anyone again. And do you want to know why?''

Wide-eyed, and apparently more surprised with every word she uttered, he shook his head. ''No. I really don't.''

''Well I'm going to tell you anyway. It's because I survived. I survived, and in the end I won. I found my brother, and the man who killed my parents paid the price. That's the way it works, Jake. In the end the truth comes out, and the good guys win, and the bad guys pay.''

''That's a fantasy,'' Jake said.

''No,'' she said. ''It's a fact. I'm living proof of it. And I'm going to convince you of it, too.''

''Not in this lifetime,'' he said.

''No. Not as long as you play their game. As long as you run from that bastard, Jake, he's the one in control. You're doing just what he wants you to do, just like I did for twenty years.''

Jake turned away from her, gripping a tree limb and steadying the boat as he stepped out onto a dry patch of ground. ''I tried it that way once, Sara. It didn't work. And I'll tell you something, lady.'' He reached his hand out, and she took it, letting him help her out of the boat. ''I'd far rather spend twenty years on the lamb than in the pen. And those are the choices. Make no mistake about that.''

''You tell me that when Vivienne's killer is behind bars where he belongs and your name has been cleared, okay?'' As she stepped onto solid ground, barefoot, his hand still clung to hers, and she met his eyes.

She saw the doubt in them, but she saw something else there too. It flashed, for the briefest instant, then faded just as quickly. She couldn't be certain, but she thought it might have been hope.

"You're crazy," he said. But she heard doubt in his voice.

"I'm right, Jake. You know I'm right."

He shook his head, muttered under his breath.

"You made a big mistake bringing me with you, you know. Because I'm going to convince you of it, too."

"No, hon. You're not. Don't go getting your hopes up."

"Oh, Jake," she said, shaking her head sadly. "You are so much better than you know you are."

He looked at her then, an odd little crease between his brows.

Chapter 8

Jake hated like hell to admit it, but he liked her this morning. Hell, he'd liked her for a long time now. But this morning he liked her even more. And it was maybe a little bit more than just "like." His admiration for her, even his respect for her, seemed to grow every time she opened her mouth. And the rest of the time there was this soft, tender feeling…this urge to protect her, that kept getting bigger, as well.

That little speech in the boat—it was chock-full of spunk. And while he didn't like spunk as a rule, he liked the way it looked on Sara Brand. He liked it a hell of a lot better than the fear and panic she'd been sporting last night. A *hell* of a lot better.

All the same, she was full of blue mud with her idealistic notions.

She stood now, bare toes curling on the cool, damp ground, her plush robe almost dragging as she squinted through the mist toward the ramshackle house. Jake had caught only a fleeting glimpse of the black negligee she had on underneath. He hadn't missed guessing that she'd been wearing it last night in her bungalow...while she'd stood by the window trying to decide whether or not she was brave enough, or crazy enough, to light that lamp. She had put it on just in case. She had put it on for him.

And knowing that didn't help matters, either.

"So where are we?" she asked softly. Her hair was fuzzy and tangled, and her eyes puffy and tired looking. She had, he guessed, a little bit of a tranquilizer hangover, and he was still wrestling with feelings of guilt for having done that to her. But if he hadn't...well, he would have been in jail before the day was out, and she would have been a sitting duck for the killer.

"Is that a house over there?" Sara asked.

Jake nodded, following her gaze to the ghostly looking, crooked house, swathed in mist. "It's abandoned. Great hideout, don't you think?"

"Yeah, great," she said. "If you happen to be a disembodied spirit."

He sent her a smirk and tugged the boat up out of the water. "Come here and grab the other end, will you?"

"Why?" she asked, even as she complied.

"So we don't leave marks on the ground. Come on, just over here." The boat wasn't heavy, despite the sack of supplies Jake had managed to throw together—mostly from Sara's bungalow. He'd taken her with him on that scavenger hunt. He'd been too afraid to leave her out of his sight even for the few minutes it would take to gather supplies. Especially asleep. Defenseless.

Together they carried the boat a few yards nearer the house and set it down amid a tangle of undergrowth. Then Jake shoved it deeper into the foliage and moved some ferns and limbs around until the little craft was virtually invisible. He stood back, eyeing it.

"You've had some experience with this kind of thing, haven't you?"

"Only as a kid, playing Huck Finn games. It's not a game now." He yanked up a fallen limb and went back to the water's edge, then brushed the moss and ferns and soil around with it, to cover up their footprints as he walked backward about halfway to the house. Then he tossed the limb aside, turned and saw Sara's skeptical gaze. "Better safe than sorry," he said.

She shrugged and turned to face the house, studying it for a long moment. "What a sad-looking place."

Jake felt his brows go up. "It's a dump. It's a hovel. But sad?"

"Mmm. Sad. And lonely. What kind of people ever lived here, I wonder?"

Jake shrugged. "Outcasts." He didn't look at her when he said it. And he didn't look at the memories that came crowding in around the edges of his mind, either. He hadn't been back here in twenty years. He'd kept them at bay all that time, and he could damn well continue to do so.

Nothing had changed. The small, square house still stood on four stilt-like poles, to keep it above the water level when the rains came. It was still a weathered, aged, brown color, built of rough-cut boards with the bark still on their edges, boards that had never been finished. Just slapped with a coat of pine pitch once in a while to keep them from rotting. It was a good place to lie low. Nothing more. This was not a nostalgia trip. This was not a homecoming.

"Come on inside, it's getting light out." Taking Sara's arm, he led her up the rotting steps, pushed open the screen door that creaked loudly in protest. The screening was hanging loose in one corner and full of holes. The inside door wasn't closed all the way. It had warped and swelled too large for its frame and was stuck in place, even though he could see through the opening. Jake shouldered it open and ordered his mind to keep quiet as he stepped inside, into inky blackness.

Something scurried away across the floor.

Jake blinked in the darkness. "Stay right here," he told Sara. "I'll get us some light."

She didn't move. He would have heard her if she had. The place smelled musty. It had always smelled musty, even when it had been lived in. He crossed the floor unerringly to the shelf on the far wall. If the place hadn't been looted—and he didn't think it had—then the lamp should still be there. And kerosene would last forever. Mamma had always kept the lamp full.

He reached up, and found it, grimy and dust covered, on the warped shelf on the wall. Blindly he picked it up, moved it in a small circle and heard the liquid sloshing in the base. It still had kerosene, then. Good. Taking off the glass chimney, squatting on the floor to set it down, he hauled a lighter from his pocket. When it flared, he heard Sara suck in a breath. Then he lit the wick, replaced the globe. Soft yellow lamplight spilled into the room. And Jake thought it had looked a whole lot better in the dark.

"How did you know that was there?" Sara asked.

"Lucky guess." He set the lamp on the shelf as Sara stepped farther inside. She was looking around now. At the uneven floorboards with their rag rugs, most of which had been chewed by whatever had been inhabiting the house all this time. Litter was everywhere. Twigs and leaves, nuts and half-rotted berries. Bits of stuffing from whatever furniture had been left here. And chewed pieces of the rag rugs. Blankets hung over the windows, letting no light in...or out, which was a condition of which he approved wholeheartedly, given their circumstances.

Against one wall an old green couch with holes gnawed in its arms and stuffing sticking out all over it stood crookedly. The rest of the furniture—what little there had been—was long gone. The ash-dusted, black potbellied stove in the corner remained, and when Jake saw a vaguely familiar-looking table leg lying beside it, he realized what must have become of the other furnishings.

Hell. Mamma had to keep warm somehow.

He swallowed the rush of regret that tried to swamp him. Tried to focus instead on Sara, who was peering through a dark doorway into what had been a kitchen once. Though not much of one, since there had never been power out here. "Not exactly the Ritz, is it?"

"Not exactly."

She moved to another darkened doorway. The one

that led into what had been his bedroom...until he'd traded it in for a more cheerful one, with bars.

"Best stick to this room, Sara," he said, his voice seeming thick. "You don't know what shape the rest of the place might be in. I don't want you falling through any holes in the floor and breaking a leg."

She turned to face him, curiosity in her brown eyes. "Aren't you curious?"

"Not in the least." He licked his lips and averted his eyes because she was probing them so deeply. "There's an outhouse around back that should be usable. That's all we need be concerned with. I don't plan to be here all that long."

"No?"

He shook his head, walked to the ratty couch and kicked it a few times, just to assure himself that none of its current residents were presently at home. Then he sat down. "No. We can hole up here until dark. Then we'll head out again."

"To where?"

Jake leaned to the side, peeling the blanket back a bit so he could peer through the grimy window. The mists were starting to burn off now. He could see clear to the water. "This runs along the backside of the highway, farther down. We should be able to make it past the county line—state line, maybe— before the sun comes up tomorrow."

Sara narrowed her eyes on him. "Which state line?"

"Texas," he told her.

She nodded slowly. Then, coming closer and eyeing the couch warily, she finally turned and sat down beside him. "So the big, bad criminal is going to see his hostage safely home before heading for the hills, hmm?''

He shrugged. ''I'm heading in that direction, anyway,'' he said. But she had it right. Miss Sara Brand, kindergarten teacher, was too damned smart for her own good. Still, Jake figured she would be just as safe as a babe in its own mother's arms if he could just get her back to that family she was always talking about, with all those cousins and that overprotective brother and cops in the family and all. She would be fine. No one could get to her there, with all that protection.

No? Not even a guy who could get to Vivienne and kill her in the bedroom right next to yours, Jake? Without making a sound? Without waking anyone? Without leaving a trace?

If only Trent had been home.

Jake bit his lip, lowered his head.

''What is it?'' Sara asked. ''What are you thinking?''

He looked up at her again. ''Just wondering if anyone has called Trent yet. Damn. This is gonna tear him up.''

Sara sat forward, looking tense. ''He…he won't believe them will he? He won't think you could have—''

''Could have what? Killed Vivienne?'' Jake shrugged. He didn't think Trent would believe that of him, but who the hell knew? Then he studied Sara's face again. ''What I'd like to know is why you don't believe it. You don't even know me.''

Sara looked down at the floor. ''I checked your hands, remember?''

"That doesn't really answer the question, though."

"I know it doesn't." Then she lifted her gaze to his. "Maybe I believe in you for the same reason you brought me along on this crazy escapade."

He looked away so fast he knew she would read something into it. The problem was, she would have read more into the rush of…of whatever the hell it was that had just passed through him, if she had glimpsed it in his eyes. And she was too damned sharp to have missed it. He got to his feet, thinking fast of something to say, anything to break the soft web her words had spun between them. "I, uh, had time to pack a few things last night. I'd best bring them inside."

Then he headed out the door, blinking in the growing light. He just stood there for a minute, waiting for the odd sensations that had twisted his gut up into knots a second ago to fade away. He didn't feel anything beyond fondness for her. And as for the wanting…well, hell, that was just nature. Hormones. Whatever. It wasn't as if there was anything more than a simple, physical attraction between the two of them, no matter what her girlish fantasies might have conjured up. And why the hell would she want to conjure up anything like that, anyway? It wasn't as if a woman like Sara Brand could ever see a man like Jake Nash as anything more than a fling.

"No," he said softly under his breath as he headed down the steps, casting nervous backward glances over his shoulder. "Not a fling. Sara Brand isn't a fling kind of girl."

Stopping by the boat, he shook his head. What

then? he wondered. What could she possibly be imagining?

Hell, it was impossible to figure her out. He hauled the sack out of the boat, slung it over his shoulder and headed back inside the house where he'd once lived.

He had been up all night. It was obvious to Sara in the way he sacked out on that filthy couch right after their makeshift breakfast of fruit and water, and fell instantly asleep. But not before warning her not to go outside or light a fire in the old potbellied stove or make any noise or do much of anything at all besides sit there and watch him sleep. He advised her to nap, too, and she really did try, but she was too wound up. Besides, she had slept like a log last night, in spite of all the excitement, which was odd. She wasn't the least bit tired now.

She looked again at Jake, lying curled up in the corner of that couch. He had left plenty of room for her to join him there, on the other end, if she wanted to.

She did.

But not to sleep.

Sara licked her lips, closed her eyes and turned away. It wasn't like her to want a man the way she wanted this one. It wasn't like her to feel the least bit attracted to a guy like Jake. A guy who was doing his best to play the role of bad boy, a guy who wanted no part of anything real and who was too busy living up to his past to get over it and move on.

But that wasn't who he really was. She had seen through it all. And she thought his aunt Flossie had, too. And Trent, he certainly had, as close as the two of them seemed to be. Even Jake's solemn, silent uncle Bertram seemed to have realized that there was a good, decent man hiding under the skin of Jake Nash.

A damned wonderful man.

Shrugging, Sara decided to explore the house in spite of Jake's warnings not to. It wasn't as if there was that much of it. She picked up the kerosene lamp, gripping it by the slender glass neck of its base, and she held it up high and out in front of her so she could see where she was going.

The kitchen, if that was what it had been, was in horrible shape. A sink with no faucets stood with an old pail underneath its drain. There were no cupboards, just shelves on the walls, some of which still held a handful of chipped plates and mismatched cups. No table. No chairs. No refrigerator or stove.

A sense of overwhelming misery seemed to permeate the musty air here. It was so palpable that Sara had to back out of the room. She took a moment to shake off the sudden sense of sadness that had overwhelmed her, then she ventured into the other darkened room. The one Jake hadn't let her enter when they'd first arrived.

It was small and square, but almost deliberately more cheerful than the others, in a pathetic way. The walls had been papered with comic strips...once colorful, but faded and peeling now. There was a cot in one corner, its mattress chewed to bits, but still identifiable despite the mess around and atop it. In one corner a pole had been fixed between two walls, and coat hangers still dangled from it. One even had a blouse hanging from it. Yellow now.

Maybe it had been white once. A wooden crate stood next to the bed, turned upside down, with a scrap of cloth thrown over it. Lying on its side atop the makeshift bedside stand was a glass vase with a long-dead stem inside. And next to that, facedown, was a tiny picture frame.

Holding her lamp out in front of her, Sara moved closer. And for some reason, as she reached for that frame, her hand trembled and her throat went tight.

She picked it up, held it to the light.

A teenage boy stood arm in arm with a thin, haggard-looking woman who had to be his mother. And though he was very young, maybe fifteen, and very skinny and gangly, Sara recognized the boy.

"I thought I told you to stay in the front room."

She turned slowly, staring at him as the golden light spilled over his features. Pained features. She held out the photo. "You lived here," she whispered.

His gaze flicked downward to the photo in her hand. He came closer, took it from her, looked at it and slammed his eyes closed.

"She...she's your mother, isn't she?"

"Yeah. She was."

"She died?"

Jake nodded once, sharply, then turned away from her and stalked back into the front room again. She hurried after him, setting the lamp down on the way. "What happened to her, Jake?"

"What the hell do you care?" he asked, and he sounded angry as he stomped across the room, headed for the door, yanked it open. Blinding sunlight spilled in, and he paused there, blinking in the brightness.

Sara came up behind him and put a hand on his shoulder. "Sorry," she said. "I didn't mean to bring up something so painful."

"It's history."

"No, it isn't."

Finally he glanced down at her, his eyes so full of hurting that she wanted to hold him and rock him against her until it went away.

"I know all about it, Jake. Don't forget, I've been there. You can move on, start over, but it's not history. It's never history. That kind of pain doesn't go away or ease up. Other people might buy that, but not me. You know better than to say that to me."

He stared at her for a long moment, and finally he said, "You're right. I do."

"So? You wanna tell me about it?"

Licking his lips, Jake heaved a long sigh, faced front again and walked outside. She followed him down the steps and around to the side of the house, where a tire swing hung from a tree by a fraying, time-grayed rope. Jake gripped the rope, stood there, silent for a while. "It's not something I've ever talked about," he said.

"And has that helped?"

"You know it hasn't."

"So?"

She watched him. The way he lowered his head, the way his Adam's apple moved when he tried to swallow the lump in his throat. She knew exactly what he was feeling. She felt it every time she remembered losing her own mother, and her father, and the horror that followed.

"I put this tire swing up for her. She used to love to have me push her back and forth." He gave the swing an experimental shove. It danced and spun in slow circles.

Moving forward, Sara grabbed hold and gave the rope a tug. "Think it's still safe?"

Jake shrugged, blinking and not meeting her eyes. "Why don't you try it and see?"

"Okay." She put her legs through the center of the tire, lowered her weight onto it, and it held her. Jake put his hands on her back and pushed her gently. Sara leaned back, looking up at him as the swing carried her slowly back and forth. She watched the emotions running over Jake's face. And she waited for him to feel ready to talk.

"Mom...Racine was her name. She was Bert's younger sister. And I guess she was always a little on the wild side. She got pregnant at sixteen, by a no-good bastard without a nickel to his name or a shred of ambition. And when her parents refused to welcome my father into the family, she ran off and married the snake."

The swing slowed, and Sara put her feet down. "I take it you didn't get along with your father?"

"He was never my father. I never even met him. He was only after the family's money, the plantation, the name. When my mother's family disinherited her, disowned her for marrying that scumbag, he walked out. So she was alone, with a kid on the way and a family that refused to take her back because she had disgraced them, as they put it."

"They...they did that?"

Jake nodded. His eyes were full of bitterness. "It didn't matter. She worked hard, we had it tough, but we got by. But then she got sick, and everything changed. She couldn't work anymore. She needed medicine she couldn't afford. I was old enough that I could have helped if she would have let me. But she flat-out refused to let me quit school and get a job.''

Sara nodded slowly. ''She wanted you to do better than she had.''

''I let her down, then, didn't I?''

Before Sara could disagree, he went on. ''We came back here. She begged her family to take her in again. But her parents were still furious, and even though by then Uncle Bert had got over being angry with her, her parents still were. So she moved us into this shack, because it was vacant and it was free and it was close to her family. She was bound and determined that they would get over being mad, if she kept trying to make amends. The worst part was she refused to tell them she was sick. She had her pride.'' He shook his head slowly. ''Right up to the end, my mamma had her pride.''

Sara swallowed hard. ''So it was all up to you, to take care of your mother?''

''It wasn't so bad. I would cut school, take part-time work where I could get it, lie to her about it. I fixed up that bedroom for her. Put up the swing. It seemed to give her a little bit of pleasure until she got too ill to come outside anymore.''

''And eventually you got so desperate to take care of her that you walked into that convenience store and tried to rob it.''

He nodded. ''She'd stopped seeing a doctor, stopped taking her medications. The money wasn't there, and she knew it.''

''What happened in that store, Jake?''

Jake lifted his head, met her eyes. ''I said I had

a gun, told the old man behind the counter to give me everything in the register. He grabbed his chest and keeled over on the floor." Then he lowered his head, shook it slowly. "I didn't know a damn thing about CPR, but I tried doing what I'd seen on TV. I called for help, tried to breathe for the old guy and pounded on his chest until the ambulance got there." He looked up again, eyes narrow with the memory. "The old bastard came around just long enough to tell them what had happened. Then he died, and I got my ass thrown in jail." Shaking his head slowly, he said, "And I never put my hands on a nickel from the old guy's cash register, either. But that didn't matter."

"But you...you didn't take the money. And you stayed when you could have run."

"And he had a son who was a cop and a grandson who was a cop and a cousin in the D.A.'s office. And I was just bayou trash." Jake licked his lips. "The only good thing that came of it was that the newspapers mentioned my mother's illness in covering the story. So her family found out how bad off she really was, and they took her back into the fold. They had her moved back into the main house with them before my trial even ended. They got her the best care there was, hired a nurse to live in. Made sure she got her medicine. She actually did better for a little while. She had three good years before she took a turn for the worse again and finally died while I was in prison."

Sara sniffed, and Jake looked at her sharply. "On her death bed," he went on, "she asked to see her brother alone. Bertram went to her, and she begged him to promise that he would give me a home when

I got out of prison. And even though he was reluctant, he agreed. I doubt he would have been able to keep that promise, except that their parents passed on ten years into my sentence. They left the place to Bert. And he honored his promise to his sister when I finally got released last year."

He reached out, gave the swing a push. "So now you know the whole ugly story."

"It's not an ugly story at all, Jake. It's one of the saddest, most beautiful stories I've ever heard." Slowly she shook her head. "If...if I ever have a son, I hope he loves me half as much as you loved your mother, Jake."

"Damn," he said, but softly, lowering his head. "I don't know why the hell I'm spilling my guts to you, anyway."

She shrugged. "Because it feels better if you let it out a little bit. Doesn't it? And because it's easier to share with someone who's been through something similar."

He didn't answer, just gave her another push in the swing. "What's that, some pop psychology you got from a magazine quiz?"

She glanced behind her at him as the tire fell toward him. He pushed her again. "No. It's the truth," she said. "Don't you feel better now that we've talked?" He said nothing, but she went right on. "You look as if you do. You're smiling, Jake."

"Am I? Maybe that's just because you're so full of funny notions."

"No. It's because you like me. You probably feel like you could tell me anything."

"Now I think you're having side effects from those tranquilizers."

"Tranquiliz—oh, Jake, you didn't!" she shouted.

But she saw the guilt on his face. He sighed, lowered his head a little. "I know it was a lousy, low-down, rotten thing for me to do," he said. "But at the time, I thought it was justified. You needed the rest. You were so wrought up and afraid."

She lowered her head. "Probably my brother would have done the same thing," she admitted softly.

"I didn't like seeing you in that state," he admitted.

"See?" She sent him a teasing smile. "You do like me. And you *do* feel as if you could tell me anything."

He pushed her again. Harder this time. She smiled as the swing sailed higher and higher. "You keep dreaming, hon."

"Well," she said on the downward arc, "I feel like I could tell *you* anything."

"Yeah, and I'll bet your life is chock-full of deep, dark secrets, isn't it, teacher?"

"I have to admit, I've already told you most of them. Though there are one or two I'm keeping to myself."

He pushed her higher and higher, and she started to laugh as she thought that lately she had lots more secrets than she'd ever had before. Secret thoughts. Secret desires. Secret feelings writhing around in her most-secret places.

He pushed her again.

The frayed rope snapped. And the tire sailed through the sultry air, carrying Sara with it. She didn't even have time to shriek before it splashed down into the murky black waters.

Chapter 9

One minute Jake was standing there thinking how unbelievably right she had been and how much better, how much *lighter*, he suddenly felt. He was pushing her on his mother's old tire swing, and he was thinking about good times, instead of sickness and bitterness and loss. He was smiling. Standing outside a place full of memories that should bring him nothing but pain, and smiling, and pushing a virgin kindergarten teacher on a tire swing. And, craziest of all, *enjoying* it!

The next minute he was standing there with his jaw lax, watching said virgin kindergarten teacher sink into the gator-infested swamp water. She came up sputtering and flailing her arms. She was still laughing, though, oblivious to how badly it had scared him to see her fly off like that and vanish beneath the muck. But she was okay. Sighing in relief, Jake kicked off his shoes and cracked a smile himself as he waded in to get her.

Then he saw the log-like shape on the far bank as it slid silently into the water. He tried to move faster. "Stop splashing, Sara!" He hurried closer, doing enough splashing for both of them, dammit, but you couldn't move through muck without it. His feet were sinking deep into the mire on the bottom by the time he reached her, snagged her around the waist and pulled her to him. The damned bathrobe was dragging in the water, and he shoved it off her, let it go, scooped her up and turned back toward shore.

She was still grinning. "My hero," she sighed, fluttering her eyes in exaggerated Southern belle fashion. But when he looked down at her, her smile died. "What's wrong, Jake?"

The shore was still ten feet away when he felt the bump against his leg, and he knew damn well the next sensation would be far less pleasant. So he shoved her forward for all he was worth, tossed her toward shore and shouted, "Run!" And then he spun around, spied the damned monster coming for him just below the surface and did the only thing he could think of to save his leg. He dove down and wrapped his arms around the brute.

The gator went into a death roll, and Jake held tight.

Sara had known something was horribly wrong when Jake had looked into her eyes as he carried her back toward the shore. His face had been drawn and tight, his jaw rigid. Then his eyes had suddenly widened, and he'd thrown her bodily toward shore, shouted at her to run and vanished beneath the water.

She picked herself up and, standing knee-deep in water and ankle-deep in mud, looked for him. There was roiling, splashing...and then the slap of a huge, scaly...tail?

"Ohmigod," she whispered. Was that...? "Jake? *Jake!*"

As if responding to her summons, Jake rose up out of the mire, but he was not alone. He was clamped to the back of a monster straight out of a Sunday-afternoon horror movie. The beast twisted and writhed, and then they both splashed down again and vanished from sight.

Sara stood there, shaking all over, staring at the smooth, mud-brown surface of the water, imagining the most horrible, terrifying things. Telling herself she should get to the shore, get out of the muddy mire before she became dessert for the alligator that was even now making Jake his main course. Telling herself she should damn well dive in and try to find him, try to help him. Horror gripped her, but she couldn't run away when he was in so much trouble. She took a step forward. She had to help Jake....

Something clamped around her ankle.

Sara shrieked at full, ear-splitting volume and yanked her foot from the teeth of that beast, hopping backward in high-speed clumsiness. And then she saw, not the beast, but Jake, pulling himself shoreward.

"OhmiGod," she said again. "Jake!" She went to him, grabbed him and hauled him bodily out of the muck and up onto the shore as he winced in pain. The muddy water sluicing down his face and arms and clothes was pink with blood. Her heart damn near burst.

She eased him down on the grassy bank. "Jake...Jake, I can't believe this. You saved my life, and that...that thing took you instead. Jake, please tell me you're all right. Dammit, I won't let you die. Do you hear me? I won't."

She tore his shirt open as he blinked up at her, looking a bit confused. No wonder. Anyone would be disoriented. And there was the blood loss, too, likely making him light-headed, dizzy.

"Where are the wounds, Jake? Can you tell? I have to stop the bleeding." She searched his front, his chest, wet with muddy water. But she saw no gaping wounds or jagged teeth marks there. As gently as she could, she rolled him onto his side and examined his back. Then she checked his arms, his neck. Seeing nothing, she clasped his face between her palms and stared hard at him. "Talk to me, baby. Tell me where you're hurting so I can help you. I'm not gonna lose you, not now. Do you hear me, Jake? You have to talk to me so I can..." She sniffled and blinked rapidly.

Jake's eyes fixed on hers and locked there. "You're crying," he said softly.

Dammit, he must be going into shock. She dashed the tears away with the back of her hand. "Where the hell is all this blood coming from?" she asked aloud, reaching for his jeans.

"From the gator," Jake said.

Sara looked at him...then looked again. *"What?"*

Lifting his hand, Jake showed her the knife he still clutched. "Had it in my boot. Hell, you didn't think I was going to wrestle a gator without a blade, did you?''

"Wrestle...?"

He smiled slightly, sat up slowly, rubbed his shoulder. "Damn. It was a hell of a lot easier when I was a kid."

Sara sat back on her heels, blinking at him in total confusion.

"I guess I didn't tell you that one of those part-time jobs of mine was in a little gator house, over in Belle Ville—"

"Belle Vee?" She repeated it as he'd said it, just like a parrot.

"It's that little Cajun village just the other side of—"

"I don't *care* where it is, Jake."

"Oh. Well, anyway, I learned to wrestle alligators there. Lots of guys my age did. Of course, we picked on smaller gators then...and we didn't kill 'em. It was a sideshow attraction for the tourists. Not all that dangerous, if you knew where to hold them." Again he squeezed his shoulder, winced. "Damn. I think I dislocated it." He gave his arm a terrible wrenching tug, made a horrible face, swore a blue streak. "There."

Sara just sat back on her heels, staring at him. "I thought you had been torn apart," she said. "You lay there and let me think you were half-dead!"

His brows came together. "Well sorry for the inconvenience, Sara. I was a little out of breath, and in considerable pain."

"And enjoying every second of seeing me out of my head with worry for you!"

One side of his mouth quirked upward. "Well, I

was enjoying the way you were tearing my clothes off. And, uh, your own outfit kind of...distracted me.''

She looked down at herself, saw the black negligee she had put on last night. God, it seemed like a lifetime ago now.

''Not to mention that I was thrown for a loop by all those tears and tender words, Sara. So if it took me a minute to get around to telling you that I hadn't been seriously injured while wrestling a monster gator to save your life, then I suppose I should apologize.''

Lifting her head slowly, she swallowed her pride. ''Thank you for saving my life, Jake.''

His smile came more fully. ''So admit it. You put that little number on for me. Didn't you?''

Her brows slammed down, and she glared at him. ''You rotten, self-centered, egotistical—''

''Shut up, Sara.'' He gripped her around the waist and, smiling at her, pulled her up against him. His arms were like wet manacles around her waist, and his chest pressed so hard to hers she could feel its heat burning her. And then he kissed her, and his mouth was hot, and wet, and he tasted vaguely of bayou water—and somehow it wasn't a bad thing. It was wild, and dangerous, and beckoning her to venture deeper.

She opened her own mouth, because she couldn't do otherwise, and he put his tongue inside, exactly the way she wanted him to. And he moved his hips against her, exactly the way she wanted him to. In fact, kneeling there with him in the swamp grass was so close to the way she'd dreamed it would be that she almost let herself believe it was a dream. A perfect, beautiful dream.

But it wasn't a dream. It was real. *He* was real. And she was falling in love with him.

She clung to his neck, nibbled at his jaw. "What are we doing, Jake?"

"What we both want to," he whispered, and his voice was raspy and deep.

She leaned lower, kissed his neck, tasted his skin.

His hands went to the straps of the small black nighty. "I like this," he said. "You did put it on for me, didn't you, Sara? Hmm? Admit it, why don't you?" He lowered his head, nuzzling her breasts with his mouth right through the fabric. When he caught one taut peak in his teeth, tugging playfully, nipping just a little, she shivered all over. "Admit it?" he asked again.

"I admit it. I wore it for you. And I almost lit the lamp."

"I wish you had...."

"I know."

He pushed the nighty down, baring her to the waist, and then he proceeded to suck at each of her breasts in turn. Sara burned inside. She wanted him so much. He pressed her down onto her back on the shore, and his mouth moved from her nipples to her navel, as his hands pushed the nighty down her legs. Then he pressed his face between her legs, and his tongue flicked out, and she screamed in glorious anguish.

"Loosen up, shy little Sara. Open for me."

"B-but..."

"Shhhh." He pressed his hands to her inner thighs, parting them until she felt more exposed and vulnerable than she'd ever imagined. And then he worshiped her with his mouth, devouring her, using his tongue and teeth on her until she was writhing on the brink of something she'd never known. Then he pushed her right over.

Sara climaxed for the first time in her life, on the ground, in a place called Gator's Bayou. And a few seconds later, still shuddering, Jake slid up over her body and pressed himself inside her. Still shivering with aftershocks, the brief stab of pain was only a momentary distraction, and then he was filling her, stretching her, moving inside her. He kissed her and muttered her name as he made love to her slowly and tenderly. And only when she once again reached the shattering precipice did he let himself join her there.

He went stiff, holding her tight to him as he thrust himself in deep, and he whispered her name when he found his release. Then, holding her close, he relaxed.

Sara sighed in contentment when Jake moved so he was beside her instead of on top of her and snuggled up close in his arms. She closed her eyes, sighed softly. "Ahh, Jake. It was wonderful."

"It was long overdue," he muttered. Then he nibbled on her ear, which tickled, and she squirmed. "I've been wanting you since I laid eyes on you."

She snuggled closer. "Me too," she admitted. "But it was better that we waited, don't you think? It wouldn't have meant anything then."

She felt him stiffen a bit. "What do you mean 'meant anything'?"

Rolling onto her back, she looked at him. He'd risen up on one elbow now and was staring down into her face. "Well, just that…that this *meant* something to me, Jake. You do realize that, don't you? *It* meant something to me because *you* mean something to me."

He sat back a little, blinking down at her. "You're crazy."

She stared at him, rapidly feeling the warm glow of contentment and sated desire fade into the dark, overcast pall of disappointment. "You can't deal with that, can you?"

He stared at her for a long moment. "I *can't* mean something to you, Sara. You're dreaming. You…you…were a virgin. You obviously just experienced something you haven't felt before. And you're confused about what it means."

"Oh." She let her arms fall from around his neck, where they had been so wonderfully locked. She lowered her head backward to thump the ground. "Well, thanks for clearing that up. I'd hate to go through life not knowing my own feelings."

"Now you're being sarcastic. Sara, can't we just enjoy this for what it was and never mind what it…meant or didn't mean?"

"No, no, I don't think we can. But I really do owe you one, for explaining my own mind—my own heart—to me. But, um…" She got to her feet, pushed him aside to do so, brushed the twigs and grass from her bare legs, snatched up her dripping wet negligee and stepped into it. "But it must be a real downer from where you stand to know that I'm only imagining things. Considering your own feelings for me, I mean." She finished putting the nightie on.

Jake had gotten up, too, and had been in the process of hunting for his lost, ruined shirt, but he spun to face her when she said those words. "Just what the hell is that supposed to mean?"

"Well, it's pretty obvious, Jake." She walked past him, heading for the house again. "You just wrestled an alligator for me."

Halfway up the steps she glanced back over her shoulder to see Jake with his head in his hands. She almost felt sorry for the big fool.

Almost.

She was smiling smugly, reaching for the door, when he called, "You're dead wrong, pretty thing. I used to wrestle gators for fun."

"Small ones," she quoted to him.

"Yeah, well, *I* was smaller then. I'm bigger now, so..."

"So you pick on bigger gators. And even *they* don't scare you as much as I do."

He sighed, shook his head, rolled his eyes. "This doesn't even bear discussing." Then he changed the subject. Typical. "Listen, there are...some dry clothes for you in that sack I brought along," he said, when she pushed open the creaking screen door.

Blinking, she looked back at him. "And it took you this long to tell me? I've been running around in that heavy robe all day long!"

He shrugged, sent her a grin, taking his turn at smugness, she thought. "I figured if it got hot enough, you would eventually have to take the robe off and give me a better look at that nightie you put on for me last night."

She made a face. "I did *not* put it on for you!"

"That's not what you said a few minutes ago."

"I was lying. I didn't want to...to spoil the mood."

"Right. And you said you thought you could tell me anything." He shook his head as if in exasperation. "You see what I mean? It's desire, Sara. It's not hearts and flowers between us. It's heat and hormones. Nothing more complicated than that."

She still had the screen door in her hand, but she didn't go inside. Instead, she slammed the door shut so hard the windows rattled and stomped right back down the steps. When she reached him, she locked her arms around his neck and kissed him hard on the mouth.

"I think I could love you, Jake Nash. Now you have to decide if you're gonna just shut up and let me, or miss out on the best thing that ever happened to you." She turned to go, then turned back again. "And by the way, if you think I'm going to let you dump me off with my family in Texas, you're dead wrong."

She slammed into the house.

Jake raced up the steps and went in after her. "What do mean, I'm dead wrong?"

"Just what I said. I don't care what *you* decide to do, because I know what *I'm* going to do. I'm going back to the plantation, and I'm going to see to it that Vivienne's killer is caught, tried and convicted."

"You're *what?*"

"You heard me." She crossed to the sack on the floor beside the sofa, leaving little wet puddles on the floor all the way. Kneeling, she started pulling out the contents. "I have to," she went on, locating a pair of her own jeans and a smallish T-shirt. "It's my duty."

"As what? An upstanding citizen?" His tone was mocking.

"As a human being," she snapped. Then she dug some more. "You obviously went to my bungalow to get my things, Jake. Didn't you bring me any underwear? A bra? Anything like that?"

"Let me think," he said slowly. "No."

She turned to glare at him. At that moment something soft and furry scurried out of the bag and up her arm. With a screech, she flung the thing across the room and leaped. Somehow or other she landed in Jake's arms.

The squirrel gave his little head a shake and scampered away, no worse for the fright. Lowering her head, Sara went to pull away. Jake was laughing, and she was mortified. How was she supposed to succeed in coming off all tough and confident when she put on displays like this?

"Put me down," she said.

"Stay," he whispered. He stopped laughing, pulled her closer, nestled her head on his shoulder and buried his fingers in her hair. "I like you right here, Sara Brand. More than is probably sane or healthy or even remotely logical. But I do."

She closed her eyes and relaxed against him. "Please don't keep running away, Jake. We can get to the truth, I know it."

"Sara…" He looked down at her, and she tipped her head up to stare into his eyes. They looked so trapped, so panicked. "Dammit, I don't want to go back to prison."

It touched her, that admission. It touched her right

to the soul. "Then we'll stay in hiding," she said quickly. "But we'll get some help. Let me get a message to my family, Jake. Let me get them involved. They'll get at the truth, I swear they will."

Jake lowered his head, sighing deeply.

"Jake, I wouldn't risk losing you now."

And when his head came up again, his eyes were even wider than they had been before. "Sara—"

"I know, I know, I don't *have* you, so I can't *lose* you. That's what you're going to say. It's bull. I know you think you believe that, but it's bull, Jake Nash."

Shaking his head, he let go of her, lowering her bare feet to the floor and turning away to push a hand through his hair.

"What would your mother tell you to do right now?" Sara asked, knowing she was hitting below the belt.

Jake went stock-still. Just as if she had shot him between the eyes. Bull's-eye, she thought. It was a cheap tactic; it was unfair; it was playing on his emotions, but to hell with that. It worked. That was all that mattered. Because if he ran, his life would be ruined. She knew that as surely as she knew her own name.

Without turning around, he said, "We stay in hiding. But…okay. I'll let you call your family. Just to tell them you're okay. Nothing more. You understand?"

Sara nodded.

"It will have to be from a pay phone. And we'll have to move fast once we hang up, because they'll probably have your family's phones tapped by now, and they'll be able to track us down in a hurry."

"Oh, we won't have to call them at the family's numbers."

"No?" Jake turned slowly.

"Nah. I imagine it's hit the news by now that a man wanted for murder has abducted me and vanished. Shoot, Jake, by now every Brand in Texas has more than likely hit Louisiana with a vengeance."

Jake's eyes closed slowly. "Oh. Good."

She tilted her head to one side. "Try not to sound so enthusiastic, will you?"

He gave his head a shake. "How do you suppose we can go about finding them?"

She shrugged. "I have a few ideas. But we probably ought to get going on this, Jake. So I can get word to them before *they* find *us*. That, um…might not be pretty."

Jake eyed her. She just smiled her most reassuring smile at him. "It's going to be all right, Jake. I just know it is."

"You've got to get those rose-colored glasses of yours adjusted, hon." He reached out, ran one hand through her hair. "Prepare yourself, Sara. I mean it. Things don't always work out the way you want them to. You've got to be ready for that, because it's a real possibility. The most likely one, as a matter of fact."

"Ah, Jake," Sara whispered. "You wait. You'll see. You will, I promise. Your life can be everything you ever wanted it to be, because you're so much more than you give yourself credit for being."

He frowned at her. "That's the second time you've said something like that to me," he told her.

"Because it's true," she replied.

Licking his lips, Jake shook his head. "Must be a woman thing. My mamma was forever telling me the same damn thing." Then he sighed. "I hope the hell you come out of this better than she did, Sara."

Chapter 10

He must be out of his freaking mind to be doing this. But he was doing it all the same. And he was damned if he knew why.

Instead of being halfway to Mexico—as any sane ex-con-wanted-on-a-murder-charge would surely be by now—Jake was bringing the oldest cliché in the book to life.

He had returned to the scene of the crime.

He crouched at the edge of the bayou just beyond the main house's sprawling lawns, peering out at the most activity Sugar Keep had probably seen since the Civil War.

Cops. Of course there were cops. Cops everywhere. Every light in the house was on, and the driveway was busier than a four-lane. Cars coming, cars going, cars shutting off or starting up. Doors opening and closing as countless people came and went.

Most of them were cops.

And the rest, he suspected, were Brands.

A few seemed to be both.

Sara clutched his arm. "That's Garrett's pickup," she said, nodding through the darkness toward the hulking thing, as two men, both befitting the truck's size, stood next to it, talking animatedly to a bunch of others. "We need to get closer, Jake."

Sure. That was just what he wanted. To get closer. "Which one's Garrett?" he asked, squinting in the darkness.

"The big one," she said.

He rolled his eyes, because that description could have fit several of the contenders. "The one with the blond ponytail?"

"No, that's Ben. I meant the *other* big one."

Okay, he saw Garrett now. A sheriff, according to Sara. And he had come to Sara's rescue, complete with the shiny star pinned to his chest. It caught the light of another approaching vehicle and winked mockingly at Jake. That same light fell on the other men who stood around, and Jake tried to take their measure even as Sara led him through the brush, closer than before.

"The dark one," Sara said, pointing. "That's Wes."

"You mean the one who looks mad enough to throttle a nun?"

She grinned. "He's hot tempered, but not as bad as he used to be."

Wes, Jake noticed, had a big, old Bowie knife strapped to his boot. How bad the guy used to be, he thought, must have been pretty damned bad. Grizzly-with-a-toothache bad.

"The one in the suit is Adam," she said.

Ah, now that one he could handle. In a physical altercation, at least. But the guy looked sharp. "Don't tell me. He's a lawyer. A prosecutor, with my luck."

"Nah. He used to be an accountant, but he runs a dude ranch now. And the one with the reddish hair is Elliot."

"Elliot's carrying a rope," Jake observed.

"Oh, that? That's just his lasso. He's good with it, and it comes in handy sometimes."

"Like at lynchings?" Jake asked. Sara didn't answer, so he went on. "He's also carrying a gun, Sara. As is the guy standing next to him."

"Jessi's husband, Lash. It's okay though. He's a deputy."

"Oh well, in that case..." Jake shook his head and turned away. "I'm getting the hell out of here, Sara. This was a bad idea. A Very Bad Idea. Possibly the world's worst Very Bad Idea."

Sara gripped his arm, tugged him closer to her as she peered over the weeds, apparently oblivious to his desire to leave. "I don't see Jessi," she whispered. "I wonder where she is?"

"I really don't care where she is. You wanted to be sure your cousins were here, now you know they are. You can call them from our next stop—which, by my calculations, should be somewhere just outside of Tibet—and tell them you're okay."

"I'm not leaving until I see my brother."

Jake sighed in frustration and lowered his head.

"And I should think you would want to see how your family is doing, as well, Jake. Oh! Look, there's Flossie."

Jake looked. Flossie stood on the wide front porch, talking to someone. Yet another physically fit specimen of manhood, and a gorgeous brunette who kept wiping at her eyes. Flossie was talking, looking shaky, pale.

"Let's get closer," Jake heard himself say. Then he, not Sara, led the way to a nearer clump of brush. He could hear them speaking now.

"…and if he's so much as mussed Sara's hair, I'll kill that son of a…" the dark, mean-looking one was saying.

Jake swallowed hard, tried to ignore the conversation near the pickup and focused instead on the one unfolding on the porch.

"That's my brother, that's Marcus!" Sara whispered excitedly. "And Casey! Oh, God, she's crying.…"

Jake knew it had to be tough for Sara to sit there and watch her loved ones this upset. He knew she must be itching to run out of the bushes right now into their waiting arms.

"I promise you, Mr. Brand," Flossie was saying, her voice floating to Jake's ears, sounding hoarse from crying, but firm, "my Jake had nothing to do with Vivienne's murder. And if Sara went with him at all…well, it was her choice to go."

My Jake. He had to look down and squeeze the bridge of his nose, because those words, and the way she had said them, touched a raw spot somewhere inside him. Flossie still believed in him. He could barely comprehend that.

"Sara would never choose to run off with a strange man," Marcus said. "Never."

"Well now, I disagree with you there, young

man. She and Jake…there was something special between those two. I saw it right off,'' Flossie said, sounding utterly sure of herself.

Jake felt Sara's eyes on him. He tried not to look at her, but wound up looking anyway.

"Are you telling me this guy was coming on to my sister?" a deep voice growled. And it was louder than it had been before. Jake snapped his gaze back to that porch and saw that now all the other Brand men were looking there, as well.

"He was *what?*" shouted one.

"He'd better hope to God the cops find him before I do," said another.

"Hell," said the redhead. "I've got a longer rope in the truck."

Sara squeezed Jake's arm. "You're right," she said. "We'd best go. We'll get to a phone, and I'll call Garrett and…explain things."

Jake stared hard at her. She had told him about her family, but, to be honest, he had been taking most of what she said with a grain of salt. Now he saw that they were just as protective, just as close-knit and every bit as hot tempered as Sara had claimed they were…and then some. And he was in more hot water than he had even begun to realize. And even with that knowledge, there was something about all this that gave him a knot in his belly. It must be something to have a family like this one. Every last one of the bunch dropping whatever they might be doing to come charging to the rescue when another one of the bunch was in trouble.

Imagine that.

Hell, if he'd had a family like that, his mother never would have been turned away without a dime.

He never would have tried that idiotic stunt he had, or wound up wasting half his life in jail.

Another voice came then, breaking into his thoughts. A deep, quiet, familiar voice.

"You won't be needing any rope, Brand, and you won't be doing my nephew any harm. I understand you're upset and worried for your Sara. But try to keep in mind that my wife and I just lost our only daughter."

Jake turned slowly. It was his uncle. Bert looked foreign standing on the porch in a dark-gray suit instead of his usual white one.

"I'm so sorry," the weeping female said. "This must be horrible for you both."

"Not so horrible that we would believe for one minute that Jake had anything to do with this. He's like a son to us, Mrs. Brand. And we aren't going to stand by and see him railroaded like he was before. I don't care if every last one of you are peace officers."

Jake couldn't believe what he was hearing.

"I told you," Sara whispered. "They love you, those two. You were just too blind to see it."

Jake blinked hard, keeping his eyes averted. This was hitting him hard. How had he not known this? How had he not *seen* it?

"Whether he's guilty of your daughter's murder or not," the big one with the badge said, "doesn't change the fact that he's a wanted man, and that he's taken Sara with him on his flight from justice."

Jake drew a deep breath, turned to Sara and, taking her hand, drew her away, more deeply into the bayou. When they were out of earshot, he said, "Go on, Sara. Go to the house, go be with your family.

It's where you belong. Just…just make sure they take you home. You can't hang around here, even for one night. You have to leave. And I mean immediately. Okay?''

She looked up at him, her brown eyes damp as they searched his face. ''Because the killer might come after me next, right, Jake?''

Swallowing hard, Jake finally gave a nod. ''It's not that I think it's likely. Just that…it's *possible*.''

''It's likely. You know something you haven't told me, don't you, Jake? Something important enough that it made you decide to take me with you in the first place.''

He couldn't look away from the hold she had on his eyes.

''Tell me,'' she whispered. ''I have every right to know if my life is in danger. You know I do.''

Swallowing hard, he knew she was right. ''That night…when I went into your bungalow to get the pills for Flossie…'' Drawing a breath, he gripped her shoulders, held them gently but firmly, wanting her to know he was right there, close to her. ''I thought I heard someone slipping out the back door.''

Her head drew backward, and her eyes flared. ''The killer.''

''I can't be sure. But…it could've been.''

''God, Jake, you should've told me!''

''You were so afraid that night. I didn't want to add to that. All I wanted to do was keep you safe, and I knew damned good and well that I couldn't do that if I let them lock me up. You would have been a sitting duck. No one would have believed me if I'd tried to tell them, and I—'' He stopped talking, because the look on her face was so…so surprised. So…misty.

"You did all this just to protect me?" she whispered.

"No. No, that's not what I meant—"

"That's exactly what you meant. Suppose you had just let them arrest you, and the killer had come after me, Jake? You would have been cleared. Don't tell me you didn't think of that."

"I…I didn't."

Sighing, she hugged his neck, resting her head on his chest, "I'm not going anywhere except back to that ramshackle house in the bayou with you, Jake. I have an idea how we can solve this whole thing. But we'll need to plan it carefully."

"Sara—"

"Don't argue." She pressed a finger to his lips. "You'll be doing enough of that once you hear my plan. So save it." Then, drawing her finger away, she replaced it with her lips. Her kiss was soft and so sweet. And he wished he could think of a way to make her understand that the things she was imagining, dreaming of, could never be.

He let her lead him back to the boat, climbed in and pushed off, and he told himself not to be so damned glad she'd chosen to stay with him.

They floated deeper in the darkness, and the only sounds around them were the deep-throated frogs and the night birds and the soothing swish of the water. The occasional snort of a boar or the roar of a gator. The steady, gentle slapping of water against the hull. Sara stared steadily behind them, her face troubled.

"What is it, hon?" he asked her.

Pursing her lips, she shook her head. "My cousin Jessi. She wouldn't have stayed behind. I know her too well not to know that. I don't like that we didn't see her there, Jake."

"Hey, don't worry. I'm sure your cousin Jessi is fine."

She frowned and looked up at him as if he were dense. "It's not her I'm worried about."

It was dark by the time they got back to the ramshackle house deep in the bayou. Twice Sara thought she heard something in the water and started, as memories of the alligator came back to haunt her. Jake, too, had tensed, then relaxed again when the sound hadn't been repeated. As before, he helped her out, then they lifted the small boat and carried it to its nest amid the brush, where it was safely out of sight. Then they walked toward the house, as, in hushed voices, they continued their conversation.

"It's out of the question, Sara," Jake said. "Trying to get to a phone to call them would just be too risky."

"Then what do you suggest we do?"

Jake opened the screen door. It creaked, and they both went still and looked around them nervously.

"It's odd out here tonight," Sara said.

"It's all in your head." But Jake hurried her through the door, and when he closed it, he took his time, as if trying to ensure that no more squeaking would result. Inside, he quickly lit the lamp, filling the musty-smelling room with soft light, making things seem just a little less scary. "But we shouldn't stay here much longer. It's risky, spending too long in one place.''

She nodded, coming inside, kicking the sofa several times and then sitting down. ''A moving target's tougher to hit,'' she said.

''Exactly. So back to the matter at hand.'' He came to sit beside her.

''Supper?'' she asked.

He tried to scowl at her, but she saw the affection behind it. It was such a small thing, but it warmed her to her toes.

''I was talking about how we contact your family without using a phone.''

''Oh, that. Well, why don't we just write them a note?'' She studied his face in the lamplight. She thought he was beautiful. Rough edges and all. He hadn't shaved since they'd been on the run, and his whiskers made him even sexier, she thought.

''How do we deliver it?'' he asked.

''Hey, I can't think of everything. It's your turn.''

Staring at her, he sighed. ''Supper. I can think better on a full stomach.''

They dined on canned meats and crackers, washing it down with sips from a bottle of fruit juice. Then Jake curled onto one end of the sofa and patted the spot beside him.

Sara looked at it.

''You like it in my arms and you know it, teacher,'' he teased.

''And you like me being there.''

''Yeah. I do.'' He lowered his eyes. ''I know we haven't really talked about...about what happened between us.''

She shrugged. ''Yeah, we did. You said it didn't

mean anything, and I said it did." She licked her lips. "I don't supposed you've changed your mind yet?"

"Sara…"

She shrugged. "I didn't think so. Well, you will. I know that…but I suppose until you do, I ought to exercise a little sanity. A little…self-preservation."

"I'd never hurt you, Sara."

She smiled sadly. "You wouldn't mean to." But he would if she let herself fall any more deeply in love with him than she already had.

"If you don't want us to…have sex—"

"Make love," she interjected.

He looked at her, frowning. "If you don't want it to happen again, it's not going to. Okay?"

"Promise?" she asked.

He nodded, making a screwed-up Boy Scout salute and muttering, "Convict's honor."

She smiled softly at him and curled up beside him. Jake tugged a blanket over them both, and Sara marveled at how cozy and safe she felt in his arms. This was perfect. Right. Why couldn't he see that? They would be so good together.

"So are you going to tell me about this plan of yours?" he asked her after a while. And she thought he was having as much trouble settling into sleep as she was.

"Well…I guess I could." She gnawed her lip, knowing he would object—and loudly. "My thought was that if we catch the real killer, you'll be free and clear."

"Makes sense." He rolled onto his back and folded his arms, resting his head on his palms. "I wonder who it is?"

"My money's on that pretty boy we saw her with at the jazz club," Sara said. "Maybe she broke it off with him like you told her to and——" She bit her lip. "Oh, damn, I didn't mean——"

"Don't think I haven't been wondering the same thing. Maybe she did take me seriously. And maybe she tried to dump the jerk, and killing her was his reaction." Jake shook his head. "I seem to have a knack for getting people killed without really even trying, don't I?"

"She slept around a lot, Jake, you told me that yourself."

He nodded. "So?"

"So it could have been any one of the men she was playing with. Don't start blaming yourself for this. It's way too early for that."

He sighed. She decided to get back to her plan, if for no other reason than to distract him from feeling lousy over Vivienne's death.

"We know the killer—whoever he is—thinks I saw him. So he wants to shut me up."

"Maybe," Jake said.

Sara shrugged. "So the solution is obvious. I go back, make sure everyone knows I'm back, hang out at the bungalow alone and wait for him to come after me."

Jake sat up so fast that Sara almost fell on the floor. "Are you out of your freaking mind?"

"No. No, you haven't heard the whole plan yet!"

"No, just the insane part, right?"

"But that's just it. It would only look insane. We could get Garrett and Marcus and all the others set up all around the place. They'd be out of sight, but close by, and when the killer came for me, they could just jump out and grab him."

"And hope he didn't bring a gun, and hope that if he did, he's a lousy shot, because he's damn well going to have time to squeeze at least one round off at your pretty head before they beat him bloody."

"Oh, for crying out—"

"No."

"But, Jake—"

"No. I won't let you put your life on the line for me. And I'll tell you something else, your cousins and your brother wouldn't let you do that, either. And if they would, then I'd have to personally kick all their asses for dereliction of duty. Now, are we clear on this?"

Sara pouted, crossed her arms in front of her and sighed. "Yes."

"You sure?"

She nodded. "It was a good idea. You're just stubborn."

"I'll come up with a better idea. One that doesn't involve putting my favorite kindergarten teacher in front of a killer with a big old bull's-eye painted on her forehead. If it's all the same to you."

She looked sideways at him.

"Sara, you want to know something?"

"What?" she asked.

"The death of that old man…it haunts me. Still, to this day, it haunts me. I can never take back what I did. I can never give him back the years or months or days he lost because of me. Now how the hell do you suppose I could live with myself if something happened to you? Hmm?"

She lowered her head and her arms. "Okay. Okay, all right. I get it."

"So you won't go trying anything? Promise?"

"I promise." She lay back down, rolled onto her side and pulled up the covers. "But you wouldn't care so much if you didn't love me," she muttered under her breath, her words barely audible.

"What did you say?"

"Nothing," she said, sounding sulky. "Good night, Jake."

"Good night, Sara."

Chapter 11

She fell asleep after another hour of tossing and turning, only to wake up what seemed like mere minutes later when nature called rather demandingly. Slipping out of Jake's arms wasn't easy. He'd wrapped himself around her, tucked her head upon his chest and was cradling her like a lover. And, God, it felt good. She tried to move carefully, not to wake him.

"Where you going?" he asked, sounding wide awake already.

"Why aren't you sleeping?" She tipped her chin up to look at him in the darkness. The lamp had burned out. Out of kerosene, probably.

He made a deep-throated sound, like a growl. "You figure that one out, honey. Besides, I asked first."

"I, um, need to use the outhouse."

"Okay." He sat up slowly, easing her off him,

never really breaking contact, though. When he got to his feet, one arm was still around her shoulders, and she rose with him. "Let's go."

"You don't have to—" she began.

"The hell I don't. You're scared to death to go out there alone in the dark. Don't even try to deny it."

Licking her lips, Sara didn't try. "I'm trying to beat those old fears into submission, Jake. It's...it's just not easy. They've been with me a long time."

His hand came to cup her chin, tipped her head up, and his eyes sparkled darkly. "I wasn't criticizing. You're one of the bravest women I've ever met. And that's no lie."

"Yeah?"

"Yeah. So come on." He walked her out of the house, around to the back and then went into the old outhouse before her, thumping around in there to scare away any unwanted visitor of the fur-bearing variety. Finally he came back out and said, "The coast is clear."

"Great." With a sigh of reluctance, almost glad of the darkness, Sara went inside and took care of her pressing needs. It didn't take her very long. She didn't much like the idea of this dark, decrepit out-house, and she didn't even want to think about what might pop up from below and where it might bite her!

She was back outside in very short order.

But when she stepped out of the outhouse into the night, Jake seemed to have simply...vanished.

Sara had only been gone for a second when Jake felt the cold barrel of a handgun pressing against his spine, and heard a very low voice whispering, "Get your hands up and keep quiet, or I'll blow you right in half."

He complied.

The gun prodded him, and he walked where it seemed to want him to walk, beyond the outhouse and into the trees just past it.

"Right there. Stop, and don't turn around."

Jake stopped. And he didn't turn around. "Just who are you, and what do you want?" he asked.

"I ask the questions here. You just answer when I tell you to. Where's Sara Brand?"

"That depends on who's asking," Jake said slowly. He wasn't going to risk that this might be the killer he was talking to.

"The person holding this gun to your spine is asking, that's who. Now tell me where she is before I run out of patience."

Something moved in the bushes. There was a solid whack, a thud, and the barrel was no longer pressing into his spine. Jake turned around, fishing rapidly in his pockets for the flashlight he hadn't dared use until now. The gunman, whoever he'd been, was on the ground in a heap, but Jake barely looked at him. His beam of light and his attention were all on Sara, standing beyond the fallen figure, a limb the size of a baseball bat clutched in her hand.

"Are you all right, Jake?" she asked. She was wide-eyed and breathless, staring down at the gunman.

"Fine, *chère*. Damn, you're something, you know that?" He moved closer, stepping over the body to hug her close, taking the limb from her hand, although she was clutching it so tightly he had to work to get it.

"Was it…was it *him?*" she asked in a whisper.

Jake turned, aiming the beam of his light down on the attacker, hoping to God it was Vivienne's killer, so this whole thing could be over before Sara went through any more trauma.

His light spilled onto shoulder-length red hair and an elfin face with high cheekbones and long lashes resting on them.

"Ohmigod!" Sara cried. "It's Jessi!" She immediately dropped to her knees beside the woman, yanking the light out of Jake's hand and aiming it at the woman's head in search of whatever damage her blow had caused to the Brand female's cranium.

"Well," Jake said, hunkering down beside her, "we've solved one problem, at least."

"What problem could this possibly solve?" Sara squeaked.

Jake had his fingers pressed now to Jessi Brand's throat, reassured by the strong, steady pulse beating there. "The problem of how to deliver your note," he said.

"You're sure she's all right?" Sara asked him for the fourth time. She sat in the small boat, looking back, though it was still too dark to see anything.

"We put her inside the house, Sara, and closed the door so no gators or wild boars will happen upon her. She was already starting to moan a bit when we left her. She'll be fully conscious in a matter of minutes. You didn't hit her all that hard."

Sara bit her lower lip, and it made him want to kiss it. "I just hope she's all right."

"If you'd taken any longer writing that note, she'd have been up and around to prove it to you," he reminded her.

"And I still didn't tell them half what I wanted to," Sara countered, finally facing him again. "Do you think she'll find her way back all right?"

"She found her way out here."

"Yes, but she probably followed us then."

"You told me yourself she was the best tracker in Texas, Sara. Don't you think she can figure out how to go back the way she came?" He watched her face, knew his words were not reassuring her in the least, knew exactly what she was going to suggest before she ever parted her lips.

"Sara, we *have* to get out of here."

"She wouldn't know what to do with a gator...or one of those ugly hogs."

"She came out to us by boat. She'll go back by boat. So long as she's in the boat, she's safe. She's perfectly safe, Sara."

"Well...what if it tips over? Or sinks or—"

"No, Sara. Just...no."

Sara tilted her head, and her big eyes were moist. And he thought for just a minute that this was insane, what he was about to do. He even spent a few useless seconds trying to figure out why he would even consider it...before he turned the little boat around, pushed off one side with the long pole and set them heading back the way they'd come.

Sara smiled softly. "We'll stay a safe distance behind her," she promised. "She'll never know we're anywhere near here, and we'll stop following just the second we know she's safe."

"Right."

She moved back to sit beside him and slid her arms around his waist, squeezing him gently. "Thank you, Jake."

His throat seemed to swell a bit when he tried to swallow and found he couldn't.

A couple of hours later, even as the morning sun broke over the bayou, spilling greenish-gold light over everything, he and Sara watched Jessi Brand beach her borrowed canoe near the plantation and climb out. As she walked, she kept her head bent, still rereading the note Sara had left pinned to her blouse.

Jake had read it, too. Sara hadn't noticed it, but he'd been determined to read what she'd written. And it had shaken him right to the roots of his hair and carved itself a place in his memory, where he knew it would always stay.

Jessi,
Take this note back to the family, but don't show it to anyone else. I need your help. Jake Nash did not kill his cousin Vivienne. Someone else did—someone who thinks I can identify him. I can't, but that's beside the point. The killer was coming after me next, and that's why Jake took me with him when he left. To protect me. He's a good man, Jessi. Damn good. And you know I can tell a good man from a bad one, don't you? I've certainly been around enough of both kinds to know the difference. You look into his prior conviction—the details of what really happened—and you'll see it, too. But I don't have time to go into that right now. Just know that I'm okay, and I'm with Jake

because I want to be. I won't come back until
he can come back with me—with his name
cleared and the real killer behind bars. You can
help me with that if you want to, but if you
don't, then just go on home. Stop looking for
me. I believe in Jake. With any luck, maybe
when this is all over, he'll believe in himself.
I hope so, because I love him, Jessi. I love him.

   Yours,

                            Sara

"We should go," Sara whispered, startling him.

He looked at her, looked at those big eyes filled
with impossible dreams staring into his. He had
never had anything good. He had, on occasion, allowed himself to hope for good things—wish for
and dream of wonderful things—only to have them
snatched away, leaving him beaten and broken. Sara
Brand…she was bigger and better than anything
he'd ever dared dream of or wish for. She wasn't
meant for the likes of him, and he damned well
knew it. If he let himself think even for a second
that this thing between them could be real, that they
could have some chance for anything…anything
good together… .

It would be the most crushing disappointment of
his life. He didn't think he would be able to recover.

He had to get away from her. Send her back to
her clean, good little life, with her respectable family
in her wholesome town. And then he could just
crawl back into the slime where he belonged.

He couldn't take her back into that slime with
him. It was rubbing off on her, contaminating her,
that swamp that had been his home. The dark cloud

he'd been born under was starting to cast its shadow on her pristine life. And, damn, but he didn't want that for her.

"We'll go on foot from here."

"You think that's wise?"

He nodded and poled the boat farther, until the plantation was out of sight. Then he banked it and helped her out. Just beyond the trees, the highway ran. Beyond that was the small Cajun settlement of Belle Ville. That was where he would leave Sara Brand. That was where he would slip away and get the hell out of here. Now that her family knew she was in danger, they would protect her. She would be safe. Jake wasn't going to let her out of his sight until he was 100 percent certain of that. But then...well, it was for the best.

For both of them.

They waited until traffic cleared, crossed the highway, then dashed through the field beyond it and through a copse of trees, into the town of Belle Ville.

It was odd that she should know him so well, see so much of him in his eyes, after so short an acquaintance. But she did. She knew he was up to something from the moment they left the small box-nosed boat behind. She sensed it. There was some sort of shadow in his eyes—and they didn't meet hers head-on, but sideways and fleetingly.

"What's wrong, Jake?"

"Nothing. Come on, I know some people here."

He took her by the arm and led her along a narrow, dusty path. As they moved closer to the cluster of dark wood buildings, she heard music. Then voices. Then the sounds grew louder, until she felt she was nearing some kind of carnival. Smells came to her, hot, spicy, fishy smells. Voices floated beneath the music. The sounds of footfalls on hardwood. It all seemed to be coming from one place— a large building at the end of the path that looked like a barn but appeared to be some kind of saloon instead. Light spilled yellow-gold from the windows, and when the door slid open on its casters, more noise and tantalizing smells spilled out at her, and Sara heard a distinctively Cajun "Aieee," coming from within and saw bodies swaying inside.

A brief glimpse, then the door rolled shut and all the noise was muffled again.

The dawning came hot-orange on the horizon, and the color glowed its reflection from the eyes of the woman who'd just exited the building. Chocolate skinned, she was, as tall and slender as a reed, with a face that gave no clue to her age. A scarf patterned in vibrant reds and yellows covered her hair, and she held herself like a queen. She glanced at them only briefly as she strode past. But then she halted, turned and said, "Wait!"

Sara almost jumped out of her skin at the urgency in the woman's tone. But she turned. "Who? Us?" she asked.

Those dark eyes narrowed on Sara. "Come here," she said, and she crooked a slender finger tipped with a nail so long it curved at the end. "Let me look at you."

"I...am kind of in a hurry."

"Oh, go on," Jake said. He smiled and urged her forward. "This is Kyra. She's a Voudon priestess. Maybe she'll tell you your fortune."

Kyra scowled at him, tossing her head in a way that made the layers of beads that dangled from her neck and her ears clatter together noisily. Her gaze narrowed on Jake, then widened again. "Jacob Nash, is it?"

"It's me," he said, stepping closer.

The woman nodded. "It has been a long time since you've come," she said. "I hear about your mamma. She was a good one. A good one." Then she tilted her head. "But you found yourself another good woman, di'n't you, boy?" As she spoke, her hand snapped out to clasp Sara's chin as fast as a snake biting. Almost as sharply, too, with those nails and her powerful grip. She stared into Sara's eyes…then her own widened, and she let go and backed away with a gasp. "Death is your shadow!" she cried.

"Knock it off, Kyra," Jake said. He took Sara's arm, turning her away. "Ignore her."

But Sara pulled away, turning back to the woman. "What do you mean?"

"He stalks you. One misstep and you will be his." Then the woman jabbed a forefinger toward Jake. "Only you can save her, Jacob Nash. If you leave her, she will die. I warn you."

"Leave me?" Sara echoed, turning to stare up at Jake. "That wouldn't be your plan for tonight, would it, Jake?"

His eyes slid sideways, away from her probing gaze.

"Not just tonight," the woman went on. "When the reaper comes for you, woman, this man will be your shield." She turned to Jake. "If you're not with her when he comes, then he'll take her with him to the underworld. Mark my words well, Jacob,'' Kyra went on, her voice lowering. ''If you let her die, you will follow—but yours will be a living death, boy. For just as you are the only one who can save the girl's life...*she* is the only one who can save your soul.'' Then she turned her hand over and opened her palm. ''That will be five dollars.''

''Oh, for crying—''

''You prefer a curse?'' she asked, cocking one narrow brow.

''Pay the woman, Jake.''

He glared at Sara, but he fished a five-dollar bill from his pocket and smacked it into Kyra's hand. ''She pulls the same scam every time I set foot in the vicinity,'' he complained.

''Is she always this accurate?'' Sara asked.

He made a face and turned to send one last, parting shot at Kyra, but by then she'd vanished. ''Another of her specialties,'' he muttered.

''She was right, wasn't she, Jake?''

He turned slowly to face Sara. ''About what?''

''You were planning to leave me tonight, to dump me off here like some unwanted stray. Don't bother denying it,'' she snapped, when he opened his mouth to do just that. ''I could see it in your face the minute the words left her lips. You were going to leave me here.''

Blowing a sigh through clenched teeth, he nodded. ''Yes. I was. You'll be perfectly safe now that your family knows you're a target. They'll take care of you, and I can get the hell out of here the way I should have done days ago.''

''And spend the rest of your life on the run?'' she asked. ''A wanted man? A fugitive? Why, Jake?''

Reaching into his pocket, he yanked out a folded piece of paper and handed it to her. "This is why."

She stared down at it. Newspaper. A clipping. "What's this?" she asked, unfolding it as she did, skimming the story about Vivienne's murder and Jake's supposed motive. Her mouth went dry as she read the latest revelations released to the press. That Flossie and Bertram had recently redrawn their will, leaving their entire plantation to be divided equally between Vivienne and Jake.

"I didn't know a thing about it. I swear to God, I didn't," Jake said softly.

Sara lifted her head, stared straight into his eyes. "I know you didn't. And…Flossie and Bert, they know it, too."

"The police think I knew about the will. They think I offed Viv so I could inherit the whole thing myself. The theory is that I was planning to murder Flossie and Bert next."

Sara drew a breath and sighed. "How long have you had this clipping, Jake?"

He shook his head. "Your cousin had it on her when you clobbered her. I found it in her pocket when I was searching her."

"And why didn't you tell me sooner?"

They stood outside the barn-like dance hall with the Cajun music pounding and the sky paling to dusky orange. "God, Jake, don't tell me you were afraid I'd believe it. Not after all this."

"Why the hell wouldn't you believe it? Everyone else does."

She blinked slowly, stepped closer. "Because…because I—"

"No." He held up his hands. "Look, it's high

time we parted ways, Sara. You hang around with me, I'm going to get you killed.''

"But Kyra said—''

"To hell with what Kyra said. Dammit, Sara, go back to Texas. Go back to your safe little fantasy life, where everything works out the way it should and happy endings abound. I don't fit there. For me, there's no such thing.''

Sara's eyes widened. His looked tortured. "Is that what you think my life is? Just a series of happy endings? Hmm? You know better, Jake. I hid in a freaking cupboard and watched my mother get blown away. I spent the last twenty-one years of my life in constant fear, being hunted and living a lie. And I still haven't shaken off the repercussions of that. If I had, I'd have come to you the first time you offered, and I wouldn't be standing here now, scared half to death of what's going to happen to me if you leave me alone.''

He gave his head a desperate shake, bit his lip. "I'm sorry. I shouldn't have said—''

"Go to hell, Jake.''

He blinked in shock and stood there, not touching her, not speaking. She sounded…mean.

"I'm tired of fighting with you. You're a grown-up. You know what you want, and it obviously isn't an ordinary life with a boring schoolteacher like me. So you just go. You just go live on the run, go have some great adventure south of the border, go hang out with a gang of thugs. And I'll go back to my boring little safe life with its built-in happy endings, and I'll try to pretend I never met you.''

She turned her back on him and walked away.

"Sara.''

She didn't slow down, didn't look back.

"Dammit, Sara, don't go."

She stepped around the corner of the building and out of sight.

Jake ran around the corner after her, but he didn't see her. She had vanished. A cold knot of panic formed in the pit of his belly as he turned, looked, searched for her and thought the worst. Kyra's prophetic words kept coming back to his mind, and he wanted to kick himself. The killer must have been watching them the whole time. Somehow that maniac had managed to get his filthy hands on Sara.

And Jake had no one to blame but himself.

Chapter 12

He stood there, not knowing what to do, feeling like the biggest fool in the history of the world...when he heard a soft sound that slapped the panic out of him like a well-aimed hand.

Sniffling. Gentle, barely audible...crying.

Swallowing the lump that rose inexplicably into his throat, Jake followed that sound. Sara sat crouched in a small, shadowed area between the barn-like building and the one beside it. Knees drawn to her chest, face pillowed on her arms.

For some reason Jake's eyes burned as he went to her. He didn't say anything. Instead he turned and sat down beside her, his back against the rough slab wood sides of the building, his side brushing hers. "I'm a real idiot sometimes," he said.

She didn't say anything, so he continued. "I mean, I'd have to be, wouldn't I? To make the mess of my life that I've managed to make. Trying to rob that liquor store...then being stupid enough to stick around afterward trying to do CPR when I didn't even know how—''

"That wasn't stupid, Jake. That was the only smart thing you did that day."

"It got me caught. And it didn't do a thing for the old man."

"It did something for you, though," she said, lifting her head, dabbing at her eyes. "You just haven't figured that out yet."

He shook his head. "All it did was land me behind bars for seventeen years."

She sighed, shook her head, looked exasperated with him, and he wished he knew why. "Then I get out, have a public fight with my cousin and wind up on the wrong end of a murder warrant all over again. Another stupid mistake."

"Running away was the stupid part," she said.

He frowned at her. "Will you let me get to my point?"

Lifting her brows, she said, "You have a point?"

"Of course I have a point!" He lowered his voice, took a deep breath. "The point is...that of all the stupid things I've done in my life, I don't regret any of them more than I regret the stupid thing I did just now."

She blinked slowly, tilted her head to one side. "And what stupid thing did you do just now?" she asked him.

"I made you cry." He ran his forefinger over her cheek, wiping away the dampness that was there. "I'm sorry, Sara. I'm sorry I was an insensitive jerk just now. I'm sorry I implied that your life had been some kind of fairy tale, when I know damn well it's been a trip through hell."

She lifted her chin, nodded at him. "It has," she said softly. "But I came out on the other side. I found my brother, my family. I'm vanquishing my demons. My life is almost perfect now."

He nodded. "I'm still working through my hell, Sara. My demons are still dogging me, and if you hang around me too long, I'll drag you right back down with me. I know I will."

"No," she began.

"You're a good woman. A decent woman," he said, interrupting her. "I'm a convicted criminal. Can't you see the difference there?"

She lifted her chin and looked him dead in the eye. "A criminal would have run away and left that liquor store owner to die alone. You stayed. You gave up your freedom to try to help him. Just the way you risked it again to try to help me, when you realized I could be the killer's next target. Don't *you* see the difference, Jake? Those aren't the acts of a criminal. They're the acts of...of a hero."

He rolled his eyes and blew air through his teeth. "Right. Some hero I am."

"Someday you'll see it, Jake," she whispered. "Someday, I'll *make* you see it."

He drew a deep breath to keep from snapping at her for her childish fantasies, then let it out slowly. "Can we please just drop this entire subject for now?"

"In favor of what?"

He shrugged, and once again the music spilling out of the barn swelled louder. "One last night of normalcy before I turn myself in and let justice take its course?''

She stared up at him. ''Would you really do that?''

Would he? It was a damn good question. He was certain of only a handful of things right now, and they were all confused and conflicting in his mind. One was that he didn't want to spend another day behind bars. Not ever. Another was that he was right and she was dead wrong: there was no way he could ever fit into her world. But she was making him wonder, making him question his own certainty. Making him doubt things he'd always been sure of before. Making him question the kind of man he was, when he'd never doubted it in his life. He didn't like that. It scared the hell out of him, in fact, because he knew that doubting the only truths he'd ever known would only result in a crushing letdown. In heartbreak. In disappointment. He didn't want to taste that kind of thing again. It was worse than the sound of the cell door banging shut on him.

He knew Sara Brand was in danger and that she would only be safe when he got her back home to Texas and into the bosom of her overprotective family. And he knew she wouldn't go, no matter what he did, unless she had no choice. If he ran, she would run with him. If he tried to give her the slip, she would probably try to hunt him down. And she would be liable to get killed doing it.

And there was one other thing, the scariest thing of all: the way he felt about her. The odd little hitch in his breathing whenever he met her eyes. The fluttering in his chest, the twisting in his belly. It was more than just lust. He'd been lying to himself for a while now about that. It was bigger and more ominous than anything he'd ever felt before. It was louder in his head than the memory of the prison cell doors banging shut behind him twenty years ago. It was more frightening than the final blow of the judge's gavel. Every instinct in him was telling him to get away from her now, before it was too late.

Or…right after tonight.

"It's the right thing to do, Jake," Sara said. "I know it will work out all right. I know it will."

"One night," he said. "Without thinking about any of this. Consider it the condemned man's last request."

"You're not condemned," she began, but he held up a finger and wiggled it back and forth. "Okay," she said, lowering her head. "We're a pair of ordinary people with no warrants hanging over their heads and no cops or killers hunting for them."

"And no Brands hunting for them, either," he said with a slight smile. Then he got to his feet, held out a hand. She took it, and he pulled her up.

"So where are we going?"

"You're kidding, right?" he said. "There's a party going on, *chère*. We'd be crazy not to join in."

Jake led her into the barn and a sea of warm bodies, all of them moving, clapping or singing along. There was sawdust an inch deep on the floor, which was littered with other items it was too dark to make out clearly. Sara took this to be a good thing. Toward the rear, a massive plank rested atop several sawhorses, its surface lined with mugs and bottles of various shapes and sizes and platters of steaming shellfish. The scents that filled the room were of mingled beer, jalapeño and seafood. And the band played and hooted, from a clear spot in the floor off to the left. Old men, bopping like rock and roll superstars, with fiddle, banjo, accordion, nose harp, washboard and spoons.

No one asked who Jake and Sara were or what they were doing there. People only smiled a welcome if they happened to meet their eye or bump their elbow, as Jake swept Sara into his arms for the fastest slow dancing she'd ever attempted. The ceiling swirled above her as he spun her around, but it was his arm around her waist and his hand clasping hers that she focused on. His body, tight to the front of hers, warm and hard, close…so close. Her hand rested on the back of his neck, and she did her best to follow his lead. But it didn't matter, because when she stumbled, he just scooped her up off her feet, then set her down again.

Her hair flew, they moved so fast, and the music had a way of working its way under the skin and singing there. She heard herself laughing out loud, felt her blood rushing headlong through her veins and her heart pounding excitedly with the thrill of it all.

Finally the music stopped, and Sara begged for a rest as a new song started up. Smiling down at her, Jake clasped her around the waist, keeping her close to his side as he guided her back toward the plank-and-sawhorse bar. He helped himself to two beers, a paper plate and heaping scoops from several of the pots of food. Setting everything down, he fished some bills from a pocket and tossed them into a big bowl full of money.

Sara blinked and looked up at him as he gathered the food and drinks up again and made his way back through the crowd.

"It's on the honor system," he explained.

"How do they keep from going broke?" Sara asked.

Jake smiled. "These kinds of people are more likely to overpay than shortchange the till."

"Like you just did?" she asked.

He only shrugged. Sara was thinking he was one sad excuse for a criminal, and she thought he knew it, but she didn't say anything. She had promised. Besides, it was fun, pretending, just for a little while, that things were normal. That she was on a date with Jake, not on the run with him. Although, the way she saw it, the "with him" part was the only part that mattered. Not where they were or what they were doing or pretending. Just so long as she could be with him.

Jake found a bale of straw in a corner and sat down on it, so Sara sat beside him. He handed her the beer, and she was hot and sweaty, so she took a long drink. Then she sampled some of the delicacies on the plate that Jake had perched on his lap.

"Crawdads," Jake said, when she tasted a nasty-looking little beggar that turned out to be mouth-wateringly delicious—but coated in spices that made her throat feel as if she'd swallowed a flamethrower. She drank more beer to wash away the burn, but it didn't help much.

That was pretty much the pattern of the next couple of hours. Dance until she was too hot and sweaty to dance anymore, then eat until her throat and her tongue caught fire and then drink until she no longer cared that all her tastebuds had been seared away.

By the time the party started breaking up, Sara was having a bit of trouble standing up straight. But her head was still clear. Clearer still when Jake led her out of the barn and she looked up to see a black velvet sky glittering with a thousand stars and no hint of moonlight. She walked close to his side. He kept his arm around her, to steady her. Or maybe just because he liked being close as much as she did.

"Are you really going to turn yourself in tomorrow, Jake?"

She felt him stiffen beside her. "Do I have a choice?" he asked in return, not missing a beat.

"Of course you do." She tipped her head up. "Was that your way of avoiding the question?"

"I thought we weren't going to talk about this anymore tonight?"

Turning Jake's wrist, she glanced down at his watch but couldn't see its face in the dark. "I think it's morning."

"It's still partly dark," he said. "Therefore, it's still night."

"Logical."

"So where are we going to sleep?"

He pointed at a crooked shack down the dirt road a bit. "There are a donkey and an old cat in residence, or there were last I knew. Hope you don't mind sharing."

"What, no rooster?" she asked.

He frowned at her.

"*The Brementown Musicians.* One of my class's favorite stories."

"Ah. Sorry, I haven't read it."

"I'll read it to you sometime."

They reached the shed, and Jake opened the door, led her inside, into inky darkness. She heard the donkey breathing, smelled him and felt his heat. But she didn't see him. Too dark. Jake closed his hands around hers and guided her to a ladder attached to one wall. "Go on up," he said. "We'll sleep up above, so the donkey doesn't step on us."

"Okay." She found the bottom rung with her feet and thought it took her an abnormally long time to climb up. But once she got there she stretched out in the hay, not a hint of fear about what might be up there with her entering her mind. No wonder they called it liquid courage, she thought.

Aah, but it wasn't the beer making her feel power over her fears. It was Jake. Being near him. Being with him. She was going to have this thing beat by the time she got back home. She knew that now. This time with him had been...healing. For her.

A second later Jake was near. She felt him, reached out and closed a hand on what turned out to be his thigh.

She could almost hear the smile in his voice. "What are you looking for, Sara?"

"A lamp," she said.

"A lamp?" He sounded puzzled.

"Yeah. You told me to light the lamp and set it in the window. That's the signal, remember? And here I am with no lamp."

He was quiet for a long moment. "You've...had too much beer."

"I didn't have any beer that night, Jake. And I was about to strike the match when you turned your light out and went to bed. I was about to light the lamp then. And if I had only done it a little sooner, none of this would be happening to you right now. You'd have come to me. You'd have been with me when Vivienne—''

"Shh." He pressed a finger unerringly to her lips. "Don't even try to convince yourself this is your fault."

"And I didn't have any beer when you made love to me out in the bayou, either. But I haven't felt you inside me since then, Jake. Not even once. And I—''

"For good reason, Sara. You said it meant something to you when we were together out there. And if we— It would mean something to you now, too. You can't deny that."

"Yes. It would mean a few hours of heaven." She leaned closer, found his mouth with hers and kissed him long and slow. She kept kissing him, over and over, even as she tugged off her clothes and began to work on his.

Jake responded after only minuscule resistance, kissing her back just the way she wanted him to. He pushed her down on her back in the hay, and he pressed his bared chest to hers and ran his hands up and down her thighs as he tasted her mouth's deepest recesses.

For a long time they kissed and touched, and then Jake lifted his head. "Hours?" he whispered. "I don't know if I can live up to that."

"Sure you can," Sara whispered. "I'll help you."

"Sara…"

She reached down to unfasten his jeans and then she touched him. The breath stuttered out of him when her hand closed tight, and when she moved it, he trembled deliciously. "Make love to me, Jake," she whispered.

And then he did.

And as they lay there afterward and the sun came up slowly outside, the rooster in the barn below them began to crow his welcome to the day. "So there was a rooster after all," Sara whispered. She burrowed closer into Jake's arms and fought to keep her eyes open just a little bit longer. Just long enough to tell him what she might not have the courage to tell him sober.

What she might not have the chance to tell him again. She sensed that very strongly.

"I love you, Jake."

"Sara...Sara, I—"

"No. No, don't say anything. I know you didn't want this. Didn't ask for it. Did your damnedest to scare me away and warn me off and everything else you could think of to protect my tender heart. But there's no help for it, Jake. I have fallen hopelessly, head-over-heels in love with you. And I'm not going to get over it. I don't *want* to get over it."

"Oh, Sara." He stroked her hair. "Dammit, I only hurt the women who love me. Don't you realize that?"

She shook her head. "Not true. And even if it were, it wouldn't matter. You don't have any choice about who you fall for, you know. And I didn't have any choice at all. The first time I saw you sitting on that porch, sipping...whatever it was you were sipping..."

"I thought you were an angel."

"I thought you were the devil," she whispered, closing her eyes.

"Yeah. Well, we were both right."

"Mmm." She surrendered to sleep, burrowing more closely into Jake's arms.

Chapter 13

Jake was in trouble, and he knew it. Lying there, as the sun came up and spilled its golden touch over Sara's face, her hair. He knew it. He cared too much about her, so much that he'd been seriously thinking about doing what she wanted—giving himself up and letting the overinflated wheels of justice have a blowout all over him.

Ridiculous.

But he couldn't just leave her, not knowing she could be next on the killer's list. So he had to take a risk he never would have taken for anyone else. Anyone...except maybe his mother, if she had still been with him.

He slipped out early, while she was still sleeping off the effects of too much beer and not enough sex. Not enough for him, anyway.

She hadn't been wrong about her estimate of

hours. It had been hours. The best hours of his life, as far as Jake was concerned.

While Sara slept, Jake went back to the ramshackle barn and located the telephone in the back. The place wasn't locked. It was, in fact, still occupied. Partly conscious bodies were relaxed in most of the shadowed corners. It sure was a party town.

With a sigh, Jake dialed.

Uncle Bertam answered the phone.

"It's me," Jake said.

Bert's voice, when it came, was quiet. "The phones are tapped, son. I'll likely get in trouble for saying so, but you're family. And I know you didn't do this thing."

"Thank you." Jake had to swallow the lump in his throat. "Are you okay, Bert? And what about Flossie, how is she doing?"

"She'll be doing a lot better when we get at the truth," Bert said. "Trent's been talking to lawyers, Jake. You'll have the best defense we can find, if you decide to come back and fight this thing. And we'll stand by you. All of us."

"That means more to me than you can imagine," Jake said softly. "Bert, I need to talk to Garrett Brand. Is he there?"

"Yes. Right here, son."

A second later, a deeper voice came on the line. "Nash?"

"Yeah, it's me. Your niece tells me you're an honest man, a man of your word. Is that true?"

"I try to be."

"I'm going to have to trust that you are. I want you to turn off the taps. I want to talk to you privately. About Sara."

"Is she all right, Nash?"

"She's—" Jake had to clear his throat "—she's incredible," he said softly, then shook himself. "Yes, she's all right, and she'll be back with you within the hour if you'll just do what I ask."

Garrett sighed, then there was a click and then Brand said, very, very softly, "call 555-7281. My cell phone. Got it?"

"Yes."

"Call me in five."

There was a click as he hung up. Jake licked his lips, nodded slowly as he checked his watch. He hadn't been on long enough for the call to be traced.

He managed to locate a coffeepot beyond the reaches of the makeshift bar, but he couldn't find any coffee to put in it and had to settle for a drink of water. He looked uneasily out at the shed where he'd left Sara. It only had one entrance, and that had never been out of his sight. No one had gone in. She hadn't come out. Still sleeping, he hoped. Hell, as much beer as she'd had, she ought to sleep for hours.

Again he glanced at his watch. Then he went to the phone and dialed once more.

Garrett answered on the first ring. "Garrett Brand," he said.

"It's me. Are we private now?"

"Yes," Brand said. "I shut off the tape before, but I couldn't guarantee they'd have stopped tracing the call even if I'd told them to."

"I appreciate your honesty."

"Appreciate this, Nash. I love my niece, and I want her back. She was taken from this family for a long time. We only just got her back, and I'm damned if we're gonna lose her again now."

Jake nodded slowly. "I know. She told me."

"She...*told* you?"

"Listen, I don't have much time, Brand. She could wake up any minute, and I don't like being this far from her."

"She's unconscious?" Garrett barked.

"She's sleeping off too much beer." Jake was offended, but he knew he shouldn't be. The guy was just worried about his innocent niece, and he had no idea what was really going on. Then Jake realized that if Garrett did know what was really going on, he would probably be just as hostile. Maybe more so.

"Sara? Drank beer?"

Jake sighed heavily. "Now you're not going to believe a word of this, Brand, but I'm asking you to please treat what I'm going to tell you as if it's the truth. You can hang me from a cottonwood tree later. After you make sure Sara's safe. Okay?"

"Safe from what, Nash? You?"

"Sara saw the killer that night, Garrett." Maybe using the guy's first name would help shut him up, make him listen. "Not enough to identify him. Just in silhouette. But the point is, he looked back at her, and he saw her clearly. He thinks she can identify him."

"And you're telling me all this...why? So I'll have a doubt in my mind that you killed your cousin yourself?"

"I'm telling you all this because the killer is after Sara. That's why I brought her with me in the first place. I heard him in her bungalow that night."

"And you didn't think telling the police would do any good?" Garrett snapped.

"The police would have had me in jail the next day no matter what I told them, Brand, and I think you know it. Even if by some miracle they listened to me, investigated my claim, they'd have done it with me behind bars and Sara sitting at Sugar Keep with no protection."

Finally, it seemed, the sheriff had run out of comebacks.

"I need to catch him, Brand. I don't plan to live my life on the run. I...thought I could, but...things have changed. I want my name cleared. I want my life back."

"So you're coming in?"

"You're kidding, right? If I come in, no one will be looking for the real killer. I'm my own only hope, Brand. But I'm damned well not going to risk Sara's getting hurt to do this. I want you to come and get her. Just you and you alone."

"Just tell me where," Brand said quickly.

"First I want your word. You'll come alone." Then Jake bit his lip. "No, wait. Not alone. Bring the mean-looking SOB with you. Just in case anything happens."

"Mean-looking—Wes? Okay. Me and Wes."

"One vehicle," Jake said.

"Got it. No cops, no weapons."

"What, are you crazy?" Jake asked. "You'd better come loaded for bear, Brand. I'm not gonna let you take Sara if you aren't prepared to protect her from this maniac. Bring weapons."

"How do you know we won't use them on you, Nash?"

"Let me worry about that. Now, listen. We've got to do this now. If she wakes up before it's done, she'll never go with you. And if she stays with me, she's at risk. Understand?''

"No. I really don't, but I'll do it."

"One more thing, Brand."

"What's that?"

"I want you to take her back to Texas. Directly from here back to Texas. Back to that ranch she keeps talking about. No stops, no nothing. If you take her back to Sugar Keep, even for just long enough to grab your brothers, she'll be a target. You have to promise me this. You can call the others from your cell phone once you get going. But you can't stop until she's safe."

There was a long moment of silence. Then, finally, "You're not kidding about this, are you, Nash?"

"Don't let her out of your sight until the killer is behind bars, Garrett. And I don't mean me. If they arrest me, fine. I'll rot in jail, but you need to know, you need to *know,* Brand, that there's someone else out there, and that he wants your niece dead. Keep her safe."

"We will."

"Good."

"Nash—"

"The town's ten miles north of Gator's Bayou. It's called Belle Ville. There's one main road. Right across from the town's barn-slash-dance-hall is an unpainted shed. She's sleeping in the loft. You ought to be able to make it here in twenty minutes."

"Try ten," Garrett said.

"Take it easy, Brand. No use drawing all kinds of attention by speeding out of there like the cavalry.

Take your time. Don't worry. I won't let her out of my sight until you have her in yours.''

There was a pause. ''You're right. Okay, see you in twenty.'' Garrett disconnected, ending the call.

Jake shook his head at the dead phone in his hand. ''No, you won't see me, friend. But I'll see you.''

Slowly he replaced the receiver. Then, bracing himself for the hardest task he'd ever had to carry out, he walked back outside into the brightening morning, crossed the dirt road to the shed and entered its fragrant dimness to climb the ladder.

She was naked and beautiful, lying in the hay, sound asleep, utterly content and totally relaxed. Not a care in the world right now. She looked even more like an angel to him than she had that first day.

She was going to hate him for this. But dammit, she would never go back home on her own. And his only chance was to find the killer himself.

He wondered, briefly, when exactly he had made that decision. Until last night he had been convinced that his only chance was to run like hell for the border.

He looked at Sara again, remembered the way she'd been with him earlier, before dawn this morning. The way she'd stared up at him with love gleaming from her eyes, and he knew why, if not when, he'd changed his mind about his options. She would think less of him if he ran. Hell, she had him dreaming about things he knew damn well were impossible. But he couldn't avoid it or deny it any longer. All the things she believed about him...dammit, he wanted to make them true. He wanted to be half as good as she—for some twisted reason—seemed to believe he was.

She was going to be furious when she realized what he had done. And he didn't know what would come next. It might be a long time before he could talk to her again, before he knew just whether he was capable of living up to her image of him...his mother's image of him.

But she was strong. A survivor. She would be okay. He only hoped *he* would.

Sitting down in the hay beside her, he gently gathered her up into his arms and began slipping her clothes carefully back in place.

"Mmm," she muttered. "Jake."

"It's okay," he whispered. "Hush, angel. Just rest. Just rest. Everything's gonna be okay, I promise."

She sighed contentedly. "Love you," she murmured before sinking back into blissful sleep.

Tears burned in Jake's eyes, hot and thick. God, tears. He hadn't shed one since they'd come to his cell to tell him his mother had died. He felt as if he were losing someone just as dear, just as precious, right now. Dammit, those Brands had better watch over her. Keep her safe.

And maybe...maybe when the dust settled...

One thing at a time, he told himself. He was still afraid to dream too big or aim too high.

"Jake?" she whispered, struggling to open her eyes. It was an effort. She tried to remember the last time she'd been awake...the loft, and Jake gently dressing her as if she were a little girl. When he'd finished, he'd held her gently in his arms, rocked her slowly, kissed her forehead. Whispered...goodbye.

Goodbye?

Sara felt a fluttering of panic in her chest. "Jake…"

A hand stroked her hair, and her head rested on a sturdy shoulder. It was okay. She calmed immediately. All of that must have simply been part of some strange dream. Because she was only just waking up now. So morning couldn't have come already, could it? She would hardly wake up to such a tender embrace, snuggled in Jake's arms, only to go back to sleep again. That made no sense at all. She'd dreamed it, dreamed his whispered goodbye.

Dreamed the warmth of a tear on his cheek when he'd kissed her.

Dread settled over her heart like a shroud. Some secret certainty she could not even acknowledge. Refused to acknowledge. That had been a dream. It must only now be morning.

Again she struggled to make her eyelids obey her mind's commands. And this time they responded with sluggish weight, opening slowly. It seemed like an immense effort to get them to open at all. And when she did, nothing made much sense. Because, even without having any focus, it was fairly obvious she wasn't in the loft, with a donkey below her and Jake beside her.

The shoulder underneath her head was… Blinking, she lifted her head, her gaze. "Wes?"

"Yeah, hon. It's me." Smiling worriedly, Wes stroked her hair. "It's okay, we're almost home."

She frowned. "Home?" Looking forward, she saw the windshield, and through it the broad, sloping nose of Garrett's pickup truck, and beyond that, vast lengths of gray pavement and yellow lines.

"But…?" Turning her head, she saw Garrett behind the wheel. "Where is Jake? What happened? What…?"

"Easy, now," Garrett said. "Don't get yourself all worked up, Sara. Everything's fine."

He spoke to her as if she were a small child on the brink of a panic attack. It made her so mad she wanted to punch him right in his nose. "Dammit, Garrett, I know I'm fine! What I want to know is what I'm doing here, in this truck with you two, and what the hell you've done with Jake! Now one of you had better start talking or there is going to be hell to pay, and don't you think I don't mean it!"

Garrett's frown was so deep it was comical, and he stared past her at Wes, who was sitting up straight with his brows arched high and his eyes registering surprise. "You sure we picked up the right girl, Garrett? Cause…this is not the Sara I remember."

She faced Wes, gripped the front of his shirt in her fists. "What have you done to Jake?"

"Nothing!" Wes removed her hands, folded them and pressed them into her lap. "We didn't even see the guy."

"He called me this morning, Sara," Garrett said softly. "He told me where to find you, said he wanted Wes and me to come and get you."

She felt as if Jake had just reached out and slapped her, from wherever the hell he was. "But…?" Then she looked at a passing road sign, recalled Garrett's assurance that they were almost home. "We're back in Texas," she whispered. Her throat was tight, tears threatening.

"Yeah. Nash made us promise we'd take you

straight back to the ranch and keep you under constant guard. He seems to think you're in danger, Sara. And frankly, he was pretty convincing.''

''He's right,'' she said. ''The killer saw me that night. He thinks I saw him, and he wants me dead. Jake could have been long gone by now if he hadn't taken me along. But I'd be dead right now if he hadn't.''

Garrett again exchanged a long look with Wes.

''Take me back to Sugar Keep,'' Sara said.

Garrett shook his head. ''No way. You just admitted someone wants you dead. Why the hell would you want to go back there?''

She looked Garrett squarely in the eye. ''Because I've spent my entire life running and hiding from someone who wanted me dead, Garrett, and I'm sick and tired of it. Now take me back there so I can find this scumbag and show him what happens when he messes with a Brand.''

Garrett's smile came so fast and so wide it damn near blinded her. ''Damn. I don't know what all happened to you back there, Sara Brand, but you sure did come back spunky.''

''Brand through and through,'' Wes said, giving her shoulder a squeeze.

''Then why isn't this oversize pickup turning around?''

The two men looked at each other.

''I gave my word, Sara. I promised this Nash character—''

''Jake. His name is Jake, and he's not a character. He's...he's... Oh, hell.'' Sara lowered her head into her hands and started to cry. The tears came harder, faster, until her shoulders shook with them.

Wes swore. "Did that son of a— What did he do to you, Sara?"

"Uh, Wes, maybe you'd best shut up and think on that some," Garrett said, eyeing Sara worriedly.

"What the hell is that supposed to— Oh, shoot. Oh, come on, don't tell me. Sara? Hey, Sara, you haven't gone and fallen for this clown, have you?"

"Uh, Wes…?"

Too late. Sara's elbow jammed into Wes's rib cage so hard all the air shot out of his lungs. "Damn!"

Then, sniffling, she lifted her gaze to Garrett's. "Did you get the note we pinned to Jessi?"

"Yeah. Who the hell hit her, anyway? She came back with a lump on her head the size of a—"

"I did."

Garrett blinked. "You did?"

"I came out to see someone standing in the dark, holding a gun on Jake. What the hell would you have done?" She rolled her eyes. "Did you look at Jake's record, like I asked in the note? Hmm? Did you?"

With a sigh, Garrett nodded. "He had a tough break. Hell, he had a run of tough breaks. But, Sara, that's no excuse for—"

"For what, Garrett? For killing his cousin? No, it isn't. But he didn't do it. For running from the law? Well, the cop on the scene that night was the grandson of the old man who died in that liquor store holdup. And when I told Kendall it was wrong for him to be on he case, he suggested I take it up with his cousin, the D.A. If Jake hadn't run, Garrett, he'd be in jail right now. And I'd probably be dead."

She made a fist and thumped it on the dash. "I have to go back, Garrett."

Garrett shook his head. "I'm sorry, Sara. Look, I can...I can make some calls. Try to get Nash...Jake...a fair deal this time. But I can't take you back there knowing someone might be taking potshots at you, hon. I just can't." He eyed her, even as she sighed and slumped lower in the seat. "Even if I wanted to, your brother wouldn't let me. Marcus...and Casey, and...dammit, Sara, there's just no way."

Sara closed her eyes. She knew this was it. She was going to be protected and safe out at the ranch whether she wanted to be or not. "Do this much for me, at least. Make them run the DNA from the samples taken from underneath Vivienne's nails and check them against a DNA sample from Jake."

"They're already planning to do that," Garrett said.

"Yeah? And who's in charge of seeing to it the actual samples get used? Officer Kendall?"

Garrett met her eyes. Sighed. "Good point. Look, I'll see to it."

She still held his gaze.

"I'll see to it," he said again. "I'll have a friend from the FBI lab go to Gator's Bayou and oversee it personally. Okay?"

"Good."

"Now...about going back to work."

She twisted to face him, lifting a forefinger. "No way, Garrett Brand. I just got this transfer to Quinn Elementary over a half dozen other applicants, and I'm *not* going to miss so much as a single day of school over this. No."

"But it would be safer if—"

"No, no, no." She grated her teeth. "Men like this one have taken enough from me, Garrett. Don't you understand? My parents. My childhood. My home, my name for twenty years. My family, my brother until I found him again. My freedom...and now the man I love." She bit her lip hard, but the tears came, anyway. "I'm not gonna let this guy take one more thing. Not one more. Not ever. When the school bell rings next Monday, Miss Brand is going to be at her desk. Bet on it."

Chapter 14

Jake had sat perched in the rafters, concealed by shadows, and watched as Garrett Brand and his brother Wes had come up into the hayloft. When they saw Sara sleeping, the two men had run to her, leaned over her, and the panic in their faces, in their eyes, had been unmistakable.

Just as the relief had been when they had realized she was okay. Only sleeping. Garrett scooped Sara up in his arms and paused to look around the place. But he hadn't called out or made any fuss. He'd simply touched the brim of his hat, a silent salute, and then he and his brother had eased Sara down the ladder and outside, to where the big pickup had been waiting.

Jake had rushed to the window to watch as they settled her on the seat between them. He'd seen Wes, the alleged bad-ass of the bunch, tenderly brush a stray wisp of hair from Sara's cheek when he climbed in beside her. Then Garrett was behind the wheel, and the truck was turning around and rolling slowly back toward the highway.

Even then, Jake kept watching. At the end of the dirt road, they could turn left or right. Left would take them back toward Sugar Keep—and the killer. Right would take them toward Texas.

Garrett Brand had kept his word so far. He hadn't arrived with a full complement of armed police officers and maybe a SWAT team in tow. He'd come with only his brother. And neither of them had tried to hunt for Jake at all. They'd done as they'd promised.

So far.

They reached the stop sign at the end of the road. Jake tensed. If they turned left, he would have to go after them. If they tried to take Sara back into the line of fire...

The vehicle turned right, picked up speed and vanished from sight.

Jake's chest hurt. His understanding of the term *heartache* suddenly became complete. "I'm gonna miss you, Sara Brand," he whispered.

The first thing Sara did when she got back to the ranch was find and swallow a handful of aspirin hoping to ease the pounding in her head. She didn't think there was anything that could help the queasiness in her stomach or the heaviness in her heart.

Chelsea, Garrett's wife, followed her into the bathroom, stood behind her at the sink and held her shoulders.

"I am so sorry," Chelsea said, meeting Sara's eyes in the mirror. "I feel horrible. I feel like I ought to close down my practice and go back to psychology school. My God, Sara, I couldn't have given you worse advice."

Her eyes, Sara noted, were red rimmed. And Sara took just a minute to draw herself out of her own misery and address Chelsea's. "You have it all wrong, Chels."

Chelsea lowered her head, shaking it slowly. "I convinced you to go on this vacation. I kept telling you there was nothing to be afraid of. That there was no one out to get you. And what happens? You witness a murder, get kidnapped by the suspect and become some kind of target all over again, according to what Garrett told me on the phone."

Sara turned slowly around. "No. You want to know what happened? I found out that I still have good instincts. And that I'm smart enough to know the difference between irrational fears and real ones. I knew Jake wasn't what he seemed. I knew it right from the start, Chels. My gut told me I could trust him, even when everything—including the big jerk himself—tried to convince me I couldn't. And I learned something else, too. I'm not afraid anymore."

"You...you're not?"

"No. Everyone else is running around trying to protect me from this killer, but I'm not worried in the least. I wish he would come for me. One of us would walk away and one of us wouldn't, but at least it would be over and done with. I'm not afraid to face the bastard. Because nothing is as bad as living in constant fear. Nothing. I refuse to do that again."

Tilting her head to one side, Chelsea studied her face. "There's something else, isn't there?"

Sara nodded. "I'm in love...with Jake. I...I thought he felt the same, but...I don't know. Maybe not. Either way, though, I'm glad for the time I spent with him." Turning around, she hiked herself up onto the edge of the sink and sat there. "In a way, it was like looking into a mirror. He'd spent almost the same amount of time in prison that I spent in my own kind of prison. We were both crippled from that, in a way. Me being too afraid of life to experience it. Him, too burned by disappointments to ever trust in anything." Then she shrugged. "That time with him...made me see that I could get past it. Move on. Be more than I was."

"And what about Jake?" Chelsea said.

"I don't know. He's the most incredible man I have ever known, Chels. And...and you know that with the men I've had in my life to compare him to, that's saying something. He's...he's magnificent. But...he doesn't know it."

"Maybe...there will be another chance, Sara. For you to show him."

"Maybe," Sara said. "I hope so."

There was a tap on the door. Chelsea opened it, and Garrett stood there, grim-faced. "I'm sorry Sara," he said. "The Louisiana State Police just called to let me know...they caught Jake before he got twenty miles from Belle Ville. He's, um...he's in jail."

Sara recoiled slightly, but then she squared her shoulders, lifted her chin. "He'll be out just as soon as those DNA tests are done. You're still gonna take care of that, right, Garrett?"

"You bet I am."

* * *

The next week was the longest one Sara had ever spent. She knew, with the practical side of her mind, that she was strong now. That she could go on perfectly fine with or without Jake Nash in her life. She'd been through trial by fire, and she had emerged like forged steel. She wasn't afraid of the killer, though he was still on the loose somewhere. Everyone else spent all their time watching over her, and God help any stranger who happened to show his face in Quinn. He would find himself subjected on sight to the third degree by a pile of suspicious, impatient and mean-looking Brands.

But that didn't bother her. The killer would be caught in time, and Jake would be exonerated, because that was the only way it could possibly be. It was right.

But Sara did still have some fears to contend with.

Every day, as she sat in the room that had once been Jessi's and wrote long, long letters to Jake, she was afraid. Because so far…he hadn't written back. Or called. Or sent a message to her via Flossie or Bert or Trent, all of whom Sara had been in contact with on a regular basis.

Her fear was that he blamed her. He wouldn't have been caught if not for her. He would have been long gone, if she hadn't made him stay, time and again, when he'd wanted to head for the border.

Chelsea kept saying he was too proud to write to her from prison. That he was likely dealing with a thousand emotions at once, being behind bars again, and that he would be much more able to deal with his feelings for her once he got out.

But Sara didn't think so. It was her fault he'd ended up behind bars. And even though she was certain the DNA tests would clear him, she was beginning to wonder if he would bother getting in touch with her when that happened.

Her other fears came at night, when she lay awake in bed and thought about Jake sleeping in a jail cell in Louisiana. She dreamed about Officer Kendall coming into Jake's cell and beating him bloody while Jake was helpless to defend himself. She dreamed that by the time Jake's name was cleared, he would be gone. That somehow the angry cop would make him disappear without a trace.

Garrett kept trying to tell Chelsea that Kendall wasn't that bad a guy…but she didn't believe him.

Then finally, a day she'd been waiting for arrived. It dawned bright and sunny and filled with promise.

The entire house brimmed with excitement, because it was the first day of school, and little Bubba, Chelsea and Garrett's son, was about to head off to kindergarten for the very first time. The entire Brand clan was on hand for breakfast that morning, all of them bubbling with well wishes for little Bubba, all bringing gifts for the big day. Pencil cases and backpacks and a baseball cap and ice cream money.

And the other reason the day dawned with such promise was the phone call Garrett received first thing. He set the phone down and turned to face the crowd around the kitchen table. "Sara, you were right. The DNA results cleared Jake Nash of any suspicion in his cousin's murder."

Sara sighed her relief, and Wes smiled at her. "Well, it seems I was wrong after all, Cuz. Congratulations."

"When will he be released?" Sara asked, nearly breathless.

"Already was," Garrett replied. "They let him go last night."

A tiny frown and a knot of worry hit Sara then, but she tried to swallow both. So Jake hadn't called her last night. It didn't mean he never would. Maybe it had been late, and goodness knew he must have had tons of other things to do.

"He'll call," Chelsea whispered, clasping Sara's hand.

Sara nodded, tried to believe it. But she was sick and tired of waiting for Jake to call her. The moment everyone seemed distracted with Bubba again, she slipped upstairs to her bedroom, which used to be Jessi's a long time ago, and used the phone there to call Sugar Keep.

Flossie picked up on the first ring.

"Flossie, hi! It's Sara."

"Oh, Sara! Oh, hon, I'm so glad you called. Did you hear the news?"

"Yes. Garrett just told me. I'm so glad...but not surprised."

"Of course not, child. We all knew Jake was innocent all along. But I can tell you, he was more surprised than anyone when he realized it had been proven and the charges dropped. Why, I think he had convinced himself that he was going to be serving a life sentence, guilty or not!"

"I know. I know. Flossie, is he there? I really need to talk with him."

Flossie was quiet for a moment. Then she said, "Hon, I...well, I'm just as mixed up as can be. He and Trent have both taken off. I thought Jake was with you."

"With me?" Sara's stomach got queasy.

"Well, he was back here last night. Bert made a special dinner to celebrate, and…oh, I wish you'd been here. But then Jake said he couldn't stay. That he had something to take care of, and he left. I…well, I assumed he was going to get you, Sara. I mean…. Well, now I'm darned if I know what that boy is up to. Surely if he were headed to Texas, he'd have made it long before now."

Sara sighed. "Listen, if you hear from him, will you give me a call? I'll be at Quinn Elementary School. I'll give you the number and the address."

"All right, hon. Just let me grab up a pen."

Sara gave Flossie the information, Flossie wrote it down and read it back to be sure it was correct. "Don't worry, Sara. I just know he'll be in touch. Why, you're all that boy has talked about since he got home. And every visiting day, and…well, he'd likely rather tell you himself."

"I'm glad you told me, all the same," Sara said. "Thank you, Flossie."

"You're just as welcome as can be, hon."

Every member of the Brand family stood at the bus stop in front of the big, curving wooden Texas Brand arch that curved high above the driveway. Every big, tough cowboy on the place seemed a little misty-eyed, especially Garrett, when the yellow bus groaned to a halt in front of the arch. Air brakes hissed. The door folded open. A round-faced woman smiled down at where little Bubba—otherwise known as Garrett Ethan Brand, Jr.—stood tall, hitching his backpack up higher onto his shoulder.

"Now you're sure you want to ride the bus?" Chelsea asked, her eyes moist, lip trembling whenever she stopped biting it. "Because Sara's driving right in, anyway, and you could ride with her, and—"

Garrett's big hand closed on Chelsea's shoulder at the same moment little Bubba said, "I *can't* ride to school with my *teacher,* Mom." He sent his dad a look that said females would never understand anything.

Garrett reached down to straighten his son's backpack. "You have a good first day, Bubba. Don't forget who you are, now."

"I won't, Dad." The boy leaned closer, tugged his father's shirtsleeve until Garrett leaned down. Way down. Bubba's whisper was loud enough for all to hear, though it was obviously meant to be just between him and his father. "Be sure and take care of Mom, today. I think she's gonna miss me something awful."

Garrett smiled fully and nodded. "I'll make her some of those brownies she likes this afternoon, keep her mind off things. How's that sound?"

Bubba tilted his head to one side. "Save me one?"

"You know it, big guy."

Bubba nodded once, turned, squared his shoulders and marched right up the steps and onto the bus. Chelsea smiled so hard Sara thought her face would break as she waved goodbye. And she managed not to burst into full-blown tears until the school bus had rolled completely out of sight, thank goodness.

By then Garrett had wrapped her up tight in his great big arms, though, so Sara knew she would be all right.

"I wish you wouldn't worry," she assured her cousin. "You know I'm going to take extra-special care with him."

Chelsea sniffed. "I know you will, hon. That's why I asked them to put him in your class. You know there's no one I trust more with my little angel. It's not that I'm worried...it's just—" she sniffled again "—it's hard letting him go."

Around them, the others all seemed on the verge of tears, too. Jessi held her toddler, Maria Michele, a bit closer than before, and Ben reached over to stroke his baby's fuzzy blond hair away from his face. Wes hugged his wife from behind, his hands stroking her swollen belly, and Elliot's wife, Esmeralda, every bit as large in the middle, gripped El's hands tight and blinked away tears of her own. Marcus and Casey, with no babies yet, and none on the way, either, only stood arm in arm. They were the only two not on the verge of shedding tears.

Everyone, though, childless or not, had someone to hold. Everyone except Sara. She thought again of Jake, wondered where he was now, what he was doing. Whether he ever thought of her at all. If a single second they'd spent together had ever meant a thing to him. Oh, he'd tried to tell her it hadn't. But she'd stubbornly refused to believe that. She had been so certain that what she was feeling inside was stirring a corresponding flood of feeling within him. So certain that he must love her, too.

Maybe he'd been right when he'd accused her of

living in a fairy-tale world, of being naive for always expecting a happy ending.

"I should go," she said suddenly. "It wouldn't look very good if the kids beat me to school the first day, would it?"

"The bus takes half an hour, Sara. You can make it in five minutes," Chelsea said. She gave a sniffle and dabbed at her eyes.

"Yeah, well…still." She left them all standing there and headed quickly to her car. "Try not to worry too much," she called back. "Nothing eventful ever happens on the first day of school, you know. It's all routine, and Bubba will be back home before you know it." She forced a smile, got into her car and started the engine and wondered why she had felt a cold chill rushing up the back of her neck as she'd said those words.

It was 2:45 p.m. Sara looked around the classroom at the sleepy eyes of her kindergartners. Chubby cheeks and baby teeth. They were still so small, so sweet.

It had been a full day for them, and they were tired now. Thank goodness it was almost time for dismissal. They could go home, get some rest.

Personally, she wanted to go home too. Call Sugar Keep again. Because if Jake wanted to cut himself off from her, well, that was fine. But he was damned well going to tell her so. She wasn't going to be left hanging, hoping, wishing, waiting, not knowing.

"You guys did great today," she told the class. "I think you're my best class ever!" A couple of faces brightened. Bubba smiled broadly at her.

"Now, have you all got your backpacks and jackets?" She scanned the room, seeing that they did, even as the children nodded. "And is everyone wearing their name badges we made today?"

Weary heads nodded again, several small hands going to the construction paper badges pinned to their shirts. Each had the student's name and bus number written on it in bright blue marker.

"All right, then," Sara said. "It will be time to go to the buses in five minutes. I want you to have some quiet time until then."

They needed it, and then some.

Sara walked around the room, stroking a head here and there, until the soft buzz of the phone on her desk distracted her. She went to it, picked it up. "Yes?"

"Miss Brand, there's a man here in the office who says he needs to see you. His name is Jake. Jake Nash."

Sara's heart leaped into her throat, and her eyes moistened instantly. "Can you give him a visitor's pass and send him to my room?" she asked. She could have waited five minutes, gone to Jake in the office after loading the children on their buses. But she couldn't wait. She just couldn't. She had to see him now. Heck, he could just walk with her out to the buses.

"Of course, Miss Brand. I'll send him right down."

"Thank you." Smiling ear to ear, Sara hung up the phone. She tried to tell herself not to be so excited. Tried to warn her heart that Jake might very well be there only to tell her that he'd decided things could never work out between the two of them. He could be there to break her heart beyond any hope of repair.

But maybe not. And she couldn't silence the joyous laughter of hope in her heart

She nervously ran her hands over her hair, smoothed her dress.

The kids got up when the bell rang and pleased her greatly by remembering to put their chairs up on top of their desks. Then they lined up at the door, just the way she'd taught them, and Sara stepped to the front of the line. As soon as Jake arrived, she would lead the kids out. He could walk beside her. And they would talk. And maybe he would hold her hand.

The school nurse's smiling face appeared at the door. A man was standing behind her, but Sara could only see his shoulders. Fiona, the nurse, wriggled her fingers in a friendly wave as Sara opened the door. She was one of Sara's favorite people at the school. Thirty-five, married to a doctor from the hospital in El Paso, she looked half her age, with her slight build, red-gold ringlets and smooth skin.

"Your friend seemed a bit lost, so I volunteered to guide him in," Fiona said, smiling.

Swallowing hard, Sara looked up. "Jake, I..." Then the words died on her lips as Trent, not Jake, looked down at her. "Trent? I don't...you're not..."

He shoved Fiona into the classroom, coming in with her and slamming the door behind them.

"Hey!" Fiona said, spinning around.

But she went still when she saw the same sight that Sara did.

Trent was standing there with a gun in his hand.

Sara lunged, acting on sheer instinct, and hit the button on the wall. The alarm went off immediately. Within seconds the entire building would be cleared.

"Dammit, what did you go and do that for!" Trent growled.

One of the little girls started to cry. Trent glared at her. Then he nodded at the school nurse. "Take the kids to the back of the room. Sit 'em down and keep 'em quiet. Understand?"

Fiona nodded. Her eyes met Sara's, and Sara saw the fear in them, but also the message: It'll be okay. We'll get through this.

Sara hoped to God her colleague was right.

Chapter 15

''Please don't hurt the children,'' Sara said softly. ''Trent, whatever has happened, I promise you, we can work through it. I'll help you through it…and so will Jake.''

Trent's face twisted in a grimace. ''Don't try to pretend you don't know what this is about, Sara. I know you saw me that night.''

Sara blinked and felt her body go cold. It was as if the heat drained right through her feet and into the floor, and she felt chilled to the bone. ''It was you,'' she whispered.

''It was me,'' he said. ''And you've probably already told the cops that. They didn't believe you then, but now… It doesn't matter. You'll never live to testify, Sara. I'm here to make sure of that.''

''Trent…you're wrong. Jake was released because of the DNA testing, not because of anything I said. The tests they did proved him innocent, and the same tests will prove you guilty—whether I testify or not.''

"You're lying! The DNA testing was all taken care of. Kendall saw to that."

Sara went stiff. "How, Trent? How did Kendall...see to that?"

"Switched the samples."

Sara closed her eyes. "And Garrett thought I was crazy," she muttered.

"What?"

"Listen, Trent, I never trusted Kendall. I asked my cousin, the sheriff of Quinn, to see to it that the DNA testing was done properly. He had a friend of his from the FBI lab go to the morgue personally and take fresh samples from under Vivienne's nails. The ones Kendall switched were never even tested."

"You lie. There is no DNA evidence, I told you. That was all just a smokescreen. So I wouldn't come after you. But it's all you, Sara. You're all they have on me, and I know it. I can't let you testify."

"I never saw your face," she said.

Trent's eyes narrowed as he lifted the gun and pointed it at Sara. "Maybe you're telling the truth. But I can't take that risk."

Another child began to cry, and then another. "Please," Sara whispered. "Not in front of the children."

Trent glared at her. "You're up to something."

"No, I'm not. I saw my parents murdered when I was a little younger than these kids, Trent. Believe me, it's the kind of thing that haunts you forever. You don't want to do that to these kids. They haven't done anything to you." As she spoke, Sara glanced behind her at the children. Most of them were crying, their faces damp. Fiona looked pale and shaken as she sat on the floor hugging as many of them to her as she could get her arms around. Several more were crowded behind her. And then there was little Bubba. He sat still and tall, clinging to no one. And the look on his face said that the five-year-old was liable to charge Trent at any moment or throw something at him. He was furious, fuming, red in the face.

Sara met Bubba's eyes and gave her head a very subtle shake from side to side. "No," she mouthed.

Swallowing hard, Sara spoke to the children. "I want you all to be very quiet and very good for me. I promise I won't let anything happen to you. Fiona, maybe you could read the kids a story, hmm?"

Nodding, Fiona reached for a book from the shelf behind her. Sara could hear the buses moving now, moving away from the school. No sirens…not yet. But there would be. It was a sad, sad state of affairs that schools had to be equipped the way they were these days. But Sara was fully glad of it at the moment. The button she had pushed was linked not only to the rest of the school, but to the Quinn Sheriff's Office, as well.

Garrett should be on his way. And he wasn't stupid. Once he saw that everyone had made it out of the school except for Sara and her class…he would know exactly what was going on.

One of the kids got up. "On the floor," Sara said quickly. There was no doubt in her mind that a SWAT team would be on hand at any moment, and she didn't want her kids in the line of fire. Fiona seemed to understand. She gathered the children closer, whispered instructions to them—probably,

Sara thought, explaining that they should not stand up for any reason.

"Now, you come with me."

Sara stood where she was. "I never saw your face, Trent. I swear, I didn't."

"It doesn't much matter at this point, now, does it? Whether you knew before or not...you know now." He waggled his gun toward the door.

Stall him, Sara thought wildly. And not with talk of the DNA tests, because he'd deluded himself into believing his scam with Kendall had worked. Stall him, because if you go with him, you're dead. The minute he gets you alone, he'll kill you.

On the other hand, maybe it would be better to just let it happen. At least the kids would be safe.

But the kids would be safe either way. She would swallow that gun whole before she would let him harm them.

"Of course it matters," she managed to say. "You were right, of course. I knew it all along. But killing me isn't going to solve a thing."

"It will keep you from testifying."

"Actually, it won't. The cops have my testimony on videotape."

Trent's eyes widened; he stared at her in shock.

"Well, hell, we knew you'd come after me. This isn't the first time I've had to deal with the likes of you, you know."

She heard the vehicles moving outside and knew perfectly well they were not the sounds of school buses this time. These were other vehicles. Their doors were opening and closing, and feet were tapping over pavement.

"You're lying. Come here."

When she didn't move, he looked toward the children. "You want me to prove that I mean business, lady? Is that what you want?"

"No, please...it's okay. I'll do what you want." She moved toward him and found herself spun around fast and clutched to his chest, with his arm like iron across her chest and his hand clamped to her opposite shoulder. "Now we'll just leave, nice and quiet. No one needs to get hurt. Do you understand?"

"Yes. Fine. Just don't hurt the children."

He moved toward the classroom door, opened it and stepped out into the hall. Five feet away was the front entrance, but he turned her in the other direction, heading down the full length of the hallway to the door in the back. But the moment he pushed it open, someone with a bullhorn yelled, "You're completely surrounded. Put the gun down and let her go!"

Sara looked around frantically, but before she could spot more than one or two officers, she was yanked back inside. Even as Trent tugged her back toward the classroom, she prayed silently that Fiona had hustled the kids out of the building by now. But there had barely been any time at all. Mere moments had ticked past.

They burst back into the classroom, Sara walking in front of Trent, his gun to her back. Fiona stood by the window, hoisting children through it.

"Stop it!" the killer screamed. "Stop it now!" He shoved Sara to the floor, pointing his gun at the school nurse instead.

Fiona shoved the little girl she held right on through and shouted at her to run. Then she spun around, putting her back to the window and facing the gunman as if she would physically block him from going after the child.

With a low growl, Trent lifted the gun toward the windows, and Sara saw with horror the children running from the school just outside. She saw what he was going to do.

"No!" she screamed, and leaped up, right in front of him, throwing herself at his chest. The gun went off as Trent toppled to the floor. Pain tore through Sara's entire upper body, but she didn't let go of him. She kicked, bit and clawed at his face. Then he hurled her off him, sending her sliding across the floor.

She lay there, vaguely aware of pain in her chest and of warm wetness spreading there. Turning her head, she counted. Only three children remained huddled in the back of the room. Bubba was one of them.

Trent was just getting to his feet, taking stock of the situation. He had an uninjured school nurse, three terrified kids, a wounded teacher, and he was completely surrounded. What could he possibly think was left for him to do but surrender?

Trent glared out the window, and Fiona followed his gaze, her own face easing in relief. "They got away," she whispered, lowering her head as her shoulders began to quake. "They got away."

"Thank God," Sara said. She struggled into a sitting position and managed to look down at herself. It wasn't an encouraging sight. Her blouse was entirely soaked in blood, which still pulsed from the upper part of her chest, just below her collar bone. She jammed the heel of her hand against the wound and pain flared anew, but the bleeding eased and slowed.

"Miss Brand?" one of the kids cried. "Oh, Miss Brand!"

"It's all right," she said, but she was afraid the pain was evident in her voice.

Fiona went to the desk, got the first-aid kit that every classroom had in the bottom drawer of the teacher's desk and came back.

Trent held up the gun, using it to block the nurse's path. "Don't even bother."

"No? You're just going to let her—?" She didn't say the last word, obviously thinking of the students.

"That's what I came here to do."

"Why?" Fiona asked, her face incredulous.

"She saw me...commit a crime."

Bubba left the other kids. He knelt beside Sara now, stroking her hair as if he were a grown man. "You'll be all right, Sara," he told her. "I promise you will." His gaze dipped down to the blood-soaked blouse, and his tears finally spilled over. "It's not so bad. I'll bet Aunt Jessi could even patch that little cut up, and she's only a vet."

Sara smiled at his courage. Dear little man, lying to her that way. Trying so hard to comfort.

Bubba then turned his head, so he could stare up at Trent, and angrily swiped at his nose. "You are gonna be some kind of sorry when my dad finds out what you did, mister."

"Bubba." Sara clasped the boy's hand. "Honey, I need you to take care of the other kids. Billy is so scared he can't move, and little Amy can't stop crying. I need you to take care of them for me, keep them calm and quiet. It's my job, but I can't do it right now, so..."

"I'll do it." He nodded hard. "I can do it."

"Thank you, Bubba."

He looked again at her blood-soaked blouse. "Be okay, Sara. Please?"

"I'll be okay," she said. "I promise."

Bubba dashed away his tears and went back to the other side of the room, where he began speaking softly, earnestly, to the other two who remained. Sara returned her attention to Trent and Fiona, who stood nose to chest with him.

"You aren't going to make it out of here alone, mister...whoever you are," Fiona said. "You know that. We are the only reason you're not dead already. Those men outside would blast their way in here without a moment's hesitation, and there would be nothing left of you, if not for us."

"I have you," he said. "I have three kids. It'll be enough."

She kept her voice very low. "You let her die and those kids are going to be hysterical. You just try managing to get out of this mess if that happens. You won't be able to hold on to them and that gun of yours at the same time, and I sure as hell won't lift a finger to help you."

"If you don't, I'll blow you away."

"Right. And deal with the kids all by yourself?"

He stared at Fiona, lifting an eyebrow and his gun. He pointed his gun right at her.

"I'm going to help her," Fiona said, her voice firm. "If you want to stop me, I guess you'll just have to shoot me. Then you'll have *no one* to help keep those kids calm."

She ·pushed past him, marching firmly toward where Sara lay.

Behind her, Trent lifted the gun, pointed it at her back and worked the action. The children began to scream.

Jake had only been minutes behind Trent. Minutes!

He'd figured it out on his last day in jail. Because he'd had a visit from the pretty boy who'd been making out with Vivienne at the jazz club that day.

His name was Gregg, he said, and Trent had been drinking, had come to his house, had threatened to kill him. Until then, Gregg said, he didn't think Trent had known about his affaire with Vivienne. But it was obvious then that Trent had found out.

And Jake started thinking back, to a conversation when he'd asked Trent why, if he didn't love his wife, he didn't just leave her. And Trent's odd reply. "You'd like that, wouldn't you, Jake?"

It had made no sense then. But now Jake knew what he hadn't before. Trent must have known that Flossie and Bert had changed their will, leaving Sugar Keep to both Vivienne and Jake. With Vivienne gone, and Jake in prison for killing her, Trent would inherit everything.

He was supposed to have been out of town that night...but Jake wondered if anyone had checked his alibi. Probably not, when they had a scapegoat ready to do the time. Why look further?

Trent. God, he could barely grasp it. Hadn't been able to even then, not fully. He'd wanted proof...because Trent had been his friend. He couldn't accuse him. He knew how it felt to be accused when you were innocent. And he also knew that, as Viv's husband, Trent would be the next-most-likely suspect. He would be investigated. Jake knew that would happen the moment word came that he'd been cleared and could go home. And he made sure of it, by insisting on talking to a cop—not Kendall, but his partner—and telling him of his suspicions.

All Jake had to do was go home and watch Trent like a hawk until he was behind bars. He didn't imagine it would take the cops more than a day to piece it all together.

So he'd returned to Sugar Keep. And Trent had seemed happier to see him than anyone else as they sat down to a celebratory meal. He wanted to call Sara. Had been wanting to call her since he'd been put behind bars.

God, her letters, every day, were full of encouragement, assurances, promises that it was going to work out. So much so that she'd practically had him believing it. But he couldn't call her. Kendall had seen to it that he couldn't make a single call the entire time he'd been inside. And though he'd written letters to Sara, he doubted the nasty cop would have allowed them to be mailed.

Kendall really had it in for him.

Back at the plantation that night, phoning Sara was topmost on his mind. But every time he went for the phone, Trent would vanish—either into another room or outside. Anywhere out of sight.

Jake figured he would have to wait until Trent was asleep to call her. But it damn near killed him to wait.

Problem was, Trent didn't go to sleep. He kept

Jake up very late, talking, acting like the best friend Jake now knew he wasn't. And sometime early the next morning Trent had managed to slip away.

Jake thought he'd only been minutes behind his cousin-in-law.

Too long. It was too long. By the time Jake crossed the Texas state line, he was deathly afraid Trent was going after Sara, just as Jake had feared he would. And he knew what was happening the second the country song on the car radio got cut off in mid-moan by a grim-voiced newsman talking about a hostage situation unfolding at Quinn Elementary.

"Sara..."

Everything inside Jake crystalized into perfect clarity at that moment. He knew. All of a sudden he knew exactly what he had to do. Save Sara at any cost. Nothing else mattered. He pressed the accelerator to the floor.

Chapter 16

Jake's borrowed car skidded to a stop a good distance from the Quinn Elementary School building. Then he got out of the car and made his way through the gathering crowds. Cops were already stretching yellow ribbon, ordering people back. Snipers were belly down atop the bus garage, and kids were crying and hugging their parents everywhere.

For fifty feet around the school building, though, there was nothing. No movement. No bodies, thank God. No sound. He homed in, seeking information, his entire body attuned for the slightest clue.

Then he heard a little girl, sobbing between broken words as she told a cop her story. "...and Miz Fiona pushed me out the window and told me to run, and then the bad man tried to shoot me!"

"But you're okay," the cop said. And when Jake looked toward the voice, he saw why it sounded familiar. The cop was Garrett Brand, and a woman who must be his wife, Chelsea, was standing nearby, looking red-eyed and shocky. The rest of the Brand family were making their way through the crowd even now.

"I think...I think he shot Miss Brand," the little girl said. "I looked back when I heard it...and I saw her fall down."

Jake closed his eyes and felt as if a fist had plowed him in the belly. He couldn't even breathe for a minute. He heard Chelsea Brand's involuntary sob, heard other Brands swearing softly.

"Who else was still in the classroom, besides Miss Brand and Fiona?" Garrett asked the little girl, his voice gentle.

"Just some of the kids," the little girl said, wiping her nose with her sleeve, sniffling loudly. "Two boys and a girl, I think."

"And do you know their names?"

It seemed to Jake, even from this distance, that the Brands held their breath as they awaited the reply.

The little girl bit her little lip. "Amy...an' Billy, I think. And the other boy said his name was Ethan but Miss Brand kep' calling him Bubba all day long."

Chelsea Brand was on her knees then, back bowed, sobs ripping through her like chainsaws. Some woman came running through the crowd, to scoop the little girl up and hug her tight. And Garrett Brand bent to fold his wife into his arms as the rest of the crowd gathered around him.

Bubba must be Garrett and Chelsea's son. Jake thought Sara had mentioned him during one of her endless talks about her family.

Her family. She loved them so much. There wasn't a doubt in Jake's mind that Sara would step in front of a bullet for any one of them. Or for any of those kids in there with her.

He hoped to God that hadn't happened. But a grim feeling in his belly told him otherwise. He slipped away as quietly as he could. He'd seen Garrett's pickup, and he figured if he needed weapons—which he did—that would be the most likely place to get them.

He found it unlocked, but he didn't see any guns lying around. Then he spotted a box on the floor and leaned in to reach for it.

A hand closed on his shoulder from behind. A big hand. Jake straightened, raising his own hands slowly.

"What do you think you're doing?" It was the mean one. Had to be, didn't it?

Jake drew a breath, let it out slow. "I'm going in there to get Sara, and if you want to stop me, you'll damn well have to kill me right where I stand."

Slowly he turned around, and he saw Wes Brand facing him. Dark, mean looking, narrow-eyed. He'd done time, Wes had. Jake recalled Sara's stories. "Listen to me, Brand," Jake said slowly. "If the cops rush this guy, he's gonna freak out and kill everyone in there. Including Sara and your little nephew. One man would have a better chance."

"You don't know that."

"I know Trent. Up until a month ago, I thought he was my best friend. Part of my family."

"Shows just how little you did know him, then."

"Yeah, well, even with that, I know him better than these guys do."

Wes's lips thinned.

"I have to get in there."

The other man still said nothing.

"I'm the best chance Sara has, and dammit, we're wasting time out here arguing about it. I'm going in. If I feel a bullet in my back, I'll know you decided not to let me."

Something came and went in Wes's eyes. He closed his hand around the small woven pouch that hung from a belt loop, held it for a moment, then sighed deeply. "You're right. You are the best chance she has."

Jake frowned.

"I think...she's been hurt, Nash. W...we don't have a hell of a lot of time here."

"How do you know that?"

Wes just shook his head. "There's a locked case in the back seat. Take it out and let's go."

"But if it's locked—"

"I got Garrett's keys." Wes held them up, then shrugged. "Hell, I had to learn something in prison. My cell mate was a pickpocket. Now, will you hurry up already?"

Jake reached into the pickup, grabbed the case and followed Wes through the crowd. They moved quickly, into the woodlot beyond the playground. Then they crouched down, and Wes opened the case. It held a handgun, a stun gun, some cuffs, ammunition and a walkie-talkie.

Wes looked at the handgun, looked at Jake.

Jake said, "I'm not carrying that thing into a school, Brand."

"No, I got the same feeling." Wes took the stun gun and handcuffs out, closed the case, locked it and hid it well. "Shall we?" Wes rose and eyed the open expanse of lawn between where they crouched and the school's rear entrance.

"We?" Jake said. "As I recall, you have a pregnant wife somewhere, don't you?"

"I've got a woman who loves me, pal. Same as you. Mine's safe and sound. Yours is in there with a gun to her head. Now, are you coming to get her or not?"

Jake swallowed hard but got to his feet. Wes yanked the walkie-talkie up, keyed it and said, "Garrett, tell your men to hold their fire or you'll be short a brother. And I do mean *now*."

Wes clipped the thing to his belt, gave Jake a nod. And they both lunged out of their cover and into the open, running full tilt.

"Don't shoot!" Garrett yelled as the two forms burst from the woodlot into the open, racing across the lawn to the building. He keyed the microphone of his two-way radio and yelled into it again and again. "Hold your fire! Hold your fire! Don't shoot!"

Then they were gone again. But not before Garrett had seen who they were. His own stupid, stubborn, bad-assed, born-again shaman of a brother, Wes, and that Jake Nash character Sara had been making herself miserable over. They were both damned lucky they hadn't been picked off by snipers.

Shoot, he didn't know what to think.

Then there was static, followed by Wes's voice over the radio. "Give us some time, Garrett."

Stupid, stubborn or otherwise, Garrett trusted his brother. "I'll do what I can, Wes, but it's gonna be out of my hands when the Feds arrive—and they're on their way."

"How long?" came the crackling reply.

"Ten minutes," Garrett said.

Sara lay on the floor and tried to keep her focus. She couldn't die so long as she kept her focus. If she started to lose it, her vision fading around the edges or her head getting fuzzy and dizzy or her body starting to go numb, she would just shake herself and force herself to focus harder. To be. To go on being. Even if that meant feeling the intense pain every time Fiona touched the wound.

The school nurse was as ruthless in her ministrations as she'd been with Trent. She tore Sara's blouse open down the front, wadded up every gauze pad in the kit, soaked them in iodine and stuffed them hard into the wound. Then she used the roll of medical tape to hold them there. It slowed the bleeding, Sara thought. Didn't stop it, but slowed it.

She wished it would stop. She was feeling very weak and light-headed.

Fiona took paper towels from the nearby sink, wet them and washed the worst of the blood away. Then she took off her own jacket, a smallish blazer that was way too pretty to be used on a bloody, gunshot victim, and slipped it over Sara's shoulders, buttoning it once in front. She made a sling from the sleeves of Sara's discarded blouse, and had her arm in it, saying the less Sara moved that arm, the less bleeding there would be.

"Enough already. What're you, the surgeon general or something?" Trent impatiently tugged her away.

"I'm a damn good nurse, and I'm married to a damn good doctor," Fiona snapped. "Maybe, if you're lucky, I'll still be around to help patch you up once those men outside get through with you."

Trent rolled his eyes. "You're one mouthy woman, aren't you?"

"Yeah, I'm a real pain in the ass," she muttered, but she went back to the children, a soothing smile pasted on her face. "Miss Brand is going to be just fine," she promised them. But Sara could hear the doubt in her voice. Damn. The wound must be even worse than she'd thought.

"You never got to read them that story, did you, Fiona?" Sara managed to ask, hoping it might distract Bubba from the fear she could see growing ever larger in his eyes.

"No, I guess I didn't. Would you like that, children?"

Bubba nodded, but they all looked doubtful. Then Sara said, "*The Brementown Musicians,* Fiona. It's...on my desk."

Fiona looked at her a little oddly, but she got the book and began reading it to the children, softly, in a soothing voice that seemed to make the pain a little less.

Sara thought about the shed in that little Cajun town. About the donkey and the rooster, and her last few hours with Jake....

And then she thought maybe she was letting herself slip again, because his face hovered before her eyes.

Focus, dammit!

She blinked and tried to shake herself awake. But he was still there. Peering at her from just outside the door. He lifted a finger to his lips, pressed it there.

Oh, God, he was real! He was real, Jake was here!

Sara blinked her eyes slowly instead of nodding to tell him she understood. His gaze moved over her body, lingering on her chest, and she saw his jaw go tight, his lower lip tremble.

Trent still crouched in front of her with his gun on her, and his back to the doorway. He was riveted to the windows, watching the men out there lining up to blow him away. He was afraid.

He should be, Sara thought. Every Brand in seven counties was probably out there by now.

Trent started to turn, as if to glance behind him toward the door.

"Trent, wait," Sara said. Too fast. He eyed her, then turned to glance at the door. Jake had pulled back, though, and was out of sight. Seeing nothing, Trent faced Sara again.

"What do you want?"

"I want to know why," she managed. "Why did you kill Vivienne?"

"Oh, come on!" His face twisted with bitterness. "She was sleeping with every man she met. Making a fool of me, spending every dime we could make at that plantation, making a huge dent in Flossie and Bert's savings. All the while never contributing a thing."

He paced, throwing his hands in the air, but was still careful not to cross in front of the windows.

"I know she wasn't a nice person," Sara said. She winced. It hurt to force enough air from her lungs to speak.

"That's putting it mildly."

"But what about Jake?" she asked, her voice soft.

Trent stopped pacing, faced her dead-on. Jake popped around the corner again and motioned to the children. Fiona saw him, nodded once, and began inching the kids closer to the door. They slid along the floor on their backsides. Fiona stayed where she was and kept on reading. Just as if they were still there. The kids didn't make a sound as they slid. Bubba was bringing up the rear, urging them along silently when they got too scared to move every once in a while.

"What *about* Jake?" Trent asked.

"He was your friend. And you were going to let him take the blame for murder."

"Hell, that was the plan." Trent tipped his head backward, staring at the ceiling. "Don't you get it?" he asked, fixing her with his gaze again. "My in-laws were going to leave that entire place to Vivienne, which meant it would have been mine. Then they changed the will to include my buddy Jake. Cutting my inheritance by half. And with Viv running around the way she was, how the hell could I even know I'd get that much? She could have up and left me at any moment!" He shook his head slowly, started to look toward Fiona and the spot on the floor where the kids were supposed to be. They wouldn't be there. Little Amy was at the door now, with Billy three feet behind her and Bubba a couple more feet away.

"So you thought that with Vivienne dead and Jake doing time for her murder…"

Trent's head swiveled back again. "They would leave it all to me," he said, his attention on her fully. "They didn't have anybody else."

An arm came around from the hallway and swept little Amy out. She never made a sound.

So Jake wasn't alone. He remained in the doorway, his eyes fixed on Trent most of the time, but darting every now and then down to Sara. To the jacket and the bandages showing in front, and the bloodstains starting to seep through, and the blood smeared all over the floor and coating her hands. Little Billy scooched closer to the door.

Jake's gaze met Sara's and held it. And she wondered again how his eyes ever got to be so brown and so perfectly shaped, so thickly fringed. His face was damp. He looked scared to death…for her, she knew. He wasn't any more afraid of Trent than he had been of that gator.

"So you were willing to let Jake go to prison just so you could have the plantation?" she asked.

"Jake should have stayed the hell away. He was…taking my place in that family. Flossie and Bert were starting—" He gave his head a shake, lowering it quickly.

"Starting to what, Trent? Love Jake more than you?"

He lifted his head and stared at her, and she had to forcibly resist the urge to look past him at Jake. Billy had made it to the doorway. Someone snatched him out into the hall. Only Bubba remained, and he inched closer and closer. But she couldn't look. If she looked, she would give it all away.

"What the hell do you care about any of this?" Trent asked her. Then his eyes narrowed on her. "You probably slept with him while the two of you were playing fugitive together. Didn't you? Hell, I thought you were different."

"So did I," she whispered.

"Well, you're not. You turned out to be just another easy tumble, like the rest of the women who throw themselves at Jake Nash."

She shrugged. The weakness was getting worse and worse now. Her mind was fading. Her voice getting softer. Maybe this was it. Maybe her words now would be her last ones. "I guess I did," she said. "But seeing how things turned out, I have to tell you, Trent, I don't regret it."

"No?"

She shook her head, managed a crooked smile. "I'd have hated to die a virgin," she whispered, hoping Jake could hear her.

Trent looked troubled by those words. Then, just as Bubba reached the door, his foot hit a chair, making it bang against a desk. A small sound, but as loud as a gunshot in the silence.

Trent whirled, lifted his gun and fired, just as Jake dove in front of the child. Wes appeared behind Jake, and Trent took aim again. But even as Sara tried to get up, tried to help, managing to lift only one arm, a chair came crashing down on Trent's head...and as he fell to his knees, Sara was amazed to see Fiona pulling it up to bring it down again.

Wes hauled Bubba out of the room, shoved him out of the line of fire, and Jake got to his feet and surged forward. He and Trent struggled, but only for a moment. It was over that fast. The gun was on the floor, Trent was on his back, Jake was straddling him, and Wes was standing above with his Bowie knife in his hand.

"You can let him up, Jake. I got him," Wes said.

Jake nodded once and got off the man. Then he

was beside Sara, even as Wes hauled Trent to his feet, turned him around, cuffed him and slammed him down into a chair. Wes spoke into a radio.

Jake knelt and cupped Sara's head, lifting her slightly, searching her face. "Are you all right?"

She smiled weakly. "What took you so long?"

"Does it matter?" he asked her. "I'm here now."

He stroked her face, and she felt herself slipping again, fought to hold on, but knew this time it was a losing battle. "You're here," she whispered. "But for me, Jake? Or for Trent?"

People came charging in then. Officers first, in riot gear, wielding rifles and ordering everyone to the floor. Jake ignored them and was shoved away from her for his trouble. That was about all she was clear on. After that she seemed to fade out, and it angered her that she would lose her grip on life when she was so close to her heart's desire.

She tried to tell Jake that she loved him. That was foremost in her mind, to tell him that she loved him, because she was pretty sure she wasn't going to get another chance. But she never knew if the words bursting from her heart actually made it to her lips or not.

Chapter 17

Jake was cold. And he shouldn't be, because he was crammed in between Wes and Garrett Brand in Garrett's big pickup truck. Chelsea and little Bubba were in the back seat, and Jake wondered if the little guy could breathe at all, as tight as his mamma was holding him. Sara's brother, Marcus and his wife, Casey, were following in their own car. The rest of the Brands were more than likely en route. But the paramedics had taken off so damned fast with Sara that Jake hadn't had time to force his way into the ambulance with her, as he'd fully intended to do.

None of the Brands had managed it, either. So she was alone, and that was killing him. Garrett could drive, though. Jake had to give him that. He had caught up to the ambulance, even though the cops had held them up at the scene for a minute or two that had seemed endless. And then he skidded the pickup's dual tires to a stop, crossways in the parking lot next to the El Paso ER.

They all piled out.

Two paramedics wheeled Sara through the automatic doors at a dead run, one of them holding a plastic IV bag above his head, another pressing an oxygen mask to her face. They blocked most of her from Jake's view, but not so much that he couldn't see the way she was thrashing around on the gurney. Jake surged forward, flanked by Brands, but the third paramedic got out of the driver's door, blocking their path.

"Is one of you guys Jake?"

Swallowing hard, Jake nodded. "I am. Why?"

The paramedic clapped him on the shoulder, looking down at the floor briefly before meeting Jake's eyes. "Hang in there, man. You've got yourself a fighter. She might just pull through yet."

"Might?" Jake's blood ran cold. He gave the man a nod of thanks, then moved past him, feeling dazed. He pushed through the hospital doors, headed straight for the room where he'd seen them take Sara and went through those doors, as well. But he saw only the pale-green scrubs that surrounded her, fighting to hold her still, and one blood-streaked, pale arm flailing wildly. He heard his name on a wheezing breath, over and over again.

Someone grabbed him, went to shove him away.

"No, dammit!" Jake shoved back, and the next thing he knew he was at Sara's side, both hands clasping hers, bending low, leaning close. "I'm here, Sara. I'm right here."

Someone grabbed him again.

Someone else said, "No, let him be! Look at this."

Sara's thrashing stopped. Her eyes remained closed, lips moving slightly, forming his name, though no sound came out. The rapid beep of the heart monitor slowed. The tension in the room seemed to ease immediately.

"I'm right here, Sara. I'm right here. It's okay."

He glanced up at the nearest face. A dark-eyed man nodded at him from behind his mask. "Keep talking to her, son."

He did, while someone fixed the IV that had been torn loose and someone else refastened the oxygen mask and a half dozen others did a half dozen other jobs. Eventually Sara seemed to sink into sleep or unconsciousness or...he wouldn't think further.

The dark-eyed doctor met Jake's eyes over his mask. "She's out. We need to get her to surgery, and you can't come with us there."

Jake still clung to Sara's limp, cold hand. "Is she...is she going to...?"

"There's a bullet near her heart," the doctor said, and his accent was Spanish. "Every time she moves, the bleeding starts up again and she risks death. We have to get it out. It's risky...she's lost a lot of blood already...but if we don't try..."

Swallowing hard, Jake nodded. He didn't need the doc to finish.

"New to the family, aren't you, son?" the man asked, guiding Jake into the hall as the nurses pushed Sara out of the room and toward an elevator.

Jake just watched her go, watched the doors slide open. "I'm...I'm not family. I'm...uh...I'm no one."

"He's family," someone said.

Jake looked up, surprised to see that the voice belonged to Garrett, who was still wearing a badge on his shirt. "Doc, maybe you could take a look at Jake's arm, there, while you tell us what's going on with Sara?"

The doctor frowned, and Jake glanced down at where he was looking. He'd only been vaguely aware of the soreness in his upper arm, and he'd attributed the blood on his shirt to Sara's injuries.

The doctor steered Jake to a chair and tore the sleeve wider to look at the wound. "What happened here?" he asked. Wes came over to stand beside Jake, looking down at his wound with what might almost have been a hint of concern in his eyes.

Jake shrugged.

"He took a bullet for my son," Garrett said, his eyes fixed on Jake's. "Yeah, Wes told me all about it. You probably don't realize it, but that qualifies you for honorary membership in the clan."

Jake sucked in a breath as the doctor poked at him.

The doctor said, "It's only a flesh wound. I'll send a nurse out to clean and bandage it, and you'll need a tetanus shot." Then he glanced past Garrett at the doorway, and his face lit up.

Jake looked, too, and he saw Fiona, the school nurse, coming through the entrance, arms open wide. The doctor ran to her, enfolded her, hugged her hard. There were tears, kisses.

"I, uh, I don't believe you've met my wife," the doctor said finally, addressing the Brands.

Garrett looked surprised. No wonder. The woman

was half "Doc's" age, by Jake's best guess. "When did you get married?" Garrett asked.

"Last month. In Vegas."

The woman looked past her husband, at Jake and Wes, and she said, "Those two...they saved our lives back there at that school. They saved the children's lives. This one, he dove right in front of little Bubba just when that man shot at him."

Behind her a camera flashed, and Jake shielded his eyes, squinting at the crowd of reporters coming into the ER waiting room.

While Jake got his wound patched up, Garrett headed to the double doors to do some crowd control. He had a few words with the reporters and apparently convinced them to leave. But the waiting room remained packed full of Brands—and one outsider who felt like a fraud.

Nurses who passed kept whispering words like "hero" as they looked Jake's way. But he knew better. Chelsea brought him stale coffee in a foam cup. Little Bubba sat on his lap and looked at him with adoring eyes. Wes and Garrett talked to him as if he were an old friend.

Marcus, Sara's brother, was quiet. Musing. Deep in thought. And finally, during a long stretch of deep silence, he said, "So are you planning to marry her, or what?"

Everyone sat there staring at Marcus in stunned silence.

Jake swallowed hard. "Don't worry, Marcus. I know damn well that I'm nowhere near good enough for your sister."

Marcus didn't say anything for a long moment. He looked at his wife, then at little Bubba sitting on

Jake's lap. Then he said, "You're right, Nash. You're nowhere near good enough for Sara Brand. Then again, neither is anyone else on the planet, in my opinion. But that's all beside the point, don't you think?"

"Is it?"

"Yeah, it is. Because if she waits for someone worthy of her, she'll be spending her whole life alone. And also, because I'm pretty sure she has her heart set on you." Then he nodded toward the TV that glared down on the waiting room from a corner shelf. "And I suppose a national hero is about as good as she could hope to do for herself."

They all turned to look at the TV screen, and Jake saw his own image there. The photo showed him sitting on a waiting-room chair, his shirt and arm smeared with blood, his hair a mess. Underneath the photo it said, "Jacob Allen Nash—American Hero. A TV10 Editorial."

"Turn that up," Chelsea said.

Someone did.

"Facts about this American hero, who today risked his own life to save two women and three children from a situation that could very easily have turned to tragedy, are still coming in. But most surprising of all, perhaps, is that this isn't the first time this man has shown such valor. Eighteen years ago, when he was little more than a child, Jacob Allen Nash tried to hold up a convenience store. Why? Because his dying mother needed medicine she couldn't afford. The result? The store owner suffered a heart attack. Nash then called for help and stayed on the scene, attempting to perform CPR on the man, until police arrived to arrest him. He served eighteen years of a twenty-year sentence. And even with that, he never lost his compassion, or his courage. The heroic soul that drove him to sit there waiting for help to arrive, instead of running away to save himself, was the same one that drove him once again to risk it all for the sake of someone else. Jacob Allen Nash…Quinn, Texas, thanks you.''

The photo of Jake vanished, the screen showed a news anchor at a desk with two coanchors. One of the coanchors, a woman, shook her head slowly. ''Men like that one don't come along every day. And I hear he's single, Mark.''

The anchor grinned. ''Not for long, I'll bet.''

Jake reached for the remote and turned the set off. A nurse leaned over his shoulder, handed him a slip of paper.

''What's this?'' he asked.

''Messages. Reporters from all over Texas want to talk to you.''

He shook his head, crumpled the paper in his fist. ''Any word on Sara yet?''

The nurse smiled gently. ''We should know soon. But I have a hunch she's gonna be just fine, hon. I don't think that ol' reaper could pry her away with a crowbar.''

Sara tore free of the grip of darkness, even though it tried hard to hold on. It seemed like an uphill battle all the way. Sounds reached her ears, but dulled, as if muffled by layers of cotton, and she had to strain to hear them at all. She had no sense of her body, felt more as if she were floating, weightless, entirely numb. And when she told herself to open her eyes, her brain couldn't seem to locate them, much less command them to move.

It was a long, slow, frightening journey back to herself. But she knew she was making progress when she managed to pinpoint a single, physical link to life. A warmth, a pressure. A touch. She focused on that touch, which was like a beacon guiding her back. She followed it and slowly identified it. A hand. Holding hers. Steadily, she made her way closer. A voice, speaking to her soft and low. She didn't know what the words were. It didn't matter. She knew the voice.

It was Jake's.

Her eyes opened very slowly. Her mouth worked, but no sound came out. She was so frustrated.

"Hey, easy," he said softly. "Easy now. It's all right." He smiled gently, and his hand stroked her hair. "You're gonna be fine," he whispered. "You hear me? Just take it slow. Don't try to talk..."

"But—" The sound came this time. It was coarse as gravel sandpaper. She tried to clear her throat.

"Here. Have some water, hon." Jake got up, moved away from her, poured water into a glass, then came back. He lifted her head, pressed the built-in straw to her lips. Sara drank.

When she finished, her throat felt marginally better.

"Better?" he asked her.

"A little." But she still sounded like a frog.

"Well, why don't you give it some time? For now, let me do the talking, okay?" he asked her.

Frowning in frustration, Sara nodded. But damn, there was so much she wanted to tell him. So much she wanted to ask him.

"Those letters you wrote to me," he said softly, settling himself ever so carefully onto the edge of her bed. "They kept me alive, Sara. I couldn't call you—they wouldn't let me. And I doubt any of the letters I wrote you made it any farther than Kendall's wastebasket."

Sara blinked. "You...you wrote to me?"

"Wrote to you, talked to you in my mind. Held you in my dreams. You were never away from me, Sara. Not really."

A bubble of emotion rose up in her chest, and her eyes watered. "Don't make me cry," she whispered. "It hurts."

"Oh, I don't want to make you cry." He stroked her hair away from her face.

"Kendall," she said as her mind slowly cleared. "He was involved with Trent."

"Yeah, Trent spilled all that when they took him in. He and Kendall are sharing a cell at the moment."

"They deserve each other."

Jake grinned at her.

"Don't look so happy. I'm still furious at you." Pain in her chest made her grimace a little.

Jake gripped her hand. "Are you okay?"

She stared hard at him. "I don't know, Jake. Am I?"

For a moment he seemed puzzled, then understanding dawned. "Oh, yes. Yes, Sara, you're gonna be just fine. They got the bullet out. There was no damage to your heart."

"That's what you think," she muttered.

He leaned over her, kissed her lips softly. "I'm

sorry. Will it help if I admit now that...that you were right all along, Sara?''

''It depends on what I was right about.''

''That the system works. That the bad guys pay. That the good guys win. Damn, I'm just sorry I didn't stop Trent before he hurt you, Sara.''

''Yeah, yeah, yeah,'' she whispered. ''But what about *us?*''

''Sara...'' Jake sighed, got to his feet and paced away from her for just a moment. Then he came back to her side. ''You were right about some other things, too.''

She managed to move her hand, swung it out, caught his in it and tugged. Smiling, he sat down on the edge of her bed again. ''Of course I was,'' she said. ''Which things?''

''I think you already know.''

''I want to hear you say it.''

He smiled. ''Okay, I suppose you've earned the right. My mother used to tell me over and over that there was more good in me than I knew. I used to believe it, before...before my time in prison. But I lost that. I don't think I ever would have found it again on my own. But you came along and...well, hell, Sara, you dragged it out of me. You beat me over the head with it until I woke up and saw it there. You made me see that I'm more than I've ever let myself believe I could be.''

''You are,'' she whispered. ''So much more. You're the man...I love.''

He smiled very slightly, lowering his head. ''Yeah, I know I am. Actually, everybody in the town of Quinn knows I am by now.''

Sara frowned at him. ''How?''

Meeting her gaze again, looking a bit sheepish, he said, "Because you kept saying it when they brought you in, in the ambulance, in the ER, in the recovery room."

She felt her face heat and considered it a very good sign.

"I thought maybe you were just...you know...delirious or something."

She shook her head. "You know I meant it. I've told you so before, Jake."

"Yeah, well, after the stunt I pulled—and what ended up happening—I couldn't be sure you hadn't changed your mind. But I sure as hell was hoping you still meant it, Sara."

Sara's breath caught in her throat, and her brows went up. "Were you, Jake?"

"Yeah. Otherwise, I'd feel pretty stupid for carrying this around with me ever since they let me out of jail. Hoping I'd get the chance...and the guts...to give it to you." As he spoke, he took something from his pocket. "I bought a new box for it, but it's not new. It was...my mother's."

He opened the little box and held it so she could see the tiny diamond ring nestled inside. "She cherished it. Never wore it, after my father left her, though. She used to say it was never meant for her, but for me someday, when I found...well, when I found you."

"Jake..." Sara shook her head slowly, felt her eyes filling with a new flood of happy tears.

"I can't believe a guy like me has the gall to ask it of a woman like you, but you keep telling me I can be whatever I want to. So what I want to be is your husband. Will you marry me, Sara Brand?"

Sara nodded as her tears spilled over and rolled slowly down her face. "No one else would ever do," she told him. "I'd have died a spinster if you hadn't come around, Jake."

"Oh, I wasn't gonna let that happen."

He leaned down, kissed her gently on the mouth. "I love you, Sara. I did all along. Right from the start."

She smiled and said, "I know."

* * * * *

Look Who's Celebrating Our 20th Anniversary:

"Working with Silhouette has always been a privilege—I've known the nicest people, and I've been delighted by the way the books have grown and changed with time. I've had the opportunity to take chances…and I'm grateful for the books I've done with the company. Bravo! And onward, Silhouette, to the new millennium."

—*New York Times* bestselling author
Heather Graham Pozzessere

"Twenty years of laughter and love... It's not hard to imagine Silhouette Books celebrating twenty years of quality publishing, but it is hard to imagine a publishing world without it. Congratulations..."

—International bestselling author
Emilie Richards

PS20SIMAQ1

where love comes alive—online...

Visit the *Author's Alcove*

➤ Find the most complete information anywhere on
your favorite Silhouette author.

➤ Try your hand in the Writing Round Robin—
contribute a chapter to an online book in the
making.

Enter the *Reading Room*

➤ Experience an interactive novel—help determine
the fate of a story being created now by one of
your favorite authors.

➤ Join one of our reading groups and discuss your
favorite book.

Drop into *Shop eHarlequin*

➤ Find the latest releases—read an excerpt or write
a review for this month's Silhouette top sellers.

➤ Try out our amazing search feature—tell us your
favorite theme, setting or time period and we'll find
a book that's perfect for you.

All this and more available at

www.eHarlequin.com
on Women.com Networks

SILHOUETTE'S 20ᵀᴴ ANNIVERSARY CONTEST
OFFICIAL RULES
NO PURCHASE NECESSARY TO ENTER

1. To enter, follow directions published in the offer to which you are responding. Contest begins 1/1/00 and ends on 8/24/00 (the "Promotion Period"). Method of entry may vary. Mailed entries must be postmarked by 8/24/00, and received by 8/31/00.

2. During the Promotion Period, the Contest may be presented via the Internet. Entry via the Internet may be restricted to residents of certain geographic areas that are disclosed on the Web site. To enter via the Internet, if you are a resident of a geographic area in which Internet entry is permissible, follow the directions displayed on-line, including typing your essay of 100 words or fewer telling us "Where In The World Your Love Will Come Alive." On-line entries must be received by 11:59 p.m. Eastern Standard time on 8/24/00. Limit one e-mail entry per person, household and e-mail address per day, per presentation. If you are a resident of a geographic area in which entry via the Internet is permissible, you may, in lieu of submitting an entry on-line, enter by mail, by hand-printing your name, address, telephone number and contest number/name on an 8"x 11" plain piece of paper and telling us in 100 words or fewer "Where In The World Your Love Will Come Alive," and mailing via first-class mail to: Silhouette 20ᵗʰ Anniversary Contest, (in the U.S.) P.O. Box 9069, Buffalo, NY 14269-9069; (In Canada) P.O. Box 637, Fort Erie, Ontario, Canada L2A 5X3. Limit one 8"x 11" mailed entry per person, household and e-mail address per day. On-line and/or 8"x 11" mailed entries received from persons residing in geographic areas in which Internet entry is not permissible will be disqualified. No liability is assumed for lost, late, incomplete, inaccurate, nondelivered or misdirected mail, or misdirected e-mail, for technical, hardware or software failures of any kind, lost or unavailable network connection, or failed, incomplete, garbled or delayed computer transmission or any human error which may occur in the receipt or processing of the entries in the contest.

3. Essays will be judged by a panel of members of the Silhouette editorial and marketing staff based on the following criteria:

   Sincerity (believability, credibility)—50%
   Originality (freshness, creativity)—30%
   Aptness (appropriateness to contest ideas)—20%

   Purchase or acceptance of a product offer does not improve your chances of winning. In the event of a tie, duplicate prizes will be awarded.

4. All entries become the property of Harlequin Enterprises Ltd., and will not be returned. Winner will be determined no later than 10/31/00 and will be notified by mail. Grand Prize winner will be required to sign and return Affidavit of Eligibility within 15 days of receipt of notification. Noncompliance within the time period may result in disqualification and an alternative winner may be selected. All municipal, provincial, federal, state and local laws and regulations apply. Contest open only to residents of the U.S. and Canada who are 18 years of age or older, and is void wherever prohibited by law. Internet entry is restricted solely to residents of those geographical areas in which Internet entry is permissible. Employees of Torstar Corp., their affiliates, agents and members of their immediate families are not eligible. Taxes on the prizes are the sole responsibility of winners. Entry and acceptance of any prize offered constitutes permission to use winner's name, photograph or other likeness for the purposes of advertising, trade and promotion on behalf of Torstar Corp. without further compensation to the winner, unless prohibited by law. Torstar Corp and D.L. Blair, Inc., their parents, affiliates and subsidiaries, are not responsible for errors in printing or electronic presentation of contest or entries. In the event of printing or other errors which may result in unintended prize values or duplication of prizes, all affected contest materials or entries shall be null and void. If for any reason the Internet portion of the contest is not capable of running as planned, including infection by computer virus, bugs, tampering, unauthorized intervention, fraud, technical failures, or any other causes beyond the control of Torstar Corp. which corrupt or affect the administration, secrecy, fairness, integrity or proper conduct of the contest, Torstar Corp. reserves the right, at its sole discretion, to disqualify any individual who tampers with the entry process and to cancel, terminate, modify or suspend the contest or the Internet portion thereof. In the event of a dispute regarding an on-line entry, the entry will be deemed submitted by the authorized holder of the e-mail account submitted at the time of entry. Authorized account holder is defined as the natural person who is assigned to an e-mail address by an Internet access provider, on-line service provider or other organization that is responsible for arranging e-mail address for the domain associated with the submitted e-mail address.

5. Prizes: Grand Prize—a $10,000 vacation to anywhere in the world. Travelers (at least one must be 18 years of age or older) or parent or guardian if one traveler is a minor, must sign and return a Release of Liability prior to departure. Travel must be completed by December 31, 2001, and is subject to space and accommodations availability. Two hundred (200) Second Prizes—a two-book limited edition autographed collector set from one of the Silhouette Anniversary authors: Nora Roberts, Diana Palmer, Linda Howard or Annette Broadrick (value $10.00 each set). All prizes are valued in U.S. dollars.

6. For a list of winners (available after 10/31/00), send a self-addressed, stamped envelope to: Harlequin Silhouette 20ᵗʰ Anniversary Winners, P.O. Box 4200, Blair, NE 68009-4200.

Contest sponsored by Torstar Corp., P.O. Box 9042, Buffalo, NY 14269-9042.

PS20RULES

ENTER FOR
A CHANCE TO WIN*

Silhouette's 20th Anniversary Contest

Tell Us Where in the World
You Would Like *Your* Love To Come Alive...
And We'll Send the Lucky Winner There!

Silhouette wants to take you wherever
your happy ending can come true.

Here's how to enter: Tell us, in 100 words or less,
where you want to go to make your love come alive!

In addition to the grand prize, there will be 200
runner-up prizes, collector's-edition book sets
autographed by one of the Silhouette anniversary
authors: **Nora Roberts, Diana Palmer,
Linda Howard** or **Annette Broadrick**.

DON'T MISS YOUR CHANCE TO WIN!
ENTER NOW! No Purchase Necessary

Silhouette®
Where love comes alive™

Visit Silhouette at www.eHarlequin.com to enter, starting this summer.

Name: _____

Address: _____

City: _____ State/Province: _____

Zip/Postal Code: _____

Mail to Harlequin Books: **In the U.S.:** P.O. Box 9069, Buffalo, NY
14269-9069; **In Canada:** P.O. Box 637, Fort Erie, Ontario, L4A 5X3

*No purchase necessary—for contest details send a self-addressed stamped envelope to:
Silhouette's 20th Anniversary Contest, P.O. Box 9069, Buffalo, NY, 14269-9069 (include
contest name on self-addressed envelope). Residents of Washington and Vermont may
omit postage. Open to Cdn. (excluding Quebec) and U.S. residents who are 18 or over.
Void where prohibited. Contest ends August 31, 2000.   PS20CON_R2

First published 1992
© Michael Basman 1992

ISBN 0 7134 6475 5
British Library Cataloguing-in-Publication Data.
A catalogue record for this book is available from the British Library

Typesetting and Illustrations by Lasertext Ltd, Stretford, Manchester
Printed in Great Britain by
The Bath Press, Bath, Avon
for the publishers,
B. T. Batsford Ltd,
4 Fitzhardinge Street,
London W1H 0AH

A BATSFORD CHESS BOOK
Adviser: R. D. Keene GM, OBE
Technical Editor: Andrew Kinsman

BATSFORD SECOND CHESS COURSE

MICHAEL BASMAN

B. T. Batsford Ltd, London

CONTENTS

INTRODUCTION

WELCOME to the *Batsford Second Chess Course*. If you are interested in improving your chess, and have progressed beyond the level of a beginner, then this is the ideal book for you!

Those completely new to the exciting game of chess are recommended to start with *The Batsford Chess Course* before moving on to this book. In that book the following basic features were discussed:

— The rules of chess
— Writing moves down
— Seeing captures
— One move checkmates
— Scholar's mate, castling, stalemate, *en passant*
— Basic mates (2 rooks versus king, queen and king versus king, rook and king versus king).

This book explains more advanced ideas of opening play, tactics and endgames that will be of great value to you in your own games. You will learn:

— The science of UFOs (mysterious ways to win and lose pieces), a hitherto unexplored dimension of the game
— How to finish off your opponent when you have a material advantage

— The fundamental positional rules of opening play
— English (or descriptive) notation
— Game analysis
— The wonderful world of king and pawn endings, where everything, or almost everything, can be worked out perfectly!
— And finally, the most important idea of tactics, quick and clever ways of winning pieces or delivering checkmate. Alert and skilful players will discover that tactics are a very useful way to speed up their victories and a very effective way of extricating themselves from difficult positions.

Each section contains a set of questions, designed to test your understanding of the important concepts. Detailed answers are given at the back of the book, along with marks for correct solutions and a score chart to record your scores. If you manage to score 75%, or more, then you have a good understanding of the Course and can confidently use these new ideas in your own games.

So now, on with the Course!

Michael Basman
Chessington
March 1992

-1-
UFOs

ONE of the most important basic techniques which all aspiring chess players need to develop during their early games is an ability to look at the piece just moved, or about to move, concentrating on the square on which it lands and the attacks it makes on the new square. This technique is a vital one in order to avoid losing pieces, but there is a further way in which material can be lost, known as UFOs.

What are UFOs? In real life, they are Unidentified Flying Objects, or Flying Saucers. In chess, they are *mysterious ways of losing pieces.* You are quietly playing chess, when one of these things swoops out of the sky and carries off one of your men. In fact, so mysterious are the UFOs, that you can sometimes lose pieces without being aware of it!

In this chapter, we will introduce you to UFOs, test you on them, and help you to spot them before they appear.

There are three types:

(1) Leaving Unguarded
(2) Focused Attacks
(3) Opening and Closing Lines.

Note that the initials of these three types of attack form the letters U F O, hence the general name, which also can serve as an aid to memory. Just remember

U = Leaving Unguarded
F = Focused Attack
O = Opening and Closing Lines.

Leaving unguarded

A very common mistake. Take the diagram:

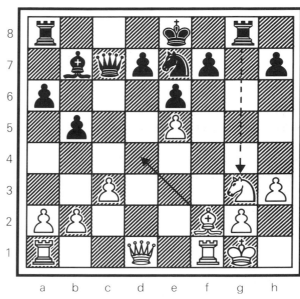

Diagram 1

White was thinking about a way to guard the attacked pawn at e5, under fire from the black queen at c7. He decided to move the bishop up to d4 from f2. What had he missed? Well, his bishop was already doing a job guarding the knight at g3 — which unfortunately is attacked by a black rook at g8. Black saw his chance straightaway and captured the knight by Rxg3.

How does one avoid making mistakes of this sort? White had done nothing wrong according to the simple concept of 'material chess'. The square he moved his bishop to was completely safe, and it adequately defended the pawn at e5. What White lacked was a sense of the whole board. Instead of concentrating solely on one or two squares, and one or two pieces, you have to learn to see the attacks and defences over all the sixty-four squares, though this ability takes time to develop.

Here are a few exercises in Leaving Unguarded; note that to do well in these tests, you must be able to see, not only where the piece is going, but also *what has been left behind.*

Exercise

Would you play Nb3 or Rc1 here? Give reasons for your answer.

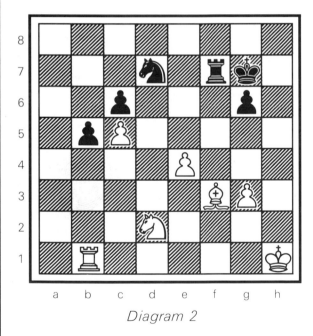

Diagram 2

Answer:

Rc1 is correct, because Nb3 leaves the bishop unguarded, and allows the capture Rxf3.

Test

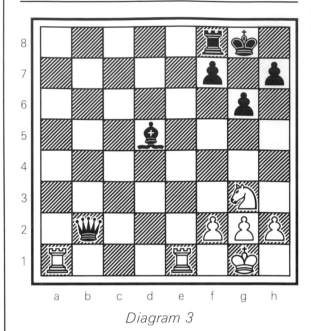

Diagram 3

White to play

Which move is better here, Reb1 or Re2? Why?

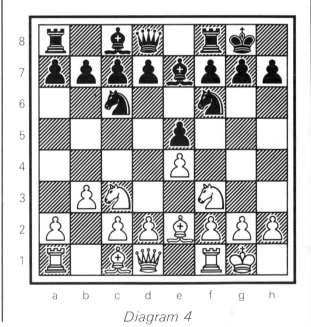

Diagram 4

White to play

Ba3
Bb2
Nd5

Comment on these three moves. Which one is best?

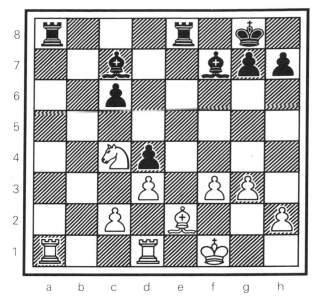

Diagram 6

White to play
Show three different ways for White to lose material by leaving pieces unguarded.

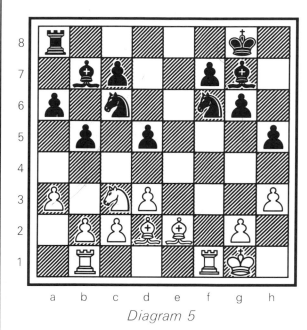

Diagram 5

Black to play
Which of these moves loses material by *leaving pieces unguarded*? Show how.

Bf8
g5
Nd7
a5
b4

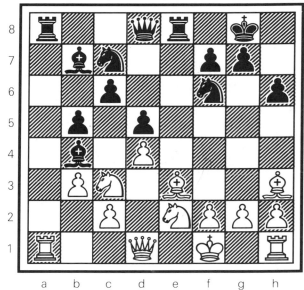

Diagram 7

White to play
Comment on these four moves. Which one is best?
f4
Nf4
Qd3
g3

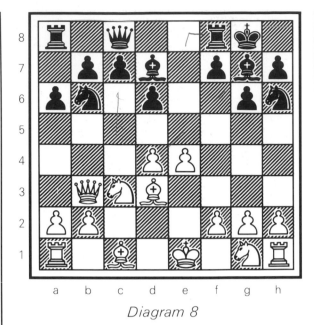

Diagram 8

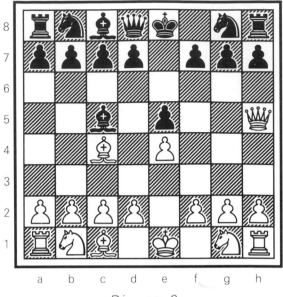

Diagram 9

Black to play

Would you (1) capture the white pawn at d4 by ... Bxd4? (2) play ... c5 to attack the white centre? or (3) place your rook on e8? Give reasons for your answer.

Focused Attacks

The next advanced type of attack we shall look at is the focused attack. This is where two or more pieces gang up on a single point. In physics, a special lens will bend the rays of light so that the focus is on one point; and in chess the player can direct his pieces so they focus on one square. A focused ray of light can burn through obstructions; and a focused attack in chess can break down strong defences.

Have a look at this position:

This is Scholar's Mate, arising out of the moves 1 e4 e5 2 Bc4 Bc5 3 Qh5. Scholar's Mate is a type of Focused Attack, which is why it is so successful against beginners. The white queen and bishop are firing in several directions, but on one particular square in the enemy camp their lines of attack coincide — the square f7. White actually threatens checkmate next move, by Qxf7, since the square is only defended once, by the king at e8.

Surprisingly enough, you can usually use MCSB to defend against focused attacks. MCSB stands for Move, Capture, Support, Block, referring to the different ways in which threats to your pieces can be dealt with: you can move the attacked piece, capture the attacker, support the attacked man, or block the attack. All these alternatives should be considered in meeting an attack on one of your men, and the most appropriate action chosen. For example, to answer Scholar's Mate, we can try

MOVE: None
(the pawn at f7 cannot move, as that would put the black king into check from the queen at h5; and even if it could, it would not help to stop the *mate* threat).

CAPTURE: None

(in this case, neither of the white pieces can be captured).

SUPPORT: Qe7, Qf6, Nh6

(all these moves defend the f7 pawn against the mate, though Nh6 is the least satisfactory as it allows the tactical sequence 4 d4! Bxd4 5 Bxh6 gxh6? 6 Qxf7 mate).

BLOCK: g6

(Black can also block by d5, but this loses a pawn to Bxd5. Note that ... g6 is not particularly good either, as White can continue with 4 Qxe5+ and 5 Qxh8 winning a rook. So our analysis shows that the best defence to Scholar's Mate is Qe7 or Qf6).

Number, value, order

With focused attacks you need to remember three things to help you solve them accurately: *Number, Value* and *Order.*

First, *number.* This is the most important thing about focused attacks; the number of pieces on both sides attacking and defending the square or piece under fire. To capture a point you will need a *greater number* of attackers than defenders; whereas if you simply want to hold on to a square or a piece, you have only to match the number of attackers with an equal number of defenders.

If it's Black to play in diagram 10, he can capture the pawn at d4, as he has three pieces attacking the pawn, and only two pieces defend it. Thus:

1	...	Nxd4
2	Nxd4	Rxd4
3	Rxd4	Bxd4

On the other hand, if it's White to play, he can match the number of attackers by playing 1 Bb2, or 1 Be3, thus defending the pawn a third time.

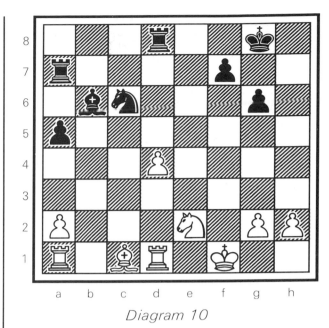

Diagram 10

Value: This is the second factor to watch out for in focused attacks, and in some cases it completely overrules the first factor of number.

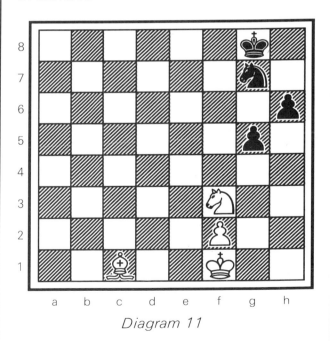

Diagram 11

We can see that the pawn at g5 is attacked by two white pieces and only defended by one. Does that mean that

Black should bring up another piece to defend the pawn? Not at all; the pawn is quite well defended as it is, due to the *low value* of the pieces under attack. If White were to play 1 Nxg5 hxg5 2 Bxg5, he would come out 1 point behind, as he loses a knight and only captures two pawns for it. (The standard chess valuation for each piece is: queen — 9 points; rook — 5 points; bishop and knight — 3 points each; pawn — 1 point.)

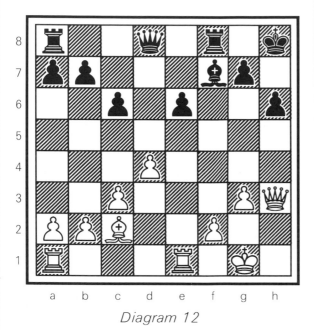

Diagram 12

In this position, too, White does not capture at e6, even though he attacks the square with two pieces, a queen and a rook, and it is only defended once. After 1 Rxe6 Bxe6 2 Qxe6, White gains 4 points (bishop + pawn), but loses 5 (a rook). It would be better in this position to pile on the pressure with 1 Bb3, threatening now to capture on e6 with a piece of the *same value* as the defending bishop.

Order: Our third important factor to remember about focused attacks is order — the order in which we are to make our sequence of captures. The rule to remember is *make your captures in reverse order of strength*, that is, capture first with your lowest value pieces, and then work upwards.

Let's look at an earlier position again:

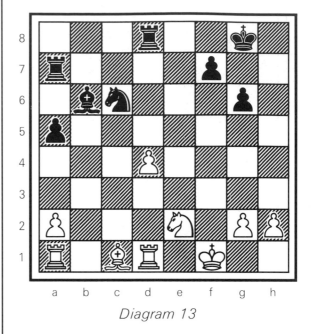

Diagram 13

Here, if you remember, Black was threatening the white pawn at d4 with three pieces, but if he neglects our rule of *order*, and captures with his *highest* value piece first, he could even end up losing points. For example:

| 1 | ... | Rxd4 |
| 2 | Nxd4 | Nxd4 |

and now White should stop capturing at d4. He has lost a knight and a pawn (4 points), but Black has given him a rook (5 points). Black should have remembered our rule *lowest value first*, and then he would have played 1 ... Nxd4 or 1 ... Bxd4.

Before tackling the exercises, here is a position to practice on.

Exercise

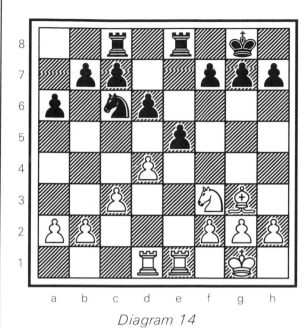

Diagram 14

Here White is attacking the black pawn at e5 four times, and it is only defended three times. If it is White to play, show the correct sequence of captures which would lead to the win of a pawn for White.

Next, imagine it is Black's move. Using MCSB (Move, Capture, Support, Block) show all the good defences for the pawn at e5.

Answers: as White to play, the correct sequence would be (lowest value piece first):

1	dxe5	dxe5
2	Nxe5	Nxe5
3	Bxe5 winning a pawn.	

White could also play:

1	dxe5	dxe5
2	Nxe5	Nxe5
3	Rxe5	Rxe5
4	Bxe5 again winning a pawn.	

And instead of capturing with the knight in these examples, he could also capture with the bishop, as these pieces are both of the same value.

Black to move, using MCSB, we have

MOVE	e4
CAPTURE	exd4
SUPPORT	f6
BLOCK	no block possible

All these moves would be satisfactory defences for the pawn at e5.

Focused attacks help to win games! So practice them in your own chess matches, and see how much they can improve your results!

Test

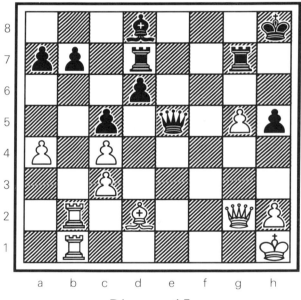

Diagram 15

White to play

He can take a pawn by a series of captures on one square. Give the sequence.

Black to play

Show a sequence of captures for Black that win a pawn.

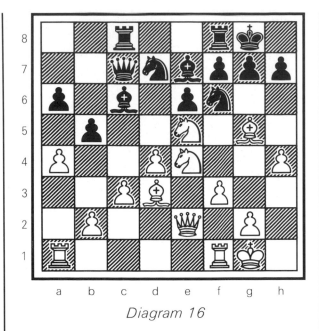

Diagram 16

White to play

He can win a pawn by a series of captures. Show the sequence.

Black to play

Show a sequence of captures for Black that win a pawn.

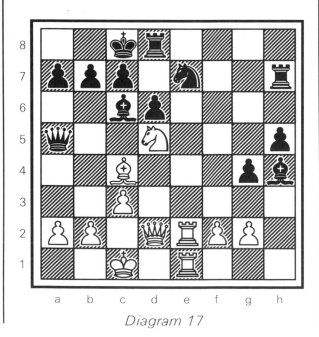

Diagram 17

White to play

White can win a piece here. Show the capture sequence that does the trick for him.

Black to play

How can Black win a piece here? Show the correct sequence of captures

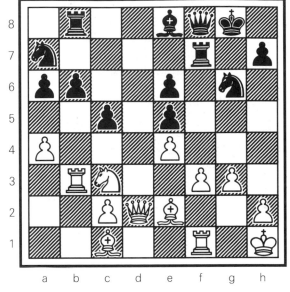

Diagram 18

White to play

Is 1 f4 a safe move? Give the sequence of captures to support your view.

Black to play

Is 1 ... b5 safe? Give the best series of captures to support your answer.

Opening and closing lines

Our third and final UFO involves the opening and closing of lines.

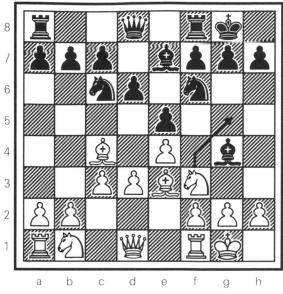

Diagram 19

Black has just moved his bishop to g4, and White, thinking his knight was threatened — or just feeling like moving it anyway — played Ng5. What was wrong? Unfortunately, the knight was shielding the queen at d1 from capture, and there is nothing now to stop Black from playing Bxd1, winning 9 points, and only losing a bishop in exchange.

As with the UFO 'Leaving Unguarded', a simple knowledge of basic material chess would be powerless to prevent you from playing a move like Ng5, since the knight itself goes to a *perfectly safe* square. By doing these exercises, you will start to make less of these mistakes, and after a while you will stop making them altogether.

To help you with opening and closing lines, look at diagram 20, and at the black bishop at g7. *Imagine* a line coming out of the bishop, crossing the squares f6, e5 and d4, till it reaches the knight at c3. That's as far as the direct influence of the

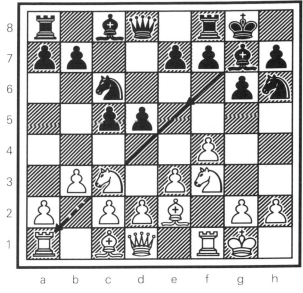

Diagram 20

bishop goes. When it gets past the knight, though, and reaches the squares b2 and a1, imagine the line now as a dotted line; this shows that the influence of the bishop is still there, but is less evident. Looking at the chessboard in this way, you will be less likely to make a move like Nb5 here, which loses the rook at a1.

The same applies to closing lines:

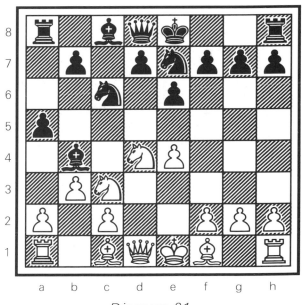

Diagram 21

In this position, Black had just played Bb4, attacking the knight at c3, and White was considering whether to defend it by playing either Bd2 or Bb2. From the point of view of simple material chess, both moves would be satisfactory, but here we have to start to look around and see how the rest of the board is affected. Turn your attention now to the *white knight at d4*, and the *white queen at d1*. Can you see the invisible piece of string that is connecting the knight to its protector at d1? And this string is necessary, for without it, the knight at d4 would fall to a capture from the black opponent at c6. Looking back to our original problem, the move Bd2 cuts the connecting string between the white queen and knight, and loses a piece, but on an entirely different square — d4, not c3!

From this piece of logic we can see that the best move is Bb2, but we can also see how much more complicated our thinking has to become, because we are starting to concentrate on other parts of the board as well.

Test

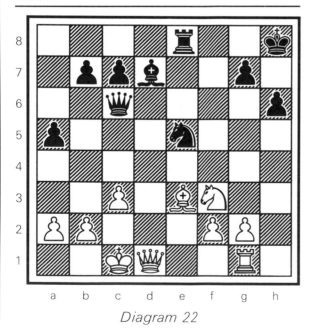

Diagram 22

In this position, would you play Be6 or Bf5? Give reasons for your answer.

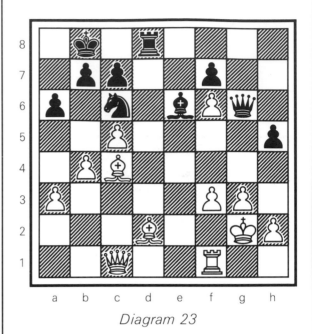

Diagram 23

The white pawn at f6 is threatened with capture. Would you defend it by Bc3 or Bg5? Why?

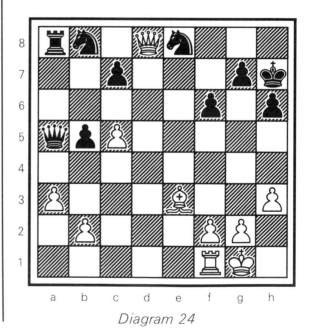

Diagram 24

Here the white queen at d8 threatens the knight at e8. Using MCSB, there is no way to save the piece, but using the idea of opening and closing lines, you can. How?

UFOs Test

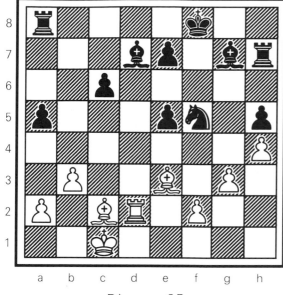

Diagram 25

Comment on each of these ways of meeting the threat to the bishop at d7.

Be8
Ra7
Nd6
Be6

In diagram 26, the white knight at b4 is threatened.

Analyse each of the defences given below:

Qb2	Nc2
Bc3	Nc6
Rb1	Rb3

Which of these defences is best?

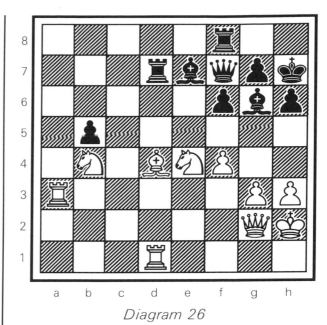

Diagram 26

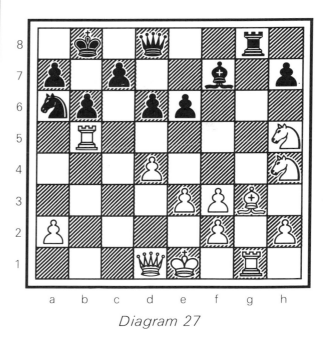

Diagram 27

White played the move Be5 here. This was a mistake. Can you say why?

-2-
FINISHING OFF

SUPPOSING you have managed to win more pieces than your opponent, how do you win the game?

The object of the game is to checkmate the king, but unless you are about a queen ahead, this will prove difficult.

If you are a queen ahead, you can just continue to attack and capture all his pieces, and then finish off with one of the basic mates, for example, the 'lawn mower', the queen mate, or the 'box mate'.

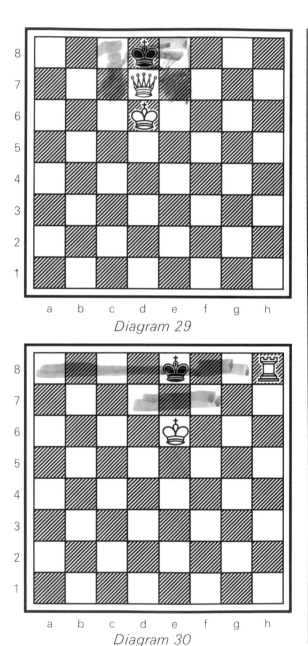

Diagram 29

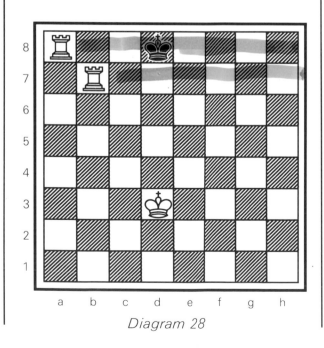

Diagram 28

Diagram 30

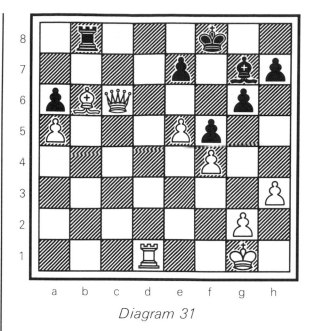

Diagram 31

In this position, White has an extra queen, so he should try to exchange as many pieces as possible, to weaken the enemy army. He can also attack the black king, as he still has his queen, the most powerful attacking piece.

White begins by exchanging off the rooks with:

| **1** | **Rd8+** | **Rxd8** |
| **2** | **Bxd8** | **Bh6** |

Black is attacking White's pawn at f4 with the remainder of his meagre army, but White need not bother to defend this and can go for a direct attack against the king.

3   Qe6

White finds a weak spot in the black position, and *focuses* his attack upon it.

The queen and bishop are now attacking e7, which is defended only once, by the black king at f8.

This type of focused attack on one square is very important in chess, and is one of the secrets of winning games.

3   ....   Bxf4

Diagram 32

In these positions, *Plan A*, would be to mop up all Black's remaining army, and then finish off with a basic mate.

But being a queen up, *Plan B* is also very attractive, to try and finish quickly with a mating attack against the black king. How would you continue in this position? (Solution on the next page.)

If you don't have an extra queen, but you do have extra material, like a rook or a knight more, it's much harder to get any mating attack going.

You should continue to try and exchange pieces, and secondly, you should try to queen a pawn.

Queening pawns

This is a great idea for winning with extra material; sometimes it even works when material is level!

First, though, you must understand what a *passed pawn* is.

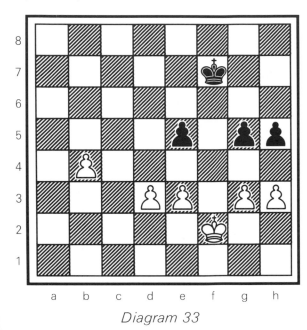

Diagram 33

In the diagram White has a passed pawn at b4. This is a likely candidate for queening, because there is no enemy pawn in front of it. On the other hand, the pawns at g3 and h3 are not passed, because they have enemy pawns directly in front of them.

What about the pawns at d3 and e3? Even though there is only one pawn facing them, neither pawn is passed, because if White plays his pawn from d3 to d4, it can be captured.

However, the pawn at d3 is a *potential* passed pawn, which is almost as good as an actual passed pawn. If White plays d4, after Black captures exd4, White can recapture by exd4 and obtain a passed pawn after all.

Example

Let's look at an example of winning pawns with extra material, and then queening them, from the London Under-12 championship, 1983.

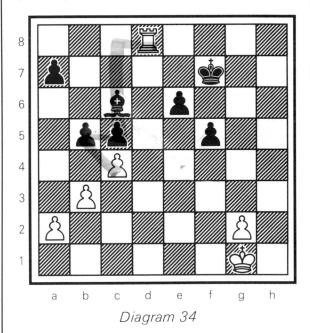

Diagram 34

In this position, White has a material advantage of a rook (5 points) against a bishop and pawn (4 points).

But White hasn't got any passed pawns, and in fact Black has the passed pawn, at e6.

Answer to diagram 32

1 Bxe7+ Kg7 (not 1 ... Ke8 2 Bc5+! Kd8 3 Bb6 mate) 2 Qf6+ Kh6 (2 ... Kg8 3 Qf8 mate) 3 g4! fxg4 4 hxg4 and Bf8 mate next move.

If White is going to get a passed pawn, he'll need to win some black pawns on the queenside, by attacking them with his rook.

His first move is to play:

1   Rc8

This attacks the bishop at c6, and the pawn in front of it.

1	....	Be4
2	Rxc5	bxc4
3	Rxc4	

Now White has two pawns to one on the queenside. He has not yet obtained a passed pawn, but he has got a potential passed pawn.

3	....	Kf6
4	Ra4	Bd5
5	Rxa7	

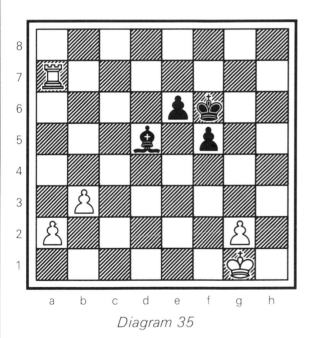

Diagram 35

With the capture of this vital pawn at a7, White has now, not just one potential passed pawn, but two actual passed pawns. These he proceeds to push down the board to queen, while Black tries to make something of his own passed pawn at e6.

5	....	e5
6	Ra6+	Be6
7	b4	Ke7
8	b5	Bc4
9	Ra7+	Kd8
10	b6	Kc8

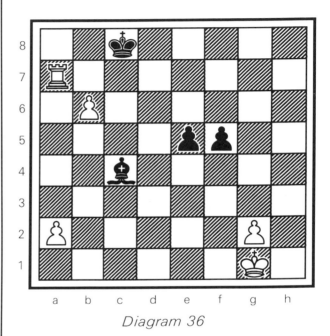

Diagram 36

The black king rushes over to stop the white pawns. In doing so he allows White the possibility of a fork by 11 Rc7+, attacking the king and bishop at the same time. However, White does not see this opportunity to shorten the game, and just continues with his main plan of pushing passed pawns — which will win in the end.

11	a4	e4
12	a5	e3
13	Re7	f4
14	Re4	e2
15	Kf2	Ba6

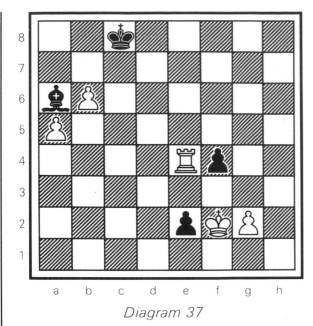

Diagram 37

Thanks to White's king on f2, the black pawn has got as far as it can go. Any move onto the queening square will result in capture.

However, Black has also managed to block White's pawns for the time being.

16   Rxf4

White captures an enemy pawn and ensures that he has another passed pawn, this time on the g-file. As the game goes, he does not need to use it.

16	.....	Kb7
17	Rf7+	Kc6

It was probably better to sit tight in front of the pawns, but even so the position was hopeless, because White has another passed pawn on the g-file that he could use.

18	Rc7+	Kd6
19	Ra7	

Forcing the bishop away from the defence of the b7 square. Now the white b-pawn can advance a step further.

19	....	Bb5
20	b7	Kc7

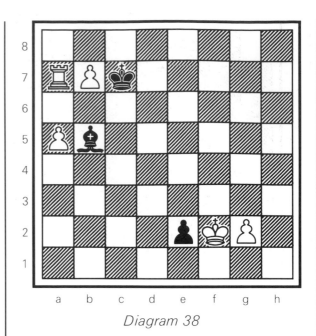

Diagram 38

Black still hangs on by the skin of his teeth, because if White now plays 21 b8(Q)+, Black can take it with his king.

21	a6	Bc6
22	Kxe2	Bxg2
23	Ra8	

The winning move. The only way Black can stop the pawns queening is by sacrificing his bishop for them, and then White can easily mate with rook and king against lone king using the box mate.

Test

(1) Name three ways of winning with a large material advantage.
(2) What methods should you use when you are a piece ahead?
(3) What effect does it have if there are queens on the board?
(4) What is a passed pawn?
(5) What is the difference between a potential passed pawn and a passed pawn?
(6) How can you create passed pawns?

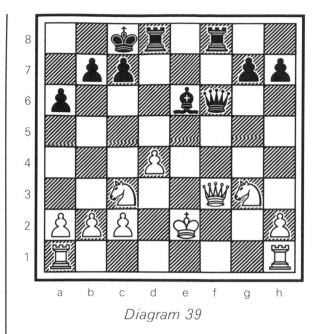

Diagram 39

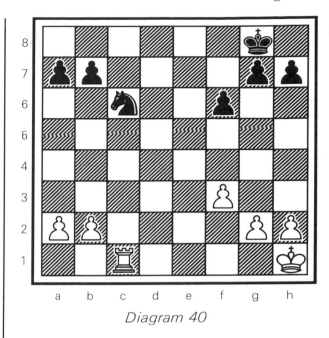

Diagram 40

(7) You are a knight ahead here as White. Would you (a) exchange queens? (b) avoid the exchange and play for the attack?

(8) You have a rook against a knight. What will be your winning plan?

–3–
POSITIONAL PLAY IN THE OPENING

Mobilisation

THE chess armies start the game inactive and far apart from each other.

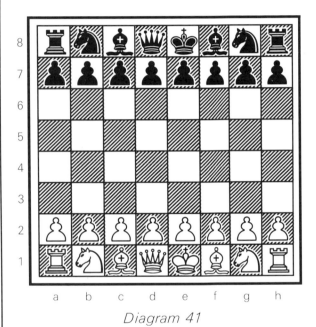

Diagram 41

If you look at the diagram, only the knights of all the pieces can move. All the other pieces are blocked by their own pawns.

So, to get the pieces out we need to move pawns.

Looking at the diagram, any pawn move would release a piece. For example, c4 would allow the queen to move out; h4 would allow the rook to move out. Can you see any moves which actually release *two* pieces?

Yes, e4 releases the bishop at f1 and the queen at d1, and d4 releases the queen at d1 and the bishop at c1.

When beginners play chess they often make three types of mistake. In the first place they might move only their pawns, and leave their strong fighting men at home; in the second place they might bring only one piece out and move it around aimlessly; in the third place they bring out only one or two pieces and try to attack with them.

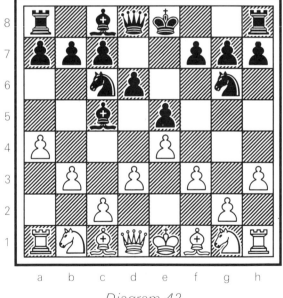

Diagram 42

After six moves: White has moved only pawns. His other pieces stay at home. Black has *released* his pieces with pawn moves.

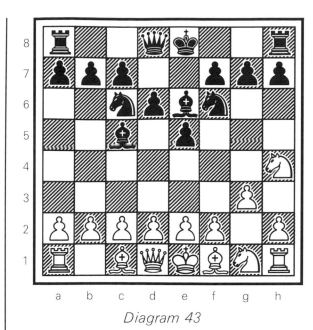

Diagram 43

After six moves: White has brought a knight out and moved it 5 times. Black has made two pawn moves and brought out four pieces.

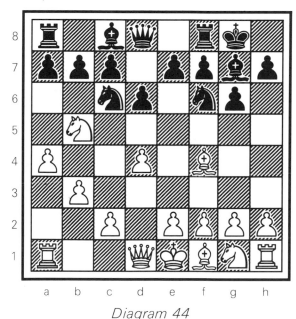

Diagram 44

After six moves: White brought out a bishop and knight and is trying to attack with them. But Black is armour-plated. Notice how well his d6 square is defended.

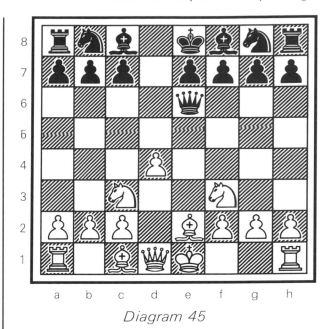

Diagram 45

After six moves: Black is attacking only with his queen. Meanwhile, White has brought out three pieces already.

So move some pawns in the opening to release pieces,

— bring the men out
— try not to move any man more than once in the opening
— don't attack too soon, before your army is properly mobilised.

Centralisation

We have learnt to bring our pieces out, but where do we put them? In fact, pieces work best in or near the centre of the board, because they control more squares and can get to any other part of the board that much more quickly from the centre.

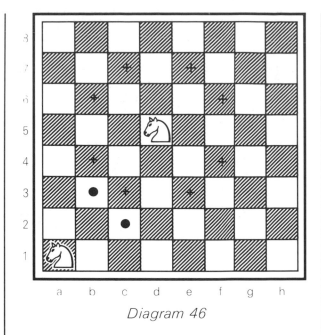

Diagram 46

The knight at a1 controls only two squares and would take three moves to get to the other side of the board. The d5-knight controls 8 squares in the centre and can reach other parts of the board more quickly.

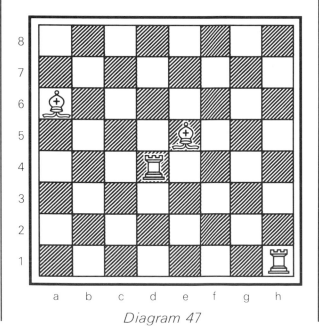

Diagram 47

The bishop attacks seven squares on the side and 13 in the middle.

An exception: the rook attacks 14 squares in the corner, 14 in the centre.

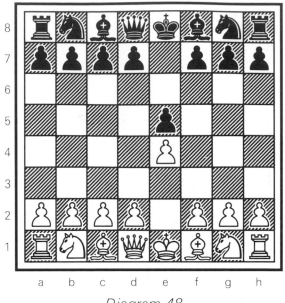

Diagram 48

Given the choice of playing the knight to e2, f3 or h3, White plays Nf3 as the knight controls the most squares there and is closest to the centre.

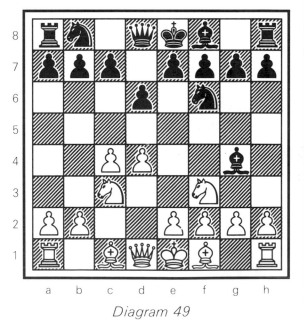

Diagram 49

Given a choice of Bd2, Be3, Bf4 and Bg5, White chooses Bf4 as the most central spot.

A further reason for placing pieces in the centre is that each key central square can only be occupied by one piece. If you can place your men in the centre first, there won't be room for the opponent's pieces and they will have to make do with interior positions.

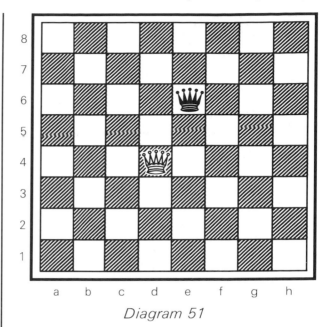

Diagram 51

The white queen stands like the sun on d4, shooting rays in all directions. The best Black can do is to stand a knight move away.

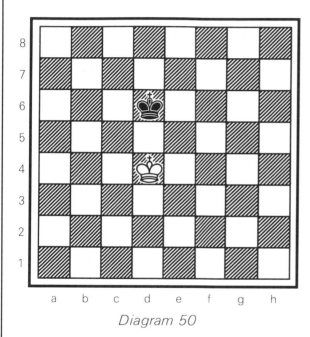

Diagram 50

The white king is in the centre and his opposite number has to skulk around the edges. Of course, because of the mating dangers to the king, we would not bring him into the middle until there were very few enemy men left. A centralised king can be a very important factor in the endgame.

King safety

One piece you do not want to develop is the king. In fact, the more pawns you move up in front of him, the greater danger he is in.

Be particularly careful about moving up for f- and g-pawns in the opening.

Here, White has even managed to get mated by playing 1 f3 followed by 2 g4, allowing the black queen to deliver check-mate on h4.

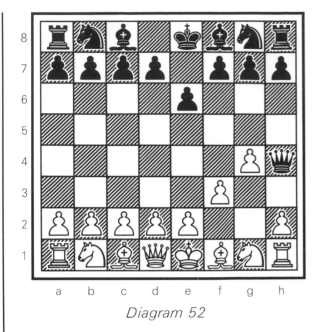

Diagram 52

One way of keeping the king safe is to castle.

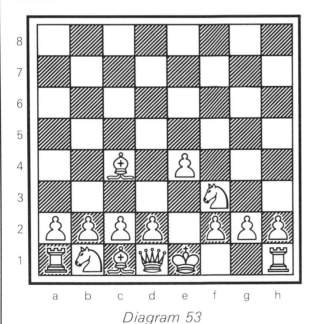

Diagram 53

White has prepared castling in only three moves. He played e4, Bc4, and Nf3, clearing the squares between king and rook. All these initial moves help to control the important central squares.

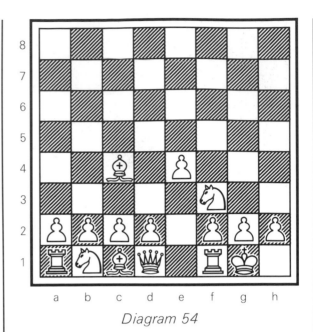

Diagram 54

Now White has castled, he will try not to move the pawns up in front of his king — the pawns at f2, g2, h2. They will stay at home as a shield for the monarch.

Test

Which answer to you think is the *most true*?

(1) In the next diagram:
(a) White is well developed because his pieces control more squares than at the start of the game.
(b) White is attacking too soon.
(c) White's king is in danger.
(d) White is badly developed because he has moved only pawns.

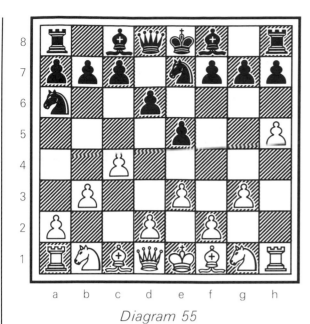

Diagram 55

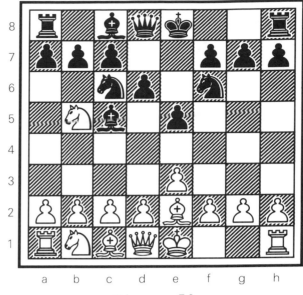

Diagram 56

(2) In the same diagram:

(a) Black has started well because he moved two pawns and then brought two pieces out.

(b) Black's knights are badly developed because one is far from the centre, and the other blocks his queen and bishop.

(c) Black should not have advanced the pawn in front of his king.

(3) In the next diagram:

(a) White has a strong attack.

(b) White has a bad position because he moved his knight too many times in the opening.

(c) White has not developed his knight close to the centre.

(4) In the same diagram:

(a) Black has a bad position because he has made too many pawn moves (two to White's one).

(b) Black should have castled by now.

(c) Black has developed his pieces centrally and has a good position.

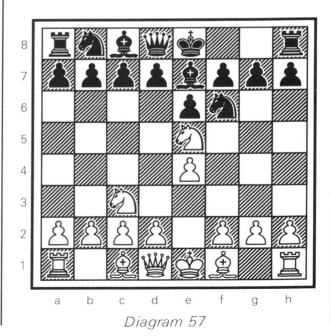

Diagram 57

(5) White has just played Ne5 (from f3).

(a) This is a strong attacking move.

(b) This is bad because White is moving a piece twice in the opening.

(c) This is good because it centralises the knight.

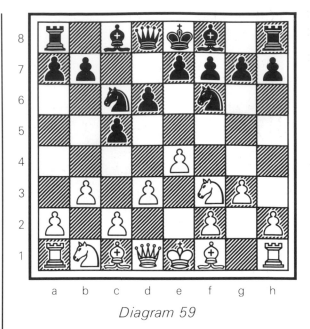

Diagram 59

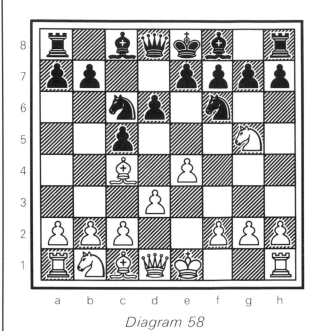

Diagram 58

(6) White has just played Ng5 (from f3). What do you think are the good points of the move and what are the bad points?

(7) In the next diagram:
White has just played b3.
What can you say about this move?

(8) In the same diagram:
Black played here g6.

(a) This is bad because Black is moving too many pawns.

(b) This is good because it helps to get the bishop out.

(c) Black should be attacking by now, and this is not an attacking move.

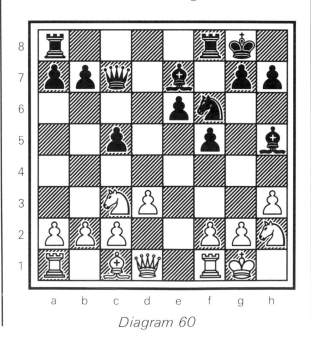

Diagram 60

(9) In diagram 60 White saw that his queen was under attack from the bishop at h5.

He played g4. Do you think this was a good or bad move and why?

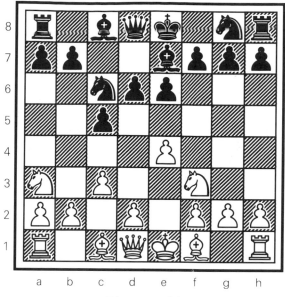

Diagram 61

(10) In this position as Black, I would like to play:

(a) Bf6, to put the bishop nearer the centre.

(b) Nf6, as this piece has not been moved yet.

(c) h5, to get my rook out.

(d) Nh6, to clear the position for castling.

–4–
NOTATION AND GAME ANALYSIS

English (or descriptive) notation

THIS way of naming the squares is still very popular in England and America, though it is gradually being superseded by the more precise algebraic notation used by the rest of the world.

It is as well to know it though. Many classic chess books were written in the descriptive notation, and it is unlikely that they will all be changed to algebraic. So if you don't know descriptive, you may cut yourself off from a vast chess heritage.

The squares are named after the pieces that stand on them at the beginning of the game. The square the king stands on is called king one and the square the rook stands on is called rook one. As there are two rooks, the square nearest the queen is called queen rook one, the square nearest the king is called king rook one. The same applies to the knights and bishops.

Shortening the names, we get the following picture:

QR1 QN1 QB1 Q1 K1 KB1 KN1 KR1

The square in front of the queen's rook is called QR2, and so on up to QR8.

Unfortunately, when you look at the board from Black's point of view (i.e. when Black makes a move) the numbers are all reversed, so White's K8 is Black's king one and vice versa.

A game would be written like this:

WHITE	BLACK
1 P–K4	**P–K4**

Pawn to king four. Pawn to king four (Black's).

2 B–B4

Bishop to bishop four. We don't say B–QB4, because the other bishop four square (KB4) cannot be reached by a bishop.

2 . . . . . N–QB3

Black knight to queen's bishop three.

3 Q–R5

White queen to rook five (king's rook five)

3 . . . . P–KR3

Black pawn to king's rook three.

4 QxBP mate

White's queen takes bishop's pawn checkmate.

Note how when we capture we don't say the square we have captured on, just the piece or pawn captured. In this case it was Black's king's bishop pawn that fell before the white queen.

Test paper: descriptive and algebraic notations

Game 1 should be translated from algebraic to descriptive.

Game 2 should be translated from descriptive to algebraic.

Game One

1	e4	e5
2	Nf3	Nf6
3	Nxe5	d6
4	Nf3	Nxe4
5	Nc3	Nxc3
6	dxc3	Be7
7	Be3	0–0
8	Qd2	Nd7
9	0–0–0	Ne5
10	Nd4	c5
11	Nb5	Qa5
12	a3	a6
13	Nxd6	Rd8
14	Nxc8	Rxd2
15	Nxe7+	Kf8
16	Rxd2	Kxe7
17	Rd5	Nd7
18	Be2	b6
19	Bf3	Nf8
20	Re5+	1–0

Game Two

1	P–K4	P–K4
2	N–KB3	N–QB3
3	B–N5	P–QR3
4	B–R4	N–KB3
5	0–0	B–K2
6	R–K1	P–QN4
7	B–N3	0–0
8	P–Q3	P–Q3
9	P–B3	N–QR4
10	B–B2	P–B4
11	QN–Q2	R–K1
12	N–B1	P–R3
13	N–N3	B–B1
14	P–KR3	B–N2
15	P–Q4	BPxP
16	PxP	PxP
17	NxP	R–B1
18	P–QN3	P–Q4
19	P–K5	N–K5
20	B–N2	RxP
21	P–B3	R–N4
22	N–B1	RxPch

White resigns

Game analysis

One of the reasons for writing your games down is that you can play over them afterwards and find out your mistakes. Of course, the next game you play may be completely different, so what use is it to find out where you went wrong in one particular game? Well, certain *types* of mistake turn up again and again and by learning to spot them, you can prevent them occurring.

They are:

(1) Basic material errors, such as putting a piece on a square on which it can be taken or leaving an attacked piece undefended.

(2) Higher material errors, which are of three types:

(a) leaving a piece unguarded

(b) making a mistake with a focused attack.

(c) losing material by opening or closing a line.

These three types were described at the beginning of this course.

In analysing beginner's games, we use special symbols to indicate mistakes:

M+   means material gain, or avoiding material errors.

M——   stands for basic material error.

M—(U)   means higher material error, leaving a piece unguarded.

M—(F)   means higher material error, making a mistake with a focused attack.

M—(O)   means higher material error, losing material through opening or closing a line.

We shall now go through a game together and try to spot and correctly describe the errors made. You might wonder at this stage why so much emphasis is made on mistakes; the reason is that chess is a very precise game, touch-move is the rule, and this can be very cruel; so it is better to see the disasters before they occur!

1	e4	Nf6
2	Nc3	e5
3	Nf3	Nc6
4	Be2	Bc5
5	Nd5?	

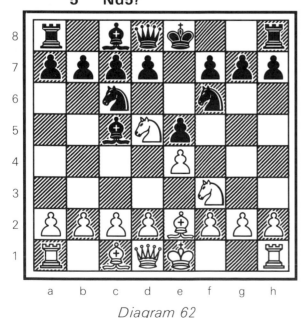

Diagram 62

This is the first mistake. White moves the knight without realising that it was guarding the pawn at e4. This is a higher material error, not a basic material error, because White did not lose the piece he moved; M—(U)

5 ...   Nxe4

Black captures the pawn at e4, and also makes an attack of his own — a focused attack of bishop and knight against the f2 square. Will White see it?

6   Bd3?

No, he doesn't see the threat, otherwise he would have played 7 0–0, which guards the f2 square a second time; M—(F)

6   ...   b6??

This move is doubly bad. In the first place, Black fails to capture at f2. Omitting to take advantage of your opponent's errors is as bad as the original mistake, and is marked in exactly the same way. So Black gets a M—(F) as well for this move.

But 6 ... b6 is also a basic material error. White's last move made a direct attack against the knight at e4.

So for 6 ... b6 Black is marked M—(F) and M——.

7   Rf1

M——; White overlooks that he can capture at e4.

7   ...   Nb4

Black still does not notice that his knight can be captured at e4, but as we have already mentioned this on the previous move, we do not continually penalise the same mistake. It is anyway a feature of beginner's games that captures are frequently left 'on' for several moves, unnoticed by either player.

Black also leaves the e5 pawn unguarded, so we should mark this move M—(U); however, White cannot capture at e5 immediately because his own knight at d5 is now under attack!

We can see that beginner's games can quite easily become fiendishly complicated as errors mount up!

8   Bxe4!

M+; White makes a good capture, winning the knight at e4 *and* defending his knight at d5 at the same time.

8   ...   Ba6

Attacking the rook at f1.

9   Rg1

White moves away; M+.

9   ...   Qb8
10   Nxb4

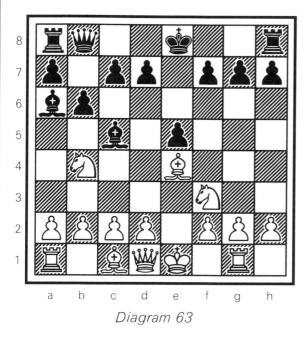

Diagram 63

By making this capture, White also discovers an attack against the rook at a8, so after Black plays 10 ... Bxb4, White can win material by 11 Bxa8. Does this mean that Black has made a *material* error? No; there are other ways to lose pieces besides making material errors. Black's 9 ... Qb8 was a *tactical* error, which we mark by T––, T standing for tactical. At this stage of the Course we are not dealing with

tactics, so we will not mark them. I'll just point out that tactics usually involve a double attack, whereas material chess concentrates on a single attack. Mistakes in material chess are always avoidable; the one move you have at your disposal is ample. In the diagram position, however, Black needs two moves to avoid material loss, and hence his *previous* move was the tactical mistake.

10   ....   Bxb4

The best of a bad job.

11   Bxa8   M+   Qxa8   M+
12   Nxe5   M+

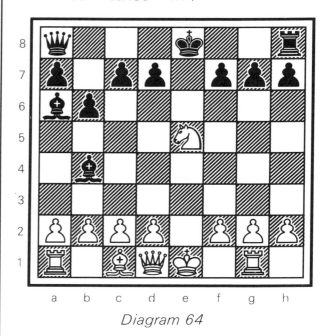

Diagram 64

White is now a full rook ahead, and he picks up another pawn here. In this case, it is an unwise choice, because Black could now checkmate him in two moves by 12 ... Qe4+ 13 Qe2 Qxe2++.

Do we hence mark White's last move as a material error? No, it is a mistake, but not a *material* mistake, as it loses the game, but no pieces. We have another symbol for moves that affect the king, and that is X (standing for exposure).

X— and X— — mean attacking or defensive errors, and X+ means a good attacking or defensive move. However, this analysis does not concern these types of moves, we are just looking for material mistakes.

12	...	Bd6

Black also misses the mating attack.

13	Nf3

M+; a good material move, though Black still has his mate threat.

13	...	h5
14	a3	c5
15	c3	g6
16	b4	cxb4
17	axb4	

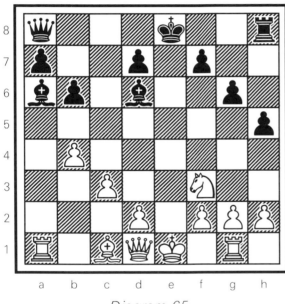

Diagram 65

Nothing much has happened over the last few moves; the mate threat is still on, and a pawn has been exchanged on each side. However, White's last capture was not entirely harmless; it opened a line of attack from the rook at a1 to the bishop at a6. Will Black see it?

17	...	Be7

No. This loses the bishop at a6; M—(O).

18	Rxa6	M+
18	...	Qc6

Another error, leaving the a7 pawn unguarded; M—(U).

19	Rxa7	M+
19	....	d5
20	d4?	

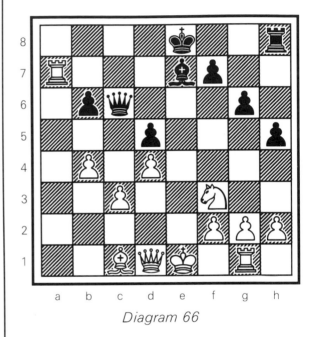

Diagram 66

White's last move, d4, is also a higher material error, leaving the c3 pawn unguarded; M—(U)

20	...	0–0?

M—(U); omitting to play 20 ... Qxc3+. and

M—(U); leaving the bishop at e7 unguarded. White could now play 21 Rxe7.

After playing through this game, and having understood the various symbols involved, you are now ready to analyse the two games given next.

In your analysis, only use the material chess symbols, not those for tactical and attacking chess.

Test

Game One

1	e4	d5
2	Qf3	dxe4
3	Qxe4	Nf6
4	Qf3	Bg4
5	Qf4	e6
6	Nc3	Bb4
7	Nb5	a6
8	Nxc7+	Kf8
9	Nxa8	Bd6
10	Qg5	h6
11	Qe3	Nc6
12	h3	Qxa8
13	hxg4	Nxg4
14	Qe2	h5
15	Nh3	Nh2
16	Ng5	f6
17	Nxe6+	Kf7
18	b3	Qe8
19	Qb5	Qxe6+
20	Qe2	Re8

Game Two

1	e4	e5
2	Na3	Nf6
3	d3	d5
4	Bg5	dxe4
5	Bxf6	Qxf6
6	dxe4	Qf4
7	Bb5+	c6
8	Bd3	Bg4
9	Nf3	Na6

10	g3	Qh6
11	Nh4	Bxd1
12	Rxd1	b6
13	Nf5	Qe6
14	Nxg7	Bxg7
15	0–0	Qd6
16	Bxa6	b5
17	Rxd6	Rc8
18	Bxc8	0–0
19	Rfd1	Rxc8
20	R6d3	c5
21	Nxb5	

Test games

Chess is an action game. What you learn in this course, you should be able to do in your own games. So for this part of the course, you need to be able to play and record 3 games of at least 25 moves without any Basic material errors (losing the piece you moved or missing a direct attack) *or* Higher material errors (the UFOs). The opponent can be another person or a chess computer, and you could ask a stronger player to mark your games for you.

Do not be surprised, or disheartened, if your games resemble the beginners' games shown above, with the blunders piling up one after another! Chess is very complicated, so you must be prepared to keep playing, and to admit mistakes if you want to improve your play.

-5-
KING AND PAWN ENDINGS

YOU already know the basic mates, and in the 'finishing off' section, you learnt how to win with a large material advantage, and how to create passed pawns and make new queens.

Now we are going to study endgames with no pieces on the board, apart from kings and pawns. Obviously, these games will all end in draws, unless one side can get a pawn through, and here you are going to learn how to queen them — and how to stop them.

Square

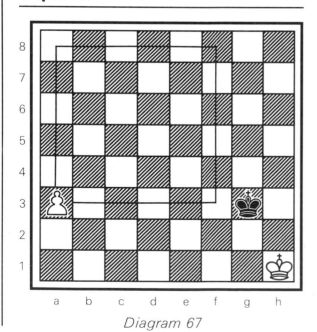

Diagram 67

In this position, a black king is trying to catch a white pawn before it reaches the eighth rank. Instead of saying to yourself 'I go here, he goes there, I go here . . .' and so on, there is a simpler way to work it out by drawing an imaginary square which stretches from the pawn to the end rank, and sideways from the pawn the same number of squares.

The rule is 'if the king can move into the square, then he can catch the pawn'.

Here, if it is Black's move, he steps into the square — either with Kf3, or Kf4, and can catch the pawn.

However, if it is White to move, he plays 1 a4, and *now the square has become smaller*. It only stretches as far as e4, so Black cannot catch the pawn.

The overworked king

Here the black king can easily stop both pawns, but not at the same time.

While he is off catching one pawn, he steps out of the square of the other pawn, and it runs through to the queening square.

| 1 | b5 | Kd6 |

Must stop this pawn.

| 2 | g5 | Ke6 |

Runs back to catch the other one.

| 3 | b6 | Kd6 |

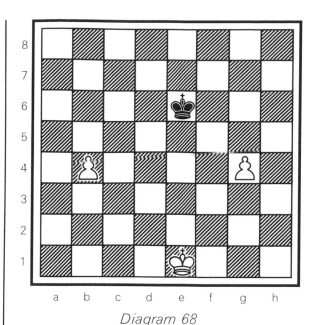

Diagram 68

Now the other one's going through.

4   g6   Ke6

He's out of the square now.

5   b7

and this pawn queens.

Active kings

When both kings are active, one side can protect its pawn, and escort it to the queening square, but the other side can still draw if it can get its king in front of the pawn.

In this position, Black's king is tied to the back rank. But he's the only thing stopping the white pawn from queening. If it's Black to move here, he must move out from his safe hole, by Ke7, whereupon White plays Kc7, and queens his pawn next move.

If it were White to play, he only has one move that does not lose a pawn, and that

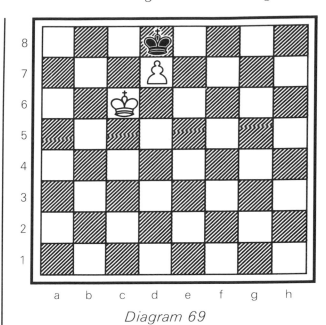

Diagram 69

is Kd6. Unfortunately, this is stalemate, so Black escapes with a draw.

These positions can be so precisely analysed, that even from a position 10 or 20 moves back, one can immediately tell if the game will end in a draw by stalemate, or whether the pawn will queen.

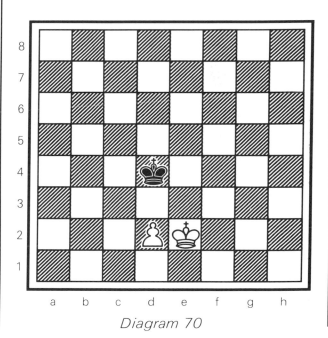

Diagram 70

This position, if defended correctly, will always be drawn, even though the pawn is only starting on its travels.

Let's move the pawn and kings up a few files, assuming that Black manages to maintain the same position with his king in front of the pawn.

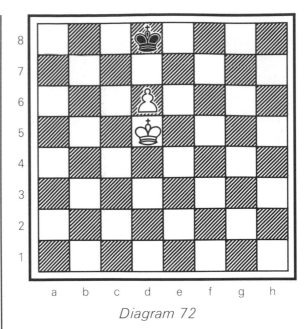

Diagram 72

3   Ke6   Ke8!

Now White has come in, Black takes a face to face position, and if White now plays:

4   d7+   Kd8
5   Kd6

it is stalemate.

Of course, White can footle around with his king and pawn before making the final advance, but Black is quite safe if he remembers this one idea — when White moves to the sixth row next to his pawn, Black must be ready to face him with his king.

The idea in the last diagram is called *taking the opposition* and, strangely enough, it is the player who has to move who has the disadvantage. Usually having the move is an advantage in chess, but in king and pawn endings everything is upside down.

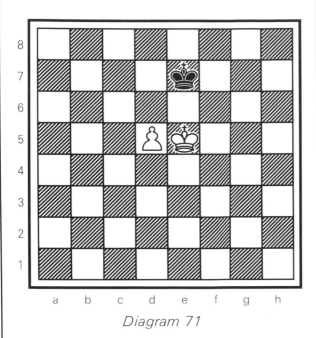

Diagram 71

White or Black to play — it doesn't matter here, the result is still the same.

Let's say White moves first:

1   d6+   Kd7

Black stays as close as he can to the pawn.

2   Kd5

Now it's Black's big moment. He has three squares to retreat to. If he chooses one of them, he draws; if he chooses either of the other two, he loses.

2   ...   Kd8!

This is the drawing move. Black steps directly back, getting ready to face White as he comes in.

One step back

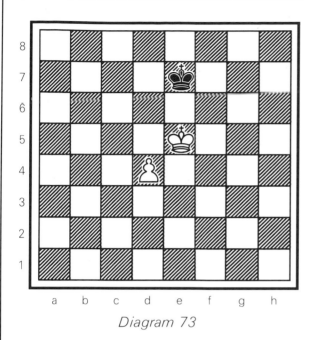

Diagram 73

Here the pawn is one step back — on d4, not d5.

Now whether the game is drawn or not depends on who has the opposition — and don't forget that we are in topsy-turvy land. That means it's the person who doesn't have to move.

If it's Black to move, he has to step aside, and White can push his king forward to control the queening square, and then bring the pawn up.

Black plays:

1	....	Kd7
2	Kd5!	Ke7
3	Kc6	Kd8
4	Kd6	Ke8
5	Kc7!	

Controlling the queening square.

| 5 | .... | Ke7 |
| 6 | d5 | |

and the pawn goes through.

What happens if it's White to move? That means he cannot push the black king aside; if he plays 1 Kd5 Black answers 1 ... Kd7, 2 Kc5 Kc7.

Of course, White can always play his pawn down from d4 to d5 on move 1, but then we get back into our previous position, which we know can always be drawn.

It is interesting how the *opposition* is used in different ways, depending on whether you are defending or attacking. If you are attacking, you use the opposition to advance your king further. If you are defending, the opposition helps you to prevent your enemy from advancing his king.

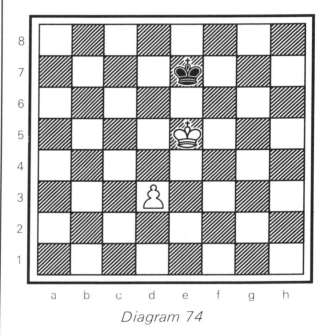

Diagram 74

With the pawn two steps back it doesn't matter whose move it is because White can always waste one move with his pawn and hand the undesirable honour of moving back to Black.

For example, Black to play here (which means White has the opposition) plays 1 ... Kd7, and White just wins by pushing him aside and bringing his pawn to the queening square: 2 Kd5 Ke7 3 Kc6 Ke6 4 d4! Ke7 5 d5 Kd8 6 Kd6! (not the careless

6 d6?? which draws) 6 ... Ke8 7 Kc7 and White wins.

With White to move he simply gains the opposition by throwing in the move 1 d4. Then Black has to give way, and White wins as we have shown before.

The rook pawn exception

When the pawn is on the edge file, none of all this applies. If Black can get his king in front of the pawn, he can always draw. And sometimes he can draw even when he *can't* get his king in front of the pawn!

The culprit in this case is stalemate. The king is at his weakest in the corner, controlling only three squares, and it is easy to take these squares away from him.

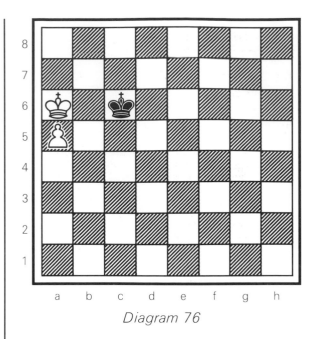

Diagram 76

What about this position? Isn't this a win? After all, the black king cannot get in front of the pawn.

No, it's still a draw, because *White* will be stalemated if he tries to push his pawn through. White's king will be trapped by the edges of the board, by his own pawn — and by the black king.

| 1 | Ka7 | Kc7 |
| 2 | a6 | Kc8 |

Now White can come out of the corner by 3 Kb6, but it would be no use — Black would simply enter it himself by 3 ... Kb8.

| 3 | Ka8 | Kc7 |
| 4 | a7 | Kc8 |

Stalemate!

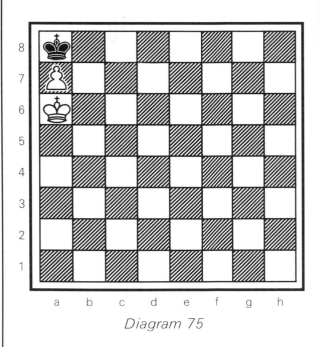

Diagram 75

Take a look at this position. It doesn't matter who is to move, it's still stalemate, unless White decides to give up his pawn.

King against two pawns

This is normally hopeless. We show two common cases.

(a) king against connected passed pawns.

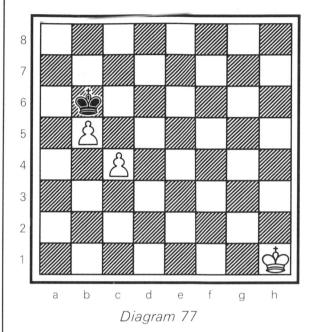

Diagram 77

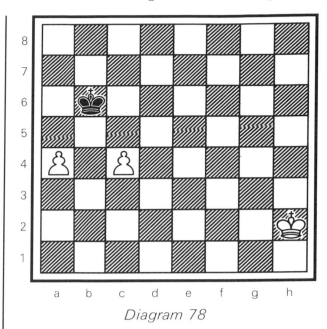

Diagram 78

With White's king far away, it looks like the pawns will fall to Black's gobbling king. But in a curious way they protect each other.

If Black here plays 1 ... Kc5, he is not really threatening to capture White's c-pawn, because that would let the other one through.

However, if Black sits tight, the pawns themselves cannot advance; White would need to bring his king up to help the pawns queen.

(b) split passed pawns.

The pawns look even more vulnerable here, but all the same, Black cannot catch one without the other slipping through.

If he plays 1 Kc5, White answers 2 a5! and Black must oscillate back to c6.

Now neither side can make progress, because if White now plays 3 a6??, Black can win both pawns safely, starting with 3 ... Kb6.

Once again, White needs to bring his king up to help the pawns through.

Test

(1) What is meant by 'the square' in king and pawn endings?
(2) If the king is 'in the square' he can always catch a pawn. True or false?

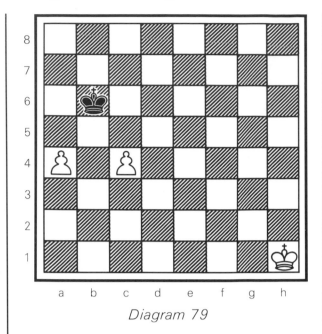

Diagram 79

(3) Is this position a win for White or a draw? If so, why?

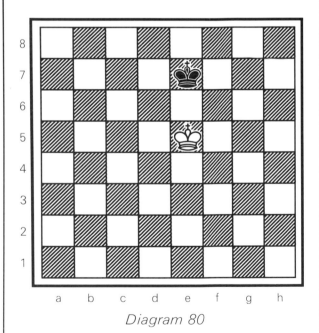

Diagram 80

(4) In this position, would it be better to have a white pawn at d4 or d5? Give reasons for your answer.

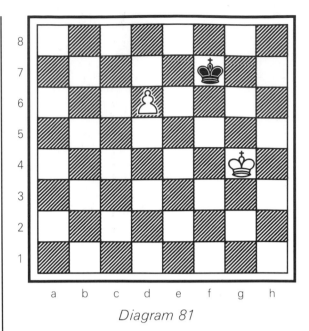

Diagram 81

(5) Can White win in this position? Give a sequence of moves to explain your answer. (It's White to move).

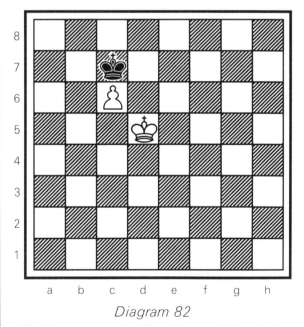

Diagram 82

(6) Your move for Black here. What is the correct defence and why?

(7) What haven't you got when you have got the opposition?

(8) Why is the opposition useful in defence and attack?

(9) If you were two pawns up in an ending, would you prefer them to be (a) connected

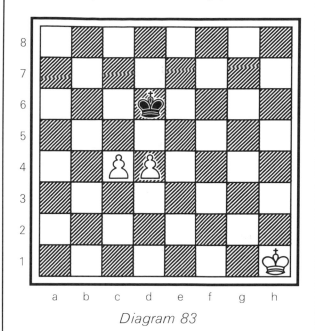

Diagram 83

(b) split

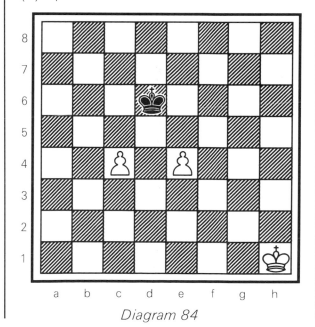

Diagram 84

(c) doubled?

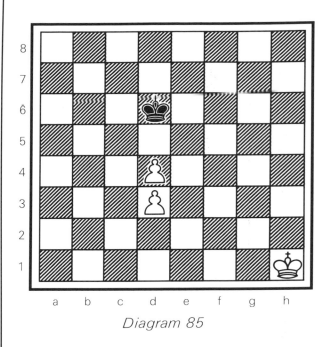

Diagram 85

(10) Why is a pawn on the a- or h-file such a menace in king and pawn endings?

Winning by decoy

This is an interesting idea that almost never fails. If you have a passed pawn on one side of the board, you can use it to lure the enemy king away, and then you invade on the other side, eat up all his pawns, and then queen your own pawns.

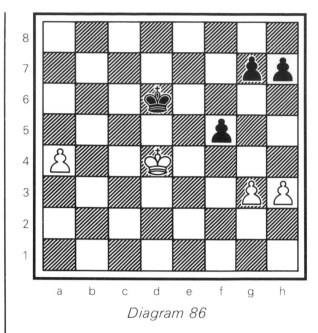

Diagram 86

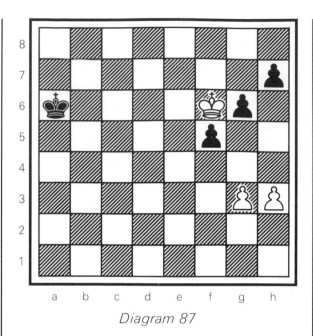

Diagram 87

Here we have our pawn on the wing, and the only thing that can stop it is the black king.

But the black king is overworked; he can't stop the white pawn queening and prevent the white king from invading his kingside pawns. At the moment, Black's king stops White from moving Ke5. But White can draw him away from the centre by the magnetic pull of his pawn on the a-file . . .

1   a5   g6

Black is still in the square, so he doesn't need to chase white's pawn yet.

2   a6   Kc6

Black must step into the square now, otherwise the pawn queens.

3   Ke5!

And now the king marches in!

3   . . .   Kb6

Black hopes to be able to capture White's pawn and then rush back to the other side to help his army.

4   Kf6   Kxa6

How should White continue now?

It would be a fatal mistake for White to go for the pawn at h7 too soon. If he plays 5 Kg7 (there's many a slip . . .) Black actually wins by playing 5 . . . g5!, followed by . . . . f4, and White cannot stop the pawn queening.

5   h4!

White first fixes the black pawns with this move, and prevents Black from ever making a passed pawn of his own.

5   . . .   Kb6
6   Kg7

Now the little pawns are defenceless against the ravenous monarch.

6   . . .   Kc6
7   Kxh7   Kd6
8   Kxg6   Ke5

Black saves one pawn, but now the white h-pawn goes through.

9   h5 and White wins.

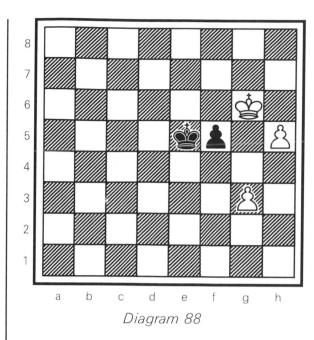

Diagram 88

Winning with the opposition

Even without a decoy, or 'outside passed pawn' as it is called, you can often win king and pawn endings if you can take the opposition, and force the enemy king to give way.

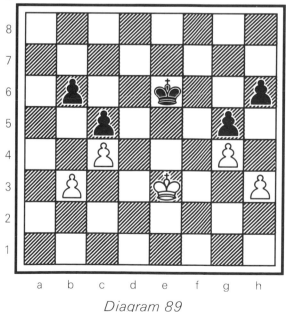

Diagram 89

In this position, *whoever moves* wins, because they can take the opposition.

White to play goes 1 Ke4, and if Black now retreats with 1 ... Kd6, White heads for the kingside pawns with 2 Kf5; or if Black goes the other way with ... Kf6, White then attacks the queenside with Kd5.

If it was Black to move in the diagram, he would win by playing 1 ... Ke5 with the same idea.

The opposition in defence

We've seen how the opposition can be used to advance our king and break through the opponent's defence. In a desperate situation, it can also be used in defence, to hold up the advance of the enemy king.

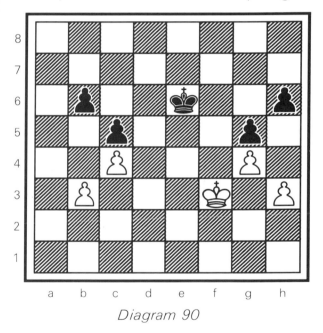

Diagram 90

This position is identical to the last one, except for the white king which is on f3, not e3. If it's White's turn he wins by **1 Ke4**, as before. But what if it is Black to move?

Black should play here 1 ... Ke5, and things look very threatening, because the next move is going to be **1 ... Kd4**, followed by ... Kc3, attacking the white pawn at b3.

But just in time, White steps in the way, *taking the opposition* with **2 Ke3**, and saying 'thus far and no further'. Now Black has to retreat and he needs to choose his move carefully. If he plays 1 ... Ke6??, White's defensive opposition is turned into an attacking opposition by 3 Ke4!, when Black must let the white king in on one wing or another.

No, Black steps back with **2 ... Kf6!** (or d6), being ready to take the opposition himself if White advances.

3 Ke4   Ke6!

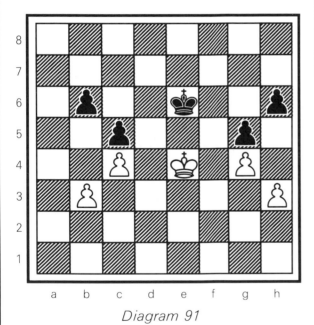

Diagram 91

4 Kf3!

The right retreat.

4 ...   Ke5
5 Ke3!

and this dance ends in a draw.

Winning by paralysis

Loss of movement is one of the signs of death, and pawns, because of their peculiar form of movement, often suffer this fate.

Pawns cannot retreat; nor can they advance if a man stands in their way. We can use this form of paralysis to win king and pawn endings, even when the enemy seems to have held up our king by using the defensive opposition.

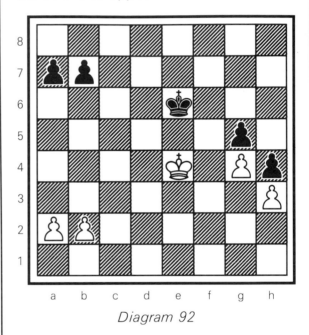

Diagram 92

White is clearly the aggressor here. His king stands poised to invade at f5 or d5 should the black king give way. But the black king has no intention of giving way, so it all depends on the queenside pawns, which will soon run out of moves as they come together.

The question is, who will run out of moves first?

If it is White to move when the pawns become blocked, Black can keep the defensive opposition and draw. If it is Black to move then he must lose.

Have a look at this position before reading on. If it is Black to move — what result?

If it is White to move first — does he win?

If you have worked out the position correctly, you'll have discovered that the same rule applies in this topsy-turvy world of the king and pawn ending — *whoever moves first does worst*.

For example: White to move:
1 b3 a5 2 a3 b5 3 a4 b4 draw.
1 a4 a5 2 b3 b6 draw.
Black to move:
1 ... b6 2 a4 a6 3 b4 a5 2 b5 and White wins.

The antidote to paralysis

The antidote to the paralysis just seen is to keep at least one piece on the board. This active unit can move back and forth and prevent further deterioration into a critical state.

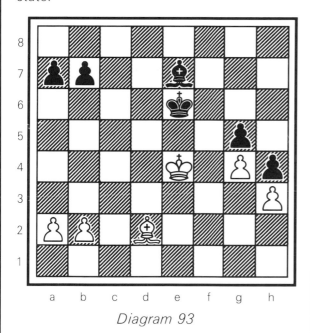

Diagram 93

The addition of an extra bishop on both sides restores Black's position to health, as the bishop supplies 'breath' to the black army by shifting back and forth on the diagonal d8–f6.

The general rule is, if you are defending, keep out of a king and pawn ending! It would be fatal, for example, for Black to head for a king and pawn ending with 1 Bc3 Bf6?? 2 Bxf6 Kxf6 3 Kd5 Ke7 4 Ke5 and White wins easily.

The pawn race

Often in king and pawn endings both sides are able to queen a pawn, usually on different sides of the board. What happens is that one king, using the opposition, is able to invade on one wing; and the other is now free to attack the pawns on the other wing.

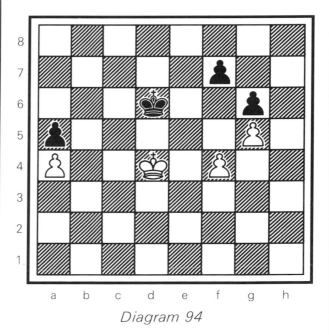

Diagram 94

Here there are pawns on both sides; Black is to play, which means that White has the opposition.

Now should Black give way by 1 ... Ke6, allowing 2 Kc5, or should he move to c6, allowing Ke5?

The way to work out these positions is to do the analysis separately. It's much less tiring. For example, after 1 ... Kc6, you first look at the white moves — the king goes e5, f6, xf7, xg6, then pawn f5, f6, f7, f8. That takes eight moves.

Meanwhile, Black would play Kc5, b4, xa4, b3, then pawn a4, a3, a2, a1 — also eight moves.

As both sides take the same number of moves, they both queen at the same time, which means the game may be a draw. If White had queened a move or two before Black, he could have stopped the enemy pawn queening with his queen.

We could also do the same analysis for Black's other move in the diagram, Ke6.

White then plays Kc5, b6, xa5, b6, then pawn a5, a6, a7, a8 — eight moves.

Black plays Kf5, xf4, xg5, then pawn f5, f4, f3, f2, f1 — also eight moves.

This method of analysis may only be the starter for a deeper search of the position.

For example, when Black plays 1 ... Kc6, White may not be satisfied with the straight pawn race, and instead decide to use the opposition to win the pawn at a5, by 2 Kc4 Kb6 3 Kd5!

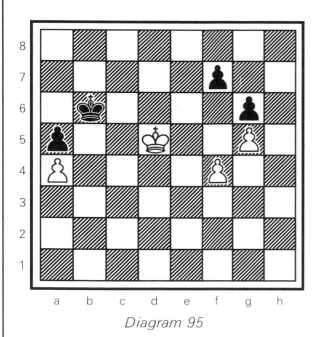

Diagram 95

Or looking again at the variation (from *diagram 94*) 1 ... Ke6, he may think of

trying to get his king back into the square of the enemy black pawn half-way through the pawn race — for example, after 2 Kc5 Kf5 3 Kb5 Kxf4 4 Kxa5 Kxg5 5 Kb4.

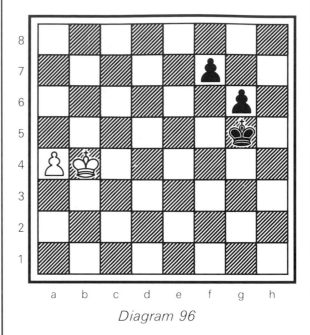

Diagram 96

A very complicated position but in fact White is still winning after 5 ... f5 6 a5 f4 7 Kc3 Kg4 8 Kd3 Kg3 9 a6 f3 10 a7 f2 11 Ke2!! Kg2 12 a8=Q+ Kg1 13 Qf8 winning Black's f-pawn.

These examples show that even simple-looking positions can involve very tricky tactics in which good calculation is very important.

Winning the pawn race

Sometimes pawn races can be very close, but even when both sides queen at almost the same time, there are still ways to win.

(1) *controlling the queening square*

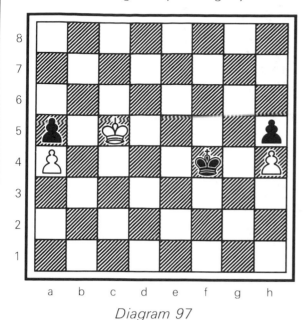

Diagram 97

It's White to move.

Both sides take seven moves to capture and queen. Does this mean that the position is a draw? No, on White's seventh move he queens and his new queen attacks Black's queening square (*Diagram 98*).

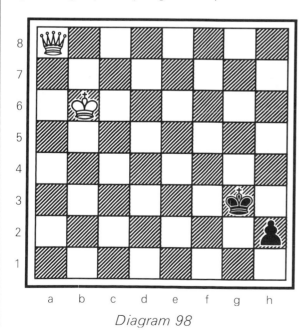

Diagram 98

Here Black cannot queen, so he brings his king to f2, but White then moves 8 Qh1 (it's vital to stop the black king reaching g1, where it controls the queening square) and White then wins by bringing his king up towards Black's last pawn.

(2) *a check gains a move*

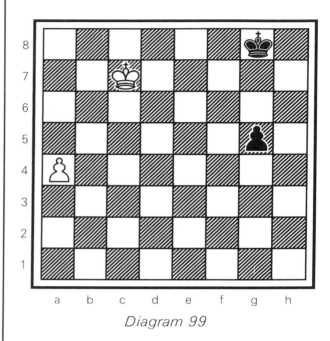

Diagram 99

White to play.

Here neither side can stop the enemy pawn, and the race looks even. However, White will queen *with check* and this gives him time to stop the black pawn.

(3) *skewering*

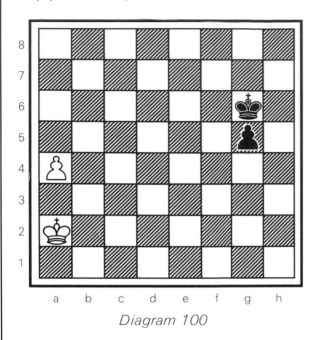

Diagram 100

This looks like an even game as well; both sides make a queen on the same move — but then White can win. Can you see how?

He can use a skewer, playing 5 Qg8ch, which wins the black queen at g1.

Look for all these possibilities, which can often make the difference between a win and a draw.

Queen against king and pawn

This is really the fourth way of winning the pawn race. It shows you how you can win against a pawn about to queen, *even when the enemy king controls the queening square.*

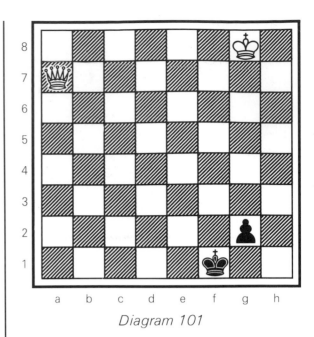

Diagram 101

White to play.

In this position, if Black's king were on e2, then White could win easily by playing 1 Qg1, putting the queen in front of the pawn, and then bringing his king up.

But here that is impossible, and the only way White seems to be able to stop the black pawns queening is by giving an endless series of checks — which would also be a draw.

And yet there is a way to win.

If only Black could be persuaded to put his king in front of the pawn, then the white king could come into the attack.

It seems unlikely that Black will do anything so stupid, but in fact with best play White can *force* this to happen.

The first task is to bring the white queen close to the king and pawn by a series of checks.

1	Qa1+	Kf2
2	Qd4+	Kf1
3	Qf4+	Ke2

Now comes the most important

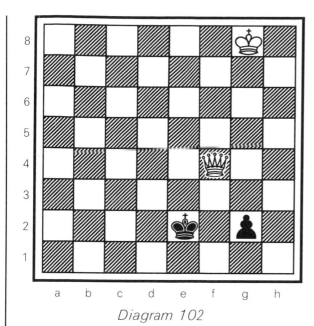

Diagram 102

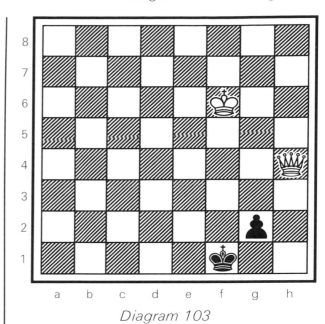

Diagram 103

moment — the part that students usually get wrong.

4   Qg3!

This move — which is not a check — forces the king back to the f1 square.

4   ...   Kf1
5   Qf3+!

White is checking from the closest possible distance, and unless Black wants to lose his pawn, *he must move underneath*.

5   ...   Kg1

Phase 1 is complete, and White can now bring his king a step forward.

6   Kg7   Kh2

Black moves his king out and renews the threat of queening. But all White does is to chase him underneath again!

7   Qf2!   Kh1
8   Qh4+   Kg1
9   Kf6   Kf1

The process continues until White's king is close enough:

10 Qf4+ Ke2 11 Qg3! Kf1 12 Qf3+ Kg1 13 Kg5 Kh2 14 Qf2 Kh1 15 Qh4+ Kg1 16 Kf4 Kf1 17 Qh3 (pinning) Kf2 18 Qf3+ Kg1 19 Kg3 Kh1 20 Qxg2 mate.

Drawing with a pawn on the seventh

The winning method described above works in all cases except when the pawn is on the a, c, f or h-files. The reason in these cases is the same — stalemate.

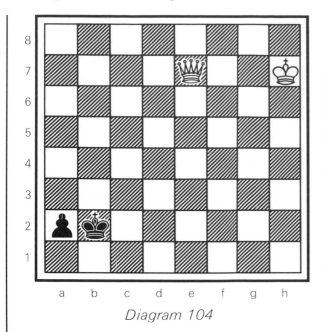

Diagram 104

Here if White tries to force the king in front of the pawn, Black is only too happy to oblige.

1   Qb4+   Ka1!
2   Kg6

Stalemate!

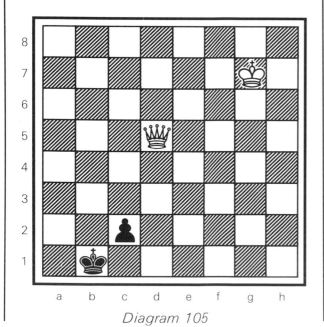

Diagram 105

And here the problem is that White *can't* force Black in front of the pawn.

1   Qb3+

Expecting 1 ... Kc1

1   ...   Ka1!!
2   Qxc2

Stalemate!

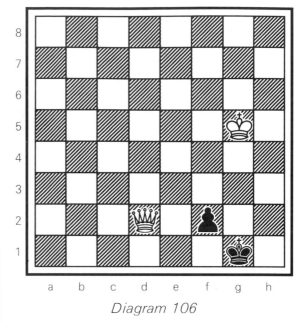

Diagram 106

And here, finally, is a little puzzle. We know from the previous section that White cannot chase the black king underneath the pawn because it is an f-pawn. But the white king is fairly close; so there is a way for White to win by a different method — 1 Kg4! f1(Q) 2 Kg3!! forces mate or wins the black queen.

Test

(1) What is an outside passed pawn?
(2) How can it be used to advantage?
(3) Name three winning methods in king and pawn endings.

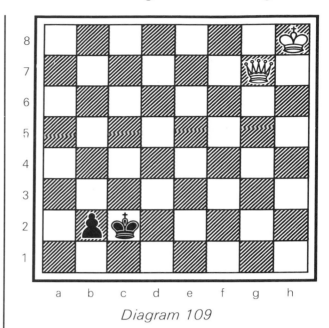

Diagram 107

(4) How would you defend this position as Black. Name the method used.

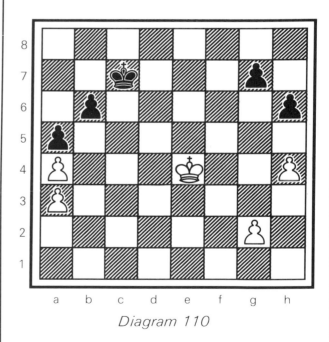

Diagram 109

(6) How does White win here? What method does he use?

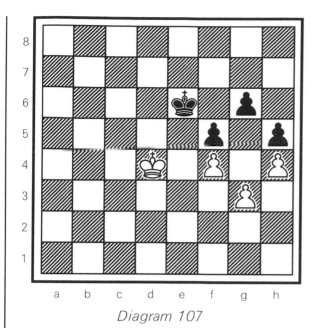

Diagram 108

(5) What is the winning move for White here? Why?

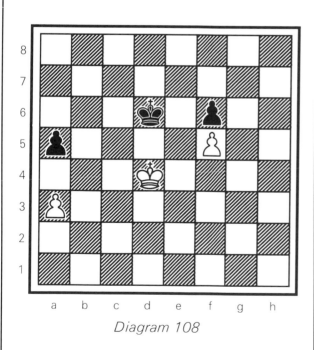

Diagram 110

(7) White goes for the kingside pawns, and Black for the queenside. Who gets there first? Give the best sequence of moves for both sides, assuming Black moves first.

-6-
TACTICS –
THE DOUBLE BLOW

Introduction

THERE is no clear dividing line between tactics and material chess, but as a general guide, tactics means the double attack, and material chess concentrates on the single attack.

Disasters in material chess are avoidable; if you have to meet an attack, you have one move to do it in, and this should be enough. The remedy is in your hands. But with tactics you, or your opponent, has to meet two or more attacks with only one move, and this is a far harder task. Often the only defence against tactics is to see it coming the move before it happens — which shows why we teach material chess first, and tactics second.

There are many quite distinct ideas in tactics, including the *fork*, when one piece attacks two or more enemy pieces at the same time; the *pin* and *skewer*, which are attacks upon pieces along the same line, and thus only used by the rook, bishop and queen. Then there are discovered attacks; discovered forks; discovered checks; and double checks, where the lines of the rook, bishop or queen are explosively opened. We have seen discovered attacks in our work on higher material chess, but in that case we were looking at a single attack arising from the opening of a line; we were not considering whether the line opening piece could also attack something at the same time.

Another major tactical theme is 'trapping', where pieces are attacked and surprisingly have no safe square; this frequently happens to knights placed at the edge of the board, where their mobility is least, or to bishops assailed by an avalanche of pawns.

Then there is removal of the defender, where a man is knocked out who happened to be defending another man; while the enemy is busy recapturing, he has no time to save his other man. Similar ideas occur in overloading, decoy and deflection, when it's not so much a double attack, as a piece being overworked by having to perform two defensive tasks at the same time.

The enemy king is often an unwilling participant in many of these tactical themes, and frequently his exposure along some line or another allows some forking check or pin. Another good reason for keeping the king safe.

There is also a whole range of tactics based on mating attacks upon the enemy king, ranging from sacrifices of pieces to force a mate, a 'king hunt', where the monarch is chased all over the board, or demolition sacrifices of, say, a knight or a bishop in order to strip away the defensive barrier of pawns protecting the king.

Having learnt the basic building blocks of tactics, you will also discover that the ingredients can be endlessly mixed to produce new ideas and combinations. Pins with forks; discovered attacks combined with piece trapping; mating threats contained in forks and pins. Sometimes a series of tactical thrusts and counter-thrusts by both sides can stretch on for several moves, causing immense complications and making great demands on your skill and imagination. Particularly important are the 'setting up' manoeuvres required in advanced tactics, when a tactical idea has to be spotted, and the correct position for the actual winning blow brought about by some forcing moves, such as checks or captures.

All the same, tactics are essentially short term operations; while your first tactical games will often make you feel like you are on a helter-skelter, eventually when you reach a higher grade your control of tactics becomes more sure, and it is the positional problems of placing your pieces that will assume greater importance. Until that time, however, tactics, especially among juniors, are the mark of a successful player, and your progress through the ranks will probably be due to your skill in tactics. Needless to say, tactics must be based on a firm grasp of material chess. If you cannot see a single attack, what chance have you against a double? If you cannot see one move ahead, how can you correctly analyse two or three?

Forks

A good fork should be against more valuable pieces, or undefended pieces.

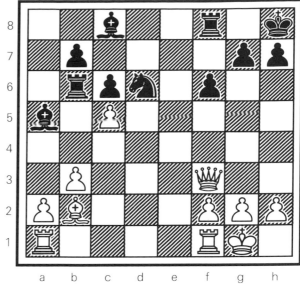

Diagram 111

A good fork; the pawn attacks a rook and a knight at the same time, and if one of them moves, the other is captured.

It doesn't matter here if the pieces are defended or not (as the black rook is here), because they are both more valuable than the pawn.

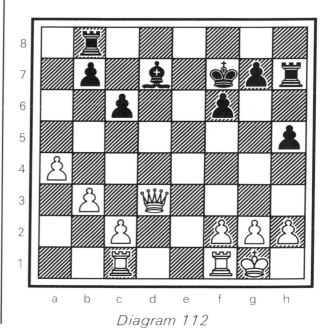

Diagram 112

Another good fork; though the queen is worth more than either the bishop or the rook, they are both undefended. If one of the pieces had been defended, this would not have been a real fork.

Let's not think that forks are only double attacks — multiple attack is quite possible — after all a knight can attack in eight different directions, so can a queen. In the next diagram, the white knight has managed a 'family fork' on the royal trio of king, queen and rook.

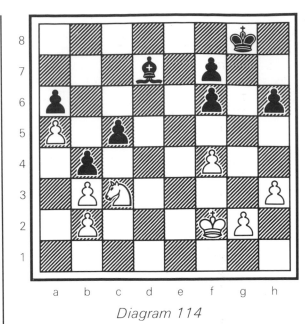

Diagram 114

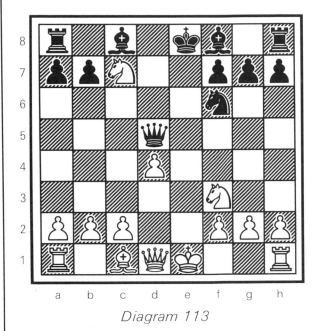

Diagram 113

Exercises

In the next two diagrams you have to find a fork for White. Answers on the next page.

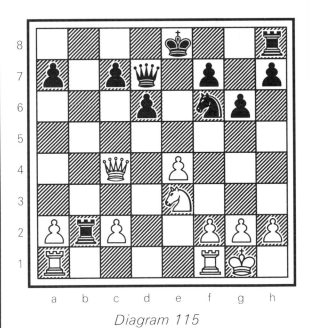

Diagram 115

Defending against forks

In defending against single attacks one has the four choices of Move, Capture, Support, Block. However, with forks we have a much narrower choice; if we cannot capture the attacker, then one of the forked pieces has to move in such a way as to defend the other forked piece by either blocking or supporting it. Usually there are many ways to combat a single attack, but with forks there is often only one good defence.

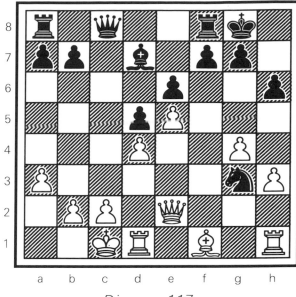

Diagram 117

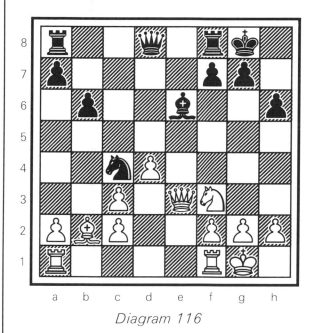

Diagram 116

White is faced by a knight fork on his queen and bishop. Fortunately he can move his queen to c1, defending the bishop at the same time.

Here White is not so lucky. His queen and rook are forked by the black knight on g3, and as they are both more valuable than the attacking knight, he must lose some material whatever he does. His best choice is 1 Qg2 (or Qh2, or Qf3) Nxh1 2 Qxh1, losing only two points.

Answers:

Diagram 114　1 Ne4
Diagram 115　1 Qd4 or Qc3

Test

In the next four positions you have landed in a fork, and you must use your wits to escape, if you can. Don't forget that in these situations, counter-attack is often the best form of defence.

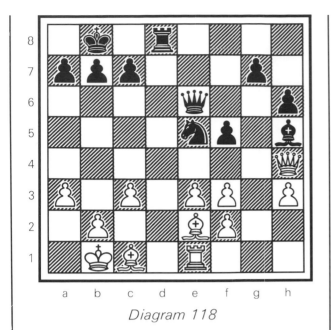

Diagram 118

Black to play

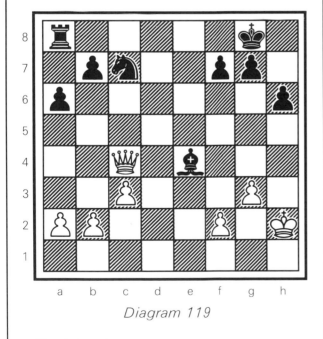

Diagram 119

Black to play

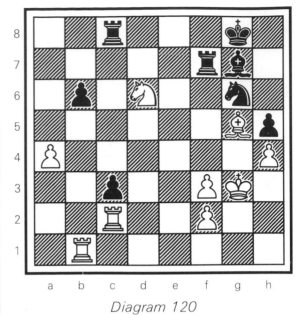

Diagram 120

Black to play

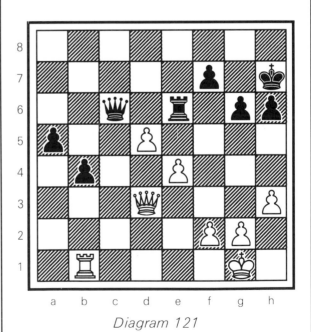

Diagram 121

Black to play

Pins

These are attacks along the same line upon two or more pieces. The best type of pin is when all the pieces are worth more than the attacking piece.

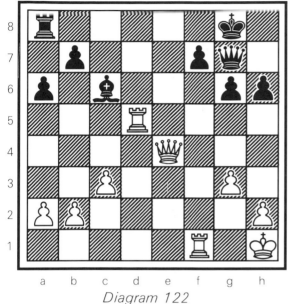

Diagram 122

This is a good pin. The bishop attacks the rook at d5; behind it is a queen at e4, and behind her is the king at h1!

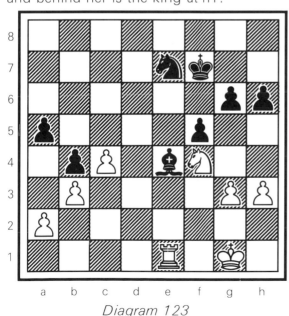

Diagram 123

This is not a real pin at all; though the knight and bishop are both on the same line as the white rook at e1, the bishop can freely move since the knight behind it is defended.

A fork is usually a way to win material. A pin, however, does not always win something. Sometimes the pinned piece is simply paralysed and unable to move; at other times we can exploit this paralysis to win the piece.

In the next diagram, Black has a knight pinned by a bishop. The knight cannot move without leaving its own king in check. White can take advantage of this to win the knight for a pawn by playing 1 d5.

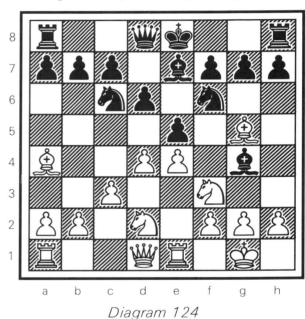

Diagram 124

Defending against pins

Pins by bishops against knights are very common on the chessboard. Sometimes they are very powerful, at others no more than a minor source of irritation.

Here, however, are two methods of dealing with pins.

Look at the next diagram. To break White's pin, Black can play 1 ... a6, and when the bishop retreats to a4, follow up with 2 ... b5, getting rid of the pin altogether. On the other hand, Black could just choose to neutralise the pin by playing 1 ... Bd7. Now the knight on c6 would be free to move. However, 1 ... Qd7 would not be so good, as the knight would then be pinned to the valuable queen.

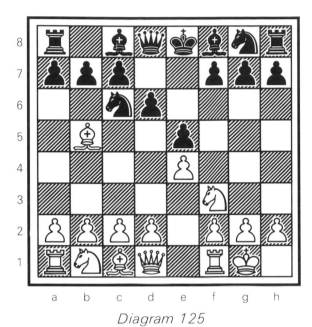

Diagram 125

Skewers

There's nothing very subtle about a skewer. Either it wins material or it doesn't. It works by attacking a more valuable piece along a line and forcing it to move out of the way. When it does so, the piece that happened to be standing behind it is captured.

The white queen and rook stand on the same line, and that gives us the clue to a simple skewer — 1 ... Re6. The white queen has to move away, but if she does, the rook on e1 is lost.

You might not have thought there was a more valuable piece than the queen, but there is! It's the king. In diagram 127 White

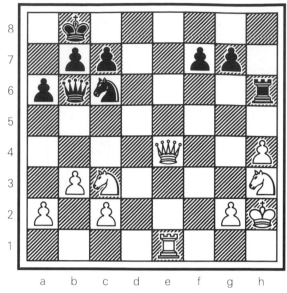

Diagram 126

wins a rook by a skewering check, 1 ... Qa6+. The king leaves the line, and then the rook at f1 is snuffed out.

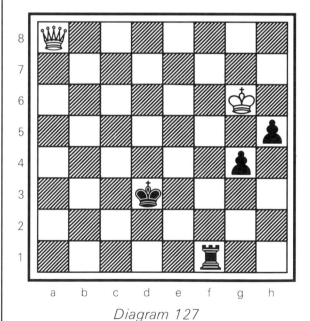

Diagram 127

Test

In the following four diagrams you have to find a skewer for White that wins material.

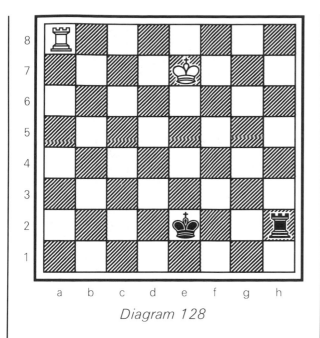

Diagram 128

White to play

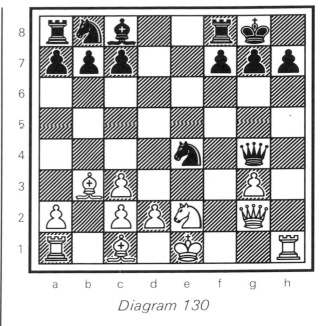

Diagram 130

White to play

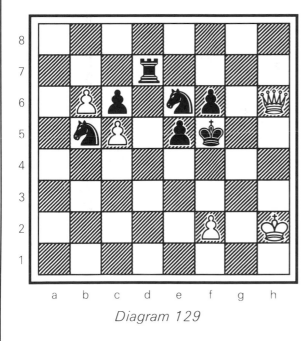

Diagram 129

White to play

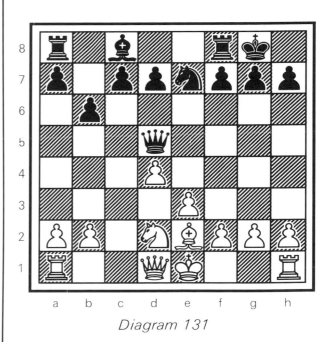

Diagram 131

White to play

Line opening

The chessboard is a small place. Pieces get in each other's way; rarely do you find a man controlling his full quota of squares. So moves where one man uncovers the fire of another are quite frequent occurrences. When the man moved also attacks something else, you get a double attack and the opponent is in trouble.

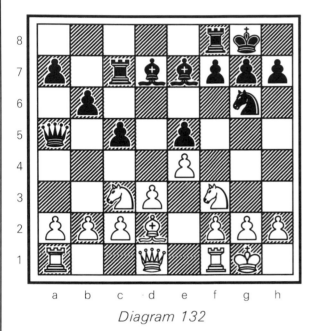

Diagram 132

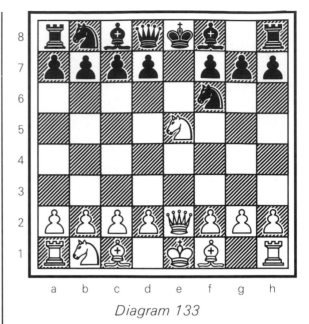

Diagram 133

This is an opening trap which is horrible to fall into. After 5 moves Black loses his queen (the moves were 1 e4 e5 2 Nf3 Nf6 3 Nxe5 Nxe4 (not good; Black should play 3 … d6 first) 4 Qe2 Nf6?? (worse and worse) reaching the diagram above.

White plays 5 Nc6, discovering an attack on the king, and hitting the black queen at the same time.

Here we have the tell-tale position of the black queen at a5, opposite the white bishop at d2. Let's move it out of the way and attack something else at the same time. Why not 1 Nd5, attacking the rook at c7? Black will have to save his queen now, and White can take off the rook next move.

Defending against discoveries

Once again, if you are quick on your feet, you can sometimes avoid disaster from a discovered attack. Sometimes you can capture one of the attackers. At other times you can move one of the pieces to defend the other. And sometimes you can counter-attack against your enemy.

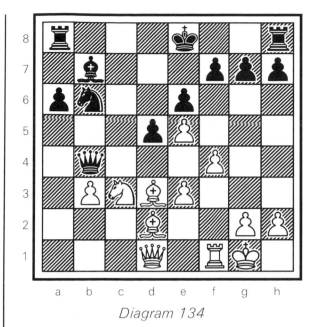

Diagram 134

Here White has an interesting choice of discoveries with his knight — it could go to seven squares.

White chose the obvious 1 Nxd5, capturing a pawn and attacking Black's queen and knight at b6 at the same time. But Black responded with 1 ... Qc5!, saving his queen and defending his knight at the same time. So Black managed to lose only a pawn out of that little skirmish.

If White had played 1 Na4!, instead, he would have won a piece, because the black queen cannot move to a safe square and defend the knight on b6 at the same time.

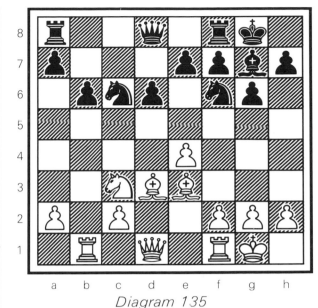

Diagram 135

This was a discovered attack, but in reality it was no more than a complicated way of exchanging pieces. Black played 1 ... Ng4, White answered 2 Qxg4, and Black played 2 ... Bxc3.

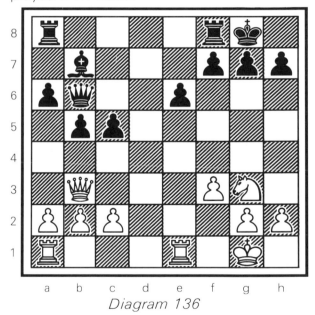

Diagram 136

This was a discovered check successfully parried. Black played 1 ... c4 dis.ch., and at the same time attacked the white queen at b3. It looked like curtains for White till he found the neat reply — Qe3!

Interference

Line opening and discoveries are attacking weapons. Less obvious, but equally strong, can be line-closing. Of course, there's no reason why you should want to constrict your own pieces, but closing the line of an *enemy* piece can have its advantages.

The spanner in the works

For an incredible example of interference, let's look at diagram 137. If White's queen were not on e1, defending b4, Black could play axb4 mate.

If White's rook were not at h2, Black could play Nc2 mate.

This suggests the following interference move 1 ... Rd2!!

If White plays 2 Rxd2, he closes his queen's line and Black can now mate with 2 ... axb4. If, on the other hand, White plays 2 Qxd2, then the rook's defence is blocked and Black mates with a further sacrifice — 1 ... Nc2+! 2 Qxc2 axb4 mate!!

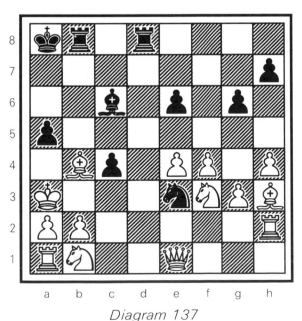

Diagram 137

This is another example of line closing, this time from the ending. Black wishes to play 1 ... a2, threatening to queen a pawn. But he sees that White could then move Bf6.

In order to close that line, Black first plays e5+. White's king has no choice but to capture the pawn, after which Black's a-pawn waltzes home to queen.

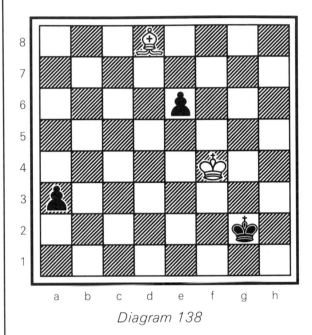

Diagram 138

Trapping

This is something that usually happens to knights and bishops, but it can happen to any piece.

Test

Here are four examples of trapping — to four different pieces. In each case the piece is attacked by a weaker piece and has no escape square.

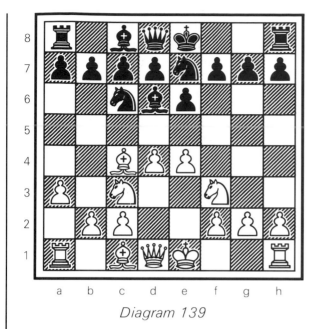

Diagram 139

White to play

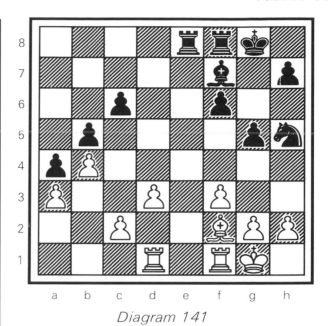

Diagram 141

White to play

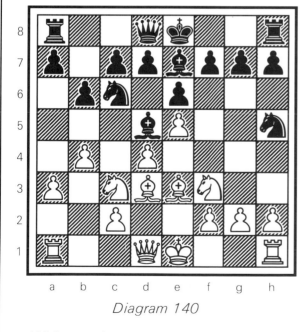

Diagram 140

White to play

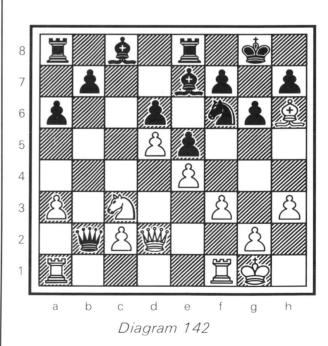

Diagram 142

White to play

Weaker pieces can also be trapped, but in that case they not only need to have no escape, but they must also be without visible means of support as well.

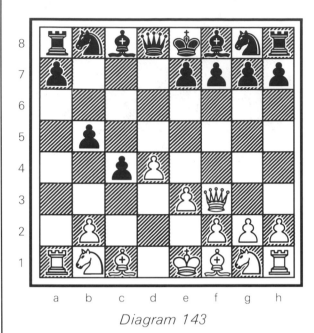

Diagram 143

Here we have a rook trapped by the queen at f3 — so early in the game! (You could call it an opening 'trap'). It comes about after these moves: 1 d4 d5 2 c4 dxc4 3 e3 b5 4 a4 c6 5 axb5 cxb5 6 Qf3!

The only way to save the rook now is by giving up a knight or a bishop by Nc6 or Bb7. After 6 ... Nc6 7 Qxc6+ Bd7, the rook is now defended, at the cost of a piece.

Removing a defender

A simple theme that can often win you a piece.

The black queen attacks the bishop at g5 which is defended by a knight at f3. What's the solution? Remove the knight at f3! After 1 ... Bxf3 2 Qxf3 Qxg5, Black wins a piece.

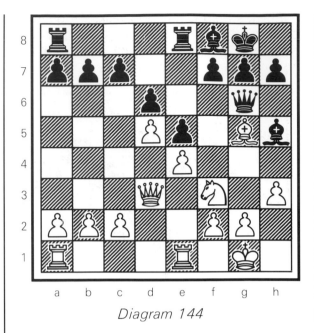

Diagram 144

Overloading

This theme crops up when a piece has more than one task to do.

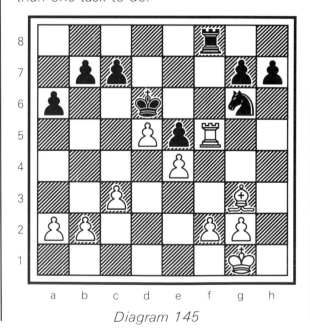

Diagram 145

Black's knight has two tasks — defend both e5 and f8. White exploits this by capturing 1 Bxe5+, as Black dare not play Nxe5 because he would lose a rook.

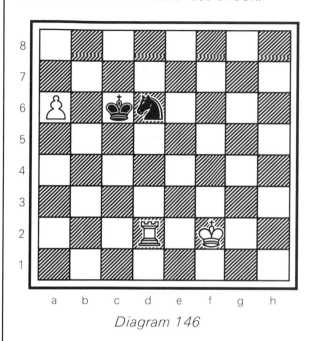

Diagram 146

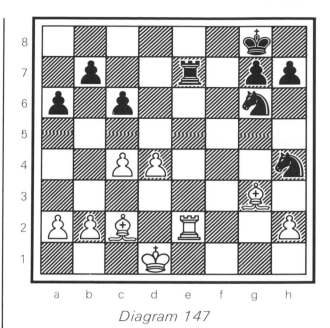

Diagram 147

Here the overworked piece is the black king. It has to stop the pawn queening and defend the knight at d6. White can play 1 Rxd6+!, for if 1 ... Kxd6, then simply 2 a7 and the pawn queens next move.

Test

Now two tests on overloaded pieces. In each position it is White to play.

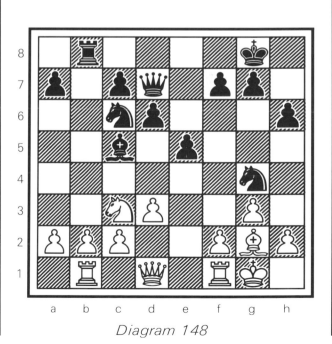

Diagram 148

Tactics involving the king

Forks, pins, skewers, discovered attacks and so on, become that much stronger, that much harder to defend against, when one of the injured parties is a king. Often it is hard to distinguish between tactical play and attacking play. Sometimes an attack may end in mate; at other times you can use an attack to gain material.

The forking check

Here a check by the black queen at a5 attacks the bishop at b5 at the same time. White's choice of defensive moves is limited: he must parry the check either by blocking or moving the king. Fortunately in this position there is a way out, Nc3, blocking the check and defending the bishop at the same time.

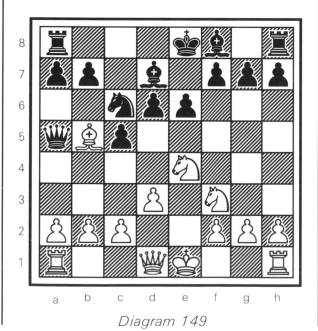

Diagram 149

The forking threat of mate

In this example we are not sure if White is trying to mate or simply win material. White plays 1 Qe4, attacking the black pawn at h7, and the knight at c6.

Which piece should Black save? Actually, the h7 pawn, because if Black allows it to be captured by 2 Qxh7, this happens to be checkmate as well.

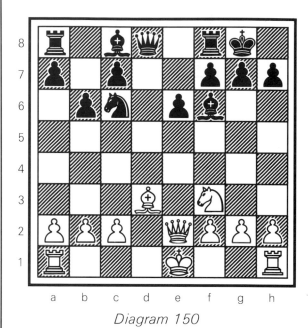

Diagram 150

Test

In these positions, you can use the black king's exposure to make a winning tactical move. Name the winning theme for White in each case.

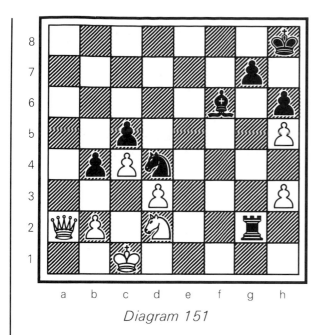

Diagram 151

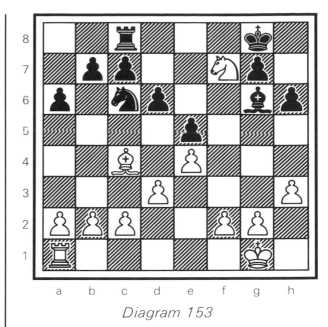

Diagram 153

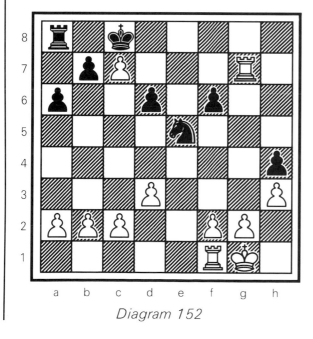

Diagram 152

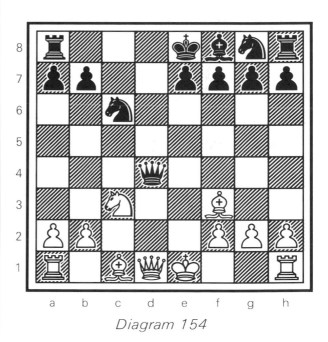

Diagram 154

Mating attacks

King in the middle

In this position, White is so many pieces down that he just *has* to mate Black. If you understand the idea of the lawn mower, you should find this position easy. How does White force mate?

1 Qd3+ Kc6 2 Rc1+ Kb6 3 Qb3+ Ka6 4 Ra1 mate or 1 Qd3+ Kc5 2 Rc1+ Kb4 3 Qc3+ Kb5 4 Rb1+ Ka4 5 Qa1 mate.

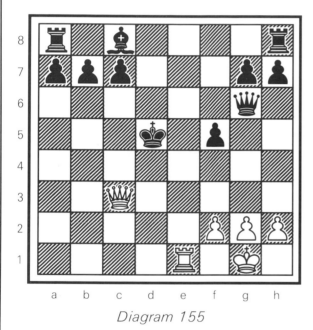

Diagram 155

Here, though, the mating attack is much more complicated. Once again you have several pieces less, but if you keep checking, and choose your checks wisely, you can once again force a mate. Can you see how? Don't forget to take into account all Black's possible defensive moves.

1 Qxc3+ Kxd5 2 Re5+ Kd6 3 Qc5+ Kd7 4 Qd5 mate; or 1 Qxc3+ Kb6 2 Qb4+ Ka6 3 Qb5 mate; or 1 Qxc3+ Kd6 2 Qe5+ Kc5 (2 ... Kd7 3 Qe6 mate) 3 Bxb7 dis. ch. Kb6 (3 ... Kb4 4 Qb5 mate or 3 ... Kc4 4 Qc3 mate) 4 Qb5 mate.

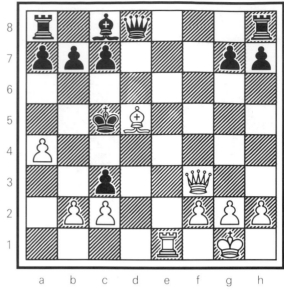

Diagram 156

King in a corner

Castling is a great way of keeping the king safe, but often with a large build up of forces around the king, a demolition sacrifice to destroy the pawn barricade can be worthwhile.

Look at this diagram.

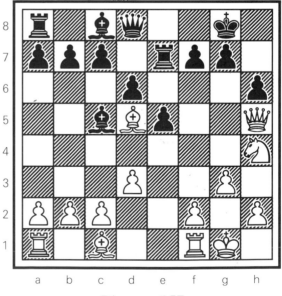

Diagram 157

White has three pieces poised against the black kingside, and he breaks in with **1 Bxh6 gxh6 2 Qxh6.**

This leads us to the next diagram.

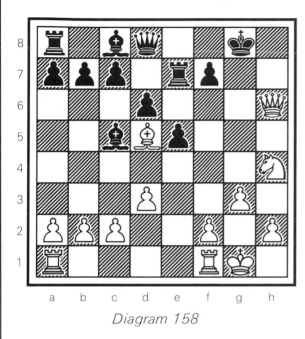

Diagram 158

At this point, if Black is to defend he should remember a good tip — exchange off attacking pieces. So he should play 2 ... Qf8, or 2 ... Be6. Instead, Black goes pawn hunting on his own, and the result is a disaster.

3 ... Bd4??

Attacking the pawn at b2. Big deal!

4 Ng6!!

A brilliant move. White takes advantage of the pin on the pawn at f7 to bring his knight in to g6. This not only threatens the rook at e7, it also plans 5 Qh8 mate. Black's only defence here was 4 ... e4! — *discovered defence* (why not? you can have discovered attacks, so you can have discovered defences as well) on the h8 square. Instead Black, all oblivious, played 4 ... Bxb2, and was mated after 5 Qh8.

Back row mate

This is one of the commonest mating attacks, and the most swift. It usually happens after one side has castled, since while the pawns are useful as a defensive barrier, they can also have a suffocating effect upon their own king.

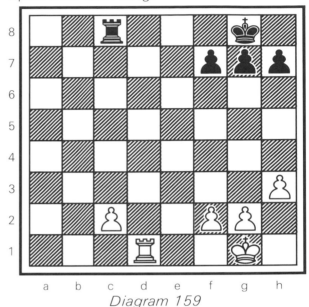

Diagram 159

Black played 1 ... Rxc2, grabbing a pawn. We have checkmate here by 2 Rd8.

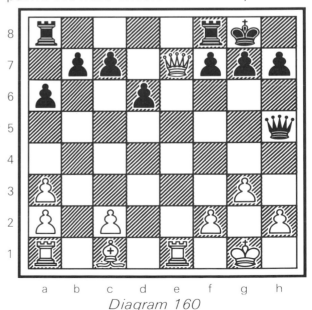

Diagram 160

This was a skewer that backfired.

Black played 1 ... Rae8, thinking that the white queen would have to move away, and then he could win a rook by ... Rxe1.

Instead White plays 2 Qxe8!! Rxe8 3 Rxe8 mate.

Such stunning reversals of fortune are part of the helter-skelter of chess and show why it is such a thrilling and hair-raising game.

Test

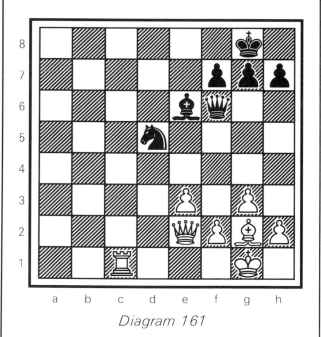

Diagram 161

Using the ideas of overloading and the back rank mate, how can you win a piece in this position?

–7–
ANSWERS

Answers to tests

1. Leaving unguarded (*Diagrams 3–8*)

3: Reb1 is better, because Re2? leaves the rook at a1 *en prise* (*en prise* means 'can be captured for nothing') to the black queen at b2. (2 points)

4: Ba3 is a basic material error, losing a piece after ... Bxa3. (2 points)

Bb2 is a good developing move. (2 points)

Nd5 leaves the pawn at e4 unguarded, and allows ... Nxe4. (2 points)

The best move is Bb2 (2 points)

5: Bf8 leaves the knight at f6 unguarded, and allows Rxf6. (2 points)

g5 loses a pawn after Bxg5, *but* it is not a leaving unguarded mistake. (2 points)

Nd7 leaves the pawn at d5 unguarded, and allows Nxd5. (2 points)

a5 leaves the pawn at b5 unguarded, and allows Nxb5. (2 points)

b4 exchanges pawns after axb4 Nxb4, but leaves nothing unguarded. (2 points)

6: In this position, three leaving unguarded mistakes would be:

Rd2? allowing ... Rxa1+. (2 points)

Kg1? or Kg2? allowing ... Rxe2. (2 points)

h3? or h4? allowing ... Bxg3. (2 points)

7: f4 allows ... Rxe3, winning a piece. (2 points)

Nf4 allows ... Bxc3, also winning a piece. (2 points)

Qd3 is a mistake because of ... Rxa1+. (2 points)

g3 is the best move, allowing the king to go to g2 to let the rook on h1 out. (2 points)

8: (1) Capturing at d4 by ... Bxd4 would be a mistake, leaving the knight at h6 unguarded

and allowing Bxh6. (2 points)

(2) ... c5 would also be a mistake, as it leaves the knight at b6 unguarded, so White can play Qxb6. (2 points)

(3) Re8 would be the best move here. It doesn't lose any pieces! (2 points)

TOTAL SCORE: 40 points.

2. Focused attacks (*Diagrams 15–18*)

15: White to play: 1 Rxb7 Rxb7 2 Rxb7 Rxb7 3 Qxb7. (4 points)

Black to play: 1 ... Bxg5 2 Bxg5 Rxg5. Now White has lost a pawn, and must stop capturing here, or he will lose more. If 3 Qxg5?? Qxg5. Black could also play 2 ... Qxg5 3 Qxg5 Rxg5 and win a pawn that way too. (4 points)

16: White to play: 1 axb5 axb5 2 Bxb5 Bxb5 3 Qxb5. (4 points)

Black to play: 1 ... Nxe5 2 dxe5 Qxe5. (4 points)

17: White to play: 1 Nxe7+ Bxe7 2 Rxe7 Rxe7 3 Rxe7 winning a piece. (4 points)

Black to play: 1 ... Nxd5 2 Bxd5 Bxd5. Now White should not capture by 3 Qxd5, or he will lose even more. On move 2, Black could also have transposed moves by 2 ... Qxd5 3 Qxd5 Bxd5, coming out once again a piece ahead. (4 points)

18: 1 f4 is safe as it is defended enough times.

If 1 f4 exf4 2 gxf4. Black should stop capturing at this point, as any further captures lose him material. For example, 2 ... Nxf4 3 Rxf4 Rxf4 4 Qxf4 Qxf4 5 Bxf4 and White is two points up. (4 points)

1 ... b5 is also safe. The capture sequence is 2 axb5 axb5, after which White may not capture without losing material: e.g. — 3 Nxb5 Nxb5 4 Bxb5 Rxb5 (or 4 ... Bxb5) 5 Rxb5 Bxb5 and Black is two points ahead. (4 points)

TOTAL SCORE: 32 points.

3. Opening and closing lines (*Diagrams 22–24*)

22: Be6? closes the line of the defence from the rook at e8 to the knight at e5, and allows Nxe5. Bf5 is the better move. (4 points)

23: Here Bg5 should be played, as Bc3? allows ... Bxc4, as the queen at c1 no longer guards the white bishop. (4 points)

24. Here Black can *open a line* in order to defend his knight at e8, by playing ... Nc6, guarding the knight by the rook at a8. However, ... Nd7 and ... Na6 would be faulty; ... Nd7 allows Qxd7, and ... Na6 cuts the defence of the black queen to the rook, allowing Qxa8. (4 points)

TOTAL SCORE: 12 points.

4. UFOs (*Diagrams 25–27*)

25: Be8 leaves the knight at f5 unguarded, allowing Bxf5. (2 points)

Ra7 is a basic material error, allowing Bxa7. (2 points)

Nd6 opens the line to the rook at h7, and White can now play Bxh7. (2 points)

Be6 is the best defence, which still keeps the knight at f5 guarded. (2 points)

26: All moves lose material, so it is a matter of choosing the least of many evils.

Qb2 leaves the knight at e4 unguarded to ... Bxe4. (2 points)

Bc3 opens the d-line, and Black can take advantage of this by ... Rxd1. (2 points)

Rb1 leaves the bishop at d4 unguarded. Black replies ... Rxd4. (2 points)

Nc2 opens the bishop's line to a3. Black can then capture by ... Bxa3. (2 points)

Nc6 does the same. Black plays ... Bxa3. (2 points)

Rb3 is a basic material error, losing a rook after ... Qxb3. (2 points)

Which is the best of all the defences? All lose at least 3 points, except Nc2, since after ... Bxa3, White can reply Nxa3, and White has only lost 2 points here. (4 points)

27: Be5 is a very bad move.

Firstly, it leaves the knight on h5 unprotected against the attack by the black bishop on f7. (2 points)

Secondly, it opens the g line so that the black rook on g8 can capture the rook on g1 with check, and next the white queen. (2 points)

Thirdly, it leaves the knight on h4 undefended against the black queen (2 points)

Finally, the bishop on e5 can be captured by the pawn on d6. (2 points)

TOTAL SCORE: 32 points.

5. Finishing off

Six points for each answer; give yourself part score if your answer is not fully correct.

1. Ways of winning with a material advantage.
    (a) direct attack on king.
    (b) swap off pieces and finish with a basic mate.
    (c) mop up enemy pieces before turning to the king.
    (d) queen pawns to give decisive material advantage.

    (Three out of four of these gains 6 points)

2. If you are a piece ahead, attack on the king is possible, but even simpler is to swap off pieces and then try to win more pieces and/or queen pawns in the ending. (6 points)

3. If queens are on the board it is harder to exploit a material advantage, as the opponent always has hopes of a successful counter-attack against the enemy king. So swapping queens when you are ahead on material usually makes the win simpler. (6 points)

4. A passed pawn is a pawn which has no enemy pawn in front of it, or on adjacent files in front of it. (6 points)

5. A potential passed pawn has no enemy pawn in front of it, *but* there is a *friendly* pawn next to it, and an *enemy* pawn opposite the friendly pawn, as in diagram 162. The pawn on d3 is a potential passed pawn.

    By advancing the pawns together, they can be exchanged off against the enemy pawn, and thus an actual passed pawn can be created. (6 points)

6. Passed pawns can be created by (a) capturing enemy pawns in the way of friendly pawns (b) advancing and exchanging potential passed pawns. (6 points)

7. White is a piece ahead, *but* his king, lacking all pawn cover, and dangerously placed in the centre, is extremely exposed. Therefore it is safest to exchange the queens and try to win the endgame without having to fear so much for the king. (6 points)

8. The winning plan in this position will be to activate the pieces, especially the white king, by

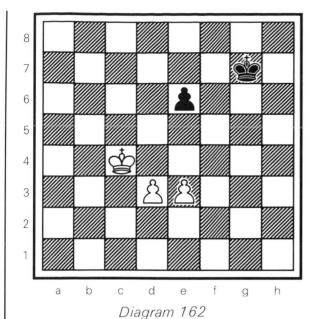

Diagram 162

bringing the king into the centre, and squeezing Black back by a general advance of the pawns and the pieces. White can also try to create passed pawns by capturing the enemy pawns on the queenside with his rook. For example, a good idea here is to play 1 Rd1, threatening 2 Rd7, attacking the pawn at b7. (6 points)

TOTAL SCORE: 48 points.

6. Positional play in the opening

1. (d) (4 points)
2. (b) (4 points)
3. (b) (4 points)
4. (c) (4 points)
5. (b) (4 points)
6. The good point of Ng5 is that there is now a *focused attack* from the knight and the bishop against the f7 square, and White threatens Nxf7, winning a pawn and forking the black queen and rook. The bad points of the move are that the attack can easily be parried, for example, by … e6, and that White will have wasted time by moving a piece twice in the opening, furthermore, to a square from which it can easily be driven away (by … h6). (8 points)
7. b3 does not help to put a pawn in the centre, so does not follow one of the positional rules. It does allow the bishop at c1 to be developed at b2, but this bishop could already have come out on the other diagonal, as White has already

moved his d-pawn. So b3 is not a very useful move, and White is guilty of moving too many pawns in the opening. (8 points)

8. (b) (4 points)
9. g4 is a good move from the material point of view, as the pawn is sufficiently well defended by white pieces, so White will not lose any material after a series of captures on g4. Positionally, though, the move is a failure, because White is *moving up a pawn in front of his king* and thus weakening his king position. (8 points)
10. (b) (4 points)

TOTAL SCORE: 52 points.

7. Descriptive notation

Game One

1	P–K4	P–K4
2	N–KB3	N–KB3
3	NxP	P–Q3
4	N–KB3	NxP
5	N–B3	NxN
6	QPxN	B–K2
7	B–K3	0–0
8	Q–Q2	N–Q2
9	0–0–0	N–K4
10	N–Q4	P–QB4
11	N–N5	Q–R4
12	P–QR3	P–QR3
13	NxP	R–Q1
14	NxB	RxQ
15	NxBch	K–B1
16	RxR	KxN
17	R–Q5	N–Q2
18	B–K2	P–QN3
19	B–B3	N–B1
20	R–K5ch	1–0

(25 points for correct score. Deduct 1 point for each mistake)

Game Two

1	e4	e5
2	Nf3	Nc6
3	Bb5	a6
4	Ba4	Nf6
5	0–0	Be7
6	Re1	b5
7	Bb3	0–0

8	d3	d6
9	c3	Na5
10	Bc2	c5
11	Nbd2	Re8
12	Nf1	h6
13	Ng3	Bf8
14	h3	Bb7
15	d4	cxd4
16	cxd4	exd4
17	Nxd4	Rc8
18	b3	d5
19	e5	Ne4
20	Bb2	Rxe5
21	f3	Rg5
22	Nf1	Rxg2+

White resigns.

(25 points for correct score. Deduct 1 point for each mistake)

8. Game analysis

Game One

1	e4	d5
2	Qf3	dxe4
3	Qxe4	Nf6
4	Qf3	Bg4?

M—(U), Black leaves the b7 pawn unguarded. (2 points)

| 5 | Qf4? | |

M—(U); White fails to play 5 Qxb7. (2 points)

| 5 | ... | e6 |
| 6 | Nc3 | Bb4?? |

M——; A basic material error, allowing 7 Qxb4. (2 points)

| 7 | Nb5?? | |

M——; failing to play 7 Qxb4! (2 points)

| 7 | ... | a6? |

M—(F); misses the focused attack on c7. 7 ... Na6 or 7 ... Bd6 or 7 ... Ba5 should have been played. (2 points)

8	Nxc7+!	Kf8
9	Nxa8	Bd6
10	Qg5	h6
11	Qe3	Nc6
12	h3	Qxa8
13	hxg4	Nxg4
14	Qe2	h5

15	Nh3	Nh2
16	Ng5	f6?

M—(U); Black leaves his e6-pawn unguarded. (2 points)

17	Nxe6+	Kf7
18	b3	Qe8
19	Qb5??	

M——; Basic material error; Black can now play 19 ... axb5; also M—(U), leaving the knight at e6 unguarded. (4 points)

| 19 | ... | Qxe6+ |

M——; fails to capture the queen at b5, the most valuable piece. (2 points)

| 20 | Qe2! | Re8 |

TOTAL SCORE: 18 points.

Game Two

1	e4	e5
2	Na3	Nf6
3	d3	d5
4	Bg5	dxe4
5	Bxf6	Qxf6
6	dxe4	Qf4
7	Bb5+	c6
8	Bd3	Bg4
9	Nf3	Na6
10	g3?	

M—(F, U); White leaves his knight at f3 unguarded to the focused attack from the black queen and bishop. Black can now play 10 ... Qxf3! 11 Qxf3 Bxf3, winning a piece, but not 10 ... Bxf3 11 gxf4 Bxd1 12 Rxd1 exf4, when White only loses a pawn. (4 points)

| 10 | ... | Qh6? |

M—(F, U); failing to capture the piece at f3. (4 points)

| 11 | Nh4? | |

M—(O); opens the line to the white queen at d1. (2 points)

| 11 | ... | Bxd1! |
| 12 | Rxd1 | b6 |

M—(U); leaves the knight at a6 unguarded. (2 points)

| 13 | Nf5 | Qe6 |
| 14 | Nxg7+?? | |

M——; basic material error, leaving the knight *en prise*; also M—(U), failing to play 13 Bxa6. (4 points)

14	...	**Bxg7**
15	**0–0**	**Qd6**
16	**Bxa6!**	**b5**

M—(O); fails to notice the line is now open to the black queen. (2 points)

| 17 | **Rxd6!** | **Rc8** |

M——; leaves the rook at c8 *en prise*. (2 points)

| 18 | **Bxc8** | **0–0** |
| 19 | **Rfd1** | |

M—(O); bishop at c8 is now *en prise*. (2 points)

| 19 | ... | **Rxc8** |
| 20 | **R6d3** | **c5** |

M—(U); leaves the b5 pawn unguarded. White can now play

| 21 | **Nxb5** (2 points) | |

TOTAL SCORE: 24 points.

9. King and pawn endings (1)

(Give yourself part scores for partially correct answers.)

1. The 'square' of a pawn in king and pawn endings comprises an imaginary line extended from the pawn to the end of the board, and then sideways from the pawn the same number of squares. These two lines are then joined up to make a box or a square. The theory is that, if the enemy king can enter the square, or is already in the square, he can catch the pawn before it queens, or as it queens. If not, the pawn will queen first. (6 points)

2. Not true always! For if, for example, a white pawn is at a2, and a black king is at g2, White can play 1 a4!, and the king cannot re-enter the square in time to catch the pawn. (6 points)

3. The position is a win for White, but care is definitely needed. The pawns can defend each other against attacks by the enemy king, until White assists their advance by bringing up the king. For example, 1 ... Ka5 2 c5! and now 2 ... Kxa4 loses to 3 c6.

   So 2 ... Ka6, after which White must not advance either pawn, as he would then lose both, but plays 3 Kg2 Kb7 4 a5! This is better than 4 Kf3? Kc6! when White loses both pawns again. White re-establishes the position, so that after 4 ... Kc6 5 a6! Black can once more not capture the backward pawn, and must oscillate between c6 and c7 until the white king arrives on the scene: 5 ... Kc7 6 Kf3 Kc6 7 Ke4 Kc7 8 Kd5 and the pawns will go through to queen. (10 points)

4. If the white pawn is at d5, the position is a certain draw, because the pawn prevents White gaining the opposition at the critical moment: 1 d6+ Kd7 2 Kd5 Kd8! 3 Ke6 Ke8 4 d7+ Kd8 5 Kd6 stalemate.

   On the other hand, with the pawn at d4, White can win *if he has the opposition*, i.e. if it is Black to move. 1 ... Kd7 2 Kd5! (king in front of pawn) Kc7 3 Ke6 Kd8 4 Kd6 Ke8 5 Kc7 Ke7 6 d5 and the pawn gets to the queening square. (10 points)

5. Yes. White plays 1 Kf5! taking the opposition. After 1 ... Ke8 2 Ke6 Kd8 3 d7 Kc7 4 Ke7, White wins, so also after 1 ... Kf8! 2 Kf6! (taking the opposition) Ke8 3 Ke6 Kd8 4 d7 Kc7 5 Ke7 winning. (10 points)

6. Black must play 1 ... Kc8 to draw, preventing White from taking the opposition, because the white pawn is in the way. On the other hand, 1 ... Kd8? loses after 2 Kd6! Kc8 3 c7 Kb7 4 Kd7, as does 1 ... Kb8? (8 points)

7. The move. (8 points)

8. In *defence*, the opposition can be used to block off the enemy king, and prevent him advancing. In *attack*, the king can be used to push the enemy king aside, and advance into an important part of the board. (10 points)

9. Connected pawns are best, as they can defend each other; split pawns are not so good, as they cannot defend each other, and are easier to pick off by the enemy pieces. However, in a purely king and pawn ending, split pawns, if they are far enough apart, can be an advantage, because one can be used as a decoy, to lure the enemy king away, while the other advances to queen.

   Doubled pawns are the worst, because they get in each others way, they cannot defend each other, and it is difficult to make a passed pawn out of them. (10 points)

10. It is much harder to win with pawns on the edge files because the enemy king, if it gets in front of them, cannot be forced out; stalemate intervenes. Even in some cases when an enemy king is not in front of the pawn, the game may still be drawn by stalemate, where it is *White* who is stalemated in front of his own pawn. (10 points)

TOTAL SCORE: 88 points.

10. King and pawn endings (2)

(Give yourself part scores for partially correct answers.)

1. An outside passed pawn is a passed pawn which stands away from the main body of pawns. (6 points)

2. It can be used as a decoy to lure the enemy king away from the defence of the pawns, while the other king invades and captures them. (8 points)

3. (a) Winning by decoy.

    (b) Winning with the opposition or by paralysis.

    (c) Winning the pawn race. (10 points)

4. 1 ... Kd6!, taking the opposition, draws. 2 Kc4 Kc6 and so on. (8 points)

5. 1 a4! White takes the opposition and forces the black king to give way, after which White invades and captures a black pawn, e.g. 1 ... Kc6 2 Kc4 Kd6 (2 ... Kb6 3 Kd5 and Ke6) 3 Kb5 Ke5 and White queens in 6 moves, Black in 7, so White can stop the black pawn. Black can also try 3 ... Kd5 4 Kxa5 Kc6 5 Kb4 Kb6 6 Kc4 and White wins by decoy. (10 points)

6. White chases the black king underneath the pawn, and then uses the time to bring his king up. When the black king emerges, White chases him underneath again, and once more brings his king forward. This process is repeated until the white king is close enough to help deliver the mate.

    The sequence could be: 1 Qc7+ Kd1 2 Qb6 Kc2 3 Qc5+ Kd2 4 Qd4+ Kc2 5 Qc4+ (White zigzags down to get close to the king) Kd2 6 Qb3! Kc1 7 Qc3+ Kb1 8 Kg7 Ka2 9 Qc2 Ka1 10 Qa4+ Kb1 11 Kf6 and so on. (12 points)

7. The sequence would be: 1 ... Kc6 2 Kf5 b5! (much better than Kc5–Kc4–Kb3–Kxa3) 3 axb5+ (otherwise 3 ... b4!) Kxb5 4 Kg6 Ka4 5 Kxg7 Kxa3 6 Kxh6 Kb4 (if 6 ... Kb2 the h-pawn would queen with check) 7 g4 a4 8 g5 a3 9 g6 a2 10 g7 a1(Q) 11 g8(Q). Black queened first but White is now a pawn up in a queen and pawn ending. White has the advantage, but Black has very good chances to draw. (12 points)

TOTAL SCORE: 66 points.

11. Tactics

Diagram 118

1 ... Qe8 defends both the bishop at h5 and the rook at d8. (4 points)

Diagram 119

1 ... Bc6! defends the bishop and blocks the attack on the knight at c7. (4 points)

Diagram 120

1 ... Be5+! meets fork with counter-fork. Black attacks the white king and knight, and instead of losing a rook for a knight, wins a knight for nothing. (4 points)

Diagram 121

There are several defences here. 1 ... Qd7 or 1 ... Qd6, by pinning the d-pawn against the white queen, prevents 2 dxe6. 1 ... Qa6! is another clever way to avoid material loss. The white queen is attacked, so 2 dxe6 is no good. On the other hand, if White captures 2 Qxa6, Black *recaptures* with 2 ... Rxa6, and simultaneously removes his rook from attack by the d-pawn. (4 points for any correct defence)

Diagram 128

1 Ra2+ and 2 Rxh2. (4 points)

Diagram 129

1 Qh3+ and 2 Qxe6. (4 points)

Diagram 130

1 Rh4 Qf5 (or Qg6) 2 Rxe4, taking advantage of the focused attack on the knight at e4. (4 points)

Diagram 131

1 Bf3! and 2 Bxa8. (4 points)

Diagram 139

1 e5 traps the black bishop at d6. (4 points)

Diagram 140

1 g4 traps the knight at h5. (4 points)

Diagram 141

1 Bc5 traps the rook at f8. (4 points)

Diagram 142

1 Rfb1 traps the queen at b2, but not 1 Na4? Qb5; nor 1 Rab1 Qxa3; nor 1 Ra2 Qb6+. (4 points)

Diagram 147

1 Rxe7! Nxe7 2 Bxh4, but not 1 Bxh4? Rxe2 (interposing move) 2 Kxe2 Nxh4, nor 1 Bxg6? Nxg6 2 Rxe7 Nxe7, when Black escapes with level material. (6 points)

Diagram 148

1 Bxc6! Qxc6 2 Qxg4. (6 points)

Diagram 151

1 Qa8+ and 2 Qxg2 (fork). (6 points)

Diagram 152

1 Rg8+ Kxc7 2 Rxa8 (skewer). (6 points)

Diagram 153

1 Nxd6+ and 2 Nxc8 (discovery). (6 points)

Diagram 154

1 Bxc6+ bxc6 2 Qxd4 (removing the defender) (4 points)

Diagram 161

1 Bxd5 Bxd5? 2 Rc8+ Qd8 3 Rxd8 mate. (6 points)

TOTAL SCORE: 88 points.

TEST SCORE CHART

		Score	Max
1	LEAVING UNGUARDED		40
2	FOCUSED ATTACKS		32
3	OPENING AND CLOSING LINES		12
4	UFOs		32
5	FINISHING OFF		48
6	POSITIONAL PLAY IN THE OPENING		52
7	NOTATION		50
8	GAME ANALYSIS		42
9	KING AND PAWN ENDINGS (1)		88
10	KING AND PAWN ENDINGS (2)		66
11	TACTICS		88
Total			550